THE ROGUE CROWN

THE ROGUE CROWN

THE FIVE CROWNS OF OKRITH, BOOK THREE

A.K. MULFORD

HARPER Voyager

An Imprint of HarperCollins *Publishers*

THE ROGUE CROWN. Copyright © 2022 by A.K. Mulford. Excerpt from *The Evergreen Heir* © 2022 by A.K. Mulford. All rights reserved. Printed in the United States of America. No part of this book may be used or reproduced in any manner whatsoever without written permission except in the case of brief quotations embodied in critical articles and reviews. For information, address HarperCollins Publishers, 195 Broadway, New York, NY 10007.

HarperCollins books may be purchased for educational, business, or sales promotional use. For information, please email the Special Markets Department at SPsales@harpercollins.com.

Harper Voyager and design are trademarks of HarperCollins Publishers LLC.

Map © 2022 Kristen Timofeev

FIRST EDITION

Library of Congress Cataloging-in-Publication Data has been applied for.

ISBN 978-0-06-329170-6 (paperback)
ISBN 978-0-06-329684-8 (hardcover library edition)

22 23 24 25 26 LSC 10 9 8 7 6 5 4 3 2 1

*For the friends who became family and made new
corners of the world feel like home*

CONTENT WARNING

This book contains themes of violence, blood, war, loss, surgery, cheating, and domestic violence, as well as sexually explicit scenes.

Okri

Murreneir

High Mount

Yexshi

Swifthill

Western Court

Sea of Callipho

N

W • E

S

Sea of Wetamuir

Eastern Court

Wynreach

Crushwold

Saxbridge

CHAPTER ONE

B riata Catullus." The elderly fae spat into the dust. "Come to seize the crown while the palace mourns? You shouldn't be here."

The prophecy plagued her, spewing from ignorant mouths since the day of her birth. At the front of the wagon, two fae scowled at her. Clearly father and son, one had gray hair and a lined face, the other a younger version with the same slender nose and thin lips. Their eyes widened, and Bri knew with her golden-brown skin, auburn hair, and eagle eyes, there was no mistaking her for anyone else. She was one of the Twin Eagles—more myth than person.

"You know the prophecy about me, but clearly not much else," she said, giving them a twisted grin as she brushed the dust from her tunic. "I don't take kindly to orders." Bri narrowed her eyes, noting a third fae popping his head up from the back of the wagon. "My assistance was requested by the Captain of the Guard herself, whose authority I am most certain supersedes your own."

"The Captain has clearly lost her mind, inviting a Catullus this far into our court," the silver-haired fae jeered. "I heard she got hacked to bits in the attack. She'll probably be dead before you get there."

Delta's urgent voice echoed in Bri's ears. She had to keep moving. Her hand moved from the reins toward her favorite dagger on her hip.

"You're not welcome in the West," the son scoffed.

He wore one knife on his belt and his father had a lone dagger. They seemed like tradespeople of some sort, untrained in fighting, but fae were faster and stronger than humans or witches. Of the three, fae were the most headstrong too. Bri moved her hands back to the reins. She wouldn't need her dagger to dispatch these three.

"Are you going to move that wagon or not?"

Her face hardened, looking at the narrow trail squeezed between the rocky outcrops of white stone. The wagon sat right in the middle of the bottleneck. She doubted she could lead her horse up and over the steep terrain. If they didn't move, she'd be forced to backtrack and wait them out. Bri guided her horse to the side and waited in the tall grasses. She prayed any snakes hiding amongst the sun-warmed rocks had slithered away. The last thing she needed was to be bucked off a spooked horse.

"Like I said, you're not welcome in Swifthill," the son hissed. The defiance in his bratty eyes made Bri chuckle.

"Gods, you're a grumpy lot." She dismounted her horse in one smooth movement. Rolling her shoulders, she grabbed the halter of the horse hitched to the wagon and led it forward. She clicked her tongue. "Come on, let's go."

"Stop!" the father bellowed, yanking on the horse's reins.

The son dropped from his seat and Bri grinned, hoping he might be reckless enough to attack her.

"Shit," the one at the back growled, jumping from the wagon bed and running to back up his friend. The father cursed under his breath and reluctantly climbed down as well.

What was it with men and fisticuffs? Every tavern brawl ended this way—one idiot bolstering the foolishness of the next until a chaotic mob erupted.

"On any other day, I'd indulge you, friends." Bri grinned as the first fae rounded on her. She hadn't had a chance to train during the last two days due to constant travel. Normally, she'd let him get a few swings in and correct his careless movements even while besting him, but not this day. She had to reach the palace and find out how bad the situation was after the attack.

The Western Court Queen was dead. That's all Bri knew for certain. Delta had frantically called upon her through the magical fae fires, begging for her help. Bri had already been on the Western Court border, fighting Balorn's cursed blue witches in Valtene. The aches of that battle still echoed through her muscles even as she rode with haste toward the Western capital.

The youngest fae swung wildly, and Bri easily stepped out of his reach. She waited for his momentum to pull him to the side before she stepped in, throwing out a quick punch. She connected with his jaw and kicked him in the gut for good measure. He tumbled backward into the scrub brush, groaning as he clutched his stomach. He'd be fine, but he was wise enough to stay down.

A hand landed on her shoulder and she grabbed the wrist, instinctively twisting until her attacker cried out at the unnatural angle of his arm. It wasn't dislocated, but it would hurt every time he moved it for the next few weeks. They didn't know how many years she and her twin brother, Talhan, had spent perfecting that move. She swept his leg out from under him, and he slammed down into the gravel. Plumes of white dust lifted around him as Bri looked up to the father.

He held his dagger out at her, wide-eyed at the speed with which she had incapacitated his comrades.

"I don't want to hurt you," she said, scowling at the fae clutching his arm and the other groaning from where he sat in the underbrush. She eyed the silver-haired fae and his dagger, her voice dripping with menace as she said, "Now, you can move your wagon, or I can move it for you. What do you choose?"

He swallowed, his hands trembling as he sheathed his dagger. Bravado gone, the two injured men rose and darted back to the wagon.

Bri nodded. "Good."

She mounted her horse, who'd been hastily grazing in the scrub. Perhaps when this horse was too exhausted to keep up with her grueling pace, stealing a new horse in the next town was better than trying to buy one. She couldn't stop and she didn't want her recognizable face to start a fight in every town she passed. The forests in the rain shadow of the High Mountains were home to mostly Western humans and witches. They barely gave a second glance, but as the forests turned to sprawling savanna, more fae towns popped up along the road to Swifthill. The closer she got to the capital, the more her presence would draw unwanted attention.

The sound of Delta's pleading voice rattled through her mind. *I need your help, Bri, please.* She would have bet a mountain of gold that Delta would never utter those words. The attack on the Western Court palace must have been devastating. How many traitors had infiltrated Queen Thorne's court? Bri would need to be wary of them all.

As the wagon rolled out of the bottleneck, clearing her path, she braced for what was to come. She would fight her way through the capital to get to Delta if she had to. The Queen's assassins had never been found, and the Princess barely survived the attack. Bri needed to reach the palace before the traitors came back to finish what they started.

~

She was ready for this journey to be over and to wash off the stink of horse, but the sight of her birthplace was no relief. The landscape morphed from forests blanketed in frost to arid red soil with spiky shrubs. The sun baked down, fighting away the winter chill. Cloak discarded, she urged her weary horse onward toward the high sandstone walls and cursed herself for coming. She reminded herself once more of who she was to these people. Briata Catullus was an enemy, banished on the first day of her life.

A towering bronzed gate guarded the main road into Swifthill. She peered between the gaps in the meshwork grating, looking out toward the city beyond. Roofs like mushroom caps dotted the skyline, starting smaller and growing larger toward the center in concentric rings. The white clay rooftops were decorated in whorls of silver and gold paint, patterned with the symbols of each household. Beyond the city walls, high on the cliffside, sat the palace.

The brown stone castle was shaped like a hexagon, with six tall towers each with needlelike bronze spires shooting toward the sky. Only one flag billowed from the nearest tower, bearing the Western crest of a ram skull above crossing axes. The palace's rooftop flickered in shades of green as seven trees shot out from the building itself, their branches billowing like clouds across the gold-tiled roofs. Each of the five palaces in Okrith had the styling of their court, but this . . . Something in Bri's chest tightened at seeing it. This place was different.

A guard stepped up to the far side of the city gate, pulling Bri's focus away from the palace on the hill. His eyes widened as he appraised her. "The Eagle," he snarled, speaking Bri's nickname with a muttered curse. "You shouldn't be here."

A scoundrel ready to seize the crown from the Western Queen—that is what they all thought of her.

"If I had a coin for every time I heard that," Bri muttered, wiping her brow as the hot midday sun beat down on her. She put on her practiced air of indifference and addressed the guard. "You're wrong. I've been asked to come by Delta Thorne."

He paused, considering her words with a glower. "The Captain was nearly killed that night. She was probably hallucinating from the pain."

Bri shook out the sweaty tunic clinging to her chest. "Do I look like I'm riding into battle?"

"You can't handle the Western sun, traitor," the guard taunted.

"You get used to it," a voice called from behind her.

A man on horseback rode up beside her. He was middle-aged with pale skin burned red across his cheeks and nose. He was lean and incredibly tall, sitting straight on his mount. She took in his cinnamon-brown tunic and the totem pouch around his neck—a witch, probably a brown witch, given this was their home court.

"Lady Catullus is needed here. I've requested her help." The witch turned to the guard. "Let us in, please, Lifa. I'll personally escort her to the castle."

The guard paused, eyeing the brown witch, and then returned his attention to Bri. He spat onto the dirt but still disappeared behind the sandstone walls to open the gate. Bri's eyebrows shot up. A fae guard taking orders from a witch? Whoever this witch was, he must be important.

"Thanks," Bri grumbled.

The bronze gate lurched, creaking slowly upward. Bri leered at the pointed teeth of the gate lifting into the sky. She didn't want to ride under them, but as the witch coaxed his horse onward, she followed, relieved the gate didn't come crashing down upon her.

Bri gave the frowning guard a wink and led her horse down the main thoroughfare into the heart of the city.

"I appreciate you doing that," she said, pulling her horse up beside the brown witch.

The witch dusted his straw-blond hair off his forehead and adjusted his golden spectacles. "That guard doesn't realize how needed your presence is," the witch said, casting his sky-blue eyes to her. "I'm Cole, head healer to the royal family."

She narrowed her gaze at him. "A male witch with enough power to be the head healer? I'm impressed."

"I think you'll find the lines between us are more blurred than our language allows." Cole's eyes crinkled. "Saying there are no powerful male witches is as ridiculous as saying there are no powerful female warriors."

"I like you, Cole." Bri huffed. "I can see why Queen Thorne picked you."

Looking to one tree peeking above the palace's roofline, he whispered the Western prayer: "May we see her spirit in the rustling leaves." He spoke it in the common tongue of Ific, but she could tell he'd translated it from the witches' language of Mhenbic.

"I'm sorry for your loss." Bri bowed her head. "I'm sure you're exhausted after the attack. How many were injured?" If anyone were to know the severity of the injuries, it would be the head healer.

"It was worse than the council let on," he murmured, gazing down along the quiet streets. He led his horse out to a side road, moving away from the bustling markets up ahead.

Bri's horse followed, clomping down the tussock-colored bricks. "How many casualties?"

"Twelve," Cole replied. "Many more injured." He tapped the saddle-bag. "I've just come from the mountains. We needed more supplies than our gardens could grow, even with the aid of green witch magic." He had a calm, warm tone, so common amongst healers.

The Western Court palace probably had teams of witches of every color—green witches who grew gardens and cooked delicious foods, brown witches who made healing elixirs, red witches who could animate objects, and blue witches who Saw the future. The violet witches of the East had long since disappeared . . . or so Bri had thought. She shuddered, thinking of the purple smoke that filled the sky during the battle in Valtene. What ancient magic had Augustus Norwood tapped into to curse armies of witches and make poisonous smoke? Worse, he'd never been found after the battle. He fled along with his remaining soldiers, his armada sailing out into the Callipho Sea.

Bri eyed the deep furrows cut into the street, giant gutters leading toward immense drains. The Southern Court had similar features, though she wasn't sure the West had quite the same monsoons. The deep gutters told her enough—when it rained, it rained hard.

"Delta? How is she?"

Cole cleared his throat. His expression darkened, and Bri clenched the reins tighter in her grip. It was bad, then.

"I was being earnest when I said you were needed here," he said. "Delta needs urgent care but . . . I think she is waiting until you arrive to let me—"

Bri's pulse drummed in her ears. "Let you what?"

His gaze dropped to his hands. "Her arm was nearly cut off in the battle. She has no feeling in it anymore. . . . It needs to be removed."

Disbelief coursed through her. "No."

Delta would be devastated. Her greatest pride was being the Captain of the Queen's guard. Bri's mind whirled, grasping for some way to ease that blow. Delta could still fight. She could train for one-handed combat. It would be okay, Bri tried to reassure herself.

"She won't let me do it," Cole said, the warmth in his voice sounding strained. "I think she's waiting for you."

Bri tapped her horse with her calf, urging it to move faster. They

7

picked up the pace, skirting around the edges of the city, where only a few curious people watched them pass.

"You want me to convince her to remove her arm?" Bri asked incredulously.

"I can't keep healing the wound forever. There is not enough *chae-wood* in the entire Western Woods." Cole let out a frustrated sigh, clearly having had this conversation before. "Fae healing can only do so much. Wounds left untreated and unhealed will still kill you."

Narrowing her eyes at the looming castle, Bri rubbed a hand over her tight neck muscles and sighed. Delta was the most stubborn sort of soldier, even worse than Bri herself.

They trotted through the open far gate of the city and up the trail toward the palace. A herd of goats scattered into the golden shrubs. The road narrowed, creating a land bridge as the earth fell into a sheer drop on either side of them. On the high plateau, the palace was protected from all angles. The attackers must have snuck in disguised as guards or servants. There's no way a cavalry would get across this bridge unnoticed, and it would be an impossible climb to scale up the cliffsides circling the palace grounds.

She looked out over the rolling landscape, filled with sawtooth plants and spindly trees, stretching out toward a strip of sapphire blue. Golden sand beaches beckoned from the white-capped ocean waves beyond. She wondered how long it would take to ride out to the sea. The heat blurred the landscape, bending it like a mirage, making the idea of a swim all the more enticing.

Bri spotted a silhouette in the gardens, a solitary person staring toward the horizon.

"And the Princess? Is she all right?"

"I think everyone is still reeling from her mother's assassination," Cole said diplomatically. "I've been prescribing many remedies to members of the council to calm their nerves ... though the Princess hasn't accepted any."

Bri understood the meaning that Cole delicately tiptoed around: Princess Abalina was uninjured but far from alright, and apparently just as stubborn as her cousin when it came to accepting aid.

She wondered if Abalina still looked the same. It had been many years since the Princess had attended a royal engagement in another court. Abalina was there the night of Neelo's poker game in Saxbridge, but Bri and Tal had waited in the parlor a floor below and never caught sight of the Princess. Her stomach tightened as her mind drifted toward her twin. They'd had long-lasting arguments before but nothing like this. Talhan had looked at her like she was a traitor for coming to Swifthill.

She shook the thought from her head and twisted back toward Cole. "Did they catch any of the attackers?"

"None remain alive." Cole adjusted his spectacles, angling his head to keep the sun out of his eyes. "There were dozens of them, though. Some escaped."

"Gods," Bri groaned.

"The witch hunters were always a problem, one the Queen conveniently ignored." Cole's tone soured. "They made themselves good money, and the West was largely exempt from the aftermath of Yexshire. I understand why the Queen did it, to stop them would have made her an enemy to Hennen Vostemur."

Bri grimaced at the name of the fallen Northern King. His shadow still hung over Okrith, even after his death. His tyranny had echoed throughout every kingdom, and his passing revealed wounds that had festered for years.

"She still should have gotten control of the witch hunters," Bri insisted.

"Agreed." Cole sighed. "She allowed so many of her people to die . . . humans, fae, and most of all, witches." His voice dropped to a whisper, and Bri wondered what happened to his own family to make his voice turn so hollow. "Now those witch hunters are rabid, and it is Princess Abalina who will have to tame them."

As they drew closer, Bri noticed the black shrouds waving through the open windows, blocking out the sun. The palace was in mourning, the Queen murdered by monsters of her own making. Bri gritted her teeth and urged her horse up the narrow land bridge toward the cliff. Too late to turn back now.

CHAPTER TWO

Bri followed the hunched servant through the darkened halls, their footsteps echoing across the stone floors. Cole had left Bri in the stables with a hasty farewell, tasking the closest servant with guiding her to a guest room. They walked through the eerie quiet, the aftermath of the attack seeming to cling to the stone. Rolling her shoulders, she shifted the straps of her heavy pack, trying to keep them from chafing against her sweat-stained tunic. The servant hadn't offered to take it, not that she would have let him anyway.

"I never thought I'd see the day," he snickered. She rolled her eyes. Even the servants were getting their jabs in. "A Catullus in Swifthill . . . Maybe I did die in the attack and this is the afterlife."

"How many attackers were there?" Bri's eyes swept across every room they passed, making note of each hall and doorway. No signs of struggle remained, no broken windows or knocked-in doors. She needed to hear as many recounts of the attack as possible. The survivors would each have a slightly different tale. In the panic, their fear would exaggerate details, and she needed to know what they were really up against.

"A dozen, not many," the man grumbled. "It was only after the Queen was poisoned that they attacked, trying to kill Princess Abalina too."

"Poisoned?" Bri's eyebrows lifted as if it were new information. "What kind of poison?"

"They still don't know." The man shrugged, turning down a gloomy hallway. "That brown witch healer is still trying to discern what they used. Three other fae at the dining table dropped dead too, but . . ." He paused, leaning in to whisper his bit of gossip, and Bri had to hide her grin at how easily she got him on the hook. "They have food tasters. So the poison couldn't have been in the meal itself."

"Then how?" Bri made a note to speak to these food tasters. "In the air somehow?"

"There were others in the room who were fine," he said. "Some say it was a magic curse that did it."

"I've never heard of such a curse," Bri murmured, reeling him in.

"Nor I," he replied. "But these are strange times we live in. Dark magic is being awakened. Who knows what magic the attackers might have wielded?"

She considered him—his balding head and scraggly beard. Had he heard about the battles with Balorn Vostemur and Augustus Norwood in Valtene? Had the news traveled to Swifthill of the odd magic that was coming back to life in Okrith? If Norwood's violet smoke could poison the air, who knew what other poisons he might be able to conjure. Rua seemed to think the Queen's assassination was his doing.

"Did you keep any alive?" Bri asked, narrowing her eyes at the decor as if she could divine the truth.

"No." The man snickered. "They met the ends that they deserved."

"That lack of restraint could cost more people their lives." Rage made fools of them all. It blinded the vengeful until they'd harm themselves to claim their due. "How can we know what they're planning if there's no one left to question?"

He turned up a spiraling set of stairs, his open-toed sandals scuffing against each step. "The Queen's council is investigating."

Bri snorted. "*Investigating.*"

"Perhaps with a Golden Eagle here they will have more luck," he said sarcastically.

"You are very forthright with your opinions." Bri bristled as if rankling her feathers. "Did you speak to Her Majesty this casually?"

"You are not my Queen." He chuckled far more than was necessary to get his point across. "You're not even a countryman. You're a foreigner here. It doesn't matter if you're fae and I'm human. I'm a Westerner, and you're not."

"Gods, I get it." She rolled her shoulders in the habitual way she did when they bunched around her ears. "Are you all like this?"

His cheeks dimpled. "Yes."

"Where is Delta?" The question had churned in her mind since she'd dismounted her horse. Despite her injuries, Bri had expected the Captain to greet her, especially considering it was Delta who had begged her to come.

"She is preoccupied at the moment." They reached the fourth-floor landing, and the man panted as if he had just summited a mountain. He hobbled halfway down the hall and extended his arm to the door. "Your room, My Lady."

Bri frowned at the title, giving the man a quick nod and thumbing him a gold coin from her pocket. He was already turning even as he caught it from midair, and she sighed at his icy reception. She needed to find the assassins and get out of this strange and unwelcoming place.

Closing the door, she entered a small hallway into her suite. The stone floor gave way to large terra-cotta tiles. They seemed perfect for baking in the winter sun and keeping cool underfoot in the sweltering summers, but the shrouds over the windows kept the room chilly, unable to absorb the strong Western rays.

The filtered light cast heavy shadows over the sitting area. Bold patterns of black, cream, and bronze covered the furniture. The room dripped in the trappings of the Western Court, from the finely crafted vases to the earth-toned patterned fabrics. Even though the Queen had banished Bri's family from the West, trinkets from the Western Court had filtered into her home over the years—painted clay pottery, woven wicker furniture, and vibrant tapestries detailed in the bronze colors of the West. The furnishings felt both foreign and strangely familiar all at once.

A scuttling noise sounded from across the room, and Bri narrowed her eyes at the far door she assumed led to her bedroom. It could be a curtain blowing in the wind . . . or it could be an assassin. The Queen had just been murdered, after all. She couldn't be too careful.

Her pack hit the ground with a hefty thwack as she unsheathed the amber dagger strapped to her hip. Moving on silent feet, she reached the far door, preparing to battle the intruder even as she twisted the knob.

Her eyes went wide as she threw open the door.

Carys lounged in an armchair, twirling her knife. A foxlike grin spread across her face as Bri gaped at her.

She smirked. "Happy to see me?"

"How in the Gods' names did you get here before me?" Bri stumbled over her words as her mind whirled to keep up. "And what are you even doing here?"

"You've been so adamant to stay out of the West that you don't know how to navigate it very well. It's only a day's ride from Valtene, if you know the right roads to take." Carys winked. "I saw Talhan's face when he returned to the tavern after you left, and I made him tell me everything." Carys lifted her legs off the chair and planted her feet down on the plush rug. Flipping her knife in her hands, she said, "You thought you could just go off without me knowing? *Me?*"

"Carys—"

"Nope," she said, cutting Bri off as she sheathed her knife. "I let you go north with Rua, but *this?* This is Swifthill, Bri. This is the place you've avoided your entire life, and I'm not letting you plunge into the belly of this beast without me."

Bri dragged a hand down her face. "What about the Eastern Court? Aren't you meant to be overseeing the election of a new sovereign?"

"The council has been assembled there now. They can handle most things, and Talhan will be there once he's recovered too." Carys shrugged as if it were that simple.

Bri quirked her brow. "Tal is going to help the council?"

"I know, his worst nightmare, right?" Carys chuckled. "But he'll keep an eye on things while we sort out the West. He's in no condition to be battling anyone right now. Besides, Augustus Norwood was last spotted heading out to sea along the Western coast. Being here is strategic for me as well. I'll keep an eye out for Norwood while you help Delta get control over the witch hunters."

Bri's lips pulled downward as she sidled to the bed. She perched on its edge, hanging her head for a moment with a sigh. "They're not witch hunters anymore. They're hunting royal fae."

"What did Augustus promise them to make them kill their own Queen?" Carys mused.

"That is an excellent question." Bri rubbed the back of her neck. "I need to find Delta."

"I bet you do."

"Quit it," Bri growled at her smirking friend. "She was a fun pastime, that's it. My Fate is to take a crown, not a partner."

Bri stared down at her boots, thinking of the words she'd heard over and over her whole life: *The Eagle will seize the crown from its sovereign.* The prophecy that loomed over her was finally less frightening now that the Eastern throne was vacant. The thought of taking the Eastern crown from the petulant child that was Augustus Norwood thrilled her. It made sense. Her Fate was to rule the East, the land she had grown up in. She would settle things in Swifthill and then go back to the Eastern Court and prove the Fates spoke true.

"I am here to help the West and then I am gone again," Bri said. "Delta has nothing to do with this."

Carys stood. "Mm-hmm."

"I hate you."

"I love you too." Carys ruffled Bri's hair. "Now let's go find some food and then some answers."

Bri stood and begrudgingly wrapped her arms around her friend, pulling her into a tight hug. "I'm glad you're here."

Carys grinned against her shoulder. "I know."

~

Bri and Carys plodded through the sprawling castle and down the labyrinth of twisting stairs. Upon each landing, short hallways greeted them, splintering out like the branches of a tree. The floors undulated from stone to tile in detailed patterns that made Bri wonder how people didn't trip.

"It makes the Eastern decor seem lacking, doesn't it?" Carys asked, eyeing the hallway tables adorned with painted clay vases and thick fragrant candles, woven artwork hanging above them. "Reminds me of your house."

"My mother created her own little Swifthill in the Eastern Court," Bri said, frowning at a painting of the savanna. The Eastern simplicity of carved wood adornments did seem lacking compared to the warmth of the Western decor. "She was so certain this was my destiny."

Carys hummed in agreement. "What do you think she'll do when she finds out you're here?"

"Celebrate," Bri snarled. "I'm sure she's buying gowns for a coronation already."

Carys moved in front of Bri, making her stop. "Are you sure you want to be here, Bri?" she asked, arching her eyebrow. Carys was one of the few people who knew about Bri's mother. She knew how Bri was treated as a child and all the reasons Bri had severed ties with her mother long ago. "We could send someone else. . . . It doesn't have to be you."

"You should have heard Delta's voice." Bri jutted her jaw to the side. "I've never heard her sound so panicked. Ever."

"Some people *are* happy you're here, Bri. I heard stirrings through the city before you even arrived." Carys gave her a wary glance.

"My mother's doing," Bri confirmed. "She's been attempting to sow seeds of dissent in the West my whole life." Bri rubbed her hand down her face, releasing a frustrated sigh. "Let's just secure the crown and get out of here, okay?"

They hastened toward the Queen's chambers, which were easy enough to find. Guards patrolled each turn along the hallways and doorways all the way to the last large wooden door. Not a single guard stopped them, clearly having been notified of their arrival.

Bri pounded on the door and stepped back. It creaked open a crack and a fae male with dark brown skin and gray hair peered out, glowering at them from his deeply lined face.

"Let them in, Father," a voice commanded from inside.

The face disappeared from the sliver of open doorway, and the room opened. It was a small reception room, but still elegant. A dozen people lined the walls, watching in rapt silence as Bri and Carys entered. A wicker chair sat empty in the center of the room while the rest of the council stood.

"I never thought I'd see the day," the fae standing in the center of the room said. He had light brown skin, hazel eyes, and a charming air so common amongst royal courtiers. "Briata Catullus, come to steal the crown at last?"

"For the last time, I have no interest in the crown," Bri gritted out, her eyes drifting to the battle-axes painted on his golden tunic. "Who are you?"

"Apologies," he said with a bow. "I'm Tem, Tem Wystron." He gestured to the gruff man who let them in. "This is my father, Darrow. We are members of the Queen's council."

"Is Lina Queen now?" Carys asked, stepping in front of Bri. It was clear from the nickname that Carys was more familiar with Abalina, having grown up in the Southern Court amongst the royalty there. She'd probably known the Princess her whole life, though she rarely spoke of her to Bri.

"Not yet," Darrow said, raising his chin. He had a deep, rasping voice, sharp and condescending. "Her mother is still unburned, her soul not even one foot into the afterlife. No ceremonies can take place until the shrouds come down."

"I understand," Carys whispered, eyes softening. "But it is a time of great turmoil and . . ."

Darrow held up his weathered hand. "We must wait for the mourning period before the coronation." He rested his hand pointedly on the back of the empty wicker chair. "One full week must pass before we can cleanse this place."

A tall figure in cinnamon-brown robes caught Bri's attention. Cole. He'd already changed and come to the council chamber. He looked as if he wanted to say something but was holding his tongue.

Carys eyed the crowd of silent, wary faces. "Where is Lina?"

"The Princess has been feeling unwell and retired early tonight," Tem said, glancing at Cole, who nodded back to him. "I'm sure she'll feel better tomorrow."

"We will speak with her tomorrow, then," Carys said resolutely.

Bri shifted. She knew what her friend was saying: there are too many people here to talk openly about what had happened.

"Whatever you need to say, you can say in front of the council." Tem gestured around the room. "We can pass on your sentiments to Her Highness."

"It is fine, Tem," Darrow said, his voice dripping with venom as he stared at Bri. "They will not be staying long. We do not need the help of foreigners."

The word grated against her skin. She knew the councilor's warning for what it was—Bri didn't belong in the West. Her mother may have birthed her in the Western Court, but apparently that didn't make her a Westerner, despite her mother's efforts to make it so. She'd been raised as if she *were* a Western Princess. Her overbearing mother trained her far more vigorously in the art of royal life than Talhan was trained with a sword. With her short hair and muscular frame, and by favoring tunics and fighting leathers over dresses and ribbons, Bri was nothing like the person her mother wanted her to be.

"We will discuss your business over breakfast tomorrow, then," Tem said, subduing both parties with an easy, practiced grace. He took a step toward his father and rested a hand on his shoulder.

Darrow's eyes closed and he nodded. "You can prepare for your departure in the morning." He waved his hand, dismissing them.

"Fine," Bri gritted out. She turned and left without a departing bow. If they weren't going to show her a modicum of respect, she would follow their example.

"You still think this is a good idea?" Carys muttered, hastening after her as they sped down the hallway.

"It was never a good idea," Bri grumbled. "But we're doing it anyway."

"Where are we going?" Carys asked without breaking stride as Bri moved in the opposite direction from which they had first come.

Bri clenched her fists by her side. "To find Delta."

CHAPTER THREE

Carys frowned at the black fabric billowing into the hallway. "I had a dream that someone strangled me with one of those things."

"Remind me to tell you about the Temple of Hunasht in the Northern Court. These bodies—"

"Nope, don't want to know," Carys cut her off. "Remy already told me what you told her, and that version of the story has already haunted my dreams. I don't need the Bri version."

A servant had pointed them to Delta's suite, not far from the Queen's own. They reached the door at the end of the murky hall. Bri lifted a hand to bang on it, but before her knuckles touched the wood, a mousy fae opened the door. Her dark brown hair framed her tapered ears as she stared up at them from wide doe eyes.

A smirk played across Bri's lips. She was exactly Delta's type— beautiful and dainty. The fae was probably leaving from a midday tryst. She wouldn't put it past Delta to woo lovers even from her deathbed.

"Oh," she said, pausing in the threshold. "Can I help you?"

Bri gave her a knowing smile. "We're looking for Delta."

"She's inside." She quirked her brow. "I was just leaving."

Bri held in her snicker.

"Are you friends of Delta's?" the fae asked, glancing between them.

"Maybe," Bri hedged. "Who are you?"

"I'm Saika," she said, pulling a lock of hair wrapped in silver thread behind her ear. "Delta's wife."

Wife.

The words kicked Bri in the gut. Delta had never mentioned a wife before. Was this new? How new? Delta and Bri had only just been together at the Winter Solstice. . . . She stared dumbly at Saika, trying to keep her expression neutral as she combed back through her memories. Delta had a wife?

"Oh, lovely," Carys said, recovering from her shock faster than Bri. "How long have you been together?"

Bri sent up a silent prayer of thanks to her friend as each question died on the tip of her tongue.

"Nine years," Saika said, smiling gently.

Bri covered her surprise with a rough cough.

"Nine years? And you've been faithful to each other that whole time?" Carys choked on her last words as Bri elbowed her in the ribs. She couldn't believe her friend had the audacity to even ask.

"Of course." Saika furrowed her brow, darting curious looks at them. "Though I don't see how that's any of your business."

"She likes to pry," Bri said with a forced laugh, yanking Carys to the side to make way for Saika to pass. "Anyway, it was nice to meet you."

"You too," Saika said, pursing her lips as she pushed past them into the hall. She turned to consider them one more time, her face softening. "Delta doesn't have many friends apart from Lina. I'm glad that you've come to visit."

Bri's bravado cracked as she watched the small, gorgeous fae saunter down the hall.

"Holy Gods," Carys whispered, knocking Bri in the side, mirroring how she was hit.

Grimacing, Bri scowled.

"We don't have to go talk to her right now, Bri." Carys scrunched her face. "Maybe we should come back later."

Bri forced her whirring thoughts to the back of her mind and took a steadying breath, just like she did when preparing for battle. She could panic later, not now. "I promise I won't kill her."

"Yeah, but I might," Carys said, balling her fists and stomping through the doorway into the suite.

"Car—" Bri called, but Carys was already stampeding off.

The chambers looked much like Bri's, except this one was well lived in. Clothes hung over the backs of chairs, and jeweled trinkets covered the side tables. Bri paused next to a charcoal sketch of two smiling people. The knife twisted in her gut at the happy younger faces of Delta and Saika.

The sound of the bedroom door opening pulled her gaze away. Delta walked out, yanking down the hem of her tunic, a flash of her smooth brown skin and muscled torso disappearing beneath the gray fabric.

Delta smirked at them, opening her mouth as she began, "Oh, hey—"

In a flash Carys was there, punching her hard enough in the jaw that Delta tumbled backward into the wall.

"What is wrong with you?" Carys shouted as Bri rushed over.

Grabbing her friend around her middle, she hauled Carys away from Delta. "She's already injured—"

"Good." Carys scrambled against Bri's hold.

"It's okay, Carys." Bri squeezed her tighter around the middle until she stopped flailing.

"It's *not* okay," Carys growled at Delta, though she stayed put beside Bri. "You are a cheating, lying piece of shit, and you had to go and drag Bri into your lies too."

"I take it you met my wife," Delta said, rubbing her jaw.

"Yes, your *wife* that none of us knew about!" Carys yelled.

Bri shifted slightly in front of her friend, readying to grab her again.

"I should have told you." Delta pushed off from the wall with a grimace. "It just got harder and harder with each year and . . . I don't know, when I'm not in Swifthill, I like being a different person—"

"A dishonest person?" Carys spat. "A liar?"

Delta turned her bronze eyes to Bri. "I'm sorry." She shook her head, tousling her coils of short hair. "This thing between us . . . I didn't want to give it up."

Bri clenched the hilt of her dagger but didn't unsheathe it. "Whatever, Del, it was only a bit of fun anyway," she snarled. "Why did you even call me here?"

"They killed my aunt." Fear seeped into Delta's gaze. "They almost killed Lina too. Gods, they were so close. They will try again; I know it."

"Do you have any leads?" Bri folded her arms, watching the way Delta hobbled to the chair and carefully lowered herself down with one arm. Her other arm was tucked inside of her tunic, a sling peeking from the collar. So it wasn't just her arm that was injured, judging by the way she limped. Delta was a fierce warrior. Her injuries must have been devastating if her fae healing hadn't fixed her.

Delta shook her head. "They poisoned the Queen, and when the healers rushed to her aid, they appeared."

"Who?"

She took a deep, wheezing breath. "The witch hunters . . . or at least we think. They wore carved wooden masks that looked, I don't know, like a lion?" Delta rubbed her shoulder as if working out a knot.

"If they wore masks, then they were probably people you know," Bri said. "Do you have a list of suspects?"

"Of course." Delta nodded. "I'll write a copy out for you."

"Lions would make sense," Carys muttered. "The patron animal of the East. Augustus Norwood is the lion cub vying for his father's throne."

"What happened after the Queen was poisoned?" Bri's eyes tracked each of Delta's shuddering breaths. Had an infection spread to her lungs? Cole was right—she needed treatment quickly.

"I got Lina out of the dining room, but the path was blocked. We hid in a cupboard, but they found us."

"Gods," Carys breathed, dropping into the chair across from Delta. All the fire in her disappeared at the sobering horrors of Delta's words.

"I fought them off as best I could, but they grabbed Lina." Delta's voice trembled and she coughed. "They nearly killed her. Darrow saved her life that day, not me."

"He seems like a real ass," Bri said. "He acts like you shouldn't be hunting the Queen's killers until after her mourning."

"He is an ass, but he loved my aunt." Delta pointed to the table beside the door. "Second drawer."

Bri opened it and pulled out a silver dagger, its hilt decorated in swirls of amethyst gems. They seemed to be symbols written in the witches' language of Mhenbic, but she couldn't discern what they were.

"What is this?"

"It was left behind by one of the attackers," Delta said. "I took it to our blue witch oracle, but she couldn't See who it belonged to."

"A witch, then?" Bri's eyebrows shot up. "Do you think this is Augustus Norwood's doing?" Her fingers traced the purple stones. "His magic, it kept the blue witches in the North from Seeing his movements. We think he may have resurrected a violet witch—or, at least, her magic."

"That would explain why we can't See the owner of the blade." Delta grimaced, adjusting her seat in her chair again.

"Norwood is working with the witch hunters," Bri said. "He told Rua as much. He said he has plans to disrupt the Western and Southern Courts and reclaim Okrith along with Balorn."

Carys gave a half-hearted smirk. "Well, at least Balorn's part of his plan didn't work out."

Remy and Rua had slain Balorn in the battle of Valtene only days prior, a battle that had so nearly killed them all. Their hold on the power of Okrith kept slipping from their grasp. When Hennen Vostemur was killed, it was a moment of hope after a decade of darkness, but the world wouldn't magically revert to one of joy—peace would come at the tip of a blade, Bri was certain of it. Augustus Norwood was a wild card no one had expected. Bri had known Augustus his whole life as a petty, sniveling brat, but now he showed surprising cunning. With whatever magic he had on his side, he always seemed one step ahead of them.

"So what's your plan?" Bri asked.

"We need to unmask the hunters, protect Lina, and stomp out the threat to the throne." Delta wheezed, her eyes filling with barely contained rage as she looked down at her injured body. "I cannot do it alone, and there's no warrior better than you, Bri."

"Ouch," Carys said, clutching her chest in mock hurt.

Bri scanned over her once friend and lover. Delta was as proud as anything. To call Bri to help her was so shocking that Bri had come straightaway, and now it was clear why. Her injury might never heal. Delta had watched her best friend and future Queen—someone she swore an oath to protect—almost die in front of her.

"Abalina won't be happy about me staying here," Bri warned. "She won't want me protecting her."

"She will let you stay, for me," Delta assured. "I'm not asking you to stay for long. Just help me find my aunt's killers, and then you can gallivant off wherever you see fit."

"That's rich coming from you," Carys hissed.

Delta rolled her eyes and then looked back at Bri. "Please?"

The pleading in her voice made Bri rock back on her heels. This wasn't the Delta she knew. The warrior was broken both in body and spirit, her fear a tangible current in the air.

"We will help you until you get better and then we will go." Bri released a long sigh. "And you make sure your people know that I do not intend to stay."

Delta hung her head. "Thank you."

Bri looked down at the ornate dagger, flipping it over in her hands. She would give them a few weeks and then she'd leave to compete for the Eastern Court crown.

Tipping her head to Carys, Bri led her friend out the door. They were hunting masked assassins and a deranged prince with violet witch magic. She snorted at the absurdity. A twinge of sorrow shot through her as she thought of the first person she wanted to tell—Talhan. He'd loved riddles and mysteries as a child. This would have been the perfect mission for him. They'd had so many adventures together: sneaking off into towns, pretending to be each other when they were little enough to look identical. They'd invented their own language, a mixture of words and actions that infuriated their mother to no end, but even a singular look exchanged between the two of them could be a whole conversation.

She shook the memories from her mind. She had work to do.

～

The pungent smell of herbs filtered down the hall, growing overwhelming as Bri and Carys neared the door. The healer's office was in the basement near the kitchen cellars. Thin windows lined the halls above their heads, sunlight beaming across the low ceilings. Bri considered the narrow rectangular panes. Too small for someone to fit through.

"Bloody brown witches," Bri said, pretending to gag on the smell.

"Behave," Carys chastised. "The sooner we figure out what's going on, the sooner we can get out of here."

She rapped twice on the door.

"Enter," a voice called.

She pushed the door open to find Cole bent over a large work desk. He peered through a magnifying glass held up on a silver stand. His magnified eyes flitted up to Bri, and he stood.

"Ah, good," he said. "Welcome to my office, Lad—"

"Just Bri," she cut in, hooking her thumb at Carys. "And Carys. We're not interested in courtly titles." Lady Catullus was her mother, someone she had no desire to be associated with, especially in these parts.

"Right," Cole said with a nod. "I thought you'd be interested to see this."

Carys sauntered into the room and leaned against the far rack of jars.

The brown witch's office was a cluttered space, filled with shelves of baskets and opaque jars. Drying herbs hung above a dresser of numbered drawers. The workbench took up the bulk of the room. Mortars and pestles, jars of oils, and metal instruments covered the surface in haphazard piles.

Bri swallowed back the odd mixture of overpowering herbal scents on her tongue and ambled over to the far side of the workbench. She narrowed her eyes at the stack of fine silverware piled in the center of the table.

"Is that the silverware from the night of the Queen's murder?" Carys's eyebrows shot up. "How can someone poison metal?"

Cole adjusted his golden spectacles. "You see this fork?" He gestured to it with the long tweezers in his hand. "Do you notice it's different from this one?"

Bri looked between the two forks lying side by side. She pointed to the one under the magnifying glass. "That one looks like it's in need of a polish."

The cutlery appeared dulled, as if a soapy film had dried on it.

"These were the ones set out the night of the Queen's murder." Cole pointed to the dulled ones. "According to the staff, they had just been shined. Watch this."

Using his tweezers, he plucked a green leaf from a potted plant beside him. Carefully, he wiped the leaf along the handle of the fork and then held it up to the light. Bri's eyes widened as the green leaf shriveled, disintegrating into blackened sand.

"Gods, is that what happened to the Queen?" Carys sucked in a tight breath.

"Internally, yes," Cole said, his lips thinning. "I examined one of the bodies. Their veins had turned black." His pale face drained of color as he looked at them and then back at his tweezers. "It wasn't as quick as this either."

"Gods," Carys whispered. "How long did it take?"

"Half an hour."

"Shit," Bri growled. Her stomach churned at the thought of that poison burning through their victims' veins for so long before it finally killed them.

"The attackers were flooding through the palace." His voice trembled and he cleared his throat. "I couldn't get to the Queen. I don't think any of my antidotes would have worked, though. All the poisons I know of are ingested. This one seems to be absorbed through the skin."

He swapped out his tweezers for calipers and picked up a scrap of fabric. He rubbed it down the handle of a dulled knife.

"It is the strangest thing. It doesn't seem to transfer to other materials." Cole wiped the cloth onto another leaf of the potted plant. They watched, but the leaf didn't shrivel. "Something about how the metal mixes with the poison . . . seems to only work on living organisms." He lifted the cloth and sniffed it. "It has an odd scent too. Kind of sweet." He shook his head, setting the cloth back on the table. "But whatever it is, it's magical. Can you feel it?"

Bri reached out and hovered her hand over the silverware, feeling the thread of magic in the air. "It's impossible to say. Your office is filled with your magic."

"It feels different to me," Cole murmured.

"I don't think I can sense the difference between the types of witch magic. It simply feels like magic." Carys looked around the room. "They probably didn't even think about it. Probably assumed it was the green witch magic in the cooking."

"Can brown witches make poisons like this?" Bri nodded toward the silverware.

"We can make all sorts of poisons, though it is highly frowned upon," Cole said, adjusting his glasses again, though they hadn't appeared to have slipped down his nose. "My great-great-grandmother was famous for her poisons." He pointed to a collection of portraits on the dresser behind him. "But I don't think this is brown witch magic."

"It can't be." Carys's brows pinched together. "You think it's violet witch magic?"

Cole crossed his arms, sighing. "I do."

"How?"

"I don't know." He took off his glasses and rubbed his eyes. "Either they found a way for other witches to wield their magic or the violet coven isn't as extinct as we all thought."

"And they're working with Norwood," Bri gritted out.

"He is technically still the heir to their kingdom," Carys said. "Maybe they feel an allegiance to him?"

"It doesn't make any sense. Why now?" Bri knew she wouldn't get an answer. She rolled her shoulders. She needed to get into a sparring ring before she punched her fist through the wall. "Right, well, we need to talk to whoever was in charge of shining the silverware."

"A boy named Francis," Cole said. "He died that night."

"You think he was in on it?"

"Why would he set these out otherwise?" Carys gestured to the soapy-looking cutlery. "The guests might not have noticed or cared, but if it was his job to shine the pieces, he would have noticed."

"We should go talk to his family," Bri said as Carys nodded. "Thank you for showing us."

They were halfway out the door when Cole said, "I'm used to treating headaches and sprained ankles. I'm glad someone else is looking into this."

"We'll do what we can," Carys replied, giving him a final bob of her head before she and Bri left and shut the door. They took a few more steps before Carys whispered, "Do you think we can trust him?"

"I don't think we can trust anyone right now," Bri muttered. "But I think he's telling the truth, for what that's worth. Still, we should keep a close eye on him."

"We should fae fire the others to let them know."

"Yeah," Bri said. "I have a feeling that gloves are going to be in fashion for the foreseeable future." She thought of that shriveled leaf on the table. The violet witches were back and with a poison that was lethal and hard to detect.

"Why couldn't this have just been a normal assassination?" Carys said with a groan.

Bri snickered. "Where would the fun in that be?"

CHAPTER FOUR

They spoke to palace staff and guards well into the evening but procured no new information. Everyone had a vague notion that it was the witch hunters who'd attacked, but no one could point the pair toward new leads. Eventually Carys relented, heading back to their room, while Bri made her way to the wine cellar. With two bottles in her hands, she climbed the twisting steps that led up to the roof, ready to finally take in the view.

She took a deep breath as her feet reached the landing, a blanket of stars stretching out above her. The panic ebbed at the endless stretch of sky. Her feet abruptly halted as she spotted a figure sitting on the lip of the red tiled roof.

Delta.

The injured warrior sat staring out at the twinkling night, the moon beaming a white glow across the land. In the far distance, ocean waves rolled into the horizon. It was as beautiful as Bri had hoped, vast and tranquil.

Glancing over her shoulder, Delta huffed. Her wounded arm hung in a sling around her neck, her other hand clutched a bottle. "Why am I not surprised?" she muttered even while shifting over to make space for Bri on the ledge.

Bri tiptoed over, careful not to trip on the uneven tiles. The weariness of the day stifled her anger toward her former lover. She was no closer to finding the Queen's killer.

Delta's eyes flitted to the two bottles of wine in Bri's hands. "Rough night or expecting company?"

"Neither," Bri said, releasing a tired groan as she sat. "I couldn't take another moment in those shrouded halls." She tipped her head to the bottle of red liquid in Delta's hand. "What's that?"

"*Avassa,*" she said, passing it to Bri. "Swifthill's finest."

It was Delta who had introduced her to the Western Court drink. The hairs on her arms stood on end as she took a swig. It was sweeter than ale and more citrusy than wine, but packed a wallop as it burned down her throat.

"The shrouds come down soon, once my aunt's spirit is sent to the afterlife," Delta said, taking the bottle back from Bri. "I'm sure my aunt's attendants will be happy to finally leave her chamber."

"Gods," Bri cursed. "I forgot you did that."

The Queen's attendants would stay with her body until it reached the pyre's flames, keeping her spirit company, singing songs and prayers for her journey into the afterlife.

"It is you Easterners who are strange." Delta chuckled. "You would just leave your family's spirits unattended? What a lonely way to begin the afterlife."

"Their spirits are gone the moment the light leaves their eyes." Bri shifted in her seat, uncorking her first bottle with haste.

"I know you're not a stranger to death, Bri," Delta said. "I'm sorry this place reminds you of her."

"I didn't say anything about her," Bri gritted out. She took a long swig of her wine, pointedly twisting her hips to move her amber dagger out of Delta's line of sight.

"Mm-hmm," Delta hummed, having the perfect way to get under Bri's skin. "I suppose you can make any traditions you want when you are Queen of the Eastern Court."

"That has a nice ring to it."

"How many people are you competing against?"

"I don't know yet, at least a dozen, probably more. My biggest competition is from Talhan and Carys, but I have Fate on my side."

"After all these years running from Fate." Delta shook her short hair out of her eyes. "You are so certain of that prophecy now, hmm?"

"It all makes sense." Bri bobbed her head. "This is my destiny."

"Careful, destinies have a way of biting people in the ass." Insects buzzed louder in the night as the stilted conversation lingered between them. Delta reached into her pocket and passed Bri a crumpled piece of paper. "Here."

"What's this?" Bri asked, unfolding the paper and glancing at the list of names on it.

"A list of whom I've already spoken to—who is in the clear, and who is still suspicious," Delta said.

Bri's eyes dropped down the long list of names and jobs, landing on the food tasters she had yet to find. "These two, I want to speak with."

"You'll probably find them at a tavern in town," Delta said with a sigh.

"None of your guards are listed in the suspicious column," Bri mused, lifting her brow.

"They're beyond suspicion," Delta countered. "I selected each one of them myself. They were all there, battling in the fray when the witch hunters attacked. If one of them was missing, I would have noted it." Bri shook her head and Delta guffawed, taking another swig of her drink. "If you don't believe me, please, by all means, interview each of them again."

"I might," Bri hedged.

Delta grinned. "I'll miss this."

Bri considered her, eyes roving her tight features and dark bronze eyes. "You speak as though you have stepped one foot out of this world already."

"Have I not?"

"The surgery will be fine, Del."

"I need you to look out for Lina," she rasped as she wiped her mouth with the back of her hand. "She's the most important person, and despite everything, I trust you."

"Your purpose isn't only in brandishing your sword . . ." Bri turned the bottle in her hands, her thumb sweeping across the smooth glass. "You've clearly got people who care about you."

"I'm sorry I didn't tell you about Saika," Delta said. Bri didn't answer. "Saika and I were best friends my whole life. I asked her to marry me when I was sixteen. My aunt refused to allow it until we were of age." She snorted, thinking of some memory. "But I was stubborn enough to wed her in secret, anyway."

Bri smirked. "Why does that not surprise me?"

"I wanted to move out of my house and go train as a warrior." Delta looked up to the bright night sky. "Plus, my parents hated her too, so of course she was the best choice for me."

Bri snickered.

"I love her, Bri. Maybe not in the right way all the time, but I love her. I know she'll take care of me and . . . I'm scared." Delta's voice broke as she lifted her bottle to her lips.

"That's not a good enough reason to hang on to someone," Bri murmured.

"I know," Delta whispered back. "And I'm sorry for it. I will miss you, though."

"Don't pine for me, it's so unbecoming," Bri taunted.

"It never would have worked between us." Delta shook her head. "I think we were both just filling the nights."

"Yes," Bri said, her eyes sweeping the form of the warrior beside her. "I'll miss you too. What we had . . . it wasn't love, but it was something."

"Yes." Delta's eyes dropped to Bri's lips.

She leaned forward, her mouth meeting Bri's in a soft, desperate kiss. Her lips felt so familiar, her scent, her taste. So many nights they'd spent together, taking their minds off their own sorrows. The feel of Delta's warm skin pressed against Bri's body flooded her veins with desire, but instead of leaning into Delta's kiss, she pulled away.

"You should go get some rest," Bri whispered, tucking the crumpled list in her pocket and standing. "The surgery will be fine."

She gave Delta one last look. The warrior's expression was hard, as if clenching her jaw might stanch out the tears Bri knew threatened to spill. She turned away, heading back down the stairs toward her room. She remembered their last night together at the Winter Solstice in Yexshire. If only she had known that moment between them would have been their last . . .

She swallowed, gripping her hand around the hilt of her amber dagger, and savored the comforting sensation of the cold stones beneath her palm. It didn't matter either way, she told herself. There was only one person who'd ever truly loved her, and she was dead.

~

The quiet grated against Bri worse than an itchy woolen cloak. If she couldn't find solace on the roof, she'd have to find it somewhere else, starting with the food tasters on Delta's list. Her pulse strummed down to her fingertips, and her pointed ears tingled. She hated this feeling that nighttime brought to her body, the sense of wrongness putting her on high alert. It was time for a much-needed distraction.

Wiping a damp cloth over her face and swirling it around her neck, she sighed at herself in the mirror.

"Off to find some guard or cook to entertain you this evening?" Carys asked with a smirk, leaning against the doorframe.

"Perhaps." Bri grinned, giving her a wink through the mirror. "Why?"

"You're cleaning up." Carys shrugged. "If you had a date with the wine cellar, you wouldn't be trying to wash the stench off yourself."

Bri huffed a laugh, shaking her head at her friend. "They don't seem to mind."

"Yes, you're a gift to all womankind, Bri," Carys taunted.

Bri chucked the wet towel at her, and the blond warrior easily dodged it.

"What's wrong with a little fun?" Carys rolled her eyes, but Bri carried on. "Besides, I'm looking for more clues as to what the witch hunters have planned." That cheeky smirk played across her lips. "If I find other diversions while I'm at it, that's not my fault."

"Hopeless." Carys shook her head. "And what bar or brothel will you be able to find where they don't know who you are?"

Bri looked at herself in the mirror again, watching her form change before her eyes. Her ears rounded, her auburn hair dulled, and her eyes turned a shade of light brown until a human stood before the mirror.

"That glamour is useless," Carys snickered. "You still look like a fae."

"In a smoke-filled room after a couple of drinks," Bri said, unbuttoning her tunic until the burgundy fabric dipped into a deep V, "you'd be surprised what people see."

"You want me to join?" Carys offered even as she collapsed like a dying starfish onto her bed.

"Nah, I'm going rogue tonight," she said, peering at her reflection as she dipped her hand into the washbasin and slicked back her short hair.

Carys nodded, stretching her arms skyward with a yawn. "Happy hunting."

Bri rolled her shoulder, giving herself a last once-over in the mirror. Her glamour dampened her muscled frame, making her slightly leaner and a few inches shorter. She seemed less like a fierce warrior and more like an everyday tavern patron.

Striding to the wardrobe, she grabbed her black cloak. Pulling the hood over her head, her face obscured in shadow, she fixed the golden clasp. "Have a good night, Car," she said.

Carys gave her a sleepy grunt and a half wave as Bri left.

Deciding to forgo riding into town, Bri opted to walk instead. Her glamoured eyes couldn't see far in the darkness, and she thanked the clear night sky for beaming its silvery moonlight down on the path. She made a point of crunching the stones loudly under her boots, hoping any animals would scatter upon hearing her. Two tails slithered off the dusty road as she approached, and she shuddered.

In the distance, a pair of eyes reflected in the moonlight. She paused, reaching for the hilt of her dagger. Those shining eyes stared at her for a moment, disinterested, before the creature turned and ambled down the road. Her glamoured ears strained for the sound of its footsteps, but she heard nothing. Bloody glamours. She couldn't imagine how Remy remained glamoured for so many years, so long that she had forgotten what it felt like to have fae magic at all. At least her witch magic had helped her survive.

Letting loose a long breath, Bri kept moving, the path narrowing until either side of the trail dropped off into sheer cliffs. No animals crossed the land bridge here, wise enough to sense it for the trap it was. Her breath escaped in whorls of steam as the air chilled. She pulled her cloak tighter, bracing against the icy evening temperatures. At midday she had been sweating buckets, debating opting for the Western warrior's garb of leathered skirts. Her fighting leathers and heavy tunic had been sweltering, along with the extensive strapping of her many weapons. She couldn't imagine how the soldiers carried battle-axes around. They looked like they weighed a ton, and on a hot day with the sun beating down, carrying one would have felt like torture.

She moved faster toward the flickering torchlights of the city ahead. Grateful for the rush of sounds, she neared the city, greeted by the clamor of people shouting and shutters being latched. The eerie quiet of that night many years ago pushed to the back of her mind. She tucked that haunted memory away. She needed the largest tankard of ale and to get lost in the drunken laughter of the humans and witches. Some had once considered Hale the prince of debauchery, but it was the Twin Eagles who could always sniff out a party. Bri stretched her neck from side to side as if preparing for battle, taking a left toward the sounds of lutes and drums, plunging into the distraction her soul so desperately craved.

CHAPTER FIVE

Three glasses sat before her, each a different liquor. With each sip, her body eased, the thrum inside her matching the hum of sound. After days of travel, the exhaustion would soon get the better of her. She'd have to sleep when the sun came up the following day. Nothing felt real when she slept so little, but the drinks helped blur the lines between life and dreaming until she didn't care which it was.

Bri wanted to get lost in the music and sounds, but when she spotted the two maidens standing in the center of the crowd, she remembered why she had chosen this tavern. They still wore the same simple dresses as the other kitchen staff, faded by wear and sunlight to the color of sand. The olive-green aprons Bri had seen the others wearing earlier were absent, along with the tea towels over their shoulders and haggard looks on their faces, but it was clear they were from the palace—the Queen's food tasters.

Bri did nothing to hide her wolflike gaze as she watched the two of them dance and sway. The look lured them over, and they edged closer with each song. Let them come to her. It was much easier to get information from people who thought it was their own idea.

"Hello," the taller one finally said. Her friend nudged her with a giggle. "I'm Terez and this is Silvie." She gestured to her friend. They seemed young, though if they were employed by the palace, they couldn't be more than a handful of years younger than Bri. Terez was tall and lean, and Silvie short and round. Opposites in appearance, and yet, clearly best friends.

"Pleasure to meet you," Bri said with a smile, gesturing to the booth beside her. "Care to sit? It looks like you've nearly danced your feet off."

The two tittered to each other, an entire conversation happening between their eyes, before they pushed in beside Bri.

"We needed to let off a little steam," Terez said, shifting so that she faced Bri. She scanned Bri's glamoured face and eyes, lingering on her lips.

Smirking, Bri knew it wouldn't take much to get an invitation back to Terez's house.

"What line of work requires you to need to let off such steam?" Bri asked, leaning her head to the side to see Silvie too. Silvie bit the inside of her lip, trying to keep from smiling at her.

Bri had this effect on people. Something about her eyes and sharp features made people nervous, but her charming swagger made her countenance endearing. She drew people in without even trying. Talhan was the same. His joviality mixed with his soldierly appearance reeled everyone into him—a fisherman who unknowingly hooked everyone on his line.

"We work in the castle," Terez replied. "In the kitchens."

"Are you green witches?" Bri asked, running a finger along the collar of Terez's dress. "I see no totem bag."

Terez's eyes fluttered closed, as if that brief touch were exhilarating.

"We're no witches," Silvie replied with a huff, covering for her friend. "The witches do the cooking. We mostly clean and taste the food."

"I understand now why you needed a night out." Bri lifted her glass of amber liquid and took a long sip, her eyes remaining hooked on Terez. "I'm sure working in the castle is taxing at the moment."

"We thought we'd struck gold when we got the jobs last year. Silvie was hired first and then convinced them to hire me too," Terez said, grinning back at her friend. "They pay far better than any of the kitchens in town. I already earn more than my older brother at the stables."

"I've heard rumors the Queen wasn't killed by a blade but by poison," Bri said, adding a hint of disbelief to her voice. Everyone loved spilling secrets to someone who was intrigued by them.

"She was, but not by the food," Silvie whispered. "We tasted everything before it got sent up—"

"And after," Terez added before Bri could ask the question.

Bri rocked back in her seat. "You tasted it again after the Queen died? That must have been terrifying."

"It was." Terez swallowed. "But they all were thinking we had something to do with it."

"We knew the food was fine," Silvie added. Her eyes implored Bri to believe her, as if she were still on a desperate campaign to convince everyone of her innocence. "A bunch of us took a bite. The servers too. Everyone wanted to absolve themselves of the crime."

"Did anyone not partake?"

"Not that I know of." Terez glanced at Silvie, who shook her head. "None of the staff at least."

Bri propped her arm on the backrest of the booth, leaning further in. "Then how was she killed?"

"I think some guards know something," Terez murmured. Her eyes darted around the room as if searching for eavesdroppers. "A few of the guards have family members who were former witch hunters. I heard the second-in-command is brothers with the witch hunter king himself."

Bri blinked at Terez, remembering how Delta seemed so convinced it hadn't been any of her guards, but Delta also hadn't shared that bit of information. Perhaps she knew Bri would want to investigate her second-in-command if she knew of the familial connection. She made a mental note to find him tomorrow.

"What poison did they use if it wasn't in the food?"

"I think it was in their clothing, maybe." Silvie mused. "Like a powder or something?"

"Then how come those other three guests died, and Francis?" Terez replied.

Bri looked between the two of them. "Who's Francis?" She already knew the answer but wanted to see if they would tell the same story or if she would catch them in a lie.

"He's one of the servers. He set the table for the dinner—the candelabras and place settings." Silvie rested a splayed-out hand on her chest. "He was gone before the guests arrived. We found him dead in the kitchens before the fighting broke out."

"You found him?"

"Well, not us, but we saw him," Silvie said with a shudder. "His blood was black, dripping from his ears and eyes. It was awful. He was stuffed into a cabinet . . ."

Bri leaned in further. "Who put him in there?"

Terez shrugged. "We don't know. We heard one of the kitchen witches scream and came running."

Bri flagged down a barmaid, signaling to her to bring more drinks. "The other attackers, what did they look like?"

"Who knows." Terez wrung her restless hands together. "We locked ourselves in the pantry when we heard the screams from the dining hall. People say they wore golden masks to hide their faces."

"Golden masks?" Bri echoed. "So they must have been recognizable, then."

"People have been mad at Queen Thorne for years." Terez leaned her head so that it rested on Bri's forearm along the backrest. "Her list of enemies is a mile long."

Bri grinned at Terez's little flirting gesture. "So who do you think did it?"

"It's the witch hunters, just as everyone says." Silvie shrugged. "They're cutthroat bastards and they had the motivation. Their witch-killing business ended with the death of Hennen Vostemur. Now they're assassins for hire. It makes sense."

"And who do you think hired them to kill the Queen?"

"Augustus Norwood, obviously," Terez said. "The people are saying that little prick has been trying to reclaim his father's throne."

"They say he's got violet witches," Silvie added.

"They seem to be saying a lot of things." Bri chuckled. "Who is this *they?*"

"You've clearly never worked in the kitchens." Terez laughed, playfully sliding her hand up Bri's shoulder. "There isn't a topic in the world that one of the kitchen staff hasn't heard a rumor about."

"But how many of these rumors are true?" Bri asked, quirking her eyebrow at Terez in a way that made her bite her lip.

"It doesn't matter," Terez said. "We gossip plenty at work. That's not why we came here tonight."

"No?" Bri's voice dropped an octave.

"No." Terez grabbed Bri's glass of clear liquid and drank it in one gulp. She screwed up her face against the potent drink and stood, twisting and pulling Bri to stand. "We came here to have some fun."

Standing, Bri chuckled as her hand settled on Terez's hip to keep her from falling. Her scent wafted off her dark hair, smelling of freshly baked bread and soap.

The barmaid placed three more drinks on the table and Bri thumbed her a silver *druni*.

"Drinks on me," Bri said, pushing a glass toward Silvie as Terez dragged her onto the dance floor.

"Why thank you . . ." Silvie paused. "Wait, what is your name?"

"Does it really matter?" Bri shouted back to be heard over the fiddle and drums. She threaded her fingers through Terez's and her eyelids drooped.

"No," Terez breathed. "It doesn't."

Chuckling, Bri lost herself in the warmth spreading through her from the drinks and Terez's soft body pressed against her own. These two would probably swap stories about the stranger in the bar for years to come . . . and she'd survive another sleepless night.

～

The pleasant hum of liquor buzzed through her limbs as Bri wound her way down the narrow paths. Her hand skimmed over the curving walls as she ducked under clotheslines.

Her mind focused on the information she had just learned. Someone in the palace knew more than they were saying. She was becoming increasingly convinced that it was an inside job. No one was beyond suspicion.

Shouts rang out from up ahead. "Stop, thief!"

Bri rolled her eyes. Of course.

The buildings were different, the food unfamiliar, but these seedy parts of a city were always the same. She turned the corner just in time to see a cloaked figure racing down the path. One snarling, muscled fae chased after them. The thief darted down a side road, one Bri knew led back the way she came.

With a smirk, she turned around, putting her plans for sleep on hold for another hour. Maybe this thief knew about the recent events in the castle. Her grin widened. It didn't matter—she loved the chase.

Leaping over piles of refuse, she barreled toward the other end of the alley. Judging by the brief glimpse of the thief, they were an entire head shorter than her, with heavy, thundering footsteps. She estimated the time it would take them to run the long way round. They were headed toward the markets. Smart. The perfect place to get lost amongst the labyrinth of stalls. First, they would have to make it down the road up ahead, and those fae chasing after the cloaked figure looked like they were gaining on them. If Bri judged it just right, the thief would be stumbling out the other side . . .

Now.

She collided with the figure, knocking them back. The cloak didn't slip from the thief's face as they yanked a hand axe from their belt, their other hand clutching a large coin purse.

A fae lay behind the thief, clutching his stomach and groaning. Despite being smaller than Bri, they had already incapacitated him before she'd caught up.

Bri smirked. "Impressive."

"Get out of my way," a feminine voice snarled.

Bri's brows lifted, expecting an entirely different-sounding person. The thief turned toward the noise of feet echoing off the cobblestones.

"What did you steal?" Bri asked, her hand drifting toward her amber dagger.

"Something that shouldn't have belonged to them in the first place," the voice hissed. Whoever this thief was, they had a deep, resonant tone—warm, yet raspy. It made Bri squint as if trying to see through the shadowed hood.

Bri toed the fallen male with her boot. "I'm glad they deserved it."

"Indeed."

Indeed. Not the tone she'd expect from a thief.

Five more lumbering fae turned the corner. They were muscular and stout, with menacing faces that fit perfectly in these parts. They were either the lackeys of potions dealers or brothel guards. Armed to the teeth, all five looked like they knew how to fight.

"Fighting or running?" Bri asked, watching as the fae horde charged them.

The cloaked figure was already turning. "Running," the thief said, bolting down the alleyway.

Bri dashed after the swishing cloak. "Good idea."

"I don't need your help," the thief growled. "Just stay out of my way."

Bri ignored their warning, darting through the narrow bottleneck of rounded houses and following them into the markets. They dove into the maze of darkened stalls. Shop owners had closed up for the night. Empty tables stretched out as far as the eye could see, covered in abandoned bare baskets and empty crates. Heavy blankets strung from ropes partitioned the stalls.

Bri kicked over a table behind her, then another, forcing the fae chasing them to leap over or go around. She followed the shadowed figure under two heavy walls of blankets. The thief panted heavy breaths, their speed dwindling, making it easier to keep up. They wouldn't outrun the fae chasing them.

"Turn right," the thief called, ducking under another curtain.

Bri's arms wheeled as she popped up from behind the curtain, nearly colliding with a thick wood pole that held up the thatched roof. That would slow the fae down. The thief and Bri careened through the stalls, setting a distance between them and their assailants. Bri spotted another square of blankets—a makeshift changing room, perhaps—and made a quick decision.

She snatched the back of the winded thief's cloak and yanked them into the changing room.

"Wh—"

"Shh," Bri whispered.

Their chests rose and fell against each other in the inky blackness. Even with her fae sight and the bright moon beyond the curtains, she couldn't see the cloaked figure a hair's breadth away.

Her heartbeat pulsed in her ears as she listened for the heavy footfall of the fae chasing them. Their footsteps faltered.

"Where did she go?" one snarled.

"She stole the night's earnings, that fucking bitch," another growled.

The sound of their boots grew closer. The pursuers kicked over a table, which skidded across the earthen floor. One brushed against the wall of the pair's hiding spot and the thief sucked in a shallow breath, tensing. Bri gripped the hilt of her dagger, her muscles coiled like an asp ready to strike. This thief seemed like a good enough fighter. They could probably take on five of the fae if they had to.

"Show your face, Airev," another shouted.

Airev. It was a Mhenbic word, though Bri didn't know what it meant. She barely spoke the witches' native tongue, and that word eluded her.

"Footprints this way," another voice shouted far in the distance. "Let's go."

The fae took off through the markets. Bri waited until her straining ears couldn't hear them anymore and she finally let out a sigh.

"What a bunch of idiots," the thief muttered, brushing their cloak against Bri to step out into the open air again. Airev sat, leaning against the upturned table.

"They seemed like they could hold their own in a fight," Bri said, leaning around the giant beam holding up the market roof. "But clearly not the smartest bunch."

"Maybe they think footprints only last for an hour," the thief mused. Bri chuckled, stooping to sit on the dusty, cold earth. "Give them five minutes to get a bit further, and then you can head on your way."

"Do you want to tell me what that was all about?"

"Not particularly."

Bri huffed. "Why do they call you Airev?"

Airev turned their axe over in their hand. It was a simple weapon—the short handle barely long enough to grip with a curving long blade that hooked at the end. It wasn't as bejeweled as Bri's daggers, but it looked like it could inflict some serious damage.

"Some people profit from the fear of others," Airev said, tossing the coin purse in their hands. "I steal it and give back to those brave enough to stand up to those beasts."

Bri cocked her head, assessing them. "A worthy pastime, I suppose."

"And what are you doing out here?"

"I've come to Swifthill to investigate the murder of the Queen."

"I know why you're in Swifthill, Briata Catullus. Why are you in back taverns of Southside?"

Bri scowled, realizing she'd let her glamour slip. The alcohol mixed with the adrenaline of the chase made her forget she was meant to appear as a human.

A thin braid spilled from the thief's hood, its ends adorned with golden rings. The thief swept the braid back into the recesses of their hood, but it was too late.

"I should have known from your sour tone," Bri huffed, "and that scent. The same one clinging to the halls."

The thief went still. "What?"

"You smell like jasmine and rose oil and wear gold in your hair. You speak like royalty," Bri said, reaching a hand out and tugging back the thief's hood. "But that's because you are, aren't you, Princess?"

CHAPTER SIX

Bri couldn't think of a single goddess more beautiful than Abalina Thorne. Kohl lined the Princess's storming dark eyes, her intense gaze framed by metallic paint over her eyelids and high cheekbones. A golden stud pierced her nose and golden hoops circled her ears to the very tips. From their brief encounters in other kingdoms, Bri knew Abalina had the confidence of a Queen even as a child, but now, she looked it. Golden coils adorned her thin braids and her neck dripped in precious gems and bronzed jewelry.

"It's been a while, Briata," Abalina said. She sat with the predatory stillness of a lion, her sharp eyes the same shape as her cousin Delta's, though a shade darker.

"Since before the Siege of Yexshire, I believe, Princess Abalina."

"Just Lina," she quickly corrected. "I hate the name Abalina. It sounds like seafood."

"I hate Briata. Just call me Bri." Bri snorted. "Briata is the name for a damsel who wears fine dresses and writes poetry in rose gardens."

"And that's not you?" Lina taunted.

"No."

"Could have fooled me." Her snicker spread to a grin as Bri scowled at her. "I nearly saw you that time in Saxbridge." She hung her axe back on the hook of her belt. "At Neelo's card game. When Hale stole the *Shil-de* ring?"

"Ah, yes. *That* time." Bri smirked. "I thought your mother kept you cloistered up in the castle ever since Yexshire?"

"She did . . . but Airev still gets out every now and then."

"I can see that." Bri's chuckle ended on a sobering thought. "I'm sorry for her passing."

"She was so certain that you would be the end of her." Lina's gaze dropped to the coin purse in her hands. "She didn't worry nearly enough about her own people."

"I'm not here to steal your crown, Lina," Bri murmured. "The prophecy of my birth is about the Eastern Court. I'm sure of it now. If I will seize the crown from its sovereign, that must be Augustus Norwood."

Lina paused before her expression softened. "I believe you."

"Do you, now?" Bri narrowed her eyes, unable to tell if Lina was being honest beneath that beautiful, stony expression. Bri had been prepared for a battle, expecting to be greeted by contempt from the Princess just as she had from the council.

"My mother was the one with a grudge, not me," Lina said, straightening the beads of her necklace.

"Hmm." Bri mused, unsure of her response. Normally, she was a great judge of character, but something about this Princess put her off-balance.

"My people already spit at you for being here. I don't need to prove my power to you." Lina shrugged. "Though your presence in Swifthill is a distraction, since your mother has made my ascension to the throne incredibly difficult by spreading her gossip and lies."

"My mother is as petty as they come." Bri grimaced, making Lina smile. "I'm glad neither of us are like them."

"Me too," Lina whispered. "Though I feel bad saying it now that she's gone."

The chilled night air swirled around them as Bri pulled her cloak tighter around her. "I saw Delta today."

"It was awful." Lina's throat bobbed, her eyes going vacant. "She took on an army by herself to protect me."

"She survived." Bri tried to sound consoling, but she knew it was little comfort.

"I think sometimes she wished she hadn't." She cleared her throat. "I don't think she would have let Cole help her until you arrived. For whatever reason, she thinks I need a replacement for her protection while she recovers, and she trusts you." Lina glanced back at Bri, the paint on her face gleaming in the moonlight. "I'm glad you came."

Bri blinked at Lina, breathing in her jasmine scent. "I never thought I'd hear a Thorne say that."

"I still think I can handle this situation without you. I have my theories as to who did it. Now I just need to investigate them." Lina twirled a golden bead on her necklace. "But my mother was too proud to accept any help. I trust Delta and Delta trusts you."

"You might be the most levelheaded royal I've ever met." Bri grinned, shaking her head in disbelief.

"I will do what's right for my people. Always." Lina sighed, resting her head back. "Even if it's not what I want to do."

"A Princess moonlighting as a vigilante." Bri looked her up and down, from her axe to the gold in her hair. "You're certainly full of surprises."

"You have no idea." Pulling up her hood, Lina winked and Bri's stomach clenched in response. "We should go before they double back. I need to be in my bedroom by sunrise."

"How often do you come out here?" Bri scanned the empty marketplace.

"As often as I can," Lina said. "Royal policy is a slow change. Sometimes more direct action is needed. Besides, I don't sleep much at night."

Bri glanced at her sidelong. "That, I understand." The inability to sleep at night was something that plagued her as well. "How many of your councilors know you aren't sick in bed?"

"None." Lina gave her a warning glance. "And you are to tell no one, not even Delta, especially not Delta. You can make a show of guarding Lina for Delta's sake, but Airev is free to go where she likes."

Bri stretched her neck to the side. "Agreed." Delta would probably panic if she knew her cousin was being chased through the back alleys of Swifthill. "Let's go." Bri looked up at the dark sky, knowing the sun would soon be on the horizon. "You've got less than an hour to turn back into a dainty Princess."

"There's nothing *dainty* about me." Lina snickered as she chucked the coin purse up in the air and caught it again. She sighed, standing up and dusting off her cloak. "Come on, then, I've got a kingdom to rule."

Bri watched as the thief Princess sauntered back through the vacant market and her heart drummed in her chest. She had expected a snobby, spoiled royal, too arrogant to accept her aid. Instead, she found a beautiful Princess and skilled fighter, cunning enough to know when to accept help. She stared up at the roof, taking a steadying breath. She could hear Talhan's taunting words in her ears even then. This was not going to end well.

~

Bri couldn't remember what it felt like to wake up without a jolt. She had gotten good at hiding it now. No one seemed to notice. Not like Rua, gasping and crying in her sleep. No, Bri's dreams were just restless. She woke with a constant fear she was forgetting something, someone. Always on alert.

"You awake?" Carys called from across the room.

Bri craned her neck up to peer at her. Her thick braid draped over her shoulder as Carys finished lacing up her boots. She turned to the pile of discarded clothes beside her and chucked them into the wicker basket. It was one of the many benefits of staying in a palace: they didn't have to wash their own clothes. With the scorching sun of the Western Court, she bet they'd be clean and dry again by nightfall.

"How was the run? Didn't get eaten by any crocodiles, I see." Bri snickered. "I've heard to steer clear of the rivers around Swifthill."

"I wasn't too adventurous." Carys laughed, buckling her weapons back around her waist. "I just ran the main road into the city and stopped in the markets. I found a place that does the best fried bread."

"You went for a run to go get fried bread?" Chuckling, Bri propped herself up on her elbow as the midday sun battled through the shrouded windows. "I'd expect no less from a Southerner."

The Southern Court was the home of the green witches, where the food was divine, the drinks flowed freely, and the parties never ended.

"I got a few trinkets for the kids too," she said, holding up three little figurines. The miniature dolls were made of flax and dressed in tiny scraps of the woven textiles customary to the West.

Ever since Carys found out about her halfling sister, Morgan, she's brought toys back for her niece and nephews on all of her travels. Carys and Morgan were instantly close, in a way that only siblings could be. Bri tried to turn her mind from Talhan, but the harder she tried to focus on something else, the more his image flashed behind her eyelids.

Bri tossed her feet over the edge of the bed and stretched. "You spoil those three."

"That's what aunts are for," Carys replied with a smile.

"You just wait for how Morgan *repays* you with your own children." Bri laughed.

Carys unbraided her hair and combed her fingers through her straight blond locks. "I don't need to worry about that because I'm not having children."

Bri twisted to face her. "Why?" she asked, waving toward Carys. "Because of that? You still bleed, worse than anyone I know."

"No, not because of this," Carys muttered, nodding down to her body. The leather cord in her mouth muffled her words. Her fingers made quick work of weaving her hair into a tighter, neater braid that she tied off with the cord. "The life of a soldier doesn't suit children, anyway."

"And what if you become the Eastern Queen?"

"Then I will name one of Morgan's children as my heir," she said with a shrug. "Besides, it's more fun to spoil them than to teach them to be good people."

Bri guffawed. "True."

Bri knew one day she wanted to have children, though she hadn't decided which route she would take to make a family for herself. The world was in too much chaos to consider it anytime soon, but the thought sat there in the back of her mind—a seed that one day would become an entire family tree.

"Hopefully, we'll settle things here soon and we can head east to deliver them," Carys said, carefully tucking the dolls in the front of her pack.

"I hope so," Bri muttered. "We need to get some more answers today. We should split up. People will be more likely to talk to you than to me."

Carys nodded. "You're doing a good thing helping Delta out, even though she doesn't deserve it."

"If I'm going to be the ruler of the Eastern Court, then this is a smart move," Bri assured her. "We have Hale and Remy in the High Mountain Court, Rua and Renwick in the Northern Court . . . The Southern Queen is a wild card, but Neelo runs the place, anyway. It's the alliances with the West that we still need to secure."

"And if I become Queen of the East, I'll take credit for this plan." Carys, so used to being attacked by her friend, ducked before the pillow even left Bri's hand.

"I'll go see what more information I can get from Delta's second-in-command," Bri said, pulling on her boots and taking out her dagger and sharpening stone. "Soldiers seem more inclined to talk to me, at least."

Carys ambled over to the bathing chamber mirror and scowled at herself. "These bloody three hairs," she hissed, yanking at the unruly hair along her jaw.

"How do you even spot those? You are so fair, you'd need to be an inch from your chin to see them," Bri countered as she sharpened her dagger.

Inlaid with amber, it felt like an extension of her own arm, its weight and length were so familiar. There was something comforting about holding it. The intricate carved knots on the handle had worn over years of use, and she never bothered to shine it. She wanted people to see it was a blade she didn't mind getting dirty.

"I need to see if that brown witch has more of that stuff Fen gave me," Carys said, rubbing her hand over the red patch on her chin where she had plucked the hairs.

Bri eyed her friend up and down. "Carys, you are and have always been a goddess." She rolled her eyes. "You could have a full beard and swathes of chest hair, and all your suitors would still swoon. You know that, hey?"

"I know." Carys paused, straightening her tunic over her bosom as she surveyed her figure. She had a powerful frame from years of training, but with an ample chest and curving hips. She moved with the stealth of a wildcat, and every head turned at the swish of her hips. Finding Bri's gaze in the mirror, she added, "Thank you."

Bri shrugged. "It takes no work for me to say it because it is true. Perhaps after a dozen more times, you'll start believing it."

"Don't you have places to be, people to interrogate?" Carys tossed over her shoulder.

"We have a formal breakfast to attend first." Bri huffed, groaning as she stood and stretched her neck. "I hope you didn't fill yourself up on fried bread."

"Never." Carys sniffed her armpits, applying a salve under them before turning to follow Bri. "Now, hopefully, the Princess deigns to meet with us this time."

Bri's lips twisted into a smirk. She wanted to tell Carys about Airev. That moment last night had flashed through her mind again and again, and something about it was too special, too rare a feeling, to share it with anyone else. Instead, Bri headed out the door, muttering, "Let's go see what the dainty Princess is up to."

CHAPTER SEVEN

When Bri walked into the room, her chest seized at the sight of Lina sitting at the head of the table. She wore a shimmering black dress that hugged her generous figure and jewels draped from her ears and neck. An ornate battle-axe leaned against her chair, just like the one on the royal crest. Bri's mind exploded, thinking of what Lina would look like wielding that giant axe in her formfitting gown.

She sat, trying to regain her composure. The sight of Lina had been a terrible, glorious surprise. She couldn't tell who was more endearing—this gorgeous Princess dripping in jewels or the axe-wielding vigilante of Swifthill.

The decor in the room was distinctly Western, from the beadwork wall art to the patterned linen napkins. Bri took another spoonful of her sweet rice porridge, dotted with raisins and spiced with ginger. Her mother had attempted to have her cooks re-create the Western dish in their Eastern home, but it never tasted quite right. As she took a mouthful of the hearty breakfast, she understood now what her mother was talking about.

Bri peeked at the Princess over her steaming mug of tea. They dined in a small room on the first floor, the table swallowing up the space.

Darrow sat to one side of Lina and an empty chair to the other. Carys and Bri sat across from Delta and Saika, Delta's face looking even more gaunt and lifeless than the day before. Bri silently thanked the Gods that Delta's surgery would happen today.

Carys reached across the table to a tray of fresh fruit and served herself a hefty scoop. "You have passion fruit this early in spring?"

The rest of the table looked over at her.

"It's the ash in the soil," Darrow said, grabbing a piece of cinnamon flatbread from the center of the table and dipping it into his porridge.

Delta snickered. "Don't let him fool you. There's a greenhouse in the gardens that holds the heat year-round." She winced, her sweaty brow bunching as she set her goblet down. The act of eating breakfast seemed to exhaust her.

"It's so beautiful out there. Have you been?" Saika leaned her arm over Delta's chair.

Bri held in her scowl at the exuberant pixie. It was not her fault that her wife was unfaithful. Still, she couldn't imagine Delta married. Saika was the exact opposite of Delta's soldierly gruffness. Such spirit would be nothing but irksome to Bri.

"We only just arrived yesterday," Carys said.

"I shall give you a tour." Delighted, Saika clapped her hands, and it made bile rise up Bri's throat.

She glanced at Delta, but the wounded warrior looked too focused on using her good arm to engage in conversation.

"Splendid," Carys said in her courtly way that only Bri knew was sarcasm.

The tightness in her chest eased slightly. At least Carys was there. They would laugh about the ridiculousness of Delta and Saika when they returned to their rooms.

Lina remained quiet at the head of the table, her focus fixed on eating her porridge. She darted a few worried glances over at her cousin but said nothing. She seemed so at odds with the carefree thief Airev. Her concern thickened the air.

Bri found her eyes snagging on all the jewelry hanging from her neck and ears, wondering if it was as heavy as it seemed. She'd have a headache within five minutes of wearing all that gold.

"Are we expecting someone?" Bri nodded toward the empty chair across from Darrow.

"My son was called away to attend to some wedding business," Darrow said.

"Wedding?" Carys asked.

Darrow quirked his brow when no recognition appeared on their faces. "To Abalina?"

Bri snorted tea back into her mug.

Carys clapped her on the back, shaking her head. "I didn't know you were betrothed, Lina. Congratulations," she added quickly.

"It's been a match made their entire lives. The Wystrons and the Thornes have always been the closest of allies. It was time we made it official." Darrow eyed Bri with a frown. "I suppose the news hasn't reached the rest of Okrith as much as we would have thought."

He looked back to Lina, who was staring daggers at the table. Her shoulders were thrown back, her chest out and her chin high in the perfectly regal posture, but she didn't comment. The hard look on her face was the picture of a stern Queen. She was so unlike the thief from the night before, Bri wondered which face was her true one. There was one thing she knew for certain: any chair Lina sat in became a throne.

Darrow reached a hand halfway across the table to her, stopping just before touching Lina, his eyes softening. "I know he blames himself for not being here to protect you."

Lina's expression tightened, but she didn't respond.

"Yes, if he had been here, that would have stopped everything," Delta said with a scowl.

Saika placed a gentle hand on her wife's forearm. It was clear to everyone that Delta had taken her aunt's death hard, possibly harder than Lina herself. The guilt and shame radiated off Delta so thickly that Bri felt like she could reach out and grab it. It was no wonder she had called upon Bri.

"So who do you think did this?" Carys asked.

Darrow frowned at her. "The witch hunters, of course."

"Yes, but what are their names? Where are they hiding? How many are there?" She shot accusing looks around the table. "How are you meant to fight a faceless enemy?"

"Apologies for not gathering more insight while they trapped us defenseless. We were trying to survive," Darrow growled.

"If my mother had allowed me my weapons at that dinner," Lina said, making everyone look at her, "I would have been able to defend myself and not needed someone else to do it for me."

Bri's eyes darted to the battle-axe that leaned against the Princess's chair. The crocodile teeth bound in leather to the shaft of the weapon added a menacing touch that sent a thrill down her spine. She wondered if Lina could truly use it. She seemed a skilled enough fighter, judging by how quickly she incapacitated the attacker in the alley.

"The future Queen can't be carrying around an axe like a common woodsman, Lina," Darrow chastised.

Lina lifted her axe one-handed, hoisting the giant weapon with the same ease as lifting her goblet. "Does this look like a common axe?" Lina set down the axe and rolled her eyes as if this were a regular conversation. "These weapons are a symbol of the Western Court, Darrow. It is an honor to wield them."

"You could practice with daggers too," Bri said, drawing Lina's midnight gaze to her for the first time. Something in those molten eyes made Bri's grip clench around her utensils. They seemed flecked in the same metallic bronze that painted her eyelids and cheeks.

"I prefer my axe," Lina said, holding Bri's stare. An entire conversation seemed to pass between them, recalling the night before. "It's a part of our crest for a reason. It is the weapon of my ancestors." She slid her gaze to Darrow. "And our people should remember it."

"You should train with Bri, Lina," Delta said, resting her head against the back of her chair. Her hooded eyes looked like she might fall asleep, as if the exhaustion of eating a meal was enough for her to need to rest. Delta looked at Bri. "We used to train each morning. She's good with that axe, so watch out." She huffed before continuing. "But she'll get rusty if she doesn't keep training. Now is not the time to be getting rusty."

Everyone tensed at that. Whatever battles the West faced were not over. The witch hunters who assassinated the Queen were still on the loose, their attempts to kill Abalina only thwarted for so long. Each court in Okrith needed to be preparing for war with Augustus Norwood. His intentions were unknowable even to their Seers.

"I'll train with her right now if you agree to let Cole treat you today," Lina said to her cousin. A flash of sorrow crossed her steely expression. "We shall train while you have the procedure."

Bri glanced between the cousins. She'd thought Delta had already agreed.

"No," Delta gritted out and the entire room tensed.

"Del—"

"Not today," she snarled.

"Right, then." Lina's fist clenched around her napkin. She looked at Bri. "My guards will help you pack your things."

Bri's mouth fell open.

"That's not fair," Delta growled at her cousin.

"You think you have no meaning if you can't wield a sword, Delta, but you are the sharpest mind I know, and I need you on my council. Which means you need to have enough energy to keep your fucking eyes open!" Lina seethed, and Bri felt every ounce of her fury that her cousin wouldn't save herself. "You told me only if Briata Catullus took the mantle of my guard while you recovered would you let Cole treat you." Lina's lips twisted into a smirk, knowing she'd won. "Well, she's here, and whether she stays or goes is your choice, Delta, so what is it?"

Delta's head hung, and Saika rubbed a slow hand across her good shoulder. That little action made Bri clench her teeth.

"Fine," Delta said, bobbing her head.

Lina glanced at Bri without missing a beat. "Then you should go get ready to train."

"Good," Bri said, trying to hide her eagerness at seeing what Lina could do with that axe. She gave Lina an approving nod, glad that at least one of them could cut through Delta's stubbornness. It was clear then how much Lina loved her cousin—hard, but caring. She pushed Delta when she wouldn't push herself. An ember of respect sparked in Bri's chest. These same qualities would make her a good Queen.

～

Bri pulled on her fighting leathers, checking and rechecking the belts with nervous hands. The tension hung heavy in the air, knowing that Delta would be undergoing the operation as she readied to train with Lina. The lines in her periphery warped, and she knew the lack of sleep was catching up to her. She'd need to rest in the afternoon. Going more than a few days like this made her shaky, and she needed to be sharp in this place.

"She'll be all right," Carys said for the hundredth time, scratching out a line in her notebook.

"She'll live," Bri gritted out. "I don't know if she'll be all right."

"It's not your responsibility to fix every broken person, Bri," Carys said, dipping her quill back in the inkpot.

Bri glowered at her. "I know."

A sound at the door made them both jump. Bri was on her feet in an instant as a servant hustled in.

"Is it done?" she asked, trying to hide the eager tone in her voice.

"No, My Lady." The servant shook his head, wringing his hands. "It hasn't even begun. Captain Thorne demands to speak with you first."

"Gods," Carys said with an exasperated sigh, wiping her ink-stained fingers down her trouser leg. "Let's go."

Bri was already heading toward the door. They rushed after the servant, who moved on long, swift legs into the depths of the castle. Turning the corner to Cole's office, the sound of shouting and clay shattering echoed off the walls. Bri broke into a run, bursting through the far door.

Her boots crunched over the shards of pottery as she took in the space. Delta lay on the table in the center of the room, Saika beside her, holding her good hand. Lina stood with her arms folded, leaning against the far wall while Cole busied himself with his potion bottle. They all seemed to freeze when Bri entered.

"Right, she's here. Now what do you want?" Lina snarled, pushing off the wall to stare at her cousin.

Delta looked worse than she had at breakfast. The beams of daylight streaming through the window revealed the severity of her injuries, the wounds festering. The urgency of this procedure seemed to press in on the room.

Delta craned her neck up to Cole. "How long again until I'm back on my feet?"

"If you let me get the infection out today," he said in a carefully even tone, "your fae healing will take over, and you should be recovered within a few weeks."

Saika gripped her wife's hand tighter, rubbing her arm up and down in soothing strokes. "No time at all."

Delta looked at Bri. "I want you to swear your sword to Lina until I am recovered."

"Del—" Lina began but was cut off by Delta's stern look.

"I need this assurance that she stays true to her word," Delta hissed. "And that you won't try to evade her." She gave her cousin a knowing look. "Please, or my ghost will haunt you forever."

"The only thing you're going to die from is stubbornness, you fool," Lina jeered. "Now let Cole put you under."

"Not until she swears it," Delta insisted.

All eyes turned to Bri.

"I'm already here, Del," Bri said, glancing to Lina, who stared at her with brilliant, unyielding eyes. "I will protect her."

"Swear it," Delta pushed.

"Gods, it shouldn't even matter," Carys said, stepping further into the room. "I'm here too, for Gods' sake."

"I know you take vows seriously," Delta said, her eyes dropping to Bri's waist. "I want you to swear on that dagger on your hip."

Carys curled her lip as Bri hardened a look at Delta. She should have never told Delta who the amber dagger had belonged to, the sentiment behind it. Delta knew a promise made with that dagger would be worth more than anything else.

"That is low, Delta," Carys said. "Even for you."

"Enough of this." Lina stormed over to the countertop of elixirs, her voice cracking as she muttered, "I won't let you die too, Delta. So help me."

Delta stared at Bri with wide, imploring eyes. "Please," she begged, scrunching her face to keep her tears from welling.

Please. She didn't know who this broken person was. Gone was the lover with the cavalier smile. The fear in Delta's eyes was like nothing she had ever seen before. Delta was so certain her cousin would be killed while she recovered. The desperation made them all uneasy.

"Damn it." Bri scowled, unsheathing her dagger. "Knowing you, you'll be better in a week, anyway."

Delta's whole body sagged, lying back down as Bri stepped up to Lina. Those dark eyes held hers, a wary look in them as Bri knelt before Lina, holding up her dagger.

As Bri stared at the amber stone on the hilt, her chest seized. "Abalina Thorne, Crown Princess of the Western Court, I pledge my blade to you for so long as you need."

Time seemed to stretch on before Lina took the dagger. It made Bri ache to have someone else hold it. A sharp pang of sorrow shot through her and she silently cursed Delta for begging her to do this.

Lina slowly touched the tip of the dagger to one of Bri's shoulders, then the other, saying in a low voice, "Rise."

Bri stood, a hair's breadth from the Princess, as her dagger was returned. The scent of jasmine and rose oil wafted from Lina as her golden earrings glinted in the dappled sunlight, but it was those endless eyes that ensnared Bri every time she looked into them. From a distance, Lina seemed cold and cunning, but this close, Bri could see the swirling emotions rise to the surface. She hated how enticing it all was—to know what lay beneath that royal exterior. Now that she had pledged herself to Lina, she supposed she had time to find out.

Lina looked at her cousin and nodded. Delta's eyes filled with tears as she bobbed her chin. Cole stepped forward, bringing a vial to her lips. Delta drank it, her body going limp within a single breath.

Cole looked around the room, adjusting his golden spectacles. "It will take a few hours. I'll send one of my aides with updates."

They made their way to the door . . . all except Delta's wife.

"Saika," Cole whispered. "You don't want to be here for this."

"I'm not going anywhere," Saika insisted, holding fast to Delta's hand.

"All right, let's begin." He nodded to the rest of them and they departed.

Lina strode off at a clip down the hall, Bri fast on her heels. She moved faster and Bri matched her speed until Lina stopped abruptly and whirled on her. "What are you doing?"

"I'm following you."

"I can see that," Lina said, rolling her eyes. "*Why* are you following me?"

Bri's brow furrowed. "Because I've sworn to protect you."

"I officially absolve you of your pledge," Lina said, glancing warily at Carys and leaning in to snarl at Bri. "You're only here to appease Delta. I don't need *you* of all people looming around when I'm trying to bring peace to my court. Now, go away."

Bri rocked back from that confession. She'd been suspicious of the Princess, and now she knew why. Lina didn't want her there at all. She was just using Bri to convince her cousin to undergo the surgery, and now that she had what she wanted, she was done with Bri.

"I can't do that," Bri pushed back, resting her hand on the hilt of her amber dagger. Delta knew what she was doing by requesting that Bri use that one. She knew it would mean too much for Bri to fob off the ritual as an act. "I'll keep my distance, just . . . let me do this until Delta wakes at least."

Lina leaned further in with a frown, easily making Bri feel small despite being a head taller. "I don't like being controlled."

"Then I promise not to control you."

Lina considered her then, surprise and amusement battling in her expression. "You may not realize this, Briata Catullus, but *you* are the biggest threat in this palace right now. The farther you stay away from me, the safer I'll be."

Bri's mouth fell open as Lina turned and marched away.

CHAPTER EIGHT

The training rings were located in the southern wing of the castle. Around the shrouds waving in the breeze flashed glimpses of sunlight and stunning ocean vistas. The Western Court was known for its golden sand beaches that stretched all along its coastline. Nothing like the craggy cliffs and stone beaches of the Eastern Court.

Bri's parents spoke of the beaches incessantly, her mother decorating the windows with dried starfish and abalone shells. They said the sandbars were long enough you could walk out until you could barely see the shore. Such sandbars also meant that the coast wasn't navigable for seafaring ships, which had to go to the trading posts in Silver Sands Harbor or Valtene at the borders for their sea trade. It made the West more cut off from the traded goods of Okrith, especially when Vostemur blocked the road to the High Mountain Court. Now, with the pass into the mountains clear, the West would pick up in trade again.

Bri didn't think Lina could surprise her any more than she already had, but when the Princess walked in wearing the traditional Western battle garb, it felt like a punch to her gut. Her braids were tied back off her face, the golden beads clinking together as she moved. She'd removed her heavy jewelry, but delicate golden cuffs still adorned her ears. She was still royalty in every way. An intricately beaded neckline decorated her vest, which corseted under her bust down to her hips in thick leather that would be challenging to pierce. Her skirt swayed with strips of polished leather and Bri eyed the smooth brown skin that peeked out from her fitted undershorts and down to her boots.

Lina's face dropped when she spotted Bri tucked into the alcove, waiting for her. "What are you doing here?"

"I'm here to train, just as you promised your cousin." Bri flashed a predatory grin, knowing her presence would irk the Princess. "Plus, I'd like to see you wield that thing." She nodded to the ceremonial battle-axe strapped to Lina's back by a leather harness, a hook shaped like a ram's skull holding it in place.

"I told you, I don't need your protection," Lina gritted out.

Bri unsheathed her sword and raised her eyebrows. "Care to prove it?"

Lina rolled her eyes. In the next second, she had unhooked her axe and was swinging it round to her front. Incredible was the speed with which she drew her weapon. Bri clenched her teeth together to keep her mouth from falling open. The way Lina's cheeks dimpled told Bri the Princess knew she was impressed.

Bri looked anywhere but at Lina, nodding to the shrouds waving in the archways as she regained composure. "These come down soon?"

Lina stepped into the painted white circle on the floor. The room was vacant, the guards probably sent away so Lina could train in private. "Yes. We will burn my mother's pyre on the bluff and say our prayers." Her eyes darkened as she choked up on the grip of her axe. "And when I'm crowned, we'll find who killed her and make them pay."

"Good," Bri said as her eyes swept over the Princess. "If you're going to wear the fighting skirt, you need the sandals too." Bri frowned at Lina's ankle boots. "Otherwise half of your leg is exposed."

Lina lifted her chin. "I move better in these."

"Better enough to not need any protection?" Bri mused.

"Care to find out?" The faintest smirk pulled on Lina's lips as she repeated Bri's words.

Bri held up her sword with a grin and nodded. She made the first move, stepping in toward Lina and sweeping her blade downward at half her normal speed. In a flash, Lina closed the gap, the butt of her axe colliding with Bri's side, knocking the air out of her as Lina's elbow collided with her jaw. Bri stumbled backward, raising her sword just in time to block the heavy axe coming down upon her. She held the block, looking down at the Princess with wide eyes.

Lina's white teeth glistened as she smiled at Bri's surprised reaction. She knew Bri would underestimate her, and Bri had fallen straight into her trap.

"Care to show me how vulnerable I am?" Lina asked, lowering her weapon and stepping back into the circle.

That smile made Bri's stomach flip, and she clenched her jaw. Now was not the time.

Bri rolled her shoulders. "Again."

Delta had trained Lina well. The Captain had always been the most evenly matched opponent to Bri in every sense—a family trait, it seemed.

Bri didn't hold back this time as she launched herself at Lina. The Princess blocked her first three strikes with a shocking ease, considering the weight of the axe she wielded. The muscles in her broad shoulders and arms flexed with each blow. Her rounded figure belied these powerful muscles underneath. Lina was a lioness masquerading as a house cat.

Bri pivoted, feinting left and then lunging right, and turned her sword just before its width smacked into Lina's calf.

"Got you." She was about to smile at her victory when she spotted the blade of Lina's axe hovering mere inches from her neck.

"And I would have taken you down with me," Lina panted, looking at the blade nearly touching Bri's skin. "I might even survive without a foot, but would you survive without a head?"

"Wouldn't it be better to not have to make such choices?" Bri watched warily as Lina lowered her axe, leaning on the handle as she caught her breath.

"I will try the sandals." Lina conceded, running her eyes down Bri's muscled legs. "Or maybe leather trousers would be better . . . though it is not our traditional garb."

"Neither are those boots you're wearing." Bri tipped her head to Lina's feet. "Styles change. You are the future Queen. You make traditions, not follow them."

Lina froze, holding Bri's stare. She seemed to war with herself, an unclear emotion bubbling to the surface.

"I suppose you will have to be making traditions too, if you compete for the Eastern throne," Lina said. "Are you ready to be a ruler?"

"Does anyone ever feel ready?"

Lina grinned. "It will be good to have an ally in the East, should you win the crown." Her smile faltered. "Though, I think you'll disappoint many Westerners who think you'll usurp me."

Dragging her hand down her face, Bri said, "I don't want this crown. I don't want to rule the court that banished my mother with newborns in her arms."

Lina stiffened. She had finally acknowledged it, the unspoken truth between them. Lina's mother had banished Bri's mother for fear of what Bri would do to her reign.

"Perhaps when the prophecy said you would seize the crown from its sovereign they meant Augustus, or perhaps . . ." Lina picked up her axe again. "Or perhaps they meant me."

"I don't know what the Fates whispered to that oracle on the day of my birth," Bri growled. "What does seizing a crown even mean? It did not say save a kingdom. Who knows if the witch's Mhenbic words were even translated properly."

"Some of my people think that's what it means, that you will save our court." Lina gripped her axe tighter as she narrowed her eyes at Bri.

"You look like you really want to hit me with that thing." Bri's lips pulled to one side.

"I really do."

"Let's go, then." Bri lifted her sword, readying to spar again.

Lina didn't wait this time. She had so much pent-up aggression, and Bri was happy to be on the receiving end of her wrath if it meant watching the gorgeous Princess rain down blows with her battle-axe.

She ducked under another swing, darting away and then back in again, trying to land a blow. Lina dropped to one knee, trying to sweep out Bri's legs, and Bri jumped, waiting for the recoil to kick out at Lina's exposed shoulder. Instead of dodging the kick, Lina ducked lower, letting Bri's foot fly past her neck and then shooting back up with Bri's knee hooked over her shoulder. She grabbed Bri's thigh, lifting her off the ground as she stood. Bri's stomach muscles barked as she sat up, the momentum making Lina fall backward. Bri grabbed Lina's neck, catching her head before it collided into the unyielding ground.

Her eyes locked with Lina's for a moment, the two of them panting in surprise at the intimate position they'd found themselves in. Lina released Bri's thigh, lowering herself to the ground, and Bri dropped to her knees beside her. They eyed each other again, surprised laughter rumbling in their chests.

"I was not expecting you to do that." Bri chuckled, shaking her head.

Lina's eyes flitted to Bri. "I wish you didn't make it so hard to hate you."

"I wish you'd stop hating me," Bri countered, her eyes dropping to Lina's parted, breathless lips.

"Keep wishing." Lina's eyes guttered. "We should go get changed before the council meetings."

"We should do this again, when you have more time," Bri said. "I need to train with someone who can actually challenge me."

"Me as well." Lina looked Bri up and down in a way that made her stomach clench. "But that person isn't you."

Bri flashed a grin, shifting on her feet at the Princess's swift rebuttal. As Lina turned to walk away, Bri followed after her, a pace behind.

"Stop. Following. Me," Lina hissed.

"No," Bri challenged, getting so close she could feel Lina's breath on her cheek.

Lina's eyes dropped to the weapon on Bri's hip. "Why did Delta make you pledge on that amber dagger?" She arched her eyebrow in a way that told Bri she knew she'd won. She knew the exact question that would push Bri away.

Bri's words faltered as she crossed her arms. "Because it was from someone important to me," she whispered, shoving away the memory and gesturing down the hall. "Now, I'll escort you to your chambers and leave you there."

～

Bri felt like an ogre holding the petite teacup. Taking a sip of the bitter liquid, she forced a half smile at Saika. She wished Lina could have joined them, but Bri had left her at the door to her private quarters, where she was meeting with her council. The wing was heavily guarded, and Bri knew her protection wasn't needed there, but still . . . she would have preferred loitering outside a closed door to having a tea party.

Bri scowled into her cup. They sat in a little alcove in Saika and Delta's chambers. The door to their bedroom was shut while Delta rested, still heavily drugged from Cole's tonics, but within earshot should she wake prematurely. Cole had said the operation went well and that he believed he got all of the infection out, but Bri's shoulders still clung around her ears with tension. She wouldn't know true relief until Delta was up and walking around again.

"Thank you for inviting us to tea," Carys offered, delicately lifting her cup from its saucer.

"Of course," Saika said, staring down at her hands. "It's a welcome distraction."

Bri narrowed her eyes at the beautiful fae. "It's understandable given all that's happened."

She wondered what Saika was reliving in that moment. Was she thinking about her wife's operation? Bri had been in many battles, and yet the gore of fighting was forever burned into her mind. She wouldn't blame this gentle fae for being upset by what she'd seen.

"I suppose," Saika mused, flicking her gaze to the shrouded window.

Bri was certain there would be beautiful views over the cliffs and out to the ocean if the windows weren't covered. Still, sunlight filtered onto the circular table, casting a golden glow over the little honey cakes and finger sandwiches. So formal and ladylike—the person her mother wished she could have been.

She regarded Saika's flowing sundress with lace-capped shoulders, her slender ears and button nose, her rouged cheeks and bowed lips. It made sense that Delta would fall for her. She was the picture of innocence . . . which also made her perfect as a spy.

"Did you witness the attack?" Bri asked, clinking her cup into the saucer.

"No," Saika replied, smoothing her hands down her cream-colored dress. "I wasn't here."

Bri cocked her head. "Where were you?"

Carys shifted in her seat, the slightest clearing of her throat telling Bri she should leave it. Saika didn't seem to notice.

"I was visiting my family in High Meadow," she said.

"How fortunate you weren't here," Bri murmured, plucking a honey cake off the tray and chucking the entire dessert into her cheek.

The sound of shuffling announced a guard entering the room and Saika rose from her chair. "Excuse me one moment," she said, skating over to where the guard waited, holding a scroll in his hand.

Carys leaned in toward Bri. "What are you doing?"

"Getting to know Saika," Bri whispered.

"You're interrogating her," Carys hissed.

"Someone in this castle played a part in the Queen's assassination."

Carys gaped at her, tipping her head to where Saika stood in the far archway. "And you think *she* is the mastermind behind the witch hunter attacks?"

"Of course not," Bri scoffed. Carys was about to nod when Bri added, "I think she's a spy for the mastermind of the witch hunter attacks."

Carys lifted her hands in frustration, her blond braid swishing as she shook her head. "And this doesn't have anything to do with the fact that she is Delta's wife?"

"No."

Carys rolled her eyes.

"I'm being sensible and considering everyone possibly linked to the attacks," Bri gritted out. "I don't care that she's Delta's wife."

"Of all the people since"—Bri cut her a look, warning Carys to choose her next words carefully—"since Falhampton, Delta's the only one you've kept any ongoing relations with."

"Relations?" Bri quirked her brow, giving Carys a smirk. "It was just a bit of fun, Car."

"I'm not saying there were any feelings, other than the expectation that your *fun* would continue." Carys held up a placating hand. "But that's still a bias."

"It doesn't mean I'm wrong." Bri's voice dropped into a growl as Saika wandered back.

"I hope nothing's wrong?" Carys asked as Saika lowered softly into her chair, her skirts billowing around her curving hips.

Saika waved the concern away. "Oh no, not at all." She laughed in that sickly sweet feminine voice that made Bri grind her teeth. "It was just a letter from the swordsmith about a delay."

"You don't strike me as someone who wields a sword," Bri murmured.

Saika's lashes fluttered to her hands. "It's for Delta." Her lips pulled up as she said her wife's name. "I'm having a new sword made for her, one that will balance better now . . ."

Now that most of her arm had been removed. Bri glanced to the closed bedroom door where Delta slept.

It was the perfect gift for Delta—a new weapon, one that would make her feel strong again when she seemed so defeated. Bri's frown deepened. Maybe Saika really did love Delta . . . but that didn't mean she couldn't be a traitor too.

Plucking another cake off the tray and eating it whole, Bri stared around the room, trying to think of who to talk to next. Cole had been more than helpful in disclosing the poison's secrets. The servants didn't seem to know anything. Darrow was gruff and mean, but in a fatherly way that told Bri he would do anything to protect Lina, and Tem seemed besotted with her. The new Captain of the Guard was top of her list now.

She leaned on the table, her eyes tracking the conversation between Carys and Saika, though she'd stopped listening. Her mind combed through the information she had and still came up lacking. Nothing was certain in this place and a looming dread hung heavy in the air. It felt as if they all were permanently bracing for another attack.

CHAPTER NINE

They found the new Captain of the Guard, Yaest, in the armory near the training rings. Bri and Carys stepped into the round stone room, cooler than the rest of the palace and filled with racks and racks of pole axes and swords. The floor had never been paved but instead left as red earth, and the room smelled of sweat, blood, and soil.

It seemed Lina was stubborn enough to stay camped out in her chambers rather than allow Bri to follow her around the grounds. Bri let the Princess stew. It would be easier to question the other suspects while the Princess was safely in her room guarded by a dozen soldiers.

Yaest stood in the middle of four haggard-looking guards as he instructed them on blade-sharpening techniques. He was tall and wide, a bear of a fae, with muscled arms and shoulders perfectly honed for swinging a long sword. The younger guards around him listened as they rested their tired arms on the hilts of their weapons.

Sweaty faces whipped toward Carys and Bri, frowns pulling on the guards' lips as they spotted the pair.

"I was wondering how long it'd be before you two came looking for me," Yaest said in a deep, gravelly voice. He casually wandered over to where they waited, muttering something over his shoulder that sent the other guards back to work.

Bri spotted the lines around his eyes and silver streaks in his black hair, though his countenance and physique were so formidable she'd have guessed he was younger from afar.

"Why did you think we'd come looking for you?" Carys asked, crossing her arms and tilting her head.

"I'm the new Captain. I stood to gain the most from Delta's injury . . ." He glanced back over his shoulder at the four guards. His voice dropped, barely audible over the *shing* of sharpening swords. "I assume you know who my brother is?"

Carys pursed her lips. "Yes."

Bri took a step backward, leaning against the far wall and letting Carys take the lead. People like Yaest responded better to someone who looked like Carys rather than Bri. The Captain's eyes roved Carys's curves and she smirked at him. Bri bit the corner of her lip, trying not to smile at how easily Captain Yaest was pulled in by Carys's beauty. He mindlessly took another step toward her. For an esteemed soldier, he should have known she was wielding her most powerful weapon.

"What makes the brother of the witch hunter king a suitable candidate for Captain of the Guard?" She cocked her head in a way that made her long braid slip over her shoulder.

Yaest's eyes trailed down to the tip of her braid and then back up to her eyes. "My brother is over a decade older than me," he said, lifting his shoulders. "I barely knew him growing up. He went a bad way—an embarrassment to my whole family."

Carys popped her hip to the side. "When's the last time you spoke with him?"

"I was a teenager, I think." Yaest shook his head. "Our mother still sends letters to him sometimes. She could never fully let him go." He folded his arms, his giant biceps proudly displayed from his sleeveless tunic. "I can give you her address if you'd like to speak with her?"

"That would be very kind, thank you," Carys said with a half dip of her head.

Bri lifted the silver and amethyst dagger from its sheath, holding it up to the filtered sunlight. "Do you know who this belongs to?"

"A purple dagger?" Yaest huffed, narrowing his eyes at the curving steel. "I can't say that I do. Not a very practical weapon." He took a step closer, inspecting it. "Those are Mhenbic symbols on the side. It's probably a witch relic stolen from some temple."

Bri frowned at the whorls of purple stones on the hilt, patterned in symbols she couldn't read. She'd need to ask Cole if he knew what it said.

"Do you think it was your brother?" Carys asked, directing Yaest back to task. "Did he kill the Queen?"

Yaest's frown deepened, the menace growing in his eyes. "If I told you I didn't think it was him, that'd make you even more suspicious of me."

"If you told me you didn't think it was him, I'd listen to your reasons why," Carys countered.

"My brother was an idiot," he growled, his eyes lifting to Bri. "And a killer of witches. But he wasn't a traitor to the fae crown. He never wanted riches and fine things, like some of his crew. He believed in Hennen Vostemur's cause—that the red witches must be washed from this realm. When they were all gone, my brother was ready to lay down his sword, and there was a lot of infighting within the witch hunters after that."

"Did your mother tell you all this?" Bri asked, her eyebrows raising.

Yaest scowled at her. "Everybody knows, traitor."

"Such a dog to the oracle's prophecy." Bri brushed the dust off her tunic. "It's really rich, you, the brother of a witch hunter, calling *me* traitor."

Carys stepped in front of Bri, blocking Yaest's view of her. "Where are all these witch hunters now?"

"Some defected and came back to Swifthill. Others broke out on their own. Many went northward to join Balorn's army once the late King Vostemur fell."

"What?" Carys straightened. "How many?"

Bri's mind flashed to the attacks in the Northern Court. Balorn had fae soldiers along with his army of blue witches, but Bri had just assumed they were all Northern Court soldiers. It made sense that the witch hunters would defect to the one lining their pockets with gold. Balorn was the one paying for red witch heads, after all. It was reasonable to assume that when the witch hunters stopped having heads to bring him, they'd try to secure their coin in other acts of fealty toward him.

"A few dozen I'd say, maybe more." Yaest shrugged. "Though I think most fell in the recent battles on the border."

"So it could be possible some of the witch hunters who returned to Swifthill were actually still loyal to Balorn too?" Bri asked, leaning past Carys and pulling Yaest's glowering gaze back to her.

"Yes," he said. "It's impossible to know who has truly given up the life and who's planted in Swifthill as a spy for Balorn—well, a spy for Norwood, now."

"Shit," Carys hissed.

Bri pushed off the wall. "We're going to need a list of all your guards and anyone who has ever been affiliated with the witch hunters."

Yaest stared at her, unblinking for a moment before nodding. "I'll get it to you by this evening." He gave Carys one more once-over and turned back to the soldiers.

Carys took a step closer to Bri as they watched him walk off. "This is not good."

"It's a mess," Bri snarled.

"Shall I go talk to his mother?" Carys offered.

"Better you than me. I'm sure I won't be warmly received into her home like you will be." Bri scrubbed her hand down her face and across her shoulder. "I'll go find Cole, see if he knows how to read the symbols on the dagger." Her frustrated sigh ended in a snarl. The assassins could be anywhere and the person she'd sworn to protect actively avoided her. "Why did we agree to come here, again?"

Carys snickered. "Because you're a good person and you care about people, even when it's not in your best interest."

Bri rolled her eyes. "Oh, right. That."

~

The sprawling gardens circling the palace were a strange mixture of local and foreign cultivars. Green witches must have kept the more delicate flowers growing in the arid soil. Plants from the tropical South and alpine shrubs from the High Mountains mixed in the garden beds.

Ambling under an archway of dazzling Northern roses, Bri arrived at a kitchen garden of vegetables from the bucolic East. The evening sky radiated a purplish hue as whining birds cawed and crowded themselves into the thistly trees. Lizards scattered off the gravel trails at the thump of her heavy-stomping boots. Everything here was different—from the musky, spiced smells to that purple evening sky, to the copper red stones crunching underfoot.

Bri had heard stories of the West her whole life, imagined what it would be like, but nothing felt right. A word jumped into her mind: "otherworldly"—the same word people so often used to describe her.

She kicked at the gravel, sending stones flying into the scrub bushes lining the borders of the garden. Bri and the West were one and the same: odd to outsiders, beautiful and strange. She trailed her fingers along the next floral display. Vibrant pinks and orange petals bowed under her fingertips, already in full bloom in the earliest days of spring.

Her breath steamed the air, the temperature plummeting as the sun lowered beyond the horizon. In one day, Swifthill could go from baking sun to freezing cold. The native plants all seemed hardy, prepared for the temperature and dry conditions, but in the other parts of the garden . . . She glanced over the hedgerow, toward the exotic beds Saika had showed them earlier in the day. Bri snorted. They were common flowers in the East, but exotic to them, she supposed.

"Gah," she cursed as her trailing hand snagged on something sharp.

Yanking her finger back, she stared at the waxy black leaves, needle-like thorns, and white flowers of the curious-looking plant.

"Careful with that one," someone called from behind.

"Too late." She scowled at the droplet of blood on her finger.

Glaring over her shoulder, she spotted Cole. The lanky blond witch meandered through the garden like a scarecrow, a wicker basket held

73

in the crook of his arm. He already wore a woolen cloak, prepared for the cold evening air.

Bri frowned at him and back to the menacing-looking plant. "It's not poisonous, is it?"

"Very, but only if ingested." He laughed at Bri's wary glare. "It's called bonebane. Native more to the temperate forests east of here, but it's hardy and can survive in these climates too."

"Bonebane . . ." Bri mused, examining the shiny broad leaves.

"My great-great-grandmother, Adisa Monroe, was the first brown witch to discover its properties." Cole plucked a few flower blossoms and placed them in his basket. "She made quite a name for herself selling her potent brews. Some called her the mother of assassins."

"I like the sound of this grandmother." Bri chuckled, moving along the fence.

At the far end of the row, two workers in green aprons scooped piles of compost into a cart. Cole entered the gate to his apothecary garden and began picking lavender.

"How's Delta?" Bri asked, leaning her forearms on the fence.

"Better than I had expected." Cole looked back up at her, clearly exhausted from the grueling surgery, with dark half-moons bulging under his eyes. "She's still asleep. She'll be resting for a few days at least before her fae healing can do the brunt of the work and my pain potions will no longer be needed. But she's a fighter. I reckon she'll be running the halls again within a week."

Bri swallowed the knot in her throat as relief warred with sorrow. She was glad Delta had survived, and that her former lover chose to save herself, pride be damned . . . but seeing Saika holding Delta's hand had hurt her in a way she would have seldom expected. It wasn't jealousy for Delta, but jealousy nonetheless. She thought about the last person she'd wanted to hold her hand. It had been a long time since she'd wanted anything more than a night of pleasure from someone.

"The late Queen was a collector of heirloom varieties," Cole said, picking a bean pod off the vine that twined around the gates to the adjoining kitchen garden.

Beetles roved the fine layer of netting covering the production gardens, and the sight of them scuttling across the gossamer cloth made Bri itchy.

"These aren't staked deep enough." Bri nudged a hole dug under the fence with her boot. "You'll have rabbit problems."

"A mongoose did that," Cole said, nodding to the warren.

"I don't think I've ever seen a mongoose," Bri murmured, snapping a green bean from the vine and biting it in half.

"If you stay much longer, you'll be guaranteed to spot a few." Stooping, he picked up a long stick off the ground. "Though there's lots of other creatures you'd have to deal with too."

Narrowing her eyes, Bri examined the item he held, not a stick but a quill, striped in black and white at the end. She shuddered. The spike was longer than her dagger. She had thought porcupines were small, but to have quills that large . . . they must be the size of sheep.

The strangeness of the landscape confronted her once more. She knew that beyond the shadow of the High Mountains the terrain changed, but it truly felt like a waking dream. When they had ventured west to find Remy, the land hadn't seemed all that different from the East. They'd slogged through rainy, dense forests, the sky filled with clouds, the trees and plants similar to the ones she had grown up around . . . but here, beyond the rain shadow, was red earth and scorching sun.

She looked out at the horizon. To the right, the city of Swifthill was built into the rolling hills. From this vantage point, she could see the sandstone walls circling the clay-covered buildings in a perfect ring. Concentric circles of dwellings spiraled into the giant open-air marketplace in the center.

In many ways, it was like the other courts, and yet it was utterly different. The scenery, the flavors, the scents all perfectly complemented each other in a way that gave her an odd sense of rightness. She could imagine what growing up here would have been like. She recognized the strange unity, though she had never known it herself.

Rua had told her there was a word for it in Yexshiri: *aviavere*. It meant a nostalgia for something that never was, and it hadn't made any sense to her until that moment.

The thought of the foreign word brought her back to the task at hand.

"Delta found something after the attack," Bri said, unsheathing the amethyst dagger. "It has Mhenbic on it. . . . Do you know what it says?"

She passed Cole the dagger over the fence, and he studied the intricate swirls of purple stone.

"It's ancient," he murmured, tracing a finger down the blunted blade.

"How do you know it's not just well-used?"

He scrutinized the scuffed hilt. "Because some things are damaged from use and others wear away gently over centuries."

"Maybe it was sacked from a witch temple?" Bri mused, watching as he inspected the dagger.

"Perhaps." He flipped it over in his hands. "This symbol here, *brik*, I know means 'gift.'"

Bri shuddered. "Like the *midon brik*?"

"Yes," Cole whispered. "The 'gift of life.' Have you ever seen it happen?"

"Unfortunately."

She'd seen the ancient witch magic in practice so many times on the battlefield in Valtene. So many cursed blue witches sacrificed themselves, each swapping their own life for that of a fae. None of them were in control of their minds enough to spare themselves. And then there was Heather. . . . The thought alone made Bri's heart ache. Heather had sacrificed her life to save Remy, swapping Remy's fate for her own, a gift to Mother Moon. That sacrifice was the reason Remy became the High Mountain Queen—because a brown witch had loved her like a daughter.

"I can't tell what this word is." Cole squinted at the faded markings. "The etched symbols on the hilt have nearly rubbed off, but the amethyst ones are clear. Heart? Crown? I'm not sure." He shook his head, handing it back to her. "A relic such as that would surely be in a witch's book, though. I can ask Baba Omly if there is mention of any such dagger in the brown witch temple."

"That would be much appreciated." Bri bowed her head. She took four steps back down the trail before she paused and said, "Thank you for saving her. She said you put yourself in grave danger fighting off her attackers."

Cole gave her a soft smile. "Helping people is what brown witches do."

She couldn't summon the will to return his smile. He was yet another brown witch willing to sacrifice everything for the fae around him. She clasped her hands behind her back, her eyes scanning over the sun boxes filled with exotic flowers. It was something so few fae truly knew the meaning of: sacrifice.

"You must have some skilled green witches to keep all these plants growing." Bri leaned against the fence and swiftly pulled away as a tiny scorpion scuttled between the beams of wood.

Cole snickered. "One thing about Swifthill—always look before you lean on anything." He placed another purple flower into his basket. "Oh, and always shake out your boots."

"Learned that one the hard way?"

"Yes." His cheeks dimpled. "But it's a habit now."

"How long have you been here?"

He blew out a long breath. "Over two decades. This place feels more like home than Valtene now."

"Valtene?" Bri asked. "I have just come from there. The battle with Norwood and Balorn was in the swamps just north of the border."

"Ah yes, the ever-moving border." His tone was even but she could sense a touch of bitterness in it. "I left before the late Northern King started pushing into our town. My father had passed, and my second eldest sister, Rose, took over the family business . . . but we needed the money, so I took a job as a brown witch's apprentice in Swifthill, and here I am."

Bri pursed her lips. Money was something so few fae ever thought about. Most of the high-class fae she grew up with had endless coffers. Their children never had to go away to work so they could send money home.

"I'm sorry," Bri murmured. "I hope you get to visit often."

"Rose has long since passed," Cole replied as if it were nothing, practice making the words seem casual. "My eldest sister disappeared when

I was a teen, and my younger siblings scattered through the courts after the Siege of Yexshire. I'm fairly confident I'm the only one still alive."

Bri ambled into the plot and squatted down to examine the mint creeping out of the garden bed. "So few families are intact anymore."

"How many have you lost?" Cole asked, dusting the dirt off his hands and rising to stand. He shook out his cloak and Bri noted the movement, reminding herself to shake her cloak out before putting it on too.

"Family? None," she gritted out. "I am very fortunate."

Cole laughed as he lifted his basket. "But you've lost someone important."

It wasn't a question. His ocean-blue eyes pierced into her at the statement as if his magic could sense her pain in the same way it could spot a wound that needed healing.

Bri's hand drifted to the hilt of her amber dagger as she looked up to the fading indigo sky. The birds had quieted in the trees and a blanket of silence began to fill the air. "We should head inside before all manner of creatures start coming out."

Cole's cheeks dimpled. "You're learning."

CHAPTER TEN

Where are you off to tonight?" Carys asked as Bri stood. "A tavern? A gaming hall? Found a new guard to woo?"

"Not tonight." Her coin purse jangled from her belt as she stretched her arms over her head. "I'm going to guard the Princess's chamber."

Carys waggled her eyebrows. "Are you, now?"

"Don't give me that look," Bri grumbled, pinching the bridge of her nose. "There are probably traitors in this castle. Don't you think it's wise to have one of us guarding her? That's why we're here."

"I thought we were here to find out who killed the Queen and see Lina on the throne?"

"And how is Lina meant to reach the throne with a bunch of assassins in her midst?" Bri asked, folding her arms and leaning against the wall.

Carys rounded on her, looking her hard in the eye. "You can't play this game with her, Bri."

"What game?"

"You're like a moth to the flame," Carys said, raising her hand to silence Bri's words of protest. "She is the future Queen of a kingdom you are prophesied to usurp. Don't get caught up in this."

"Car—"

"Pick someone else to heal," Carys warned.

They stared at each other in a silent standoff.

"Is that all?" Bri finally asked.

Carys narrowed her eyes, scanning Bri from head to toe. "Seeing as I can't convince you otherwise, yes."

Bri nodded, turning to the door. She looked over her shoulder with a smirk and winked at her friend. Carys grinned and flashed her a lewd gesture in return. It was what made Carys one of her best friends. They could tell each other hard truths and get in each other's faces, but there was never any doubt that their friendship remained.

As Bri wandered the halls, ambling toward Lina's chambers, she thought about her twin. She felt that way about Talhan too, despite how they left things. They would always have each other. Even when they hated each other, they loved each other more. It was a strange sort of tether that held their group together. Perhaps that was why she gravitated toward people like Remy and Rua, always pulling more rudderless people into their circle. She couldn't imagine the pain of not having that assurance, that confidence that someone would always be there.

The candlelight flickered across the red stone walls as she padded quietly up to the westernmost tower. Despite those friendships, she still knew the pang of loneliness all too well. A vacant spot festered within her even a handful of years later. In the whispered quiet of the night, she felt it more acutely. She hated that stillness. In the quiet she could remember things she wished to forget: the smell of her hair, the sound of her voice, the feeling of being loved.

A shroud billowed into the hall, revealing flashes of the city. Bri ducked under it, looking out to the firelight brightening Swifthill. The stars seemed different here than in the East. The night sky was brighter, peppered with flickering white stars. Movement below the window caught her eye. Guards swapping posts?

She trained her fae eyes to the shadows and spotted a black cloak walking toward the front of the castle, carefully avoiding the torchlight. She knew that cloak, that shape, that gait.

"Shit," she hissed, turning and running to the front entrance. She'd forgotten about Airev.

~

Bri put on her calm, cavalier mask as she finally spotted Lina.

"And what exactly is Airev up to tonight?" Bri said as she swaggered up to the open tavern window.

Lina whirled and, despite her shadowed hood, Bri could tell by the slump of her shoulders she was glowering back. The tavern in the center of town was much finer than the seedy ones in Southside. Fae in delicate dresses and furs chatted in a riot of sound, but Lina clung to a far doorway, hidden in the shadows.

Bri grinned, leaning her elbows onto the window ledge. "Surprised to see me?"

"Why are you here?" Lina muttered.

Bri raised her eyebrows and placed a hand on her chest in mock offense. "Am I not allowed to frequent taverns in my free time?"

"Why *this* tavern?" Lina stepped closer to the open window frame, the torchlight illuminating her full lips as a frown pulled them downward. "There's mostly fae here, loyal to the Crown. I can't imagine a Catullus would have a warm reception."

Bri waved away the thought. "I'm used to the mean looks that your mother so readily encouraged."

"My mother wouldn't have needed to if your mother wasn't constantly plotting to overthrow her." Lina scoffed. "I'm sure she's holding feasts right now to celebrate the death of the Queen."

Bri lowered her head, careful not to hit the sill as she leaned through the window. "I am not my mother."

Lina's hood slipped back an inch, revealing her fiery eyes. "Nor am I."

A smirk pulled at Bri's mouth as she cocked her head, scanning Lina's smooth skin and painted lips. "So why *are* you here?"

"I'm busy," Lina said, turning and leaning against the wall beside the window. "And you're distracting me."

Bri grinned. "I have that effect on people."

"Please." Lina snorted. "If your head got any bigger it might explode."

A tall, slender fae at the end of the bar moved toward the back door and Lina straightened.

"Is that your target?" Bri asked, tipping her head toward him. "You're going to steal from him?"

"Go get a drink, or find a maiden, or go back to the castle; I don't care," Lina snapped. "Just leave this to me."

Bri guffawed. "What did he do to deserve the wrath of Airev?"

Lina pushed off the wall as the fae disappeared from sight, exiting the door beside the window. Bri took a single step, pivoting in front of her.

"Move," Lina hissed.

"Let me come with you," Bri implored. "I told Delta I'd protect you."

"You told her you'd look out for the Princess." Lina folded her arms. "She knows nothing about Airev."

"That is a dangerous distinction, one I'm sure Delta won't care about if Airev gets killed." Bri leaned in and whispered, "I promise you I'm more at home with thieves and bandits than I am with Princesses."

Lina craned her neck past Bri, trying to spot the figure she was tracking, and Bri sidestepped her again.

"Fine." Lina grimaced, clenching her fists. "Just don't get in the way."

Bri flourished a bow, stepping out of Lina's path and following her into the moonlit alley. The spring air was crisp—frost clung to doorways and their breath whirled steam from their mouths. Bri wished she'd thought to bring a cloak.

She kept in step with Lina. "What did he do?"

"He stole something," Lina muttered. "I'm going to steal it back."

"What did he steal?" Bri chuckled as Lina gave her a sideways glance and pulled her hood lower. "Something you don't want to share with me?"

"Because I already know what you're going to say," Lina growled.

Their target wove through the back alleys behind the fine fae restaurants and inns that made up the wealthiest part of the city. They kept several paces behind, dawdling at the turns to give him enough of a lead. They were about to turn the corner when Lina grabbed Bri's sleeve and yanked her to a halt.

The fae had stopped at a back door, midway down the alley. He laughed loudly to the woman who opened the door. When the creaking door slammed shut again, Lina and Bri leaned down the alleyway.

Bri sighed, spotting the red lantern hanging inconspicuously above the door. "A brothel. Of course."

Lina peered up at the second-floor window, where candlelight flickered beyond the half-drawn curtains. "You go distract the matron and I'll sneak in and grab the necklace."

"Necklace?" Bri tilted her head. "He stole a necklace?"

"He nicked it from Tem in the bathhouses," Lina whispered. "I saw him wearing it this morning in the castle. It's Tem's necklace, the lying thief."

"Right." Bri snorted.

Lina's lip curled as she leaned closer. "What?"

"Aren't you a hero, rescuing your betrothed's stolen necklace," Bri teased. Lina's hot breath skimmed Bri's cheek as Bri held her hard stare.

"This is why I didn't want to tell you." Lina turned the corner, looking back over her shoulder at Bri. "Now, do you want to help me or not?"

Bri frowned but followed. Lina rapped on the brothel door, shoving Bri in front of it and disappearing into the shadows. Bri's scowl into the darkness morphed into a feral smirk as the matron opened the door.

"I know you," the matron said, clasping her hands in front of her and blocking the narrow threshold. "You're that one they call the Golden Eagle. The one they say is here to steal the crown."

Bri let her eyelids droop, pretending drink had overtaken her senses. She dropped into a swaggering bow. "The one and only."

The matron cocked her head. "I thought you were a twin?"

"Well, 'the two and only' doesn't sound as good." Bri leaned her forearm against the frame, pinning the matron with her smoldering gaze. "I heard your establishment is the best place to come for those with a pocketful of gold who are looking for a good time."

The matron grinned at the word "gold," dropping her eyes to Bri's pockets. She stepped backward, permitting entry into the foyer. With a drunken guffaw, Bri stumbled forward, pretending to trip into the matron. Her hands bracketed the woman's body as the matron gasped. Caging her in, Bri dipped her head down into her neck and breathed deeply, making her shudder. The whoosh of air behind her told her that Lina had successfully snuck inside, and she pushed away.

"Apologies," Bri said, straightening her tunic with a playful laugh. "I might have had a few glasses before I came here."

"It's quite all right," the matron said, brushing a brown curl off her forehead and swallowing. Her cheeks were flushed as she pressed her hand to her chest and took a steadying breath. Bri grinned at her flustered expression.

"Please, do come in." The matron gestured to the sitting room.

Bri sat on the red satin couch and crossed her ankle over her knee, the picture of ease. A woman entered in nothing but a sheer, gauzy slip. Her dyed red hair spilled over her shoulder and covered most of her chest. She carried a golden tray with a single silver goblet, gracefully gliding across the lush crimson carpet and proffering the drink to Bri.

Taking it, Bri grinned at the woman, who peeked at her through her curtain of hair.

"Abigail is free tonight, should you so wish," the matron said, gesturing to the redhead.

The courtesan's eyes flickered a brilliant scarlet, and Bri's mouth dropped open.

"A red witch?" Bri cocked her head at the witch and then turned to the matron. "How?"

"My staff are all witches," the matron said with a proud smirk. "And if you've never been with a red witch before, believe me, you're missing out."

Abigail flashed a carnal grin.

"I thought all the red witches were gone from the West," Bri murmured. "Weren't the only ones who survived hidden in the High Mountains?"

"Not those with powerful enough employers to protect them." The matron lifted her chin, her face hardening. "This lounge became a safe haven over the past many years. Even now that witches no longer need a refuge, many have chosen to stay. People fear looking in the dark corners, afraid of what they might find, but that is where we have thrived."

Abigail nodded, perching herself on Bri's knee and biting the corner of her lip as she leaned back into Bri's chest. She was overly perfumed but still had that magical scent of the witches hiding underneath. Bri's hand snaked around to her belly as she gave the matron an approving nod.

She took a long swig of wine, spotting Lina's peeking hood from the stairwell. She snorted into her drink, coughing to cover her surprise. Lina tipped her head in a gesture that indicated she had gotten what she'd come for as she gave Bri a pointed look.

Bri let the goblet slip from her grip, wine pouring down both her and Abigail. The courtesan leapt up as Bri muttered a string of apologies. The matron rushed over, grabbing a napkin from the side bar, and Lina bolted back to the door unseen.

"I'm so sorry," Bri said again, wiping down her stained tunic.

"It's no problem," Abigail cooed. "It happens all the time."

"I think I've had a bit too much." Bri chuckled, dropping four gold coins onto the table.

The matron's eyes widened at the coins, far more than Bri would have been charged. Bri hugged Abigail one last time, pressing two more gold coins into her palm and giving her a look. The matron would take most of the gold on the table for herself. These coins would be Abigail's alone.

Abigail smirked and nodded. "I do hope you visit us again."

With a wink, Bri headed toward the door and waved over her shoulder. "Have a lovely night, ladies."

She heard Abigail's excited whisper from behind her. "I can't believe that just happened. Briata Catullus!"

She'd never get used to people's excitement at seeing her, as if she were an oddity, her fame and reputation preceding her actual personality. In Swifthill, she was infamous—a threat to the Crown.

She stumbled back into the alleyway but Lina was already gone. She cursed, scanning the vacant road and jogging off in the direction she suspected Lina was heading.

CHAPTER ELEVEN

Bri pulled her sticky, wine-soaked tunic off her chest and waved it, trying to dry the fabric. She should have known Lina wouldn't wait for her.

"Insufferable," she muttered, grimacing as the cold fabric touched her skin again. "This is what I get for helping."

Jogging down the road, she finally spotted Lina's black cloak winding its way toward the manor at the far end of town. She caught up with Lina in a few strides and, even though she didn't say anything, she could sense the Princess's disappointment.

They hiked up the gravel road in silence for a few more paces before Lina finally said, "I figured you'd rather stay back, since you were so *comfortable*." She picked up speed, rushing up the hillside as if expecting Bri to fall behind. "You seemed quite at home in that place."

"That's just my nature." Bri snickered, easily keeping up. "I seem quite at home everywhere."

"But brothels especially."

Bri flashed a toothy grin. "Jealous?"

Lina twisted her head and Bri was certain of the exact scowl that would be on the Princess's shadowed face. "I'll remind you, even with this cloak on, you are speaking to royalty."

Bri's smile widened. "And I'll remind you, I don't care."

"Insufferable," Lina muttered, and Bri had to bite her lip to keep from laughing at hearing the same word echoed back at her. Lina gripped a simple silver necklace in her hand, a pendant of a paw print etched in gold hanging from the chain.

"Is that Tem's necklace?" Bri tipped her head.

"You're a sharp one, Catullus."

"Why a paw print?"

"The wolf is on the Wystron family crest." Lina clenched the chain in her fist. "Tem said it was a gift from his uncle in Saxbridge."

They reached the towering manor, the door painted in shimmering gold and the word "Wystron" carved above the arched stone doorway. Bri raised her eyebrows at the monstrosity—gold and silver painted into every corner of the intricately carved walls.

Bri huffed, shaking her head. "A little garish, don't you think?"

Lina shot her a look. "Says the fae who grew up in the second-largest castle in the East."

"Good point." Bri grinned, thinking of the gaudy castle her mother had decorated until it screamed that it was a Western home. "You seem to be going to great lengths for Tem—"

"He's one of my oldest friends," Lina cut her off. "Apart from him and Delta, my mother didn't really let me socialize much. After the Siege of Yexshire, she forbade me to leave the West and she mistrusted many of the fae families in Swifthill."

Bri folded her arms, the wet, wine-stained fabric bleeding into her sleeves. "But you do go south, like that time in Saxbridge."

"My mother didn't know," Lina said. "She thought I was holidaying at the seaside along the fishing villages by Silver Sands. Many of the richest fae have summer homes there for when the heat becomes stifling in Swifthill. Delta would cover for me, make up extravagant lies about our trips to the sea . . . but I haven't been anywhere besides Saxbridge since I was a child."

Lina looked up to the night sky and her hood slipped off her head. She didn't reach to lift it, seemingly caught up in a memory and peering at the stars. Bri shifted closer beside her and looked up as if she too could see Lina's drifting thoughts.

When Bri spoke, her voice felt too loud cutting through the silence. "Where would you go?"

"What?" Lina glanced over, her brown eyes glinting with reflected moonlight.

Bri's gaze dropped to Lina's parted lips. "If you could go anywhere, where would you go?"

Lina shook her head. "I don't know . . . everywhere—the High Mountains and the ice lakes in the North. The Sea of Wetamuir and the Rotten Peak. I'd like to see it all."

"It's all overrated." Bri bit the inside of her lip, holding back her smile.

"I'd like to judge that for myself, thank you," Lina said, lifting her chin. "One day . . ."

"Rua is having a Spring Equinox celebration in Murreneir," Bri said, the words coming out a bit too eagerly. She cleared her throat. "I'm certain you're invited. Why don't you accept her invitation?"

"Because my kingdom is in disarray, and I need to restore order before indulging in banquets and balls." Lina's expression hardened, resolute. "Nothing else matters until my people are safe and a crown is on my head."

Bri pursed her lips. "Sensible."

"You should try it some time." Lina winked and walked up the steps. She gingerly placed the necklace through the letter slot and stepped back down.

That wink echoed in pinpricks all over Bri's body. No matter what Bri volleyed at her, Lina always seemed ready to throw it back. The Princess sauntered back down the stairs, and Bri wished she could see the swish of Lina's hips hidden under her cloak. She hadn't realized someone could have such an alluring walk until she met Lina—the rock and sway of each step rhythmic and powerful.

Bri pressed her lips together and swallowed, heat rising in her cheeks as she asked, "Where to next, Airev?"

~

By the time they returned to the castle, the sun had crested the horizon, and they'd barely managed to sneak back in before the long shadows yielded to daylight. Once Lina had safely snuck back into her rooms, Bri headed straight for her own chambers and collapsed into her bed. Carys was already awake, preparing for her morning run. The moment Bri's head hit the pillow, sleep overtook her, but her rest was short-lived. It seemed like only minutes had passed before Carys returned and woke her. Wiping the sleep from her eyes, Bri rolled her shoulders and readied for another day.

"You really can't let this Saika thing go, can you?" Carys muttered as they trudged down the spiraling stone steps and onto the red tile floors.

It was the day of the Queen's weekly reception and Lina's first time taking up the mantle. With crowds of city dwellers coming to air their grievances and watch the rest of society, Bri knew she needed to be in attendance. There were too many risks for Bri to sleep through it.

She trailed her fingers along the western wall, which radiated heat from the midmorning sun. "I am investigating everyone."

"Mm-hmm."

Guards and servants paused to watch them pass by. A few guards even openly sneered. Bri gave one a wink and chuckled when his sneer deepened.

"Who do you think was behind this, if you're so certain it wasn't her?" Bri asked, ducking around a large planter of white flowers.

"I think Darrow has a part in this," Carys said. "He's defensive and angry, not how you'd expect someone in mourning to be."

"Is that not how they mourn in the South?" Bri cut her a glance. "Not everyone dabs their eyes with handkerchiefs when someone dies. His Queen was killed."

"So you don't think he's suspicious for acting gruff and standoffish?" Carys asked, looking at Bri sideways as she narrowly avoided a servant holding a basket of oranges. "But softhearted Saika is?"

Two kitchen staff clad in green aprons approached, carrying heavy trays of cutlery. The taller one stopped, her eyes widening at Bri, and Bri realized she recognized her: Terez—the food taster from her first night in Swifthill. Silvie stood beside her, her brows knitting in confusion. Bri wasn't the human they'd met in the tavern anymore, but she probably looked similar enough to spark some recognition. She watched as it dawned on them all at once that they had spent the night dancing with none other than Briata Catullus. Bri flashed them a grin and kept walking, hearing the two tittering as they walked away.

Carys snickered. "I don't want to know."

They reached the side door to the grand hall and Bri lowered her voice. "I still think it's worth talking to everyone who was here the night of the Queen's murder."

"The assassins are probably long gone and their poisons with them," Carys whispered as Bri placed her hand on the handle. "They wouldn't stick around to be found out."

Bri's hand stilled as she looked back over her shoulder at Carys. "They would if they haven't finished the job."

Carys's lips thinned as Bri cracked open the door and they slid in behind the gathering crowd of courtiers and guards. They pushed into the throng, leaning until they spotted Lina upon the dais.

Once again, Airev was transformed into a goddess on her throne. She wore a patterned bronze and gold dress that hugged her figure, the thin fabric pooling around her sandaled feet. A beaded chest plate draped over her large bosom and down to her belly and hips. She wore golden cuffs on her arms and bronze metallic paint highlighted her eyes, making her dark skin shimmer with iridescence.

"Holy Gods," Bri breathed, her hands clenching at her sides.

Carys produced a handkerchief from her pocket with a flourish. "For the drool."

"Shut it," Bri snapped, watching Lina preside over the gathering.

The Princess sat rod straight, no flicker of mischief on her face, though Bri knew it lay just below the surface. She seemed a dutiful ruler in that moment, not a rogue Princess, as she listened to a human airing his grievances.

A line of people—human, witches, and fae alike—waited in a long line to speak with her. The rest of the crowd gathered on either side, making an aisle for those wishing to speak to their sovereign. A pile of mismatched flowers dotted the steps below Lina's feet.

"Thank you, Your Highness," the human man said, bowing his head and putting his cap back on. He moved off into the crowd as another man stepped forward. He wore a black totem bag around his neck, denoting that he was a witch.

With a bow, he placed a pale orange flower into the growing pile. His straight black hair fell into his eyes and he brushed it away.

"Rise," Lina said, lifting her hand. Thin chains of gold ran from her ring fingers up to her wrists, and her fingernails looked dipped in a gold leaf that dusted up to her knuckles. Bri cleared her throat. Even Lina's fingers were utterly enticing.

"Apologies, Your Highness, but I need your help in settling a dispute between the baker, Maxfeld, and me." He wrung his hat in his hands as his eyes and fingers flared a magical green. He blinked and it was gone—a green witch, then.

Witches couldn't always control their magic when their emotions were heightened. Bri had seen the same happen to Remy and Rua several times—their eyes flashing red. Even though they weren't witches by blood, red magic ran in their veins so emotions revealed it just the same, especially when they were glamoured. Bri shifted, grateful she didn't have witch magic. How annoying it must be to not be able to lie.

"What is your grievance against the baker?" Lina asked. Her voice was smooth and warm, the snark from the previous night gone.

Bri shook her head again. Lina was clearly the same person and yet she felt like a stranger too, each mask she wore more endearing than the last.

"He hired me to help with the breads. He promised me a witch's wage, but when payday came, he gave me the same as the humans. He refuses to pay me my worth even though I exhaust my magic by making his bread the best in town."

The crowd murmured as Lina assessed him. She lifted two fingers off the armrest and the crowd silenced. Bri's skin rippled with gooseflesh at the way Lina commanded an entire room with the smallest flick of her fingertips.

Lina cocked her head. "And what was your employer's reasoning?"

"He said I don't have a stitch of green magic, that the bread I bake tastes the same as all the others . . . but it's not true. Here." The witch took a tea towel out of the satchel on his shoulder. He unwrapped the fabric and held up two rolls.

"Darrow," Lina said, flicking her hand to the side.

Darrow pointed to one of the guards beside him and the soldier stepped forward from behind the throne. He walked down to the witch and accepted the food.

"First is the regular bread." The witch's voice trembled as the guard took a bite of one of the rolls. The guard frowned as he chewed, assessing, and gave a nod before turning to the second roll. "And this is one that I made."

The guard took a second bite, his face unreadable as he turned to Lina. "The witch's bread is significantly better, Your Highness. Worth the higher price."

A sigh of relief spread through the onlookers. Green witches were some of the most well-paid of any coven. To retain their services cost many human coppers, but it also meant an employer would run a roaring trade.

"Darrow, send one of your people to speak with this Maxfeld," Lina said, darting her kohl-lined eyes to her head councilor. "I will not make any one-sided decisions. If they suspect this is all true, have them see that the witch is reimbursed for his current wages."

"Thank you, Your Highness." The witch bowed deeply again, his cheeks flushing.

"But I would advise you," Lina added, turning her gaze to the witch, "to find a better employer once your contract is fulfilled. There are many businesses in Swifthill that would be eager for your magic. Don't settle for less than you're worth."

The witch swallowed and nodded again, scurrying away to the back of the line.

Bri peered down the row of waiting townspeople—at least another dozen to go. This would be the tedious part of court life. She remembered nearly falling asleep watching King Norwood receive people. Even though the fallen Eastern King received only high-class fae, they tended to prattle on. She and Talhan took turns leaning on each other and nodding off. Their mother would poke them in the back to make them stand straight again. Bri could still feel the itch of lace, the ribbons in her long hair, the tight bodices her mother would force her to wear to pull her body into an hourglass long before she was mature enough to have such a figure. It had taken her too long to realize she could refuse her mother . . . even if it meant ending their relationship.

This will be you one day. Pay attention, her mother's scolding voice echoed in her mind.

Bri's gaze hooked on Lina again. The Princess didn't seem the least bit tired, though she'd been running through the streets of Swifthill only hours before. If she was exhausted, she hid it better than anyone.

A couple approached next, the woman holding a swaddled baby in her arms. The gruff, bearded man threw a rose onto the pile, the petals already bruised from his tight grip.

The woman bobbed her arms up and down to keep her baby quiet as the man pushed her back into a bow. The woman flinched at the touch of his hand, such a subtle movement covered by her flustered smile, but Bri knew instantly. Lina's eyes narrowed too. She must have spotted it as well.

"Speak," Lina said to the man.

"Thank you, Your Highness." He wiped a hand down his greasy beard.

The blood vessels in his dark-ringed eyes were burst from drinking or shouting . . . probably both. Bri knew his type. They darkened every tavern doorway.

"We had a fire at the shop," the man said. "Half my tools are gone. I can't work. We don't have enough money for food or to fix the damage."

The baby in the woman's arms let out a soft whine and the woman jolted, bouncing as a sheen of sweat broke out on her brow.

The baby cried again and the man scowled. "Keep her quiet," he growled.

"That won't be necessary," Lina cut in, narrowing her eyes at the man. "All of my people deserve to be heard, especially the children. They tend to be the most honest of all."

The man's brow furrowed. "All right, then," he said, dismissing what was clear to everyone else as a warning. "Will you help me with my shop?"

"I will send someone tomorrow to survey the damage and see what we can do." Her eyes darted once more between the man and woman, lingering on the woman's lean frame and jittery movements.

The couple bowed and scuttled off. Bri watched Lina's shrewd, assessing eyes and already knew who she was going to send. Airev would be taking to the streets of Swifthill again.

CHAPTER TWELVE

Bri's knuckles rapped lightly on the door, and she heard the shuffle of feet from inside. When Tem answered the door in nothing but his trousers, Bri regretted coming without Carys.

She clenched her jaw, her eyes dropping to the small silver pendant around his neck. He must have already retrieved his stolen necklace from the manor in town. He was leaner than a soldier but still carved with muscle over light brown skin, more brawny than Bri had expected.

"Sorry to disturb you."

"Not at all," Tem said, grabbing his tunic from somewhere behind the door and hauling it over his head. "I was just getting changed. How can I help you?"

Bri crossed her arms. "I wanted to ask you some questions about the attack."

"Oh." His dark eyebrows lifted. "Of course."

He stepped back, opening the door for her, and she paced into a lavish formal sitting room. It was far more sumptuous than hers, with gold-embroidered curtains, woven fabric chairs, and clay vases of freshly cut flowers.

She eyed the sword hanging over the mantle, its hilt dusty enough to denote it as decoration and nothing more.

"Do you reside in the palace?" she asked, dropping into the seat that Tem gestured to.

He perched on the armrest of the opposite chair. "We have a family home in the city that I sometimes stay in, but most of the time I'm here, serving on Her Highness's council." The thought of him living in the palace rankled Bri for some reason, but she hid her frown. "Do you want a refresh—"

"No," Bri cut him off, and he shrugged, dropping into his plush chair. "Where were you when the attack happened?"

"I was in Saxbridge," he said, leaning his elbows on his knees.

"Why?"

He huffed, looking down at his bare feet. "You're going to think I'm really petty."

"Clearly you haven't met my mother."

"I've heard plenty about her." Tem chuckled, rising from his chair again and walking over to the mantle. "Lady Catullus is famous around these parts."

Bri ground her teeth. She wasn't the least bit surprised. Her mother probably fueled half the gossip in Swifthill, her spies spreading rumors far and wide.

Tem turned the wooden dial on his intricately carved cigar box and the lid popped open. He pulled one out and looked at Bri. "Do you smoke?"

She crossed her arms. "Not like that."

He grinned and put the second cigar back down, shutting the lid with a click. He snipped the end and leaned into the candle flame, twirling the cigar as he puffed on it.

"Your necklace, what is the symbol?" she asked, nodding to the silver chain that dipped below his neckline.

"A wolf paw," he said. "The wolf is part of the Wystron family crest."

"Of course it is." He was so slick and mannered, exactly like the courtiers she had grown up with in the East. The high-class fae trained their children to be lyrical in their movements and words, equal parts poise and power. Bri's eyes roved the room and landed on the shrouded windows. "So why were you in Saxbridge?"

"I was shopping for our wedding." Smoke trailed in circles from Tem's cigar as he gestured. "My family is close with the Southern silk merchants. My personal clothier resides there, so I was going for a fitting."

He leaned against the mantle and crossed his legs at the ankle. Bri fought the urge to roll her eyes. Of course the richest family in Swifthill, aside from the royals themselves, would have their own personal clothiers.

"You're right," Bri grumbled. "That does seem petty."

"I didn't realize the dinner would end in tragedy." His cheeks dimpled as he puffed on his cigar. "It pains me every day that I wasn't here to protect Queen Thorne and my betrothed."

Bri's lip curled at the words "my betrothed." From what little Bri knew of Lina, she didn't seem to be anyone's anything. She belonged wholly to herself.

"Do you love her?" The words flew from Bri's mouth before she could take them back.

"More than I should, probably," Tem replied instantly. His chuckle was tinged with sorrow as he hung his head. "It's unrequited, I'm afraid."

"Did Lina tell you that?"

"Not in so many words, no, but I've known Lina her whole life. I know her type, and trust me, I'm not it." Tem let out a long sigh. "My father was the Queen's closest advisor. The joining of our families made logical sense. Our marriage was planned in our infancy, and I would have married her for duty's sake alone, but . . ."

"But you really fell in love with her," Bri muttered.

"How could you not?" Tem grinned. "You've seen her."

Bri didn't reply, unwilling to admit that she understood the magnetic draw of the Princess all too well. She thought back to their training, the sight of her in her battle leathers, wielding that heavy axe as if it were a feather. Never had anyone bested her so quickly . . . or looked so good doing it. Lina was magnificent.

"Who do you think was behind the attack?" Bri cocked her head at Tem as halos of smoke circled his head.

"The witch hunters seem the most likely," he said. "But I wouldn't put anyone beyond suspicion right now."

Bri nodded—at least in that they could agree. "Some of the guards have connections to the witch hunters. Why have they not been dismissed?"

Tem let out a mirthless laugh. "Because the witch hunters and the Western fae are mostly one and the same at this point."

"How?"

"There's not a corner of the West that they don't touch." Tem frowned, inspecting the smoking embers of his cigar. "Whether through friends or family, everyone knows at least one fae who was once a witch hunter."

"Once? But not anymore?"

"The smart ones abandoned the hunts years ago," he said. "Once they realized there were no red witches left, the money became considerably less. And selling other types of witches into the North was frowned upon." He shook his head. "Awful business. Truly the worst sort of people nabbing any kind of witch and selling them into servitude. Even Cole might have been grabbed were it not for the Queen's dogged protection."

"But many of the Western fae thought it was okay to hunt the red witches?" Bri glared at the wall, thinking of the attack on Remy when they'd found her in the Western backcountry. Hale had been in such a murderous rage after that attack. Standing there amongst the bloodied fallen like the God of Death, she should have known then that he and Remy were Fated.

"I can't condone it," Tem said. "But I can say that it was heavily *encouraged* by Her Majesty."

Bri's eyes widened. "What?"

"Queen Thorne encouraged the red witch hunts throughout the West." His lips curved downward as his carefree mask slipped. "She wanted to drain the Northern Court of as much of their wealth as possible. She knew Vostemur was desperate for red witch heads and wouldn't think twice in spending all his kingdom's gold to ensure he got them." He held his cigar between his lips, his voice muffled as he took another drag. "In some ways it was a clever plan, though a ruthless one. The West stayed out of the wars and became tentative allies with the North, all the while draining them of their coin."

"So it was true that Queen Thorne was hoarding her gold," Bri murmured, thinking of the gossip spread around her household as a child. Her mother had said the Western Queen had amassed two courts' worth of gold in her bloody trade with the North.

"I believe it was your mother who took that truth and turned it into something larger than life," Tem said, his eyes assessing her as if hearing her thoughts. "That our people were dying of hunger while she sat on a mountain of gold." Bri's gaze dropped to her hands as she picked the dirt from under her fingernails. "A half-truth of sorts. Queen Thorne accrued an incredible amount of wealth, but most of it was earned and kept by her people. The witch hunters became rich as thieves . . . until all the red witches were gone and the money stopped coming."

"Not a very wise long-term strategy," Bri growled. "Killing innocent people."

"Queen Thorne allowed an army of bloodthirsty and moralless fae to rise up in this kingdom," Tem said. "And then the gold stopped coming. . . . Over the last few years they've become more reckless and violent—raiding towns and selling our own brown witches into the North."

"And what did Queen Thorne do then to get them back in control?"

"Nothing," Tem growled. He took another puff and sighed. "I shouldn't speak so ill of the dead. She was my Queen."

"I don't blame you." Bri waved away the cloying cigar smoke as a heavy haze settled over the room. "She made her people into monsters and then they turned on her."

"It was the cost of falling from that high—the glory days of witch-hunting." Tem's voice filled with disgust. "They became more and more desperate, more and more angry. The smart ones turned to other jobs, but the core group remains to this day at a camp in the woods."

"Ah yes, with a fae who calls himself the witch hunter *king*," Bri snarled. "And whose brother is now the Captain of the Guard."

"Yaest hasn't spoken to his brother in years. He's always been loyal to the Crown," Tem said, waving off her concern. "Like I said, if we condemned every fae associated with the witch hunters, there'd be none left."

"So, what now?" Bri asked. "What would be your plans to prevent another attack if you were in charge?"

Tem considered her for a moment before he spoke. "I would increase the guard on the palace, train more soldiers loyal to me, and not the former Queen, for whatever is to come." He stared at her through the cloud of smoke. "But what I would do isn't important. Lina is the future ruler of this kingdom, and I will follow her no matter what she decides."

Bri snorted at his stoic proclamation. "You really love her, then."

"Don't tell her."

Bri stood and gave Tem a half-bow. "I won't."

He mirrored the motion, walking her to the door. He was a fool, but he wasn't a threat. She needed to find out more about the witch hunter king and organize a visit to their camp. Now she just needed to figure out how to convince Lina to stay behind.

The first snick of the window latch made Bri push off the wall and crane her neck up. She grinned, proud of herself for figuring out how Lina was sneaking out. Though surely there was an easier way than climbing down from her chambers four stories above.

This Princess would be the death of her. Bri watched from the shadows as Lina found her footing on the rocky outcroppings of stone. She moved in a practiced way, knowing where each nook and cranny would be. She leapt the last few feet, her cloak flying back as she landed.

"Hello, Airev," Bri said, stepping out of the darkness.

Lina whirled, and fast as lightning, her hand axe appeared in her grip. Bri looked at the simple weapon, a common tool, nothing like the one Lina wielded as a Princess. She wore simple breeches and a thread-bare tunic, her cloak a muted gray. The hand that held the axe was bare of jewelry, but flecks of gold dust still clung to her fingertips. At a single glance, she was a commoner, but with a little more scrutiny, it was clear she was something else.

"Gods, it's you." Lina released a slow breath and lowered her axe. "What are you doing out here?"

"I swore I'd guard you," Bri said with a shrug. "So, I'm guarding you."

"I don't want or need your chivalry," she hissed.

Bri's brow arched. "And if Airev gets killed, what am I meant to tell Delta then?"

"Royals have to be fair and tempered, but thieves can pass out judgment as they see fit." Her voice dropped to a biting whisper. "I won't hide behind closed doors when I could be out there helping my people."

"I'm not telling you to hide behind closed doors," Bri grizzled back, looking past Lina to see if any guards patrolled the northern side of the castle. "I'm just asking to come with you."

Lina narrowed her eyes and Bri gave her a wolfish grin. The top of Lina's head came up to Bri's chin but the Princess seemed so confident that Bri kept forgetting she was shorter until they were this close.

"Fine. I'm sick of this debate," Lina muttered, hooking her axe back on her belt. "Just don't get in my way and don't talk."

"Excellent." Bri grinned, following after her. "Guarding your door all night would have been torture."

"What you're doing right now is talking," Lina growled. She pulled her hood up again, hiding in its shadows as they rounded the corner. High torches flickered in a semicircle of light from the sandstone promenade. "Seeing as you're here," Lina whispered, "go be a distraction for me."

Before Bri could respond, Lina shoved her, causing her to stumble into the circle of light. She snarled, wishing Lina would stop pushing her into these harebrained schemes. The guards gripped their pole axes, straightening their posture as they spotted her. Bri leaned into her stumble, putting on a drunken swagger, just as she'd done at the brothel.

"I think I've drank the cellar dry." She slurred her words as she smirked at the guards, moving further into the light so that they had to turn away from Lina's direction.

"Briata Catullus, the Eagle of Death," the first guard snickered.

"Eagle of Death?" Bri smirked. "I haven't heard that one before, but I like it. Maybe I should change the family crest to an eagle holding a skull. My mother would be so proud."

"Why don't you go and do that in your Eastern homeland, then?" The second guard set her weapon back on the ground, leaning against it as she leered at Bri.

"But think of all the fun we could have if I stayed here." Bri looked her up and down and winked, relishing in the flustered look on the guard's face.

The other guard cleared his throat. "Get out of here, Catullus, we're working."

"Fine, fine." She chuckled, gesticulating wildly as she spoke. "I'm heading into town. Any good pubs I should visit?"

"The Rattling Bone," the first guard called out as Bri stumbled her way toward the outer torches.

The other guard snickered.

"For some reason, I don't think I'll take your word on that," Bri said, waving a drunken hand at them. "I hope you two have an exceedingly boring shift. Come find me when you're done, Goddess."

The first guard snorted and then paused, looking to the fae beside him. "Oh, come on. That can't have possibly worked on you."

Bri swayed over the lip of the patio and back onto the dusty road as she heard the guard defensively reply, "She's charming."

Her lips twisted up as her boots crunched over the loose gravel. She was halfway down the narrow land bridge to Swifthill when she spotted Lina's cloaked figure up ahead. She'd already made it most of the distance down the road and didn't seem intent on stopping.

"Curse the Gods," Bri muttered. She should have known that Lina was trying to lose her when she shoved her in front of those guards. Anyone with skill could have snuck past them without need of a distraction.

She picked up into a jog as Lina disappeared into the streets of Swifthill. She rushed into the city and down the first alley that she saw

Lina shoot down. Nothing. She gritted her teeth. Delta would kill her if she found out, but she suspected she knew where Lina was going.

A drunken man stumbled down the alley, fumbling for keys in his pocket. Clenching her fists, Bri willed the glamour to shift her fae body into a human one.

"Do you know where the Mesons live? A husband and wife and a baby?" Bri asked.

The man jolted. "What does he owe ya?"

"Nothing, I need his help," Bri hedged.

"I think he's had a lot of your kind of *help* lately," the man chortled, flipping through his ring of keys. "But I don't want any trouble at my door. He's three roads down. Third house on the right. If it looks abandoned, that's the one."

"Thank you."

The man gave her a wary nod. "Don't tell him it was me."

"I don't know who you are," Bri replied with a grin, patting him on the shoulder and grabbing the keys from his hand. She selected the one his trembling hands had struggled to grip and unlocked the door for him.

"Thanks," he muttered, a surprised look on his face.

Bri tipped her chin to him and dashed off down the road. He probably would have fumbled with his keys all night if she hadn't intervened. Walking as quickly as she could without drawing suspicion, Bri rushed down the streets of Southside. It was still early in the evening, and the streets were filled with people. Luckily this seedy part of town was populated by people who also hid in cloaks, and Bri fit right into the crowds . . . but so did Lina.

CHAPTER THIRTEEN

She ducked down the poorly lit road, reaching the third town-house on the right. Sure enough, the paint chipped from the clay walls and the roof looked one heavy rain from collapse. The door was shut by a piece of string hooked on a nail. Clearly the lock had been broken so many times it wasn't worth replacing. Bri stared at the door for another breath, grimacing at the foul stench from the brown fluid that flowed down the open gutters.

"Of course," Lina's voice growled.

Bri turned toward the voice with a wicked grin. "Thought you could get rid of me that easily?"

An elderly witch appeared beside Lina, her weathered brown hands touching her totem bag as she looked at Bri.

"It was worth a try," Lina huffed. "How did you know I'd come here?"

"You said thieves can pass out judgment as they see fit." Bri's tone filled with menace. "And of all the people you received today, this man is the one I'd like to see judgment passed out on the most."

"Agreed," Lina said, gesturing to the witch. "This is Baba Omly, High Priestess of the brown witches. She knows who I am."

Bri's eyes widened as she looked at the elderly witch. She had short coils of gray hair, a warm face, and glowing brown eyes.

"That I do, Airev," the witch said with a deep, rasping chuckle.

"What's a High Priestess doing in Southside?" Bri furrowed her brow.

Baba Omly gave a calm smile. "I am a healer. This is where our magic is needed most."

Bri considered the High Priestess. She had expected her to be presiding over a grand temple somewhere, not a rancid back alley. Royal fae and High Priestesses were known to work together, but this . . . It was foolish for a ruler to be gallivanting around without protection, so headstrong, and yet, she respected Lina for it. Bri glanced into the shadows of Lina's hood. She would probably do the same thing if she were in Lina's position.

Stepping forward, Lina rapped on the door. A delicate, light knock—an odd sound in this part of town, where people were probably more used to hearing pounding fists. Not a peep came in reply, but the door string was tied to the inner nail, signaling someone had shut the door from inside.

"I wouldn't open the door for strangers around these parts either," Bri muttered.

"Hello?" Lina slipped her hand through the gap in the door and unhooked it. "We're not here to hurt you." She took another step into the dark room.

The sight of the space—an overturned table, splinters of wood, and glass shards scattered across the muddy floor—made Bri's chest tighten.

"Gods," she whispered.

They pushed further into the room. Straw poked from the bed on the floor and the curtains were torn to shreds . . . apart from one. She and Lina exchanged glances, spotting the telltale bump behind the curtain.

Lina carefully stepped over the broken glass and gently pulled the curtain aside.

The woman flinched, lifting her hands to shield her face. Her baby slept wrapped against her chest, none the wiser. But her face . . .

"It's okay, it's okay," Lina hushed, crouching down beside her.

Bri swallowed the bile rising up her throat. The woman's hair was matted with blood, her right eye swollen shut, and her lip split. Bri had seen soldiers on the battlefield and tortured blue witches with far worse injuries, but the sight of the sleeping babe on the woman's chest—a stark contrast to the state of her wounds—made white hot fury fill Bri's body. She was certain she'd never forget the sight.

Baba Omly rushed over to the woman, extracting elixirs from her robes even as she crouched.

"Do you know who I am?" the witch asked, dabbing a droplet of ointment onto her finger.

The woman swallowed. "Baba," she croaked, barely able to speak.

Bri's eyes fell to the revealing bruises around her neck.

"Yes," Baba Omly whispered in a soothing voice. "Is it okay if I treat these wounds?"

The High Priestess paused, waiting for the woman to nod before dabbing magical balms onto her eye and lip. Baba Omly's hands glowed a flickering bronze as her healing magic poured from her, heightening the power of her remedies.

The woman sighed, leaning her head back against the wall behind her.

"There," Baba Omly said as her magic soothed the woman's wounds. "Breathe."

Bri breathed along with her, taking another deep breath as that tight knot of panic eased into sorrow. The woman's eyes welled.

"I think we all know who did this," Bri gritted out.

"He swore he could get the money back." The woman shook her head. "I convinced him we should lie about how we lost it and ask the Princess for help . . ." She rubbed a shaking hand up and down the fabric that wrapped her baby to her. "I thought maybe if people saw, someone would come."

"I saw," Lina said, pulling back her hood.

The woman gasped. "Your Highness."

"I'm sorry I didn't help you sooner." Lina's voice was tight and Bri felt every ounce of the responsibility in her words. "I won't let this happen to you again."

"I . . ." A heavy tear slid down the woman's cheek and Bri braced for the refusal of Lina's help. Baba Omly continued applying ointment to the woman's face, the minty scent of the balm filling the stale air.

"Is your baby injured?" Bri asked.

"No. He didn't touch her." The woman shook her head, trying to take another deep breath, but it caught in her throat. Her baby let out a sleepy groan, her tongue fluttering as if she were drinking in her sleep. "That's all that matters."

"That's not all that matters." Lina's voice was barely leashed with restraint as she took the woman's hand in her own. "*You* matter too." More tears poured down the woman's cheeks and Lina waited for her to look up again before she repeated, "You. Matter."

"Where would we go?" The woman could hardly get the words out.

"With me," Baba Omly said. "You'll come to the temple. We'll get you back on your feet."

"You'll be safe there," Lina promised as the woman looked nervously at the High Priestess.

"We may dry flowers and sing songs to the moon," the Baba said, "but no one messes with a coven of witches; I promise you that."

The gravity of her words made Bri want to shudder. She wouldn't underestimate this Baba.

Lina and the High Priestess helped the woman to stand. She squeezed Lina's hand one more time.

"Thank you," she mouthed through thick tears. She bounced up and down on her toes, keeping her baby asleep.

"Better days are on the horizon. Hang on to that," Lina said, her soft voice dropping into one of promised vengeance. "Now, tell me where he is."

~

Bri shook out her hands, her knuckles numbed from years of practice. They'd found the man, Meson, already tied up in a back room of the local gambling hall. It seemed Bri and Lina weren't the only ones wanting to dole out judgment on him. They'd paid a bag of coins to the owner to *speak* with him privately, and the owner was more than happy to oblige.

Meson was a ruddy-cheeked man with skin the color of rotten ham and pale, hateful blue eyes. His arms were tied behind a wooden support beam, his face already swollen, and his tunic stained in dried brown blood. How long had he been left here? Judging by the putrid stench, several hours.

"Are you the one they call Airev?" he asked, resting his head back on the splintering beam.

"I am," Lina said, keeping her hood tucked low over her nose as she took another step forward. He didn't seem to recognize her voice, probably too preoccupied with surviving this encounter. "We've just come from your house, Meson."

Fear flashed in his icy gaze. "I'm sorry," he muttered, scrambling for a meaningless apology. "It'll never happen again."

"No," Lina said, wailing a blow down on him. His head snapped to the side as he let out a bark of pain. "It won't."

Bri rolled her shoulders. Meson understood using violence as a weapon to prey upon innocent people. There'd be no good outcome to letting him live. She took a step toward his pathetic, crumpled body, held up only by the ropes tying him to the beam.

"Wait! Please!" His pitiful voice trembled as Bri approached, her golden eyes stabbing into him.

"How many chances have you not taken, Meson?" she asked, unsheathing her amber dagger.

"I know about the Queen's murder," he blurted out, darting glances between Lina's hooded face and Bri. "Please. I'll tell you what I know."

He spat blood onto the floor as Lina held up a hand, staying Bri from taking another step.

She cocked her head. "What do you know?"

"The assassins," he panted. "They wear golden masks that look like lions."

Bri crossed her arms, keeping her dagger in her grip. She toed an empty bottle lying at her feet. "Of course Norwood would choose a lion."

She'd grown up seeing lions carved into every corner of the Eastern capital of Wynreach; the castle was covered in lions and crashing ocean wave iconography.

"How did they get in the castle that night?" Lina asked.

"They were already there." Meson huffed a laugh. "Half of them already worked as guards and soldiers of some sort." Bri's heart thundered in her chest. "The smart ones fled after that."

"How do you know all this?"

"I was tasked with procuring something," he wheezed. "I wasn't meant to see the lion mask in his bag but I was . . . looking for some coins." Bri rolled her eyes. "It was his fault for leaving his bag with me!"

Lina leaned against the far wall. "What did he ask you to procure?"

"Seeds," Meson said, shrugging. "A flower that's used in perfumes. I . . . I can't remember the exact name. He gave me a drawing and asked me to pick them up from a trader at the southern port."

"Seeds?" Lina looked back at Bri. "Do you think that's how they made the poison?"

"To sow the seeds of rebellion," Meson whispered, making Bri's eyebrows shoot up. "This is so much bigger than either of you realize."

"What else do you know?"

His breath rattled in his throat. "Nothing."

Bri raised her dagger, making him flinch as she took a pointed step closer.

"Nothing!" he exclaimed frantically. "Just the seeds. I was told to drop them off at a spot in Southside by Maxfeld's. That's all I know. I don't know who they were for."

"What is the purpose of these seeds?" Bri crouched, surveying her blade.

"I don't know," he pleaded. "I try to stay out of it. The less I know, the better. If you were smart, you'd stay out of it too. Keep a low profile until this all blows over, Eagle. The palace isn't safe right now."

"A lot of places aren't safe anymore," Bri said, her lip curling. "Your home, for example."

Meson's throat bobbed. "Is she okay?"

"That's none of your concern anymore," Bri snarled.

"Where is she?" He yanked on his restraints, a fire starting to brew within him. How quickly he morphed from a whimpering mess to a wrathful fool.

In two steps, Lina was in front of him, kicking him in the gut. The air whooshed from him as he doubled over with a grunt. "That's none of your concern either."

"She's mine!" he seethed, veins popping from his neck and sputum flying from his lips. There it was. The beast who lay beneath the lies.

"I knew I shouldn't have let her leave with you." Lina's fist silenced his protest, one blow, then another. "I knew it in my gut and I didn't do anything about it." His head flopped to the side, unconscious, but she didn't stop. "I should have done more to protect my people. My mistakes could kill them."

She rained her fury down upon him, punishing him for every ounce of guilt burning in her soul. It wasn't about Meson anymore; it was about Lina and the momentous undertaking of ruling a kingdom.

Bri grabbed Lina's cloak and hauled her backward, but Lina fought against Bri, scrambling to land another punch even as she stumbled away.

"Enough." Bri slammed Lina against the far wall, pulling her hood back. Bri's forearm pinned Lina to the wall as she stared her down. "Breathe."

She knew Lina could easily escape the hold, but the Princess didn't move, her storming eyes boring into Bri's. Admiration bloomed in Bri as she watched the Princess regain control. She was so powerful, so mighty, but she also clearly cared so deeply about her people that any of their suffering she'd feel within herself.

The fire faded from Lina's eyes, her gaze dropping to Bri's panting lips as she slowed her breathing. It was strange how anger and lust seemed sometimes one and the same. They should be opposites, but they both stoked a fire—two warring flames. She smelled the sweet tang of Lina's breath on her cheek, sparking a blaze within her. The urge to close the distance between them was overwhelming, the need to know what those full lips felt like upon her own strong. Bri's heart thundered with adrenaline and desire.

The owner of the gambling hall stumbled in, surveying the room, the unconscious man, and up toward them. Bri pushed away the second the door cracked, stepping into the center of the room, and Lina quickly yanked her hood back up.

"Did you get what you're looking for?" he asked in a thick Southern Court accent.

Bri shook her head. "Yes and no."

She needed to know more about these seeds, but Meson seemed more like an errand boy than a true member of the witch hunters' organization. His knowledge was probably limited to what he'd already told them, if that was even true.

"What are you planning on doing with him?" Lina tipped her hood toward Meson.

"He owes more than he'll ever repay. The best thing he can be now is a lesson to the others." The owner's eyes darkened and he flashed a crooked grin. "I'd ask that you don't intervene. People who wrong me have a way of disappearing."

Lina pushed off the wall and placed another two gold coins in the owner's hand. "Good."

She left without waiting for Bri, the owner's wide eyes tracking her as she walked away. Bri watched the way she threw back her shoulders and lifted her chin, knowing it was all a carefully constructed facade. This was the burden of Queens—choosing who lived and who died. Whether by official decree or paying off a ruffian, the choice was the same.

Bri followed silently, knowing she'd make the same choice. Meson could have been put in the stocks as a lesson, but never would she have allowed him to return to the people he hurt nor find others to replace them. She knew it was their lives or his, but that didn't mean having to choose didn't chip away at someone's soul.

Lina's voice echoed in her mind. *My mistakes could kill them.* Bri thought she could handle sending armies into battle, but things like this . . . bearing the burden of them alone seemed an impossible task. A begrudging respect grew in her as she watched that cloak wind back toward the alleyway. Lina feared not being a good enough Queen, and it was the exact reason she'd make an excellent one.

CHAPTER FOURTEEN

The shrouds had come down, the white spring sunlight brightening the castle at last. Life was breathed back into the halls as the dreary darkness lifted. Bri had found herself spending the better part of the morning wandering the palace, learning it anew, appreciating its beauty—the warm reds and copper earth tones, domed roofs and beaded tapestries. The castle had a heartbeat, so distinct she could almost feel it under her fingertips. It was the first time in her life she felt saddened that she'd never gotten to know the place as a child. Something about the Western Court had a different kind of magic than the rest of Okrith.

Carys cleared her throat, pulling Bri's attention back to the ceremony in front of them. They stood on the flat field outside the western wing of the palace. Eddies of wind blustered up from the cliff's edge, whipping their hair in the breeze. A large pyre was perfectly constructed to hold up the weight of the body that lay atop it.

Holding her torch aloft, Lina stood alone in front of the pyre. Her bronze ceremonial robes flowed in the wind as the crowd watched her whispered prayers.

Bri nudged Carys with her shoulder and Carys elbowed her back—a silent conversation flowing between them. It was something they did often during these long, drawn-out ceremonies. How many times had they been forced to stand and listen to lengthy prayers and kingly diatribes? Such was the life of royal fae and the two of them were always circling the fringes of that world.

Bri glanced over to her friend. Carys would have made a good Queen—never dragging on long ceremonies, kind, fair—nothing like Bri . . . or Lina. She thought back to the vengeance meted out the night before. The Princess seemed just as confident leading this ceremony as she did raining blows down upon Meson, and Lina did it all with grace, power, and heart. Bri hated the feeling stirring in her chest, like each moment spent with the Princess placed another hook within her soul.

Lina lifted three fingers to her lips, her forehead, and then the sky. As she did, the crowd mirrored her actions, mumbling an Ific prayer that Bri didn't know.

She and Carys whispered their own: "May their spirits blow freely through the wind. May we see them in the waving grasses and the falling leaves and the mighty ocean waves. Rest in eternal peace."

It was an Eastern prayer, uttered at many funerals over the years. Bri's chest ached and she grabbed the hilt of her amber dagger. . . . Too many. She remembered kneeling at the freshly turned earth below that oak tree. The battles at Falhampton had been bloody and brutal, neither the Northern nor Eastern Kings acknowledging the bloodbath despite having ordered it. Now, Bri wondered if they had been working together this whole time to destroy Hale. Had the hundreds of soldiers lost on both sides been collateral in their plot to kill Norwood's illegitimate son? It was horrifying, and yet, not surprising coming from either of them.

Carys used to say her Southern prayers when she first joined their retinue, but they swiftly became the Eastern words as soldier after soldier died. Carys was fleeing her own sort of battles when she swore her sword to Hale's army. It was clear she needed a fight to get lost in, and after the battle of Falhampton, she was able to come out the other side of it.

Darrow stepped up beside Lina, an unlit torch in his hand. He touched it to the flames of Lina's own and turned to light the corners of the waiting pyre. Delta hobbled up from where she had leaned against Saika. Her weakened gait made Bri want to protest. Delta still looked gaunt and sickly, only a hint of brightness back in her face. Standing for that long had probably drained all of her energy, but Bri knew even if they produced a chair for her, Delta wouldn't have accepted it.

Delta's arm trembled as she lifted her torch to Lina's. She moved to light the top of the pyre but her arm lowered in a shaky arch. With a scowl, she released the torch to the hay-filled underbelly of the pyre and hobbled away. No one else would have noticed or cared, but Bri knew that Delta was burning with shame. Only she was stubborn enough to have her body hacked apart and still manage to fulfill her duties as the Queen's niece.

One by one, Tem led the rest of the crowd. He grabbed a dried witches' palm leaf from the mound beyond the pyre. The pointed tips of the giant brown leaves waved in the wind. The mourners formed a line, stepping forward toward Lina and lighting their leaves. With a prayer, they placed papery leaves on the growing flames. The fire crackled, thick clouds of smoke billowing into the air.

As Tem stepped up to Lina, he leaned in and kissed her cheek, whispering words lost on the wind. Lina's face creased as she offered him a restrained nod, his words clearly moving her as she held in her tears. Then he continued on and she received the rest of the line, acknowledging each mourner with a bob of her head.

Bri couldn't imagine bearing all of those conciliatory words by herself. Her mind wandered to Talhan. When their parents died, he would stand beside her. They would hear the pitying and patronizing commiserations together, and then they'd drink and laugh about it afterward. She tried not to dwell on the disappointment on his face when she'd said she was going west. They'd been separated many times over the years for one journey or another . . . but they had never parted like this.

She glanced at Delta, hobbling with her arm over Saika's shoulder back to the palace. Even Delta had finally admitted defeat and gone in to rest. Perhaps Bri was the most stubborn of them all.

As the line dwindled, Carys and Bri stepped up to the end, picking up the tattered palm leaves from the bottom of the pile. The pyre roared with life, the flames growing at an amazing rate. The smell was overwhelming as they approached, like meat over a campfire. It made Bri's stomach churn. Pyre ceremonies were more beautiful and poetic but messier than burials. The placement of the pyre had been perfected, though, set on an outcropping on the cliff, where the winds carried the smoke off toward the rolling golden savanna and out to sea.

As they advanced up the line, she watched the thick black trail of smoke drift long into the horizon instead of up into the ether, as if the Queen's soul strained toward the ocean waves. By the time they reached Lina, her arm holding her torch aloft was shaking but her face was hard. She gave Carys the barest of acknowledgments, and then her brow dropped heavy over her eyes as she glared at Bri. A whole conversation seemed to flash between them as they stared at each other— Lina's eyes had the same hard, pained look from the night before. *The decisions of rulers are never easy.*

Bri wished she hadn't let Carys convince her to attend. Not paying her respects to the fallen Queen would be dishonorable, and she'd sworn to protect Lina, but showing up and laying leaves on the pyre of the Queen she was prophesied to usurp felt like an insult as well. There was no winning. With Delta hobbling off to the castle, Bri needed to stay here with Lina until she returned to her rooms, protected in the palace. Delta's pleas to protect her cousin wouldn't be in vain, even if Lina hated Bri for it, especially at that delicate moment.

Bri didn't say anything as she lit her leaf, the papery golden palm catching fire instantly. Flames licked high into the air as she set it on top of the pile. The structural wood of the fire was now well-fed and the body of the Queen wrapped in white was invisible through the flames.

Carys and Bri retreated a few steps and studied the constellation of embers scattering toward the sky. Carys watched through watery eyes, and when she sniffed, Bri slung her arm around her friend and pulled her into a side hug. Carys knew the Western Court better than the rest of them. She'd probably visited Swifthill often as a child. Even if she hadn't known the Queen well, the sight of the royal pyre, burning on the ledge of the steep cliffs, was enough to move even the darkest souls. Carys wrapped her arm around Bri's back and gave her a tight squeeze then released her—a silent thanks.

The Princess finally stepped forward, placing her torch through the soaring flames to where her mother's body would be. She took a few steps away from the fire, keeping her back to the rest of them, and just stared, motionless as the fire burned. Even from several paces away, the heat blanketed Bri's skin. Lina must have been sweltering.

As time ticked by, the crowd dwindled. Mourners each took their time and left when it felt appropriate to them until only a handful remained. The sun fell toward the horizon as the sunset brushed the sea, illuminating the clouds above in streaks of gold. Bri and Carys watched as the gold bled to blue, the indigo dye of nighttime staining the sky. In silence, they waited until the fire and the stars were the only light, Lina silhouetted against the diminishing flames.

With a mighty crack, the wood fractured and the pyre collapsed, tumbling over the cliff's edge and down into the valley below. Carys gasped, watching as the pyre plummeted and embers drifted in the air.

Lina stood in the darkness, still unmoving, watching the space where the pyre had been. Bri took a step forward, but Tem beat her to it, striding up to Lina and wrapping her in his arms. He held her for a long moment, her arms never holding him back.

"At least she has him," Carys whispered, new tears springing to her eyes.

Bri clenched her jaw, her eyes tracking each step as Tem ushered Lina back toward the castle. She couldn't deny the burning in her gut as she bowed her head and silently followed behind.

～

"Remy's going to kill you!" Carys gaped at the glowing green of the fae fire.

Rua's snicker echoed through the magical flames. "She already knows."

A breeze wafted through the sweltering room and Bri was grateful that the shrouds had finally come down. The fae fire room in the Western palace was a round stone space with built-in bench seats and a giant fire flickering up toward the open domed roof.

"You wed in secret?" Bri knew that Rua was smiling even without seeing her face. "Without me?"

"That's what 'in secret' means, Bri."

"Don't you start with me," Bri snapped, even as a grin stretched across her face. "I invented—"

Carys elbowed her in the ribs, making Bri bark out a laugh. "So no one else was there?"

"Baba Airu officiated," Rua said mildly.

Rua and Renwick had always done things on their own terms. It shouldn't have surprised Bri that this would be no different. She'd seen Rua at Remy's wedding; she looked like she'd rather gnaw off her arm than be there for one more minute.

"Aneryn and Laris were there too," Rua added.

"Oh, so Aneryn got to come," Bri said, not ready to let it go. "And who the fuck is Laris?"

"You know her, the green witch from the ice lakes?" Bri racked her brain trying to place the green witch. She thought to the witch with straight black hair, pale skin, and round face who would bring out the breakfasts at the camp. That was probably Laris. The rest of the green witches she remembered were too old. She chuckled, wondering if Aneryn and Laris were an item or if the two of them were just close friends.

She stared into the flickering green flames. She doubted Rua would even consider that Bri wanted to be at her wedding. She knew she didn't seem like the type to care, but she was proud of Rua for how far she'd come since that day in Drunehan when Bri had found her staring lifelessly at the Immortal Blade.

"I didn't want it to be a big thing," Rua said, finally breaking the awkward silence between them.

"We wouldn't have made it a big thing." Carys clutched her chest in mock offense. "Just some gowns, flowers, catering, jewels, drinks . . ."

Bri snorted. "You've got a point, Ru."

If Remy and Carys came within a mile of the festivities, they'd have wanted to change it, make it more elegant and fantastical and less like Rua.

"We'll celebrate together during the Spring Equinox festivities," Rua said. "You're still coming?"

"Three days of wine and revelry? Gods, I hope so." Bri shoved her hands in her pockets and rocked up on her toes with eagerness. It sounded like the exact sort of thing she'd love, far more than chasing wayward Princesses through city slums, at least. "I want this thing solved before then. If not, maybe we can convince Lina to come with us."

"Good luck with that." Carys chortled, her braid swishing as she shook her head. "I assume she's invited?"

The fire flickered in silence before Rua finally said, "Of course."

Bri grinned, knowing Rua hadn't even considered inviting her until they'd brought it up.

"It would probably be good to get her out of this court for a while," Carys said. "It's a mess here."

"Her mother wanted her to stay cloistered in Swifthill," Bri added. "But she found her own ways out over the years."

"I like her already." Rua's voice echoed around the room.

Bri's lips pulled up at the corners. "You would like her."

Lina fit right in their group—brave, cunning, cheeky, and somewhat brash. She could hold her own in any conversation and in any battle. Plus, she was already close with most of the royal fae of Okrith. She grew up with Hale, Renwick, Neelo, even Carys, when they attended parties and events hosted in Swifthill. Only Bri and Talhan weren't there, their stories slightly skewed from those of the others because of their banishment.

"How is everyone?" Bri asked, hoping Rua would tell her about her twin.

"Good," Rua hedged. "Is there someone you want to ask me about in particular?"

"You're cruel, Ru." She knew Rua would be grinning on the other side of the flames.

"I don't have any news," Rua said. "Remy's caravan has only just returned to Yexshire since they were going at such a slow pace."

Because of Talhan's injury. She knew that's what Rua meant though she didn't expressly say. She hated that Talhan was wounded; it made being at odds with him even more frustrating. She'd still not recovered from the shock of seeing his drawn, bloodless face, his eyes searching the skies as if the Gods were coming to claim him. She'd never felt horror like it, not even on that blood-soaked night many years ago in Falhampton.

"Any leads?"

She realized Rua and Carys were still talking but she hadn't heard a single word, not as her own voice roared in her ears. *Tal, come on!* she'd screamed, shaking her brother as he held that mortal wound in his gut.

"Bri?" Carys's voice snapped her attention back. "That purple dagger?"

"I've still got it." Bri tapped her hip. "But I'm planning on giving it to Lina." Carys arched her brow and Bri added, "It's the only clue as to who killed her mother. I thought she should be the one in possession of it."

"An amethyst dagger has Augustus Norwood written all over it," Rua said.

"When did that little brat become the lord of the violet witches?" Bri gritted out. "His father hated the witches, was happy to treat them the same way the North did."

"I doubt Augustus cares for them any more than his father," Carys said. "But if building an alliance with the witches means building an army . . ."

"So there are violet witches still alive?" Rua asked. "Aneryn said the last known violet witch died over sixty years ago."

"Who knows what he could be doing with that blue Witches' Glass," Carys muttered.

Bri frowned, thinking of the ancient blue witch stone still in the possession of the Norwood Prince. A flicker of an idea sparked in her. "Do you think the amethyst stones on the dagger we found are the same?" she wondered. "Just as the rubies in the Immortal Blade or the Witches' Glass can be used to cast witch magic?"

"It would make sense," Rua said. "All the covens seem to have magic talismans."

"How are they? The cursed blue witches?" Bri asked tentatively, remembering the faces of the Forgotten Ones as the spell lifted from them, morphing them from feral beasts to frightened souls in an instant. The thought made Bri shudder. How awful to have someone controlling their minds like that. She wondered if they'd remembered all they'd done while under Balorn's curse.

"They're healing," Rua said softly. "Slowly. Baba Airu has taken them in. The blue witch coven is working together again now to heal their sisters, but so much damage had been done before they were even cursed. There is no going back for them, only, hopefully, a better way forward."

Bri's mind flashed with memories of the attack in the blue witch fortress. To be locked away in such an awful place . . . Even before the curse, those scars would never fully heal.

"Augustus said something to me when he captured us," Rua said, pulling Bri from her swirling thoughts. "He said his plans for the West and South were already in action. One nudge and it would all come crumbling down."

"If he had a hand in turning the witch hunters on the Queen, it was a smart move," Carys said. "The kingdom is too preoccupied fighting against one another to mount any meaningful defense against Norwood."

"And the South?" Rua asked. "What would his plans be for them?"

"They're too busy with partying and revelry." Carys shook her head. "He'd only need to send through a few more casks of wine and he could stomp through the capital unnoticed."

"I need to talk to Neelo during the Equinox celebrations." Rua sounded deflated. "They need to prepare for whatever Norwood has planned. If Augustus senses the South is weak, he'll exploit that."

"I know the Equinox is meant to be a party." Carys gave Bri a look.

"But I think we should hold a few meetings with the crowns of Okrith, given the current threat."

"Agreed," Rua said.

Bri pinched the bridge of her nose and sighed. "That's probably the wise thing to do."

"There'll still be plenty of time for partying, Bri," Carys snickered.

She glanced back at her friend. "Then we need to convince Lina to come. It's not safe to leave her here."

"I'll leave that to you," Carys shot back. Bri rolled her eyes and Carys turned to the fire. "Be safe, Rua. We'll see you on the Equinox."

"Don't die, Ru," Bri added.

"If I steer clear from any more purple clouds, I think I'll be just fine," Rua said, the flames ebbing from vivid green back to orange as her voice called, "Good luck."

CHAPTER FIFTEEN

A soldier stood at the end of the hallway, guarding the ornately painted doorway framed in dented bronze. He looked Bri up and down and then unlocked the door.

She opened her mouth to question the action, but the guard interrupted her by saying, "Her Highness said if you were to arrive tonight, that she requested an audience with you."

Clenching her jaw, Bri stared at the cracked doorway. She had planned to stand watch outside the door and have a night of stilted conversation with the other guard, peppering him with questions about what he knew of the witch hunters. Throwing aside her investigative plans, Bri nodded and entered.

The anteroom was a circular space with smooth tiled walls and curved bench seats hugging the sides. Sheer curtains framed the benches, creating private alcoves. Vibrantly colored beaded cushions dotted the seats and the nighttime breeze whispered through geometric cutouts in the walls, but it was the centerpiece that snagged her attention—a glorious living tree. It was a miniature version of the trees stretching out across the savanna and similar to the ones breaking through the roof of the palace, but this one was only as tall as Bri. She paused to examine the perfectly pruned tree, its clusters of lime-green leaves shaped like low, rolling clouds.

The far door creaked open and Bri jolted, lost in her thoughts staring at the tree.

"It's why it's there," Lina said by way of greeting.

"What?"

She stepped out of her chambers, circling round the other side of the centerpiece. "The tree, it's there to let your mind wander."

She wore long, flowing robes, her hair tied up in a matching silk scarf and her jewelry and makeup taken off in preparation for sleep.

"It's beautiful," Bri murmured, though her eyes never left Lina.

Lina only hummed, peering at the top branches.

"No Airev tonight?" Bri asked.

"No, not on the day I sent my mother into the afterlife." Her midnight eyes dropped to find Bri's amber ones. "Can't sleep?"

"Never." Bri smirked. "You?"

Lina sighed, and, gathering her robes to the front, she sat on the cushioned bench behind her. "I don't sleep much either since the attack," she said as Bri moved around the tree and came to sit beside her. "I hear you have plenty of ways of distracting yourself, though." Lina chuckled, but it was half-hearted. She seemed exhausted, drained from the long ceremony and the grief that surely followed. "It seems you've already stolen the hearts of half my guards. I suppose that's a better diversion than a night of heavy drinking."

"I keep myself busy." Bri grinned, looking at the tree in front of them. The words rose within her before she could take them back. "I suppose you'll have more distractions once you and Tem are married."

"No." Lina snorted. The solitary word rang out between them. "He's not my type."

"And who is your type?" Bri's pulse drummed in her ears as Lina's stormy gaze held hers.

She knew exactly what she wanted Lina to say: *you.*

Lina's eyes dropped to her hands. "It's not that kind of marriage," she said finally. "It's business. Tem is a good person from a good family. He'll make a good consort."

"Because he's rich?"

Lina cackled, a spark of her spirit coming back into her tired face. "Yes, but I'm ten times as wealthy. I'm not concerned with his gold." She shook her head. "Our two families are stronger together. He pulls back into the fold the ones who've had your mother's whispers in their ears." Lina's voice turned bitter as her gaze dipped to her feet. "Tem will convince the people that think I am too weak to be their ruler. The ones that think *you* are a better person to take the throne."

"I don't want your throne," Bri growled, dropping her head in her hands. "I don't know any other way to say it. The prophecy was that I would seize the crown from its sovereign ... and I am about to enter in a competition in the East to seize a crown from its sovereign. How clearer can my intentions be?"

"I believe you. But whether I do or not, your presence here puts doubt in my sovereignty." Lina clenched her hands together in her lap. "This is exactly what your mother wanted all these years. You, here, with your cavalier attitude and rugged good looks, the perfect swaggering royal to take the crown."

Bri's lips twisted up. " 'Rugged good looks'?"

"You know what I'm saying." Lina scowled. "How could they not compare the two of us and find me lacking?"

"Then you clearly don't see yourself the way that I see you." Bri paused, hooking into Lina's stare. "I've seen you wield that axe. You're utterly fearsome." Bri grinned at Lina's begrudging smile. "And more than that, I've seen the way you hold court and address the needs of your people. Do you think Gedwin Norwood or Hennen Vostemur ever asked themselves such things? Even before the crown has been placed on your head, you are already ten times the ruler that they ever were."

Lina considered Bri for a moment and said, "There's still too much dissent amongst my people. I need the Wystron family as my allies."

"That's what you have councilors for," Bri muttered. "You can have them as advisors. You don't have to marry them."

"Tem will be a good partner, like Saika is for Delta," Lina insisted, glancing sideways at Bri. "Sorry, I knew you two were together at one point."

"Is that how she phrased it?"

"I love my cousin. She is the most loyal person in my life," Lina murmured. "If only her loyalty extended beyond that. She married Saika young and they've had their ups and downs, and . . . When they had their rough patches, Delta would go away, acting as an ambassador for the West in other courts while she worked out her feelings."

"How lucky for her to have someone to *work out her feelings* with," Bri gritted out.

"I didn't know about it then," Lina said. "What she did was wrong. I'm sorry she hurt you."

"Please." Bri rubbed her hand down her neck and shoulder. "I was never heartsick over Delta."

"You don't still care for her?" Lina asked tentatively. It was such a gentle move coming from someone so formidable, as if she were nervous to hear Bri's response.

"No," Bri said, wanting so badly to reach out and grab the hands Lina clasped together.

"But she was also your friend and she lied to you," Lina said. "That hurts."

Bri shrugged. "I've been through worse."

"As have I," Lina whispered, looking back up at the tree.

Bri unbuckled the amethyst dagger from her belt and passed it to Lina. "You should be the one hanging on to this."

Lina's brows pinched together as she accepted the weapon, turning it over in her hands to inspect it. "Have you been able to decipher the inscriptions?"

"Not yet."

"I'm going to the brown witch temple tomorrow," she said. "I'll ask Baba Omly."

"Then I'm coming with you," Bri replied, smiling as Lina rolled her eyes.

"Of course," she muttered. "My shadow."

They held each other's gaze for a long time before Lina finally looked away.

"There are five trees growing through the palace rooftop," Bri mused, nodding to the tree in front of them. "Plus this one here. Why five?"

"My mother planted this tree on the day of my birth," Lina whispered. "Just as her parents did for her and her sister, and their parents before them. . . . Not all of the trees grow, fewer still crack through the ceiling toward the sky. But if they survive and thrive, it is a good omen for the West. Those trees bursting along the roofline of the castle are the spirits of my ancestors, a reminder to my people that the Thorne legacy lives on. I've always wondered if my tree will reach as high."

"It will," Bri whispered.

Lina's cheeks dimpled. "Over two decades this tree has grown into what it is today." Lina craned her neck up to the domed roof high above the canopy of leaves. Star shapes cut into the ceiling, making holes to let in beams of moonlight. "I thought it would be bursting through the roof before I would be wearing her crown." Lina's voice wobbled and she swallowed back that betraying sound. "I thought I'd be planting the seeds of my own children long before I took her place."

Bri leaned closer, lifting her arm to wrap around Lina's shoulders. Lina was soft and warm against Bri's side. She thought Lina might pull away, or go still as she had with Tem, but instead she leaned into Bri's touch ever so slightly. The contact seemed to make Lina's eyes well.

"My mother and I didn't get along. At most, we respected each other," Lina said. "This idea that she would have ever been a doting grandmother is ridiculous but . . ." A thick tear slid down her cheek. "She will never get to meet my children." Lina pressed her lips tightly together as if to stop the tears spilling from her eyes. "Sorry."

Bri squeezed Lina's shoulder as if she could absorb her pain. It made her ache to see such a strong person so broken down. "You farewelled your mother today," she whispered. "It's okay to mourn her."

"I thought I had mourned her in every way and then a new kind of sorrow pops into my mind . . . ," Lina whispered as if trying to keep her voice from cracking. "And I know—I know I'm mourning a future that would have never been."

Bri pulled her in tighter, letting Lina's soft curves mold into her side. "I know what it is to mourn the relationships you know you'll never have." She reached up with her thumb and gingerly wiped the tear trailing down Lina's cheek. "You're not just mourning her loss; you're mourning the hope that it could have ever been different between you two."

Lina sniffed, wiping her eyes with her knuckles. "Yes."

It was the simplest word, and yet, it meant more than any other: Yes, she understood. Yes, she saw her pain. Yes, she was the same.

"I don't normally cry," Lina muttered.

"Nothing about your life right now is normal," Bri said, placing her lips atop Lina's head and speaking into the soft fabric of her scarf. "The world right now is a giant unknown."

"If only the people knew what we were doing right now." Lina let out a half-hearted chuckle. "Me crying and you comforting me."

"It would make it very hard for the people to pick sides if we were friends."

"Your mother would be furious," Lina said, resting her head on Bri's shoulder.

Bri's eyes shut, and she savored the feeling of Lina's warm skin against her neck and grinned. "All the more reason to do it, then."

Sunlight filtered into the atrium as Bri's eyes peeked open. She blinked a few times, realizing she wasn't asleep, waking without a jolt. No nightmares had roused her from her slumber. A soft chest rose and fell against her hand, the heady scent of jasmine swirling around her.

Lina's head rested on Bri's thigh, her chin tucked into the fabric of Bri's trousers as her loud breaths echoed off the tiles. Birds twittered, flitting in and out of the holes in the atrium roof. Bri inhaled, her brows knitting together.

She'd slept.

She'd slept through the night without any drink. No lust-filled evening or long day's training was required. She'd merely fallen asleep with the warmth of Lina pressed against her. She shook her head, staring down at Lina's peaceful face. She traced the delicate outline of Lina's pointed ear, her calloused fingers dropping down to the bow of her lips. Gods, those lips.

Lina let out a soft groan, grumbling as she turned her face further into Bri's lap. Bri grinned, sweeping her hand gently down Lina's back. The soft fabric of her robes bunched at her hips and she hummed.

Bri savored that feeling—deeply calm for the first time in many years. She wished she could bottle it up and take it with her when she left Swifthill—to be able to tunnel into that steady peace, like dropping below the roiling ocean waves to the calm below the storm. Maybe then she'd be able to sleep without exhausting herself first.

Lina stirred again, this time opening her eyes and sitting up. "Oh."

"Good morning," Bri said with a sleepy grin, stretching her arms above her head.

"I slept," Lina murmured, rubbing the sleep from her eyes. Confusion addled her expression. "I can't believe I slept. I don't even remember falling asleep."

"Nor I." Bri chuckled. "But for the first time in as long as I can remember, I didn't wake to a pounding headache."

Lina blinked at her. Bri pressed her lips together to keep from laughing at the Princess's bemusement.

"The funeral must have drained me more than I realized," she muttered, regaining her composure—that sharp personality pulling back into place. "I need to get ready for the day." Lina swept a hand down her robes and stood, grabbing the amethyst dagger from the bench. "We're meant to be at the brown witch temple for their morning prayers."

"I'll go get ready." Groaning, Bri stood, stretching again. "I haven't actually *slept* with anyone in a very long time. I appreciate the rest."

Lina paused, cocking her head as she considered Bri. "Perhaps we bring each other luck in that endeavor."

Bri's voice dropped an octave. "Perhaps."

"Maybe you should come back tonight to see if it was a fluke," Lina suggested, making Bri's mouth drop open. "Just to sleep." Lina narrowed her sharp eyes.

"An interesting experiment." Bri flashed her foxlike grin. "I'm in."

"Fine." Lina folded her arms. "I'll see you at the front entryway in an hour."

"You're not going to try to escape from me this time?" Bri taunted.

"I'm sure Delta will be monitoring the royal procession from her window." Lina huffed. "This is a formal visit into town by the Princess, not Airev. Your presence will be expected and it would look poorly if I tried to evade you with so many people watching."

Bri nodded, struggling to contain another smile. She wasn't sure if she'd smiled this much in her entire life. Something about Lina made her lose control of herself, this odd giddiness building in her every time Lina was near. This was not who she was. Bri cleared her throat, cursing herself.

She gave Lina a half-bow. "I'll see you in an hour."

CHAPTER SIXTEEN

They walked in the middle of the royal procession, guards in front and behind, as they wended their way through Swifthill. Lina held a parasol over her head, her mauve gown billowing in the breeze. Elaborately beaded necklaces hung over her bare shoulders and draped down her chest toward her scooped neckline. Her hooped earrings ended in golden tassels that matched the gold bands snaking up her arms. To top it all off she wore a thick leather belt with an ornate golden buckle, the amethyst dagger Bri had gifted her resting on her hip. It took every ounce of Bri's effort to keep her gaze fixed on the crowd and not the gossamer fabric that whispered from Lina's figure.

The crowd oohed and aahed at her extravagant outfit, but it was clear to Bri that Lina's choice of garments was both to delight and to distract. Gods, was it working. People would spend more time talking about her attire than the tumultuous lead-up to her coronation. The glorious sight of her would fuel their gossip with something sweeter than the morbid mutterings of her mother's assassination.

In the far distance, children splashed in a magnificent bronzed stone fountain. Thin waterfalls spilled from high spigots in the walls above, cascading down a sculpture of the Moon Goddess and into the basin.

The children's delighted squeals carried over the clamor of the pressing crowd. Vendors walked up and down through the crowds, holding aloft trays of boiled candy sweets, salted green mangoes, and skewered sticks of spiced pineapple.

Bri considered Lina's each step, each wave and smile. A natural at royal life, Lina undoubtedly was trained since infancy to rule the Western Court. She had an undeniable drive to prove herself worthy of her title and convince her people that she'd be a better ruler than her mother.

Carys and Bri followed along with the retinue of other guards, feeling the soldiers' scrutinizing eyes upon them. The crowds swelled as more people gathered in the street, waving and bowing to Lina, Darrow, and Tem. Bri quirked her brow, surprised that Darrow and Tem received such adoration. The Wystrons, the second family under the royals, unmistakably held sway within Swifthill as well.

A child darted out in front of Lina and handed her a pink flower. Lina crouched, grinning at the child as she accepted the flower and gave it a long sniff. Bri couldn't hear what Lina said but the child beamed up at her, nodding with wide saucerlike eyes. The crowd cooed at the motherly interaction.

Bri so easily envisioned what Lina would be like with children of her own, and she wondered how many new trees would grow up through the palace within Lina's lifetime. She eyed Tem, waving to the crowd and flashing his charming grin. Even though their relationship seemed mostly platonic, would he still father Lina's children? Lina had made it clear she wanted them one day. . . . Bri's gut clenched and she cleared her throat. She'd be long gone before any trees were planted and it didn't matter beyond that.

The deeper into Swifthill they wandered, the more opulent the buildings became, until they reached the brown witch temple. The rough bronzed walls seemed constructed out of sand, the porous material reminding Bri of a sandcastle. Intricate paintings of gold and silver swirled along the rough outer walls, Mhenbic symbols etched into the steps and the archway. Potted flowers sat on every step and a curtain of colorful glass beads separated the outside from the temple atrium.

Stopping on the first step, Tem took Lina's hand and kissed it. "I'll let you say your prayers in peace." He grinned, his lips lingering on her skin before releasing her. Bri's eyes narrowed at the movement, and she bit back a scowl. "We would only be a disruption."

Lina's face softened at his words and she bowed her head, her beautifully adorned braids slipping over her shoulder. "Thank you."

"Come," Darrow said, clapping his son on the shoulder. "We'll go sample some wines for your wedding." The crowd cheered as he glanced over his shoulder at Lina. "We'll see you for dinner tonight."

The muscles in Bri's jaw tightened as she watched them wander off. Her hard expression morphed to one of surprise as half of the guards followed the father and son. She was about to question the action when she spotted the wolf silhouette carved into the guards' armor—the Wystron family crest. They brought their own personal guards to the parade? They must have known they'd be breaking off from Lina, but why did they need their own guards? She wondered if any of them accompanied Darrow and Tem into the palace too.

When Lina's foot hit the landing, she turned and pulled Bri's attention back to those hypnotic dark eyes. "Are you coming?"

"I thought guards weren't allowed to enter witch temples," Bri said, looking from Lina's inquiring face down toward the hilt of her dagger.

"You aren't official guards," Lina said with a scoff as if it were an honor far beyond Bri's reach. "You're guests of the palace, currently, who happen to be good with a sword. You may enter."

Bri frowned at that distinction but relented, climbing the steps and following Carys and Lina into the atrium. The high, windowless walls stretched up into an open roof. They walked around the mirrorlike reflection pool and into the temple proper, where Baba Omly waited for them.

She greeted Lina with a hug. "Hello, my dear." She had a warm, steady tone, the kind so common amongst brown witches. She craned her neck toward them all and smiled. "Welcome."

Bri and Carys nodded to the High Priestess. Two witches in flowing brown robes walked slowly past, a human standing in between them. The human hobbled, leaning on one of the witches as she bore weight on her bandaged leg. The witches whispered words of encouragement to her and she grimaced but kept moving.

Bri quirked her brow. "I thought this place was a temple."

"It is," Baba Omly said. "A temple to brown witches and our healing magic. A hospital is the greatest way we can honor our gifts. Many of our coven reside here as healers along with the patients. All those in need of healing are welcome here—witches, fae, and humans." She clasped her hands together and turned toward Lina. "She'd welcome you if you'd like to visit with her."

Lina pursed her lips together and nodded, following after the High Priestess.

"Who?" Carys whispered, though Bri already suspected she knew.

They followed Baba Omly down the winding corridor, past rooms filled with cots, dining halls, and garden courtyards. The whole space smelled of *chaewood* smoke, a cleansing herb found in the Western woods.

Bri leaned into Lina and whispered, "You seem in good spirits today."

Lina's thick lashes lifted and she smirked at Bri. "I slept well last night."

"As did I," Bri murmured, her eyes searching Lina's gaze, but Lina broke their stare, her face unreadable as she followed the High Priestess deeper into the temple.

As Lina pulled ahead of them, Carys snickered and Bri elbowed her. Her friend didn't miss a thing. They climbed the spiraling sandstone steps to the second floor and arrived at a door halfway down the hall.

"Nelle?" Baba Omly's knuckles tapped on the door. She opened it and they stepped inside. "May we come in, *mea raga?*"

"Yes, please do," a warm voice whispered.

The woman, Nelle, sat on the bed, her shirt dipped down to one side and her baby nursing at her breast. Sunlight beamed in a halo from the window above her, casting the room in its warm golden glow. Her face was purpled with bruises but the swelling had gone down, and Bri could make out her true visage once more. The brown witches' healing balms had worked wonders on her already, though Bri knew some wounds would take far longer to heal.

"Is it okay if we sit with you for a while?" Lina asked tentatively, waiting to cross the room until Nelle bobbed her head. Bri was struck by that gesture. Lina was soon to be the future Queen, she could take on an army with a battle-axe, and yet, she waited for this human's permission to enter her room. It was such a small gesture, but it told Bri everything about what kind of ruler Lina would be.

"I'll leave you to chat," Baba Omly said with a bow and ducked out of the room.

Lina sat in the wicker chair beside the bed, while Carys and Bri leaned against the far wall. The room looked nothing like the hospital beds in the East. This room was warm—painted in rich earth tones, delicate woven tapestries hanging from the walls, and potted plants of lavender and sage along the windowsill.

"This is Carys," Lina said, gesturing to them. "And you remember Bri."

Bri crossed her arms and then uncrossed them, trying to make her usual stature less threatening. Carys chuckled at her and she had to force herself not to glower at her friend. She was better at interrogating people than she was at comforting them, and she thanked the Gods that Lina and Carys were there. Nelle had been through enough. Bri didn't want to scare the woman, and something about her face and demeanor seemed to put people on edge.

Nelle nodded to them, a half smile tugging at her lips. Her baby unlatched and she tucked her breast back into the low hem of her nightgown. The babe's eyelids fluttered, the warm milk lulling her to sleep.

"Did you find him?" she asked in a hushed tone, rubbing a hand rhythmically down her child's back.

"Yes." Lina's brows dropped heavy over her eyes. "You won't be seeing him again."

Nelle swallowed and nodded as her eyes welled.

"But we need to ask." Lina leaned forward. "He mentioned that he was acquiring seeds for someone."

"He *acquired* all sorts of things for all sorts of people," Nelle whispered.

"Can you remember any of them?" Lina asked.

"They never came to the house." She shook her head. "He always went out, kept us separate from his business."

"Did he give you any names?" Bri asked, trying and failing to soften her words. "Anything would be helpful."

"I know he used to work with the witch hunters, long ago back when they were still looking for red witches," Nelle murmured. "He'd brag that the witch hunter king used to send jobs for him personally." She frowned. "Whether that's true or not is anyone's guess."

"We should go there," Carys said. "See if it's truly them behind this."

"Venturing into the forest to interrogate a bunch of criminals isn't a wise plan," Lina countered. "We need more information first, information we can attain from the safety of Swifthill."

Bri stretched her neck to the side. "We can take a few witch hunters."

"And if they aren't involved in the attacks?" Lina's jewelry clinked as she whipped her head at Bri.

"Then they'll know you are not to be trifled with." Bri grinned back, delighting in the way she got under Lina's steely exterior. "That you won't suffer fools like your mother did."

Carys kicked her with her heel and Bri smirked.

Lina ignored them, turning back to Nelle. "Any other things you can remember?"

"I'll try to think . . ."

"It's okay," Lina said, resting her hand on Nelle's forearm and smiling down at her baby. "Take your time."

"Would you like to hold her?" Nelle asked, holding out the sleeping babe.

Lina lit up as she gingerly took the baby. Leaning carefully back in her chair, her arms instinctively bobbed the bundled infant up and down. The way Lina smiled down at that baby was nothing like the normal masks she wore. Her expression was open and vulnerable, as if the shrouds had been pulled back and the sunlight finally beamed from her soul, and something in Bri ached to see her with her own children one day—that beautiful duality of motherhood—gentleness mixed with the ferocity that would burn the world down to protect those she loved.

A flicker of recognition crossed Nelle's face. "I don't know if this is helpful, but Meson did sometimes bring home bread from the baker. . . . What was their name?" She looked up at the ceiling. "Maxfeld, I believe. I don't know if he knows anything, but maybe."

"We'll look into it, thank you," Lina said with one final sweep of her thumb down the sleeping baby's cheek. She passed her back to her mother. "You both need your rest. If anything else comes to you, you can let Baba know."

"I don't know how I can ever repay you." Nelle's voice quavered as she looked back at Lina. "You saved us."

"You saved yourself, by making him come to me," Lina said. "And you'll teach your daughter how to be brave like her mother too. Be proud of who you are, Nelle."

Bri's chest tightened and she shifted on her feet. Lina cared so deeply for this person she hardly knew. Even when she was acting as a nighttime vigilante, that goodwill and courage was inextricably tied to who she was.

Lina rose from her chair. "I'll come visit again soon," she promised, and Nelle offered the three of them a soft smile as they left.

They got three steps down the hall before Carys growled, "Please tell me you killed him."

"No." Lina straightened, rolling back her shoulders and lifting her chin. That royal mask slipped back over her face as she led them back down the stairs. "But we didn't stop his death either."

CHAPTER SEVENTEEN

On the fifth floor, Bri peered from the window of Baba Omly's office to the conservatory below. Narrow paths wound through lush green trees bursting with vibrant flowers—an oasis in the heart of the temple.

Baba Omly sat at her modest desk, flipping the amethyst dagger over in her hands. "It looks like a relic from a violet witch temple." She gazed up at the three of them, her eyes lingering on Lina. "I don't know what these symbols say . . ." She pointed to the one in the center. "Except this: gift."

Carys's shoulders drooped. "That's what Cole said too."

"This one may be the symbol for 'heart'?" Baba scrutinized the hilt. "Or maybe 'crown'? The words are quite similar. I would need more context to know for certain."

"Do you have any witches' books here on ancient relics?" Lina asked, crossing the room toward the High Priestess. "Anything on the violet witches?"

"Nothing here, I'm afraid." Baba Omly slid the dagger back across her desk. "Occasionally such books are donated to us—books about other covens, old tomes and witches' letters, cookbooks and witches' art. We send it all to the archives in Silver Sands."

"The archives?" Bri asked.

"It's a collection, a memorial of sorts, to the witches' way of life before the Siege of Yexshire," Baba Omly said. "The books important to each coven stay within their own temples, but others get sent there. . . . Why just yesterday someone donated to us an old apothecary ledger that we delivered to Silver Sands."

Carys leaned against the far wall. "Do you think they'll have anything on the violet witches?"

"There is no 'they.'" Baba Omly tilted her head toward the window. "The archives are no longer cared for by anyone. We bring things there, we shelve them, and then we leave."

Bri traced her finger over the tiled vase holding a bouquet of brilliant pink and yellow flowers, their smell filling the room with a sweeter scent than the incense and pungent elixirs on the bottom floor. "Why didn't the guardians stay?"

"The world wasn't safe for witches anymore," Baba Omly said. "The smart witches pledged themselves to fae families, protecting themselves with their patronage, but in a kingdom rife with witch hunters, the archives would have been an easy target I'm sure."

Bri noted the way Lina folded her arms at the mention of the witch hunters. It was her mother's doing, and now, her mess to clean up.

"I'm surprised the archives haven't been sacked if they're unprotected," Carys said.

"A fae family has taken guardianship of the archives." Baba Omly sifted through a stack of papers on her desk. "I don't think they do much for it other than attaching their name to the property, but no one wants to mess with the Hemarrs."

"The gold miners?" Bri asked. "Bern's family?"

Carys lifted her chin to the sky with a sudden realization. "His family lives just over the Southern border of Silver Sands and are as rich as thieves. It makes sense that they would look after the archives."

"The fae probably disliked that they protected the archives," Bri huffed. "But no one argues with the endlessly wealthy."

"We should fae fire Bern and ask him about it," Carys offered, pushing off from the wall.

"Good idea." Bri nodded. "He'll be in Yexshire, and I haven't spoken to Remy in a while, anyway."

Lina walked to the desk, picking up the amethyst dagger and sheathing it.

Baba Omly cocked her head at Lina. "Perhaps a trip to Silver Sands would be good for you, my dear."

Lina's eyes snapped up. "No."

The lines on the Baba's face deepened as she gave a knowing smile. "When was the last time you slept?"

"Last night," Lina said tightly.

Bri straightened, remembering their night together—waking with that woozy, warm feeling, confused at her surroundings but also blissfully calm. She hadn't felt like that ever before, not even before Falhampton, as if one foot was in a dream. She was certain she wouldn't soon forget the feeling.

"I'm needed here," Lina insisted. "My coronation is only a handful of weeks away. Augustus Norwood is still out there. My people need a Queen now more than ever."

"They will always need you." Baba Omly held up a hand to stop Lina's protest. "When you've lived as long as I have, you'll understand that there will always be something to worry over. Every battle feels deserving of sacrificing yourself for, but if you destroy yourself over every problem, *mea raga*, you won't be around long enough to lead them through it."

Lina's eyes sharpened as she clenched her jaw. Bri knew that feeling all too well—so desperate to burn herself to cinders in order to fix the wrongs of the world.

"I was born to make sacrifices for my people," Lina muttered.

"Perhaps you've taken the prophecy of your birth too literally." Baba Omly's eyes flicked to Bri and Bri quirked her brow in confusion, wondering what Lina's prophecy was. "Both of you." Bri scowled but the Baba continued. "I told Queen Thorne the same thing and she had the same reaction. She was so certain she could defy Fate by sending your family away."

"The Goddess of Death comes for us all," Lina gritted out. "Fate or no."

"Unfortunately, I have no potion or elixir to deal with headstrong young fae." Baba Omly made a straining groan as she pushed herself to stand and gestured for the door. "But such is the way of youth to ignore the wisdom of your elders."

Lina gave the High Priestess a begrudging hug as she rounded the desk. "Thank you for looking after Nelle."

Baba Omly cupped Lina's cheek with a smile. "You are already a better ruler than your mother, Lina. You don't need to try so hard to prove you are so different than her."

Lina's eyes guttered, the weight of the Baba's words crashing into her. The Baba had said the thing that Bri had been thinking since the moment she met Lina. It was evident in every choice and action Lina made: she wanted to prove herself worthy of her crown, but in her people's eyes, she already had.

"Take care," Lina said, ignoring the Baba's comments and heading out the door. She didn't wait to see if Carys or Bri followed.

Baba Omly looked between the two of them. "I'm glad she has you."

Bri swallowed the hard knot in her throat, bowing to the High Priestess and leaving. She wanted to protest, but it wasn't worth her breath. Baba Omly was wrong—soon they'd be gone.

～

Bri wished for the hundredth time that evening that she had declined the invitation to dine at the Wystron family manor. The residence took up half a city block, nearly the size of the brown witch temple itself. Everything dripped in unparalleled opulence, more so than even the palace. Where the castle was tasteful and rich, the manor bordered on gaudy—the eye having no place to rest amongst the riot of rich fabrics, gilded baubles, and gem-studded trinkets.

"You're rich; we get it," Carys whispered into Bri's ear, making her snort.

They sat on one side of the long dining table, Tem and Lina across from them and Darrow at the head. It felt strange not to have Delta there too, but at least she was finally healing.

Lina narrowed her eyes at Carys. Whether she had heard Carys or not, her eyes warned Carys to behave.

"Your home is beautiful," Carys said louder, and Bri covered her mouth with her napkin to keep from laughing.

"Thank you," Darrow said with a bow of his head. "It has been our family's main residence for seven generations."

"Main residence?" Bri asked, pushing her spiced rice around with her spoon.

The green witches at the palace had far superior cooking skills. She wondered if Darrow had instructed his witches to over-spice the food. She rubbed her turmeric-coated tongue along the roof of her mouth, trying to scrape off the flavor. Nothing from the decor to the food was created with a delicate hand. Clearly the Wystrons knew nothing of moderation.

"We have a beach house on the coast, a townhouse in Saxbridge, and a hunting cabin just outside Silver Sands." Darrow set down his goblet and picked up a forkful of greens. "Though the one by Silver Sands was abandoned when the road into the High Mountain Court was blocked." He looked at his son. "We should refurbish it now that the road is open again."

Tem nodded. "It would be a fun project."

"Fun?" Bri asked incredulously.

Lina leaned forward with a frown. "Not everyone delights in sharpening weapons and battle training."

"But you do." Bri held Lina's gaze, her beautiful dark eyes painted with kohl and streaks of shimmering silver. "More fun than shopping for jewelry." Bri leaned back in her chair and folded her arms. "I know a few thieves who would think the same."

Lina blinked, the only indication that she understood Bri was speaking of Airev. Bri's lips twisted into a smirk, knowing she flustered the Princess with the threat of revealing her secret.

"I think jewelry shopping is a splendid pastime for a future Queen," Darrow said, pulling everyone's focus back to him. "You work so hard on city planning and council meetings, receiving the people, and running an entire kingdom," he huffed. "Why not enjoy a few pretty trinkets? You've earned a moment of enjoyment."

"I haven't earned anything yet," Lina said, taking the smallest nibble of her bread.

Bri had to hold in her snicker at that dainty, minuscule bite. She was certain Airev didn't eat with such manners.

"Soon, my dear." Darrow took another sip from his goblet as servants came to take the half-eaten plates and replace them with servings of poached pears and honey-glazed nuts. "Your coronation is only a few weeks away—"

"We should move it forward," Lina cut him off, and Darrow gave her a sympathetic smile as if this were a conversation that had happened many times before. "We don't need to wait for all the decorations and festivities. We can crown me now and then celebrate later. The kingdom will be tense until I am the official ruler."

"Your people have suffered." Darrow set his fork down and steepled his fingers. "They're frightened from the attack. Their Queen has just died. Right now they need a calm, steady leader. Frantically crowning yourself will bring just as much unease. Let them see you have it all under control. Let them know they can trust your capable leadership."

Lina released a long-suffering sigh and turned back to her dessert.

"What would you advise, Tem?" Carys asked, glancing between Darrow and Lina.

Tem draped his arm over the back of his chair. "I think Lina was born to rule the West." He looked pointedly at Bri with a grin and she frowned back at him. "And whether it is made official tonight or in two weeks that won't change. But I support her decision wholeheartedly regardless."

"No, you're right," Lina growled, stabbing at her pear. "A tempered approach is best right now."

Lina could take whatever she wanted, do whatever she wanted, and no one would stop her, but she had more self-control than most too. Her desire to do what was right for her people superseded her desire to claim her throne.

"Good." Darrow tossed his napkin onto the table. "I know we have family from all over Okrith coming for your coronation. I'll admit, I'd be disappointed if they missed your wedding because it wasn't scheduled for the same time."

"A coronation and a wedding," Carys mused. "Like Remy and Hale did."

"Yes," Lina said with a nod. "I'm sorry I wasn't able to attend. I heard it was beautiful."

"Now that you're the ruler of this kingdom, do you think you'll travel more?" Carys asked.

Tem crossed his ankle over his knee. "We plan to do a tour of Okrith for our honeymoon."

"How appropriate," Bri muttered, and Carys kicked her under the table. "I mean, it's a smart move to rebuild relationships with the new rulers of the courts."

"Yes," Darrow said with an approving nod. "There's a new King and Queen in the High Mountain *and* Northern Courts now, and soon the Eastern Court will elect a new sovereign too."

Bri grinned. "You're meeting with her already."

"So confident you'll win?" Lina asked, cocking her head. "Will you use your prophecy to your advantage and seize the Eastern crown?"

"The people will love it." Tem chuckled, gesturing at her with his napkin before dropping it on his plate. "You've already built the image in their minds. Your crest should be an eagle with a crown in its talons."

"Oh, that's good," Carys snickered. "I have my work cut out for me if I want to beat that."

"When do the games commence?" Darrow asked.

"Not until autumn," Carys replied. "We were planning on the summer but it can get too hot in Wynreach, and we worried that the people wouldn't be able to gather for the events."

"Hot in the East?" Tem laughed, his eyebrows raising. "The sun is weak on that side of the continent."

"Well, they're not accustomed to it," Carys gritted out. "And we want to make the competitions available for all citizens to watch. They'll be voting for their future ruler, after all."

"I still can't believe you're letting the witches and humans vote,"

Darrow said with a disapproving laugh. "They can select their own local officials; why do they need a hand in fae leadership?"

"I think you'll find they're invested in who rules their kingdom." Carys frowned. Clearly Darrow didn't know that Carys had a halfling sister. "The fae sovereign affects them all."

Tem yawned, stretching his arms over his head. "It's getting late. We should retire."

"Thank the Gods," Bri muttered, pushing back from her chair. She had no interest in hearing Darrow and Carys spar about politics.

"Are you staying here tonight?" Lina asked Tem as she rose.

Bri's eyes snagged on Lina's curving figure, the fabric of her dress perfectly hugging her hips in a way that made Bri's throat go dry.

"Yes." Tem stood and kissed the back of her hand. "Why don't you stay too?"

Bri bit down on the growl that rumbled in her chest.

"I'll sleep better in my own bed," Lina said with a careful smile as she pulled her hand from his.

A smirk pulled on Bri's lips at the way Lina diplomatically rejected the invitation.

"We'll escort you back to the castle," she said, gesturing for Lina to lead the way.

"Thank you for the delicious dinner," Carys said with such warmth that Bri knew it was sarcasm.

They gave Darrow a half-bow.

"We'd love to have you again sometime," he said with a gruff nod, his expression not matching his words.

Bri snickered, following Lina out of the room, Carys beside her.

"Ugh." Carys licked her sleeve. "That was so gross."

Lina shot her a sharp look. "Tell me again why you think you'd make a good Queen?"

Carys gave a mock flutter of her lashes. "Because I waited to wipe my tongue until I'd left the table."

Lina tried to maintain a steely expression but her cheeks dimpled and she pressed on faster out of the foyer.

Of all the parts of courtly life, this would be Bri's least favorite. If she were to become the Queen of the East, she'd need to get used to fae families like the Wystrons. She exchanged glances with Carys, who smirked and rolled her eyes in a silent conversation that told Bri she felt the same. They'd have each other, regardless. So long as someone was there to roll her eyes at, Bri would be able to handle it.

CHAPTER EIGHTEEN

The guards didn't stop Bri as she strode into the atrium of Lina's chambers. She paused, admiring the tree as her heart thundered in her chest. The night was unseasonably balmy and Bri waved out her tunic, which still clung to her chest with sweat. She'd anticipated the normal evening chill when she donned the thicker layers, but now wished she'd worn something lighter.

Groaning, she scrubbed a hand down her face. She turned toward the door and then back to the tree and then to the door again, pacing like a trapped wildcat. What was she even doing here?

Before she had time to question her intentions any further, the far door opened and Lina peeked out. Bri scanned her from head to toe, taking in the cerulean silk scarf in her hair that matched her flowing silk robes.

"Come in," Lina rasped, her voice already scratchy with sleep. The sound of her voice made Bri thrust her hands in her pockets, trying to regain composure.

Why was she so nervous? She'd just come to sleep.

Lifting her chin, she strode into Lina's chambers in her soldierly way and surveyed the grand bedroom. The gigantic bed took up most of the far wall, easily sleeping four people comfortably. It was covered in finely woven pillows, detailed in the colorful patterns that the local artisans sold in the markets. An ornate fireplace of bronze-flecked red stone climbed up the opposite wall. Two logs sat in the blackened belly of the fireplace, unlit. Bri was grateful that the already humid room wasn't heated with a fire. To the left, floor-to-ceiling curtains covered the darkened windows. The door to the right led toward what appeared to be a bathing chamber. She spied a copper tub through the cracked door and her eyes drifted to her own wide-eyed expression in the floor-length mirror.

Lina wandered to a sitting area beside the plush gray curtains.

"Are we having a tea party?" Bri teased as she tipped her head to the steaming teapot and two mugs.

"It helps me sleep," Lina said, her eyes tracking Bri as she dropped into the chair across from her.

Bri cocked her head. "I thought you don't sleep?"

"It helps me pretend I'm doing everything in my power to try to sleep," Lina corrected with a smirk.

"Now that I understand." Bri picked up the warm mug, cupping it in her hands. "I've gotten more superstitious about sleep over the years. Trying to perfectly re-create the things I did on the nights I was able to rest . . . but I don't think any of it really matters."

She studied the intricately painted ceramic, the outside grooved to perfectly fit fingers, as if the artist who created it knew how soothing it was to feel the warmth radiating from within.

Bri took a sip, tasting the zesty rooibos flavored with vanilla. It reminded her of the scent of spice tables in the markets all around Okrith. This popular calming brew was served in every court, though it originated in the West, and Bri wasn't sure if it was all in her head, but she did feel drowsier after even a single sip.

Her eyes snagged on the way Lina blew on her tea—the way her bottom lip pressed to the rim of the mug, her top lip curling over to blow on the whorls of steam. Lina's eyes lifted and Bri dropped her gaze into the swirling red liquid in her hands.

"Why can't you sleep?" Lina's voice dropped to a low whisper as she surveyed Bri.

Bri shrugged. "When you've been attacked in the night enough times, it stops making sense to do so."

It wasn't the real reason and she was certain Lina knew so as well, judging by the curious look on her face. It hadn't been all the nights they were attacked in Falhampton; it had been one night, one attack, that caused her to be on high alert when the skies darkened. Normally, lies rolled easily off Bri's tongue, but they felt strange and awkward in front of Lina, as if the Princess could see straight to the core of her.

"I had my guards go investigate that baker Meson spoke of," Lina said.

"Any news?"

"He's as slimy as they come," Lina sighed. "He's mixed up in all sorts of misdeeds, but he's a middleman like Meson. He doesn't know what the seeds are for or who they're going to."

"Which errand boys came to claim them?" Bri asked. "Maybe we can follow the trail—"

"I'm working on it." Lina's voice was weary and rasping.

"Maybe we'd be able to resolve this faster if we worked together." Bri took another sip. "We're both investigating the same people, doubling the work."

Lina hummed. "I suppose."

"I'll agree to tell you which leads we're chasing, if you share with me if you've found anything important." Bri crossed her ankles and leaned back in her chair. "I promise not to leave you out of anything we're doing. You don't have to take this on alone."

"I know that. I'm trying," Lina growled, exhaustion and frustration making her voice rough. "But I'd rather trust no one at all than trust the wrong person." She stared down into her mug. "My mother trusted a lot of the wrong people." Her voice softened as if her mind was drifting to a far-off memory.

"I'm not the wrong person," Bri whispered.

Lina's eyes lifted, something like sadness flickering through her sharp expression. "I wish you were."

The moment stretched on in silence, Bri contemplating the weight of each of those words, until finally she tipped her head toward Lina. "Why can't you sleep?"

"It's a recent affliction," Lina said, pulling back into herself. She let Bri piece together the rest.

"I don't blame you, knowing there are people around who want you dead . . ." She blew on her tea. "It would make anyone want to stay up." Bri tapped the hilt of her amber dagger. "It's why you should train with daggers; you can't sleep with your battle-axe under your pillow."

Lina huffed, rising from her chair and sidling over to her bed. She reached under her pillow and pulled out the hand axe that Airev wore on her belt.

Bri grinned. "I stand corrected."

Abandoning her tea, Bri walked around to the far side of the bed and slid her dagger under the last pillow. She kicked off her boots and slid beneath the sheets, a groan pulling from her chest as the soft mattress cradled her body. The sheets were softer than any she'd ever felt before, the light duvet just the right amount of weight for the temperature.

"You're sleeping in your clothes?" Lina asked, perplexed as she replaced her axe. "Aren't a tunic and trousers uncomfortable to sleep in?"

"I don't usually sleep that long," Bri said, staring at Lina as she tucked her face into the supple pillow. Her eyelids grew heavy, and she was certain this bed was magic. "Changing isn't really worth it for a nap. Besides, it's this or nothing, so . . ."

Lina rolled her eyes. "Turn over."

"What?"

Lina's fingertips hovered on the silk belt of her robes. "Turn. Over."

Bri rolled over to her other side and listened to the sound of the fabric pooling on the ground. The sheets rustled and the bed dipped as Lina slipped beneath the sheets. When the movement halted, Bri rolled back over, her eyes dipping to the thin straps of Lina's nightdress.

"Why'd you make me turn over?" Bri chuckled. "You're still clothed."

Lina's eyes narrowed. "I didn't want you getting any ideas."

Bri flashed a wide grin. "You're very confident in the effect the sight of you in a nightdress would elicit."

Lina adjusted the strap that had slipped over her shoulder, a peek of black lace pulling above the sheets. Bri's eyes dropped to it, lingering on the curve of her breasts.

"Am I wrong?" Lina asked, arching her brow as Bri's eyes snapped back up to her own.

Her cheeks flushed and she muttered the word "no" through clenched teeth.

Lina smirked, looking rather pleased. She closed her eyes and then peeked one open at Bri. "I feel like I should light a candle or say a prayer or make a wish or something. . . . I don't think this is going to work."

"Me either." Bri sighed, nestling her cheek into the pillow. "Though if any place would, it would be *this* bed."

"And with a guard sworn to protect me sleeping by my side," Lina whispered. "One with a dagger under her pillow."

Bri waited to speak until Lina opened her eyes again. She held Lina's midnight gaze as she whispered, "I won't let anything happen to you. I promise you that."

"Of all the people I shouldn't believe, it's you." Lina yawned, her eyes fluttering closed again. "But I do believe you, for what it's worth, enemy or no."

"I'm not your enemy," Bri whispered, her eyes drifting closed.

"No." Lina's voice grew distant, the undertow of sleep pulling on her every word. "But neither are you my ally. You are something entirely your own, Briata Catullus. I just wish I knew what."

CHAPTER NINETEEN

The week passed uneventfully, each lead becoming a dead end. Maxfeld's runners had no useful information and neither did any of the guards' family members. Carys and Bri continued to lobby the council for permission to go investigate the witch hunters camped in the woods, but the council shut them down every time. The only part of Bri's days that weren't endlessly frustrating were the evenings, when she'd fall asleep next to Lina on that lush bed, the smell of jasmine lingering in the air along with Lina's steady breaths. Her dreams were serene. Not once did she jolt awake, nor did her hands mindlessly search the darkness for that lifeless body. It was the first time in many years where those unblinking, hollow eyes weren't the first thing she saw when she awoke.

They fell into an easy routine, Bri appearing late in the evenings, climbing into the empty side of the bed and closing her eyes. Sometimes they'd whisper to each other, debriefing about the day, other times they'd only murmur good night. Airev hadn't taken to the streets that whole week and Lina looked as bright and energized as Bri felt. The tightly wound strings that normally squeezed her skull had loosened, the sleep finally making her vision clear and the colors more vibrant. Everything that had once felt underwater was now full of life within her.

On that night, as the early evening descended, she decided to go visit Delta. The air in Delta's room was thick with burning *chaewood*, the healing smoke clinging to the fabric of the chair where Bri sat. Vials covered in Cole's scribbled handwriting dotted the bedside table. Delta propped herself up against her pillow. Her eyes seemed clearer, her mind sharper than it had been when Bri arrived.

Bri nodded to the flowers in the vase beside the bed. "These are beautiful," she said, trying to make light conversation and failing miserably.

"From Tem," Delta said with a smirk. Bri frowned at the purple flowers crushed at the bottom of the bouquet. "He's not much of a florist, but it was thoughtful."

Bri chuckled. "I'm surprised he sent something as simple as white and purple wildflowers, seeing how grand the Wystrons' manor is."

"That place is such an eyesore. And the food . . ." Delta grinned as Bri pretended to gag. "I hope I won't be invited to dine for some time." She gestured to her sleeve, knotted at the elbow. "I'll use what I can."

Bri snorted. "You'll be using that excuse to escape a dinner even when you're in the midst of battle again." She glanced at the sword leaning against the bed frame. "Speaking of thoughtful gifts."

"She made me promise not to try to train with it until next week," Delta said, her eyes scanning the beautiful, narrow weapon, viciously sharp and featherlight.

Bri arched her brow. "But you have, haven't you?"

"Of course I have." Delta laughed. "It's good. The weight. The balance. It'll take some time and getting used to . . . but don't count me out just yet."

"Never." Bri leaned back in her chair. "You could be tied up and blindfolded and I'd still bet on you, friend."

Delta's cheeks dimpled. " 'Friend'?"

"Yes," Bri said, folding her arms.

"I'm glad." Delta leaned her head back against the headboard.

The word had come tumbling out of Bri's mouth. Even as she said it, she realized that's what things between her and Delta felt like now. There wasn't any fire in her, no spark of yearning that made her want to throw herself at Delta. There was no urge to feel the brush of her lips . . . but that burning feeling was far from gone, replaced by another face in her mind.

She let out a long breath through her nose, trying to push the image away of Lina's softly sleeping face—a face that only Bri got to see.

"Where's Saika?" Bri asked, desperately trying to move her thoughts away from the images crowding her mind.

"Visiting her family in town," Delta said. "She should be back soon."

"I should be going." Bri rose from her chair, stretching her arms. "You'll be all right?"

Delta tipped her head to the stack of books on her bedside table. "I'll give you one guess who sent me those as a get-well-soon present."

Bri's lips twisted into a smirk. "Neelo Emberspear."

"They said this should be enough to keep me entertained until I'm out of bed." Delta laughed, sizing up the massive stack of books. "I suspect Neelo thinks I can read books as fast as they can."

Bri grinned and shook her head. "Ah, well, enjoy." She patted Delta on the shoulder, her friend giving her a nod in farewell as she left.

The halls were crowded with servants bustling about in the early evening. She kept close to the wall to avoid the flurry of activity as they closed down the castle for the night—hauling baskets of linens, carrying trays of food, lighting the torches along the walls. She weaved through the hubbub, making herself a shadow as she twined her way back toward the great hall.

Bri ducked out of the way of a harried-looking servant by tucking up against a door. She heard voices from the other side of the painted wood. At first they were murmured, then one voice she heard more distinctly. Her brows dropped, her face scrunching as she recognized it.

She quietly tested the handle but the door was locked. Grabbing her smallest knife from her belt, she inserted it into the lock and twisted. Once the lock was disengaged she opened the door and stepped into the front room.

What she saw made her freeze. Saika gasped, hauling a blanket up to cover her bare chest from where she sat straddling none other than Captain Yaest.

Bri snarled and turned back to the door.

"Bri, wait!" Saika called, climbing off Yaest and wrapping the blanket around her shoulders. She scurried over to Bri with a panicked look on her face. "Don't tell Delta, please."

"The two of you truly deserve each other." She huffed a bitter laugh, glowering at Saika. "I think you and your *wife* need to talk."

"I love her, Bri, I do, but—"

"Spare me," Bri grumbled. "That is a conversation for you and Delta." She glanced to Yaest, who covered himself with a pillow, watching Bri warily. "This makes everything you've told me all the less believable."

"I haven't lied to you," Yaest said with a haughty shrug. "You didn't ask me if I was sleeping with anyone."

"Gods, each one of you is worse than the last," Bri gritted out. She flung her hands in the air. "I don't care. Leave me out of it."

"Delta didn't leave you out of it," Saika hissed. She clenched her blanket around her shoulders as Bri's eyes widened. "You think I didn't know?"

"You knew?"

"Of course I knew," Saika snapped. "We'd have a falling out and she'd go off and find a new lover and then come crawling back, again and again and again. It broke my heart the first few times. . . ." She glanced over her shoulder at Yaest. "But then I stopped waiting for her to grow up and come to her senses. I was going to confront her about it when she came back from the wedding in the High Mountain Court . . . but then everything happened and I couldn't."

"Delta would *hate* that you stayed with her out of pity," Bri snarled. "She . . . ugh, I don't want to be involved—" Bri cut herself off, pinching the bridge of her nose in frustration.

"I just wanted you to understand," Saika pleaded.

"I don't want to understand," Bri growled. "Have a dozen lovers, I don't care. But don't promise to someone that you'll be loyal only to them and then break that promise. That is something I'll never understand. Both of you . . . just . . ." She clenched her hands into fists, trying to rein herself in from the lengthy rant desperate to spill from her lips.

With a final glowering look, she turned back to the door and grabbed the handle. "Sort your shit out, Saika."

Bri stormed back into the hall, uncaring as she nearly bowled over a guard on her way back to her room. She needed to find Carys and tell her what had just happened. They would need to double back and reinvestigate Yaest given this new information. A low growl rumbled in her chest.

There'd only been one person she'd ever wanted to be faithful to, and Bri couldn't have imagined ever breaking that promise to her. Even now that she was long gone, it felt wrong to ever love another. The steady rotation of women in and out of Bri's bed all knew that it was a casual, one-time thing. She'd always been very clear on what she wanted from them, and they'd always been eager for one night of mischief with her.

She couldn't understand why Saika and Delta couldn't have just decided to openly live that way too. Lies rotted relationships from the inside, and she knew if they didn't talk to each other soon, it would all crumble down around them.

When Bri threw open the door to their room, Carys's eyebrows raised and she dropped the book in her hand. Perching her elbow onto her knee, she leaned in.

"Oh, this is going to be good," she said, already intrigued from the way Bri stormed into the room.

Bri swept her hair off her forehead and pinned Carys with a look. "You know a court is messed up when its Princess is the most trustworthy person amongst them."

～

Bri mapped out the halls in the methodical way she did most nights, learning each corner and dip in the floor. She knew where each passageway led, which doors were cupboards and cellars. Each castle was different, but some things were always the same. The kitchens and dining commons were always near each other, the stables close to the training rings and armory. The most important residents slept on the higher floors, where the air was sweeter and the nights caught the breeze during the hot summer.

There was an intuition to these layouts she had learned over the years during her many travels alongside Hale. They'd stayed in many Lord's castles, exploring every corner of Okrith . . . apart from the West.

She skimmed her hand along the beaded tassels of the artwork on the wall, reminding her of the one in their sitting room back home. The Easterners had scoffed at it, preferring their intricately carved doors and wooden furniture. The Eastern houses had clean lines, jewel-toned colors, and oil paintings lining the walls, but Bri's parents had insisted they uphold the Western traditions, even though neither were native by blood. Her mother and father both grew up in Swifthill, as had their parents before them, but her mother had the Yexshiri warm brown complexion of the High Mountains, and her father the golden-olive skin of the Eastern fae . . . and Bri and Talhan came out looking like neither parent.

They carried the blood and traditions of three courts inside of them, those of their ancestors and those of their birth. As such everything about the West seemed eerily familiar to her. She meandered past the woven curtains, covered in brilliant geometric patterns of color, the same style as those in the castle she had grown up in.

"Remind you of something?"

Bri knew it was Carys without turning. Her friend's light footsteps always sounded like a dance.

"She was meticulous," Bri mused, tracing a finger along the patterns of the curtain.

As a child she'd spent hours hiding behind curtains just like it when she and Tal played hide-and-go-seek. Everything from the bedding in her rooms to the tile floors to the scent of cooking reminded her of her childhood in a foreign court. It was clear now how hard her mother had worked to preserve those traditions for her children. She had taught them of a place they had never seen.

"Your mother made a miniature Swifthill in the East," Carys said, stepping up beside her.

"People always commented on how accurate it was, but I hadn't really understood until now." She shook her head, turning to her friend. Carys knew what it was to seem like a foreigner in her home court. Her parents were Northern but she grew up in the South. "The Easterners scoffed and laughed at my mother, but she had always tempered their taunts by telling them one day she'd be the mother of the Queen. That shut them up."

"People don't mess with the Fates." Carys chuckled.

"No, they don't." Bri frowned. Some fae even doted on her mother in the hopes of currying favor with a future royal. She had done well for herself, Helvia Catullus. She was probably in her castle in the East now, gloating as the news traveled to her of where her daughter had ended up.

Carys's voice dropped to a whisper. "When was the last time you spoke with her?"

"Many years," Bri replied.

The pair didn't talk about her parents often. Carys had met them a few times at celebrations in the East, but even when they were in the same room, Bri had kept her distance, treating them like strangers. Her mother's plotting and scheming had grown out of hand. The second Bri and Tal had turned sixteen, they pledged their swords to the Eastern Crown Prince. Her mother's outrage was larger than any hurricane. Gone were her sixteen years of planning to put Bri on the throne in the West. She had been hiring spies and sowing seeds of discontentment for years, and with Bri's pledge, all the results of her mother's actions vanished. No one could have known that Bri's lifetime pledge would be transformed toward fealty to the High Mountain Court or that Remy would absolve Bri and Talhan of it.

Bri scowled and kept walking down the hallway, Carys a step behind.

"What?" Carys asked.

"I can't help but wonder how much of this is my mother's doing," Bri grumbled, marching toward the stairs that led to the wine cellar. "She's been trying for years to create distrust in the Crown. She's been whispering in people's ears for years that Queen Thorne was unfit to rule."

"I don't think she did this, Bri," Carys said. "She might have ruffled a few feathers, but Queen Thorne was the one who let the witch hunters off their leashes. She was the one who befriended Hennen Vostemur."

"But perhaps her people would have set her straight." Bri balled her fists as she jogged down the steps and threw open the cellar door. "Perhaps there would have been more faith in her."

"She is one person, kingdoms away," Carys said, eyeing Bri as she grabbed the first two bottles of wine off the rack. Carys considered the bottles and rolled her eyes, leaning past Bri to grab another for herself.

"Never underestimate the power of a plotting mother's whisper," Bri warned. "Now, where are we drinking these?"

"I vote somewhere inside," Carys snorted. "All the nighttime creatures around here seem to want to eat us."

"Our room it is," Bri said, hastening back up the steps.

She had another few hours before she could sneak off to Lina's quarters for the night. Her tired body already looked forward to the familiar comfort of those soft sheets and plush pillows, sleep finally accessible like a key turning in a lock.

Bri turned the corner too quickly, smacking into a person rushing down the hall. She looked up to the wide-eyed fae, who was wearing riding clothes and had a heavy bag slung over his shoulder.

As they collided, the bottle in Bri's left hand slipped but she caught it before it shattered on the ground. The fae's bag smacked onto the floor, its contents spilling across the tiles. Stooping, Bri and Carys both moved to help him scramble after his belongings.

"Sorry, about th—"

"No, no, I can do it," he cut them off, reaching for the object that had tumbled the farthest just as their eyes landed on it.

Bri's hand froze midair.

There, on the floor, was a golden lion mask.

The second they spotted it, he knew the jig was up, dropping it and dashing down the hall.

"Shit," Carys cursed, dropping her bottle of wine. It shattered around their feet as she raced after him.

Bri set her bottles on the ground and sprinted after Carys, catching up in three easy strides.

"Just put it down, Car. You don't have to be so bloody dramatic," she snapped, more disappointed in the wasted wine than concentrated on the ensuing chase.

"Can we focus, please?" Carys replied as the fleeing fae darted down a hallway to the right.

He tumbled a table behind him, clay shattering across the floor. Carys hurdled over it in one stride, leaping like a gazelle. Bri thundered through the debris, her boots crunching across the shards of clay. The escapee fled to the end of the hall, vaulting up to the open arched window and sliding out the other side. Carys was there in a heartbeat, jumping up to the window after him as Bri darted through the door to the left.

"Round him up," Bri shouted to her friend as she sped into the darkened servants' passage.

Mapping out the castles hadn't been just a mindless practice. There was a reason she knew where every pathway led, and that the arched window led to the training rings, and the only way out of the training rings . . .

She pulled her dagger from her belt as she dashed through the maze of halls, halting at the far wooden door. Her chest heaved. She needed to take Carys up on her offer to go on more runs. Bri preferred training with weapons, and, though she had stamina for hours, sprinting was not her forte. She took one last gulping breath as the door was thrown open.

Arms wheeling, the runaway's eyebrows shot up as he skidded to a stop. Bri grabbed him by the collar of his tunic and slammed him into the wall.

"Before you go," she said, pinning him with her dagger at his neck, "we've got some questions for you."

Bri's eyes widened as she recognized him—the one she and Lina had followed to the brothel that night, the one who'd stolen Tem's necklace. Her lips curled up into a smile. Finally, they were getting somewhere.

"Gods!" A hiss from down the hallway had them turning. Saika stood at the end of the hall, a basket of dried flowers resting on her hip. "So they are hiding in the castle."

Carys tucked the golden mask behind her back. "We'll figure out what he knows, don't worry."

"You can't just question him here in the halls," Saika whispered. "Take him to the dungeons. I'll go warn the guards."

"No," Bri cut her off, lifting a hand and halting her steps. "Speak of this to no one," she warned. "I have questions that need answering."

Saika narrowed her eyes at the three of them but nodded and kept walking. Carys and Bri exchanged glances, wondering if they could trust her to keep this secret. If any other guards showed up, they'd know Saika had tipped them off.

"Take him to the dungeons," Bri muttered, shoving the cowering suspect into Carys's grip. "I need to go find Lina."

CHAPTER TWENTY

T he brown-haired fae sat on a narrow canvas cot with his wrists shackled together. As he stared down at his hands, his face was unsettlingly neutral. Carys and the fae hadn't passed a single soldier as they reached the far end of the dungeons; there were no prisoners to guard in the dark catacombs. Carys had waited outside the cell for Bri and Lina to arrive. Bri felt the anticipation buzzing through Lina's body. She hoped this would be the person who would unravel the rest of the answers they'd been circling.

"You," Lina snarled as she strode into the room. "The thief. What is it you do in the castle?"

"Stablehand," he muttered, not meeting her gaze. His tone was eerily calm for someone just caught with a lion mask.

Bri tried to think over the list of suspects Delta had given her. She hadn't gotten through the whole list of names, but she'd started with the ones in the highest positions, the most suspicious. Stablehands would have been low on her list of people to question. They had limited access to the upper floors and couldn't go near the Queen's chambers. Unlike maids, stablehands would be easily spotted in a location they weren't supposed to be.

"How many of you are there?" Bri folded her arms and leaned against the stone wall.

The dungeons were cleaner than most she'd seen, the smell not as rancid as in the ones in the East, probably because the Thornes didn't make a habit of keeping prisoners. Their judgment was swift.

The traitor hung his head. "Many."

"And where are they?"

He shrugged, looking at his fingers with vacant, haunted eyes. "In the woods, out at sea, above the clouds, I don't know."

Bri unsheathed her amber dagger, flipping it back and forth in her hands. "And how many more are here in the palace?"

"I'm the only one who works here."

"You're not even good at lying," Lina snarled. She leaned against the iron door, holding the carved golden mask in her hands. "So Augustus Norwood holds the leash to the witch hunters now?"

The expressionless fae didn't reply.

Carys crouched, opening his bag and dumping the contents across the floor—clothes, weapons, dried meat . . . The toe of her boot paused over a little brown packet. She bent and picked it up.

She read the curling words. " '*Veliaris Rudica.*' " She opened the flap and peered at the contents inside. "Seeds."

Bri's eyes darted to the packet, her mind flying back to Meson's confession in the gambling hall.

"What is the purpose of these seeds?" Bri asked.

"To sow the seeds of rebellion," he whispered in a chanting way as if he'd said the same thing many times before. It matched what Meson had said.

"Is it a symbol?" Carys asked. "Are they what killed the Queen?"

He swept the dust off his knees. "If I tell you anything they'll kill me."

"If you don't tell us, *we'll* kill you," Lina seethed, taking a step forward. Bri's muscles tensed, readying to hold her back if she must. "You played a role in my mother's murder. I'm offering you only one chance to save yourself."

The traitor shook his head, dropping it into his hands.

"Enough of this." Bri scowled, pushing off from the wall and lifting her dagger. "I know how to get him to talk."

"Wait." His voice was steady as his eyes shot up to her. His chains rattled, and he lifted his hand to the necklace dipping below his tunic. "I can give you the note. It will tell you everything you need to know."

"The note?" Carys cocked her head at the locket the man lifted into his shackled hands. "You keep a note in there?"

The silver metal locket was scuffed to the point that she could barely make out the gold etched onto the front. It didn't open like a regular locket; instead he twirled the center like a dial. He rotated the scuffed blotches of gold all the way around and pushed down, and the locket divided into two. He bent to the opened necklace and sniffed deeply as if smelling a flower.

"Stop!" Bri shouted, realizing too late what was happening.

His eyes rolled back in his head, a guttural choking sounding in his throat. Black blood dripped from his ears and the corners of his mouth. Bri reached for him as he fell backward, his head cracking against the edge of the cot. She touched his neck, feeling for a pulse but there was none.

"He's dead."

"No!" Lina growled.

"He inhaled it...." Carys took a step backward. "So it's different than what killed the others?"

"Go find Cole," Bri commanded. "He'll want to investigate this poison."

Carys nodded and left, leaving Bri staring down into the lifeless eyes of the poisoned man.

Lina clenched her fists and gritted her teeth. With a bellowing shout, she punched the stone wall. She raged as she wailed her fists into the hard stone. Bri rushed over to her, putting herself between Lina and the wall. Cupping Lina's cheeks, she forced Lina's eyes to meet her own.

"We will find who did this," she promised, slowly, carefully. The contact of Bri's palms on Lina's cheeks seemed to pull her back into her body. "We will find them."

"You were right," Lina panted, biting back the venom in her voice as she looked down to her bloodied knuckles. "We need to go find these witch hunters, see what they know." She let out a shuddering sigh, her anger seeming to ease with each breath. "I thought I had a handle on this."

"No one does," Bri whispered. "The world is changing faster than any of us can keep up with. Magic that wasn't meant to exist is being used against us now. New enemies we never even suspected have sprung up. We *will* figure this out, Lina."

Lina's eyes guttered as Bri whispered her name. "We?"

Bri searched her gaze, trying to parse apart every emotion that seemed to flicker like constellations in the night sky. "Yes."

They rode on horseback out of Swifthill with a retinue of twenty guards. Carys and Bri positioned themselves on either side of Lina, on high alert, suspicious even of the guards who journeyed with them. Each hour through the forest felt more and more like they were being led into a trap. Every cracking branch and rustle of leaves made Bri's hand drop to her dagger.

The West was filled with liars and spies. Bri insisted that she kept the night watch; she and Carys were both on high alert during the day. Between the two of them, there was always at least one loyal guard around Lina. Still, after finding that traitor in the castle, she understood even more why Delta was so frantic for her to come. The best way to stop this threat was to cut off the head of the snake. If Augustus Norwood fell, then his witch hunters would stop—stop the flow of Norwood's coins and see how many of them remained loyal then.

The air cooled as they ventured farther into the forest, the clouds that clung to the High Mountains in the distance providing a welcome reprieve from the scorching sun. Inland, the terrain changed from red rocks and spiky shrubs to moss-covered stones and swaying trees. The buds of spring greened their bare branches, the promise of new life peeking out from every stem. Soon the forest would be covered in the first flowers, the heavy spring rains coaxing them alive once more.

A white-breasted crow cawed overhead, and Bri shifted on her mount, her muscles tightening. Of course it had to be the ominous sound of crows and not the twitter of songbirds punctuating their silent travels. If the Goddess of Death walked out of the fog right then, Bri wouldn't have been surprised.

A fine sheen of mist blanketed their skin, the weather turning sour as they continued their trek. The canopy above provided protection from the worst of the rain, but they hadn't worn enough layers to shield themselves from the wet conditions.

Bri wiped damp hair off her forehead. "How much farther?"

"Less than an hour now," a guard called from up ahead.

Bri scowled, wiping the droplets dotting her forearms.

"At least we're finally cool," Carys said, smirking at Bri. Little curls of wet hair escaped her braid as she wiped her face with the collar of her tunic.

"Can't take the heat?" Bri jested.

"Please," Carys snickered. "I grew up in the South. It's not the heat, though the sun does seem harsher in the West. It's the thin air that makes it so onerous."

"You'd rather the humidity of the South?" Lina mused, still looking everywhere but at the two of them, and Bri wondered if she was think-ing about what had transpired between them.

We. She hadn't elaborated on what that meant, only that it meant something, and Lina had seemed . . . angry and pleased at the same time, as if she were mad at herself for what was building between them. Bri studied the Princess, wishing she could read her expression, dying to know the thoughts swirling under that sharp face.

"Yes, I suppose I would prefer the humidity." Carys smiled at the frown on Lina's face. "Though the West is lovely to visit . . . for brief periods of time."

"A diplomatic answer, Carys. I would expect nothing less," Lina said with a huff, adjusting the leather belts of her shoulder harness.

Bri had to hold in a groan. Lina's battle-axe perfectly framed her shoulders, its lethal blades flaring out behind her like wings. Bri's gaze lingered on the beautiful weapon then moved down to the straps that pulled back Lina's posture and framed her large chest. Bri had the sudden urge to invite Lina to train again, to watch her wield that monstrous weapon. So evenly matched, so unexpected—Bri couldn't stop thinking about that day in the ring.

Instead, Bri found herself saying, "I will make you my ambassador when I am Queen of the East, Car."

Carys cackled. "When *I* am Queen, you can be the captain of my army, Bri," she said, winking. "No ambassadorship for you."

"So eager to play Queen," Lina muttered more to herself than to them.

They both looked at the Princess riding between them. Bri could see the restraint in her expression, hear the control in her voice. The weeks since Lina had taken up the mantle of Western ruler, title or no, were wearing on her. Bri understood why the Princess was so eager for a coronation. She even begrudgingly understood why Lina was so eager for Tem to become her consort. Leading a court alone was an incredible burden, but if anyone could handle it, it would be Lina.

"Ruling a kingdom is no easy feat," Carys conceded. "We didn't mean to belittle it."

Lina waved her hand in dismissal. "When you have citizens lined up waiting to air their decades-old grievances to the new sovereign, you'll see then how fun it is to wear the crown."

She said it as if in jest, trying to sound lighthearted and failing. At least she was sleeping at night now—one burden Bri could help with. Bri had given up trying to keep her mind from drifting toward images of Lina's sleeping face. It happened so often throughout the day, in all of the quiet moments when normally anxiety would prickle across her skin. She wasn't searching the darkness for threats anymore, but instead she listened for the steady rhythm of Lina's sleeping breaths, like a heartbeat outside her own body.

"I'm sure the people of Wynreach will have complaints that stretch beyond the start of Gedwin Norwood's reign," Carys said. "None of the Norwood Kings cared a sniff about the humans and witches of their kingdoms."

Clenching her jaw, Bri studied the canopy above them.

Bri wasn't excited about the council meetings or the parties . . . but receiving the citizens she would look forward to. She watched her whole life as the royalty around her dismissed the needs of everyone but the richest amongst them, and soon, she'd finally have the power to make a difference. Tal could handle the parties and Carys could run the council meetings, but Bri would listen to the people of the Eastern Court. A twinge ran through her thinking of her brother. She needed to talk to Talhan.

They descended into stilted silence once more as Bri's mind wandered toward the competition. The challengers would each vie for the Eastern crown based on strength and fighting skills, yes, but also on public speaking and plans for the future of Wynreach.

She thought of Carys's half sister, Morgan. The halfling led a human life with her human husband and children. Morgan saw the underbelly of the city and the dark side of the fae who wished she didn't exist. Her ties to Carys would make Carys Bri's biggest competition. Carys would surely have the humans' vote, maybe the witches' too, but the fae would probably vote for Bri or Tal. The twins grew up in the courts and attended the fae's weddings and birthday celebrations. Their mother had relationships just as deep in the East as she did in the West. Perhaps now that the Eastern throne was vacant, she would shift her meddling away from the West entirely.

The line of horses veered from the thin trail onto a wider worn path, drawing closer to the witch hunters' camp. The forest reminded Bri of trekking through the backcountry to find Remy not so many months ago. How the world had changed in such a short span of time. The red witch in that seedy little tavern was now a fae Queen, her little sister now the Queen of the Northern Court. Bri shook her head. It was impossible to know what Okrith would look like in another year's time. Would there ever be a future when all five crowns of Okrith were allies, when the continent wasn't at war?

They passed a splintering sign nailed to a tree, the white paint of the skull and crossbones nearly flecked off. A single carved word was barely legible in the rotten wood: "RED." Below that were notches in the tree, moss growing over each split in the bark. Bri swallowed the bile rising in her throat. They were tallies—hundreds and hundreds of tally marks that scarred the trunk.

"We didn't come here to kill anyone," Lina reminded them. "We . . ." She eyed the tree again. "At least let's get the answers we need first."

Bri snarled at the trunk as she passed. How close had Remy come to being a tally on that tree? She bet it filled the witch hunters with pride every time they got to mark another line. Another witch head. Another bag of gold. Now, the tree was covered nearly down to its roots, a coven gone. She thought to the red witches back in Yexshire. Mere dozens had survived and were now back at the temple in the High Mountain Court. Others had emerged from their hiding spots around Okrith upon hearing the news that the High Mountain fae had returned, but there were still so few of them. It would be many generations before their numbers matched what they were before the losses from the witch hunts.

"Bri?" Bri snapped her head up at Lina's voice. Lina's eyebrows lifted as if she was waiting for a response to a question Bri hadn't heard.

"I'll try not to kill anyone until we have answers," Bri gritted out, giving Lina a hard look as she guessed what the question was. Judging by Lina's grim nod, she'd guessed correctly. "And I'll try to keep you from doing the same."

Lina flashed a menacing grin, nudging her horse forward. The riders fell into a single-file line to navigate the narrowing path.

Fury filled Bri's chest as she rode past that tree. With a burning desire to avenge the fallen witches, her fingers twitched for her dagger. Schooling her expression, she promised herself she wouldn't make a hasty grab for her weapons. She needed to get answers and protect Lina . . . no matter how much she wanted to ram her blade through the witch hunters.

CHAPTER TWENTY-ONE

Signs of life started to pop up along the road. Discarded wagon wheels, tattered scraps of fabric, broken glass, and rusted steel lined the edges of the path, bleeding into the dense underbrush. Were it not for the trail of smoke rising above the canopy, Bri would have thought the site was abandoned.

The travelers twined their way through the narrow trail, the forest opening up to reveal a ramshackle dwelling covered in climbing weeds and moss. It was built like a hunting tavern, constructed with giant beams and stag antlers adorning the outer facade. The windows were shattered, the door falling off its hinges and the thatched roof caving in. No one greeted them as they dismounted.

Lina held up her hand to the other guards waiting with their horses. "Stay out here. Keep watch," she commanded stiffly.

Bri wondered if Lina didn't want the guards to overhear any conversation between Bri, Carys, and herself. The palace was a leaky vessel, secrets spilling from its hull. It was wise to control the flow of information to the guards. Lina moved to enter the decrepit building but Carys stepped in front of her, her hand resting on her sword, and entered first.

Bri blinked, straining her eyes to see in the darkness of the musty room. Cobwebs brushed across her forehead as she stepped through the threshold and into a rundown front room.

Five fae silhouettes clung to the far wall, watching in the shadows as Bri surveyed the space. Hints of the reception room's former beauty flashed in the firelight. A rusted chandelier hung high above, beautiful swirls of gray and black stone covered the paving, and an elaborately carved wood chair with a crotchety-looking fae sitting atop it was positioned at the far end of the room.

"A *king* on his throne," Lina spat, stepping up toward him.

He looked similar to Yaest in his face and build, but the lines on his face were deeper, his hair faded to a dark silver. He wore a thick fur mantle and tatty dark clothes that looked like they should have been replaced many years ago. He looked one cold day away from death. His eyes were sunken in and his lips cracked, and sores marred his skin. It looked like a malady easily treated by a skilled brown witch . . . but not even the kindest witch would ever help these monsters.

The whole site was like a ruin from years past, as if the people who resided there loomed in a purgatory, unable to die or move on.

"Princess Abalina," the king said in a deep, booming voice, still strong despite his weakened appearance. "Might I say your beauty is unparalleled. Very pleasing."

"You males are insufferable," Lina hissed, throwing back her shoulders in a way that made the witch hunter's eyes land on her axe. "Even when you're speaking to a Princess, you think the highest compliment is that we might please you. *Nothing* I do is for your benefit nor any male's."

"So I've heard," he said with a knowing smirk. She scowled but he pressed on. "I've heard many secrets being whispered throughout the realm of late."

Lina cocked her head. "And what secrets have you heard?"

"Why would I tell you?" He waved his hand across the derelict room. "You've ruined us."

"I think you'll find you did this all to yourself," she snarled. "Now, tell me what you know."

He crossed his arms and leaned back in his chair with a smile. Bri's palm rested on the hilt of her dagger. She knew an easier way to get him to talk.

"He wants money," Carys muttered before Bri could take a step forward.

"Not just that," he said, looking Carys up and down. "I suppose you don't remember a little town on the western road called Guildford? Your master killed my friend and his nephew."

Bri's mind flashed back to the attack on Remy. Bri and the others had arrived just in time to see Hale hacking apart the last of the witch hunters trying to capture Remy. Bri turned her golden stare on the witch hunter before her. "Your *friends* tried to behead my friend."

He shrugged as if it were nothing. "They were doing a job sanctioned by the Northern King."

"And my comrades were doing a job ordered by the Eastern King, and here we are in the Western Court and none of that fucking matters," Bri growled.

"You can be angry that they're gone, but blaming Hale for defending his Fated is ridiculous," Carys said with an even, steadfast tone.

"I suppose you're right, Southerner," he said, pointedly sneering at Carys.

Carys didn't even blink.

"You are supposedly the king of the witch hunters . . . a *sovereign* with no nation." Lina took another menacing step toward him and the other fae in the shadows visibly tensed, as if preparing for a battle they were all itching to start. "Tell me, were you there the night my mother died?"

His eyes flitted to Lina, a smile pulling up his cracked lips. "I wasn't there that night." He bellowed out a laugh, smacking the armrest as he slung an elbow over the back of his chair. "You still don't realize it, do you? How muddled up in this your mother was all these years?"

Lina stilled, narrowing her eyes at him.

"The Northern King might have been the one lining our pockets with gold," he said with a wolflike grin, "but it was *your* mother we worked for. She commanded the hunts and organized our crew. She willingly built the wealth of your kingdom on the heads of red witches."

"No," Lina whispered. "She didn't stop it, but neither did she sanction it. That can't be true."

"I think deep down you know it is, Princess," he snickered, reading Lina's hollow expression. "We are not interested in allying with Augustus Norwood. His kingdom's wealth is controlled by Hale now while the East waits to choose its new ruler. Queen Thorne knew the red witches had too much power in Okrith, that they threatened the fae way of life, and now they are gone. Our job is done."

"It was you. It had to be," Lina insisted.

"Does it look like we have a wealthy patron?" The king scrubbed his hand along his stubbled jaw. "*If* we'd been paid to kill the Queen, do you think we'd still be living in this squalor?"

"I wouldn't be surprised," Bri snarked. "Squalor suits you."

The king glared at her. "Hennen Vostemur understood what a threat the witches could be. He knew what would happen if their leashes grew too long." He waved a hand to one of the fae behind him and they stepped forward with a goblet in their hand. It was a beautiful, gilded cup, so strange-looking in the sore-addled hand of the ailing witch hunter. "There's an order to this world, one in which the fae are meant to be at the top. King Vostemur cemented that legacy for generations to come. The five crowns of Okrith will always be controlled by the fae. Queen Thorne understood that too. It's why she let us hunt."

He took a long sip, watching Lina stew. This *king* had completely lost his grip on reality if he believed the lies he spewed. The red witches never showed any ambition toward ruling a court. They respected the High Mountain fae and the High Mountain fae respected them, ruling congruently for the betterment of their kingdom. That was what Hennen Vostemur couldn't handle—a world where he didn't have complete power. He hoarded it like a little boy hoarding his toys, throwing a tantrum at any sign that he couldn't keep them all for himself. He would stand on the corpses of an entire coven to make himself feel even an inch taller.

A log cracked in the fireplace and they all turned toward the sound, so loud in the looming silence.

"If it wasn't you who attacked the palace, then who?" Lina asked.

"I'm sure some of my men who've deserted over the years were pulled into Norwood's cause," he muttered. "But they aren't true witch hunters, not anymore. I believed in making a better world for the fae. The future dominion of our kind was won by my men and their blades, but not all of them were true to the cause. Some of them were only in it for the coin. I wouldn't be surprised if Norwood has his claws in quite a few of them by now." He looked between the three of them. "But that has nothing to do with me."

"Whoever started the attacks," Lina asked, "are they still in the West?"

"Your guards did a good job knocking them out from what I hear," he replied, taking another sip from his goblet. "Though it's impossible to know if you've stamped them out once they've taken root."

"If you help us find who killed my mother," Lina said carefully, "we can give you more money than Augustus Norwood would offer you."

He guffawed, clutching his belly. "Do you think I have a death wish?"

"Clearly you do," Lina snarled, surveying his gaunt face. "I could get you the remedies you need." Her eyes lifted behind him. "I'm sure your crew hiding in the shadows looks as dreadful as you. If you help me, I can get you aid."

"The winter was hard," he muttered with a dismissive wave of his hand. "We'll be fine come summer. We're fae. We don't need brown witches to heal."

Bri frowned at his sunken in eyes. "Your face says otherwise."

"Augustus may have no money, but he has magic like I've never seen and the Witches' Glass to boot." He shook his head, looking at them like they were the delusional ones. "Just because Renwick Vostemur broke his curse, doesn't mean Norwood isn't a threat to all of Okrith still. He could curse the witches anew for all we know."

"He'd need witches with weakened minds to do that," Bri said, her gut clenching at the memory of the cursed blue witches in the North, the Forgotten Ones. They were the perfect group to prey upon, their minds shattered from years of torture in the blue witch fortresses. There wasn't any other group like it—a collection of witches too far gone to fight off a mind-controlling curse. "The blue witches are safe now; who could he possibly use?"

"I can think of a few." The king chuckled, wine dribbling down his tunic as he gulped back his drink. He passed the empty goblet blindly behind him to be refilled. "All I know is he has a powerful witch stone and a witch who knows how to use it on his side."

Lina inched forward. "Who is this witch?"

He shrugged. "I don't know."

"You claim to hear the secrets whispered throughout the realm and you don't know?" Bri reminded him as she chucked him a pouch of coins.

He caught it one-handed, sharp and fast, despite his glassy drunken eyes—a reminder that a monster existed beneath the surface, one that had killed many people.

He mused at the coin purse and then extended out his hand. Rolling her eyes, Carys tossed him another coin pouch. He weighed the second bag in his hands.

"I don't know her real name," he said. "But they call her Baba."

"Baba?" Carys gasped. "As in, a High Priestess?"

"They say Balorn's witches were just a swarm of ants to Augustus," the king said, pocketing his coins with a satisfied smirk. "He had a witch of sound mind helping him too."

"Who are they?" Lina pushed. "What kind of witches? Where are they from?"

"Isn't it obvious? You've seen that purple smoke." His eyebrows lifted as he flashed an unsettling grin. "The violet witches are back."

CHAPTER TWENTY-TWO

aba. The word whirled through Bri's mind. How many violet witches were there still in existence?

The whinny of horses up ahead made Bri's mare buck. Bri lifted her head to find the source of the disturbance, but the road ahead was clear. The ride back toward Swifthill was a somber one. The wrathful vengeance that had swarmed through her died the moment she saw the witch hunter king's face. He and those that stayed with him were no longer a threat to anyone. It probably would have been a mercy to kill him; his punishment now would be to live with all that he had done and slowly wither away. His fae healing would keep him going, only extending his misery, until he finally succumbed to whatever disease plagued him. She shuddered, making a note to get a cleansing tonic from Cole.

Another horse whinnied up ahead. Bri exchanged glances with Lina and Carys. "The horses are spooked," she murmured. "That can't be good."

Lina straightened on her mount, her eyes narrowing to survey the shadowed forests. A deep growl rent the air and Bri jolted, her head snapping toward the sound.

The trees swayed as something prowled through the underbrush, appearing on the path before them. Her breath caught in her throat.

What strange sort of monster was this?

At a passing glance, it looked like a lion with a billowing black mane, but it was larger than a horse and had tusks that curled toward its whiskered nose and gnarled horns twisting out from its skull. It looked similar to an Eastern mountain lion, crossed with some sort of beast she didn't know . . . but what was it doing in the Western Court?

Her horse bucked again and she struggled to regain control. With a final kick she tumbled from her mount into the gravel. A sharp pain shot through her shoulder as it took the brunt of the fall. Lina shouted her name, dismounting her own horse before Carys could stop her.

Lina appeared, crouching next to Bri and grabbing her arm. "Get up," she commanded.

Before Bri could move, a bellowing growl boomed through the trees and the horses screamed, bolting into the forest. Lina dropped over Bri, shielding Bri with her own body, their heads tucked together as they narrowly avoided being trampled. Lina pulled back and Bri panted, her eyes hooking into Lina's for only a split second, but that one look made lightning skitter across her skin. It was the Queenly thing to do . . . it was the soldierly thing to do too, but Bri knew that's not why Lina covered Bri's body with her own.

Another snarl broke their gaze, and Bri unsheathed her amber dagger at the same moment Lina pushed off Bri and grabbed the axe off her own back.

Shouts rang out through the forest as the guards tried to regain control of their horses. Carys and her mount had disappeared too, leaving only Lina and Bri standing before the giant monster.

Yellow sputum dripped from its snarling maw. Its quicksilver eyes flared at the pair as its claws tested the earth beneath its feet.

"What in the Gods' names is that?" Lina hissed, her fingers squeezing tighter around her axe as she and Bri slowly stepped backward.

"No clue," Bri panted, reaching for Lina's hip and unsheathing the amethyst dagger with her free hand. She held the two blades—one silver and purple, one golden and bronze—out toward the creature and it retreated a step. "What the . . ."

She held up just the amber dagger and the beast took another snarling step. She lifted the amethyst dagger and it retreated again.

"Whoever created this beast," Lina breathed. "I'm guessing is the owner of this dagger."

Baffled, Bri looked from the purple hilt back to the glowing pewter slits of the creature's eerie eyes. "Sit," she commanded, but the lion didn't move.

"It's not a fucking dog," Lina gritted out.

"It was worth a try." Bri lifted the dagger higher in the air and took another step forward.

The lion lowered into a crouch, its ears plastering back as it looked to the ground.

Carys came barreling through the woods on foot, skidding to a halt when she spotted Bri approaching the lion. A handful of guards stumbled up behind her and she held up a hand to stop them from advancing.

The creature's giant claws dragged rivulets into the soft earth. Its ears perked up, twisting toward the west just as a murmured chant echoed from the same direction.

People were coming.

The voices grew as a violent thread of magic shook the earth and whipped through the trees.

"Run!" Carys screamed and they all turned and bolted.

The beast chased after them, snapping up the closest guard into its giant jaws. The deep snarl rattled her ribs, the pulse so low it made the leaves tremble. The retinue of guards stopped as the creature closed in, turning to fend off the beast.

"Protect the Princess," one guard commanded.

Lina, Bri, and Carys raced off the trail and breached the tree line, diving into the thick forest. Branches scratched along their arms and faces as they stumbled over the uneven terrain.

"Look out!" Carys shouted, and they skidded to a halt.

A line of six masked figures stood in front of them, swords drawn. Their attire was a mismatch of fighting leathers and armor, dented and worn from years of use. Their weapons looked one bad swing away from breaking but their stance told Bri they knew how to use them. Only their masks were pristine—the carved wood face of a snarling lion painted over in gold.

Were these witch hunters? Had that ailing fae who called himself king been the one to send them? How could they not be? It was far too convenient and unlikely to encounter another foe only hours after confronting the witch hunter king.

Bri couldn't breathe, couldn't think, as a snarl sounded behind them, accompanied by the screams of their guards.

The masked attackers charged and the three of them quickly moved, placing their backs to each other, readying for the onslaught.

Lina connected with the first attacker, their leathers no protection against the heft of her axe. Bri sliced into the second, shifting as their trio sidestepped in a circle, whirling in a dance of steel and blood.

One leaned in too far, leading with his face as his sword swing brought his momentum forward. A careless mistake, Bri thought, as she plunged her dagger through the eye slit of his mask. His mouth opened on a voiceless scream as she kicked him back with her boot.

The yelp of the beast signaled the turning tide, just as the last assailant dropped like a stone as Carys stabbed him straight through the neck. The trio panted, staring down at the six bodies around their feet. Carys stooped and pulled one of the masks down. Lifeless eyes stared up to the canopy above.

"Do you recognize him?" She gulped deep breaths, looking up at Lina.

Her chest heaving, Lina shook her head. "No."

They pulled the rest of the masks down but didn't recognize any of the faces. The assailants weren't from the palace. Bri wasn't sure if that was a relief or not. She looked through the woods at the guards surrounding the furred heap. Only five still stood, others groaning and wounded on the ground.

"The witch hunter king must have tipped them off," Carys said, wiping her bloodied hands down her trousers.

"Or they already knew we were traveling this way." Bri sheathed her weapons. "We haven't done the best job of keeping Lina's movements quiet. All her guards knew she was coming out here today."

Lina looked between the two of them. "The witch hunters didn't know we were paying them a visit until we arrived, but the palace did." She swiped the back of her hand across her sweaty brow. "Do we really think that sickly fae who calls himself king could have orchestrated this attack on such short notice?" She tipped her chin to the bodies around their feet. "None of them have the sores. If they worked for him, they'd be ailing as well."

Bri eyed Lina and bobbed her head. This seemed to be a problem coming from within.

"We're rounding up the horses, Your Highness," a guard called through the trees. "We should be—"

His voice was cut off by a loud pop. The sky darkened and they craned their necks upward to see a dark purple cloud descending through the trees. Another round orb flew into the sky and an arrow shot it down directly above the guards. Purple smoke exploded, filtering down through the air.

The first guard screamed, clawing at his eyes and throat. The whole group of guards began choking and gasping as the noxious smoke billowed over them.

"Go!" Bri shouted, shoving Lina out of her stupor.

Another horde of masked attackers appeared through the mist, bolting after them, seemingly unaffected by the smoke.

Bri moved to unsheathe her dagger again and Carys snapped, "Wait until we've cleared the smoke." She raced liked a bolting deer through the deep leaves. "If that shit touches us, it won't matter how many of them we take down with us."

They dipped over the crest of the hill, down into the valley and up the other side. The undulating landscape made it difficult to set any distance between them and those looming purple clouds.

"Over the river!" Lina shouted, and they darted toward a rotten log wedged across a roaring river.

The water rushed under the beam in white-tipped rapids. Lina leapt onto it, holding her arms out to balance. She made it across in three bounds and Bri and Carys quickly followed. When Carys reached the other side, Lina unhooked her axe fast as a striking asp and brought it down in one powerful strike, cleaving the log in two. Bri's mouth dropped open at the power and fury in that one move as the split log flew away on the roaring current.

Three masked figures ran downhill toward them, plunging into the cold mountain river. The first one's feet swept out from under them; a scream faded into the distance as the raging river carried them downstream. The other two moved at a snail's pace, inching forward to keep their footing but not stopping.

"Keep going until we're out of shooting range," Carys called, pulling on the back of Bri's tunic.

Bri narrowed her eyes at the thinning smoke in the distance. How many more poisonous explosives did these attackers have? She turned, hustling up the far bank. The three of them wheezed as the weight of their weapons and the near vertical incline of the hillside slowed their speed. Bri's thighs burned as she urged them onward.

More pops echoed in the distance, the poison smoke filtering above the trees and raining down on the masked figures crossing the river. They didn't choke or scream as the smoke swirled around their bodies; they continued to push forward across the river. Bri crested the next hill, and down toward the other side, seeing a twin river rushing from up ahead. The spring rains had flooded the banks of the two rivers on either side of them, trapping them on the hill between.

"Shit." Carys unsheathed her sword. "We'll have to fight them off here."

"And the smoke?" Bri hissed.

"And pray they've used up all their poisons already."

The two masked assailants emerged from the hillside, wet from the waist down. Their shoulders and hair were covered in a fine dusting of purple powder.

Lina arched her eyebrow. "Why doesn't the poison work on them?"

"Maybe it's the masks. Maybe they drink an antidote beforehand," Carys replied, waiting for them to reach striking distance before charging forward.

Bri and Lina converged on the second masked figure while Carys squared off with the first. The masked figures' movements were slow and sloppy, exhausted either by the river crossing or ingesting the poison smoke, Bri didn't know, but in two strikes the second attacker was down. She glanced over to see how Carys fared. Carys barely had to blow on her attacker before her opponent collapsed at her feet as well.

She shook her head. To cross the river and climb the hill, only to fall in two easy blows . . . She wondered if they were similarly compelled by magic like the cursed blue witches. These weren't the actions of a person in control of their mind.

They looked back toward the tree line but there was nothing but silence, the last of the smoke having cleared from the sky.

"Looks like we're heading back to Swifthill on foot," Carys panted, looking at the roar of water behind them. "We'll find a crossing upriver."

Bri and Lina nodded in unison. "That was too close."

Their breathing was the only sound as they surveyed the two bodies at their feet.

"They knew you were with us," Carys said to Lina, staring at the masked figures, blood strewn across the leaves.

Lina wiped a crimson hand down her leathers, swapping her axe to her other hand and repeating the action.

"How many more do we think there are?" She glanced at Bri. "Surely this is most of them."

"How many witch hunters did the Queen let run rampant over the years?" Carys toed the body closest to her, the violet powder shaking loose from his body. "There were hundreds at the battle in Valtene. Even with the massive casualties, who knows how many of them managed to flee into the forest. At least we outran the smoke."

Bri pulled her tunic up over her nose, exposing her muscled torso as she approached the second masked body. She noted the way Lina looked at her flash of skin but hid her smirk under her clothing.

Carys's face twisted. "Rua said you needed to breathe in the kind they used to capture her in the North."

Lina slid the handle of her axe back into its hooks. "It's violet witch magic for certain, then," she said. "They work in powerful perfumes, incenses, and aromas. . . . Maybe the blue Witches' Glass that Augustus has is enough to resurrect their magic?"

"But who would read the spells for him?" Bri frowned. "Who is this Baba the witch hunter king spoke of?"

"Perhaps one of the old violet crones survived the past sixty years," Carys grumbled. "Witches have been known to live longer than humans, some as long as fae, with magic to aid them."

"Maybe." Lina rubbed her temples, smearing the bronzed paint that dotted above her eyebrows.

Crouching over a body, Bri reached for the carved mask. "These masks seem made in the East. The lion for one, and the way it's carved . . ."

She pulled back the mask to reveal wide, bloodshot eyes.

Then they blinked.

CHAPTER TWENTY-THREE

Before she could withdraw, the assailant slashed out with his knife, nicking Bri in the hip. He booted her in the knee, sending her toppling as Carys brought her sword down through his chest.

Flailing, Bri flew backward, tumbling down the rocky hillside. She faintly heard her name being screamed by her two comrades as she scrambled for purchase on the sliding blanket of leaves. The roar of the river filled her ears as her fingertips scraped against jagged stone. The icy shock of the frigid water knocked the air from her lungs as her legs hit the rapids. The water still bore the sting of the snow-capped High Mountains, staggeringly cold despite the warm air.

"Hang on!" Lina shouted, rushing down the steep slope.

The river sucked more of her body into its chilled depths as her torso was swallowed by the mighty currents. Her raw fingertips dug tighter into the stone. She couldn't pull herself up against the force of the rushing water.

Lina reached her first, Carys right behind. Grabbing Bri's forearm in a viselike grip, Lina hauled her up an inch and then another.

Bri looked up the bank to see a figure looming on the hillside above them.

"Look out!" she shouted.

Carys was already unsheathing her sword before the words escaped her lips, the look in Bri's eyes warning enough.

His arm was barely hanging on to his shoulder, blood gushed down his body, and yet, he stood on two feet. What magic possessed these attackers? How was he still alive? Were these fae turned into monsters like the lion with the tusks of a boar?

The soldier's glassy eyes looked vacantly through the trees. Before Carys could reach him, he stumbled down the hillside. He had no weapon in hand, and his intentions became suddenly clear.

"Gods," Carys cursed, sheathing her blade and dodging out of the way of his battering-ram body. She reached out to yank him to the side, but her fingers grasped nothing but air as he careened into Lina.

Lina and Bri smashed into the water, the force of the collision hurtling them into the icy currents.

"No!" Carys's scream was cut off as Bri's head plunged underwater.

The current shoved and jostled her up and down as she kicked wildly to breach the surface once more. Her head popped up, warm air filling her lungs, as the river pushed her to its center. She spotted the body of their attacker first. He was limp as a doll, bobbing to the water's erratic whims. Scanning the white foamy waves, she spotted Lina upriver, her arms flailing to keep afloat.

"Drop the axe!" Bri bellowed as her fingers fumbled with her belt.

The heavy weight of her weapons pulled Bri's body under again. Her boots brushed a rock and she used it to bounce back above the surface of the water. Finally, her slippery fingertips unbuckled her belt and it dropped like a stone off her body. She didn't have time to think about what it meant—to lose those weapons—not as she heard Lina's desperate gasp.

She spotted Lina's head breaching above a choppy wave. Lina moved her arms out of her leather harness and the axe fell away, her movements calming slightly now that she didn't have to battle its weight. Even in her distress, Bri was impressed how quickly Lina gave up her family heirloom in order to save her own life. She knew too many people who, in panic, went after their possessions even when doing so was a death sentence.

Bri's stomach plummeted to her feet as she tumbled over a dip in the river and dropped through the air to the rapids below. She needed to get to the side, but every attempt eddied her straight back to the middle of the churning river. Glancing ahead, there was not a single rock to grab, and the river soon bent around a corner.

There.

"We'll kick to the side at the bend," she called back to Lina, finding her close enough that Bri could nearly reach her.

"Don't mess it up this time," Lina breathed, spitting water from her panting mouth.

Bri guffawed. Even in mortal danger Lina was teasing her—a fae after her own heart for sure.

As they rounded the bend, Bri reached out and grabbed Lina, shoving her toward the shoreline. Lina's strong legs kicked with an easy grace and she made it to the side, reaching back to grab Bri, but their fingers slipped and Bri was pushed away from the banks once more.

Lina's eyes filled with horror. "No!"

Bri turned to look in the same direction to see the river twisting around the bend, and then . . . ending in nothing but air.

She prayed it was another small waterfall, but judging by the forest far below . . . Growling, she kicked and dug with her arms, battling against the relentless swells and not gaining an inch. She kept pushing until her arms burned and her breath was ragged, and still, she only moved backward. Each attempt shoved her back again as water pummeled into her like a wall of bricks.

Bri kept fighting, her muscles beginning to fail her. A snarl escaped her mouth as she pushed harder, even as a bud of doubt bloomed in her mind. This might be it. Of all the ways she thought she'd die . . .

She would miss seeing it all—Rua's celebration, the competition for the Eastern Crown. She wished she had said goodbye to her brother. She hoped he'd find that ring she still kept in her pack for these many years, waiting for him. She knew Talhan would blame himself somehow for her death. Of all the mistakes in her life, this was the one she wished most she could change.

As the rapids readied to swallow her whole, Bri prayed that they would all be well—Rua, Remy, Hale, Carys, Talhan, and Lina—the ones who mattered most. More than anything else, she wished she hadn't been such a coward when it came to one person in particular. She should have known time was never a given—it stole from everyone. She shouldn't have waited.

She released her tight grip on reality, fading her mind to those important things as she stopped fighting the river.

A body collided into hers, seconds from the edge, grabbing her around the torso and hauling her to the side. The force of that arm around her waist sparked new life into Bri. Her body sprung back into action, kicking in the same direction. Lina's wrist circled around the loop of her belt, the other end tethered to a tree protruding from the precipice of the waterfall. The gnarled roots clung to the ledge, its trunk bowing under the weight of Lina's tugging. Bri grasped a sharp rock that protruded like a tooth from the gaping maw of the waterfall, pulling herself further out of the current. The feeling of that grip sent a thrum of relief through her.

Lina pushed off from the rock to the shore, her fingers digging into Bri so hard she knew she'd have bruises. Each inch forward, Lina circled her wrist again, tightening the belt around her wrist until she pulled them onto the muddied shore. They collapsed in a breathless heap, lying side by side as they stared up at the swaying green canopy. The mist of the waterfall swirled around them and the warm air revived Bri's numb limbs.

Bri turned her head to Lina and spoke between gasping breaths. "You saved me, you bloody idiot. You could have died."

Lina panted even as she feigned nonchalance. "A simple thank-you will suffice."

"I'm meant to be protecting you."

"And I wasn't going to watch you die when I knew I could save you," she said, lifting her exhausted arm, still wrapped in her belt. Her knives and daggers sat unceremoniously discarded around the tree trunk. How quickly she must have dashed to this last tree on the cliff and fastened her lifeline. It felt like an eternity that Bri was battling the current, but it was probably mere seconds.

"You are so infuriatingly stubborn," Bri growled.

"Maybe I should have let you die," Lina snickered. "Then I wouldn't have to put up with this lecture."

Bri propped herself up on her elbow, leaning over Lina. "I'm just saying that a future Queen shouldn't be following her guard over a waterfall."

"Fine," Lina said, narrowing her eyes at Bri. "Jump back in the water, then."

Bri's lips twisted up. She dragged her eyes over Lina's breathless face and Lina flashed a matching grin as she reached up a hand and swept away the wet hair plastered to Bri's forehead. Bri's eyes trailed Lina's smooth brown skin, water beading on her cheeks and forehead, tracing up to her beautiful dark eyes, an endless world swirling in them like a moonless night sky.

Lina's gaze dropped to Bri's lips and it was Bri's undoing. Leaning down, she brushed her lips across Lina's warm, full mouth. Breathing in Lina's heady jasmine scent, she groaned at the sensation, that singular touch heating her chilled body. Lina's hand came up to cup the back of Bri's neck and pulled her closer. Their kiss deepened, Bri's tongue dipping into Lina's mouth. The quiet, low moan that she pulled from Lina sent tingles through Bri's body, and she was suddenly filled with a desperation to elicit that sound again. She pressed her chest tighter into Lina's, her knee curling over the top of Lina's thigh.

"Bri? Lina?" Carys called, her swift boots stomping through the leaves.

The two of them broke apart, staring at each other wide-eyed.

"We're here," Lina yelled. She looked back to Bri, her face seeming to contort between confusion and surprise as she shook her head.

Lina rolled to the side and stood, climbing her way up the riverbank as Bri dropped her head into her hands. She'd nearly died—it was just the giddiness of surviving that made her heart race, nothing more. Who wouldn't want to kiss their savior in relief? The memory of that heated look in Lina's eyes made Bri quaver. The way Lina pulled Bri's mouth closer—Lina had *wanted* to be kissed too. The river had revealed truths that she couldn't whisper even in the quiet of her own mind. Cursing all the Gods, Bri stood, wringing out her sodden clothes and following Lina up the bank.

~

The exhaustion of the day warred with the adrenaline still pumping through Bri's veins as they gathered in the council chambers. The brilliant orange and red sunset cast a golden glow over the savanna, its final glorious rays beaming into the cold stone room.

The council stood around a table, surveying a map of the Western Court. Lina pointed to where the witch hunter camp was and where they were attacked, retelling the assault to Darrow, Tem, Delta, and Cole. She traced the twin rivers and down to the waterfall that had nearly taken both her and Bri's lives. It had been too close. Bri hated the feeling of being one step behind, not knowing the attacker's plans.

"Hallis," Lina called and a guard marched in from beyond the far door. "I want you to gather five of your best and ride out to the witch hunter camp." Lina's face was sharp as she directed her guard.

"You're going to kill them after all?" Tem asked.

Lina gave him a soft look, as if knowing he was too gentle to make such hard decisions himself. "We should have never allowed them to live," she said, considering her words carefully. "Even if their connection to the attacks is dubious, there can be no room for doubt. Not anymore." She turned back to the guard. "Gather any information you can but make it quick. The witch hunter king's reign ends tonight."

Hallis bowed deeply to Lina and was one foot out the door when Lina said, "And Hallis?" The guard paused. "Burn down that tree."

The guard's brows pinched in confusion but he bowed again and left. Bri should have thought to do it herself—that tree scarred with the notches of dead red witches, a proud display of their slaughter—she should have taken Lina's axe and chopped it down herself.

"Where's your dagger?" Carys muttered out of the corner of her mouth.

The two of them stood off to the side while Lina reported back to her councilors. Lina's eyes lifted to Bri and dropped to her beltless hips, even as she continued speaking. Bri shifted, folding her arms as Lina turned back to the map.

"Lost in the river." Bri's voice was a growling whisper.

"Gods," Carys cursed. "Are you okay?"

"I've got three more in my pack," Bri gritted out. "I'm fine."

"Do you want to train later?" Carys offered.

Bri smirked. Her friend knew her too well. Even a few weeks ago, she would have needed to pummel her fists bloody to recover from the sting of losing that precious weapon, but now . . . She tried to summon the sharp pain she was certain she should feel, but instead there was only a distant sorrow, old and steady, as familiar to her as the feeling of that hilt in her palm.

"Seriously, Car, I'm fine," Bri replied. "Nothing a bottle of wine can't fix."

Carys tutted.

"I will *not* abandon my city," Lina hissed, pulling their attention back to the table.

"Swifthill isn't safe—"

"You're not abandoning anything," Delta cut off Darrow. "You're finding the right weapon. The witch hunters don't want the castle, they want *you*. Don't make yourself an easy target."

Lina leaned on her fists over the table. "They have yet to get to me."

"And how many people died to see that happen?" Delta asked, her voice softer than Bri had ever heard it. She knew it would hurt her cousin to say it, and, judging by the look on Lina's face, the blow landed just as she anticipated.

"I need to know more about these poisons," Cole interjected, snapping the stare down between the two cousins. He turned over the golden mask on the table. It had been brought back from the attack, along with a dusting of the purple powder for him to examine. "I think I might be able to find an antidote. With a remedy, you can return to

189

Swifthill without that constant fear." He looked at Lina, his blue eyes softening. "Even if they managed to try something, you'd be able to protect yourself and any others against it."

"The witch temple in Silver Sands." Darrow's voice was a deep rasp, easily carrying over the others'. "The library has collections from all of the witch covens; perhaps there are some violet witch tomes amongst them."

"It's worth a try." Cole nodded. "I'll leave at first light."

"You should go with your brown witch," Tem said, taking a step closer to Lina. "If there is an antidote to this poison, I want you to be the closest to it at all times." Lina's eyes softened at him, making Bri's stomach clench. "My father will look after Swifthill just as he did for your mother during her official trips."

Lina's shoulders bunched and she took a breath. Lowering them back down, she morphed her expression from irritation to one of calm. "I'll go, but we should crown me before I depart."

Darrow bristled at the idea. "Do you really think that's wise, given—"

"I know you're eager for your coronation," Delta said, shifting in front of Darrow and effectively silencing him. "But you are already Queen in every way that matters. That isn't the coronation you deserve, Lina, nor does it show your true power. What's a couple more weeks to protect a lifetime reign?"

Lina narrowed her eyes at her cousin, frowning at the wisdom in Delta's words.

"I want you to report back to me," Lina said carefully to Delta, her eyes dropping to her cousin's thin sword. "You've been promoted from Captain to head councilor and I expect you to honor that duty."

Delta's eyes searched her cousin's and she bowed her head. "Bri and Carys will go with you," she said, considering the map. "I'll stay back and keep things in line here for you."

Lina's lips thinned into a half-smile. She was giving her cousin a purpose. Delta might not be able to guard Lina, but she was still one of the most important fae in the Western Court, and Lina wasn't going to let her forget that.

"If anyone else asks, I'm traveling into the Southern Court to visit

Saxbridge." Lina eyed each one of her councilors. "Fae fire Neelo Ember-spear. I want them to be aware of this ruse. No one else is to know we are stopping in Silver Sands, is that understood?" One by one the councilors nodded. "Cole can drive the carriage. Have the servants pack for Saxbridge, formal attire, gowns, everything."

"We will find who did this, Lina," Delta vowed. "I promise."

"Whether you succeed or not, I *will* return by the coronation date." Lina straightened. Lifting her chin, she cut Bri and Carys a look. "Go get ready. We leave at first light."

CHAPTER TWENTY-FOUR

Bri wasn't sure what it was about a wine cellar that was so comforting . . . well, apart from the wine. The earthen smell, the cool air even on a hot day, the stillness and quiet. It was like a cave, a womb in the depths of every castle. It felt safe—the exact thing that usually grated against her, forcing her into the clamor of packed bars and parties. Only in these dark caverns, or with a sleeping Princess beside her, did Bri enjoy the calm.

The cellar door opened, and Bri squinted against the blinding light of a lone candle. For a moment she thought it might be Carys, but then she smelled the heady waft of rose oil, the one that tugged her into its undertow.

"I knew I'd find you in here," Lina snickered, lowering her candle and stepping into the cellar.

Bri wondered if Lina had been waiting for her to show up at her chambers or if she was planning on sleeping that night at all, given that they were leaving so soon.

She leaned against the shelves, shrugging as she clenched the half-empty bottle in her hand. "We were nearly killed by poisonous smoke and a giant beast today. Can you blame me?"

Lina rested against the opposite beam, just out of arm's reach, and pinned Bri with a look. "Are you okay?"

Bri gave herself a quick once-over. "Yep."

"That dagger that Delta made you swear upon?" Lina clasped her hands in front of her, and Bri's eyes dipped down her figure-hugging dress before dropping to her sandaled feet. "I'm sorry you lost it."

"You dropped your axe too."

"I have many," Lina said, waving her hand as if abandoning the axe was no great loss. "But that dagger obviously had some special meaning to you, otherwise Delta wouldn't have made you swear on it."

"Yes." Bri swept a hand over her short hair. The darkness pressed in from all sides as she held Lina's gaze.

"Talk to me." Her voice was barely a whisper, her soft eyes pleading, so unlike her normal sharp, regal demeanor. Bri knew this was the Lina that existed under the mask. She'd seen it in the way Lina treated Nelle, in the way she fiercely protected her cousin, and in the way she cried for her mother the day of her funeral. Even when she was sleeping by Bri's side, she rarely let that mask slip fully.

Bri held out the bottle to Lina. "There's nothing to say."

Setting her candle down on the shelf, Lina accepted the bottle and took a long swig. "Why is that dagger so special to you?"

"It's not a happy tale."

Lina wiped her mouth with the back of her hand and passed the bottle back to Bri. "I can handle it."

Bri let out a long sigh. "Her name was Aurella," she murmured, surprised by how easily the words came out of her mouth. Words she had choked on for many years suddenly flowed out of her with ease, as if they were inevitable. She knew it wasn't so much about the words themselves, and more about *who* she was saying them to. Propping her boot against the shelf, she looked at the ceiling. "We were young, barely of age, and . . . I loved her, so madly. Every moment with her felt like I was soaring. I'd never felt anything like it before. I would have been convinced she was my Fated, were it not for the prophecy." She rubbed the back of her neck. "My only Fate was that of a thief—to seize the crown from its sovereign, whatever that means."

"My Fate was similarly obtuse—*Sacrifice will bring honor and glory.*" Lina snickered. "No Fated for me, only a cryptic maxim, easily twisted to fit the plans of everyone around me."

Bri chuckled, flashing a toothy grin. "So you understand my frustration."

"You have no idea." Lina's cheeks dimpled. "Was Aurella an Eastern fae?"

Bri blinked at the strangeness of the name coming from another person. She'd spoken about Aurella with so few people—Carys, Delta . . . Talhan and Hale knew, but she'd never allowed them to speak of her. Some wounds weren't meant to be prodded.

"Yes," Bri said. "The daughter of an Eastern nobleman and a good fighter too." She smirked, looking at the wall as if looking back through time. "She had my heart the second she unsheathed her sword."

"She sounds magnificent," Lina whispered.

"She was."

Lina took the bottle from Bri again and drained the last drops, setting it on the ground beside her with a clink. She leaned back against the beam, watching Bri, waiting for her to speak. The longer the silence stretched on, the more Bri felt compelled to do so, knowing Lina would wait all night to hear her story if she asked.

"We were in the Battle of Falhampton with the rest of Hale's army," Bri said, shaking her head. "I begged him to include her. I couldn't bear the thought of leaving her behind in the capital. It was purely selfish. She would have been safer guarding the castle with the other highborn soldiers, not mucking through the border towns fighting a pointless battle with the King's illegitimate son."

Lina blinked slowly, her cheeks dimpling. "I bet she was more than eager to join you."

"Yes." Bri grinned. "She was glorious, fearless, headstrong. . . . We both were. We'd sneak off into the forests at night to be together. Our relationship was the worst kept secret in Falhampton."

Lina chuckled. "First love."

Bri's countenance darkened. "One night we snuck off west of the camp. We fell asleep under the stars. . . ." Her voice thickened. "We were ambushed in the night and I was knocked out." She parted her auburn hair, revealing a thin scar that ran from her hairline down to her ear. "When I came to . . ." She clenched and unclenched her fists, unable to steady herself. "Her throat was slit."

Bri looked up to find a tear trailing down Lina's cheek as if she already knew what Bri was about to say. Lina absorbed the story, pulling the poison from Bri's soul.

"I never knew for certain why they didn't kill me too," Bri whispered. "Though I suspect they recognized me. I was still a powerful player in their prophecies. Perhaps Norwood and Vostemur ordered their soldiers not to kill me, in case I became their future ally."

"That's awful," Lina breathed.

"I kept her amber dagger and buried her there, under that tree." Bri took a long breath. "Hale reported her death as part of the casualties in the melee. Her family never knew it was because we'd left the camp in the middle of the night. They never knew she was special to me at all." She rubbed her hand down the side of her face. "Nights have been hard ever since."

"I can see why that dagger was so important to you," Lina said. "I'm sorry it's gone."

"I thought losing that dagger would break me." Bri struggled to control her voice. "I thought letting go of her would shatter me into a million pieces."

Lina cocked her head. "Why are you mad?"

"Because I didn't feel it." Bri clenched her jaw. "It was the last part of her and I let it go and it didn't hurt."

Lina's brow furrowed. "Holding on to that pain doesn't honor her memory."

"Yes it does," Bri gritted out. "But when it came down to reaching for that dagger or reaching for you . . ." She clenched her fists so tightly, her nails dug into her palms.

"You chose me." Lina stared into Bri's stormy eyes. It wasn't a question. Time seemed to stand still, the air so thick between them she could hardly breathe. Lina's lips parted. "I can't tell if you want to choke me or kiss me right now."

"I wouldn't do that."

Lina lifted her chin. "That's a shame."

Bri's eyes flared, Lina's words like the spark to a flame. Bri pushed off the beam, grabbing Lina by the throat and pinning her back against the shelf. Bri's lips crashed into Lina's, enveloping her in a scorching kiss. Lina didn't miss a beat, one arm snaking around Bri's hips, the other threading through her short hair, pulling Bri's muscled form tighter against her own soft curves.

A moan escaped Lina's lips, unleashing Bri further as one hand bracketed Lina's jawline and the other skimmed over her side and down to her ass. Bri pressed her fingers into Lina's soft flesh groaning as she dipped her tongue into Lina's mouth.

"Your Highness," a voice called from beyond the door and the two of them flew apart.

"What?" Lina snapped, her words breathless.

"Your carriage is ready," the guard said.

Bri scowled, the absence of Lina's soft body against hers making her muscles tense. "I thought they wouldn't be ready until dawn."

"It is dawn," Lina said, panting from her swollen lips. She straightened her dress, wiping at the smudged paint around her lips. She glanced at Bri. "This isn't over."

Bri's eyes widened but she found herself nodding anyway. Those words were a promise. Lina wanted Bri as badly as Bri wanted her. She watched as the Princess's hips swished out the door, her heart stuttering with each step.

"Catullus," a voice echoed down the hallway.

Bri adjusted her pack on her shoulders, veering toward the sound as her boots scuffed down the quiet passage.

She looked down the hall to find Tem leaning against the doorframe to his chambers. Bri muttered a curse and followed him into his sitting room, dropping her pack with an unceremonious smack on the floor. It was too early and she was too exhausted to deal with a charming courtier like Tem.

"What?" She frowned at him.

Amused, Tem chuckled at her gruff countenance. "I just wanted to thank you for saving Lina's life. It sounds like it was a close call."

"First off, I swore I would protect her." Bri folded her arms. "Second, she saved me."

Tem dropped into his leather chair, firelight flickering behind him. The curtains were still drawn but beams of sunlight illuminated the painted vase sitting between the windows. The room filled with the cloying scent of wilting flowers.

"Why am I really here?" Bri asked, slumping further down in her chair.

Tem raised his eyebrows. "You think I don't know about the two of you?"

Bri shifted under his look. "There is no two of us."

"Of course." Tem smirked, raising his hands in defense before Bri could argue. "I'm not angry. I always knew Lina would never care for me in the way that I cared for her. I just want to see her happy. She deserves some happiness after all she's been through."

Bri's eyes darted awkwardly around the room—the lush rug, the tapestry on the wall, the carved wood box on the mantle—there wasn't anywhere her eyes could land as her feelings betrayed her. There was something between her and Lina, something that others could see.

Bri thought of that shared moment in the wine cellar, how she had grabbed Lina the same way that she'd wanted to after interrogating Meson those many weeks ago. Bolts of fire shot through her at the thought of pinning Lina to the wall again, of her hand dipping under the hem of Lina's shirt and down between her legs.

Bri cleared her throat. "You seem surprisingly even-keeled about this," she muttered.

"Lina is far from the first royal to have other lovers," Tem said, grabbing a glass of amber liquid from the table beside him and swirling it in his hand. "But you don't seem like the type to be a Queen's mistress."

"I'm not," Bri growled.

"Then make sure Lina knows that." Tem gave her a look. "You still plan on going to Wynreach and competing for the Eastern crown, yes?"

"Yes, and Lina knows that."

"As long as she understands what you are to each other." Tem took a swig of his drink. "I don't want to see her any more heartbroken than she already is." He lifted his long lashes. "And you, Catullus, seem like the type to break hearts."

"That's not what I'm trying to do," Bri gritted out.

"No?" Tem cocked his head. "What are you trying to do?"

"I'm trying to find who killed the Queen and make sure Lina is safe on her throne."

Tem bobbed his head. "Well, then, you and I have a shared goal." He stood, gesturing toward the doorway. "I'm sorry to have troubled you. I only wanted to ensure Lina would be safe on her travels. You must be heading to the horses now."

"Right," she muttered, hauling her heavy pack back onto her shoulders.

She didn't say a parting farewell to Tem as she headed down the hallway. She passed Saika and Delta's door and her gut clenched. Was she just as bad as them? She had no plans to stay in the Western Court, but Lina knew that, and she felt helplessly drawn to the future Queen. The feel of Lina's lips on hers tugged on her thoughts and she already yearned to repeat the action, consequences be damned.

CHAPTER TWENTY-FIVE

The looming rain clouds chased them all the way to Silver Sands. The monsoon season was nearing, the heavy spring rains bringing life back to the arid savanna. Cows lay under trees and birds sheltered in the rustling branches, signaling the brewing storm.

Bri looked over her shoulder to Cole driving the single-horse carriage. She wondered if Lina managed to sleep during the ride. She must be as exhausted as Bri felt.

They left Swifthill in a promenade, the two guards at the front and the brown witch healer driving the carriage. A little holiday to escape the rainy season, Lina had told her staff—a fun diversion in Saxbridge before her coming coronation. She said she didn't want to take too many people or distract them from readying the castle for the wedding. It was a believable enough lie that no one seemed to question her further.

Bri looked back to the twisting dusty road ahead. Carys's horse kept in line with her own. The barbed shrubs slowly gave way to leafy greenery as they headed out toward the coast. The air thickened, a blanket of humidity covering the warm air.

She glanced at Carys but the lithe blonde was already staring at her. "Don't look at me like that."

Carys shrugged, sweeping her braid over her shoulder. "I'm not looking at you like anything."

"I know what you're thinking."

"No, you don't," Carys snorted.

"I'm sure someone told you about the wine cellar." Bri's voice dropped an octave even though there was no one around to hear.

"It's always a wine cellar with you," Carys jeered.

"It's—"

"Spare us both the lies," Carys cut in with a laugh. "Why can't this be a good thing?"

"Because our families are enemies," Bri said, tightening her grip on her reins. "Because there's too much at stake for casual flings. Because I have my own crown to win in the East."

Carys shook her head. "You're so afraid of your destiny, you'd ruin a good thing just for spite."

"This isn't a *good thing*, Car," Bri grumbled. "I won't be taking any crown from Lina and I won't interfere with her plans. She deserves better than that. I will make my own destiny."

"And if you stayed with her," Carys hedged, "you fear you wouldn't?"

"It was one kiss." Bri rolled her eyes. "Well, two, but still."

Carys pressed her lips together to keep from laughing.

"Stop it."

A chuckle escaped her mouth. "I didn't say anything."

"Oh Gods," Bri groaned. "This is such a mess."

"It's nice to see you panicking for once." Carys grinned as Bri shifted in her saddle. "I mean, I get it. She's like a pretty version of you."

"Hey."

"Oh please, you're not offended." Carys huffed, arching her brow. "Would you like me to call you pretty too?"

"No. Gross."

Carys chortled, her braid swinging behind her as the horses trudged downhill. "You're normally so even-keeled. I like that she sets you off-balance."

"You say that like I'd want to be off-balance," Bri scoffed.

"Sometimes you should." Carys's expression hardened and she

looked down at her horse's mane. Bri knew she wasn't thinking about her and Lina anymore. "Sometimes it's worth it. Even if it ends badly."

"I'm sorry."

"You didn't bring up Ersan," Carys said with a sad, half-smile. "I did."

Bri ducked her head. "I thought for a long time that Aurella was my Fated."

Carys's head whipped toward her. It had been many years since she'd uttered her former lover's name in front of Carys, but once she said it to Lina, she realized she could—that it wouldn't break her the way she had feared.

"The blue witches said they didn't feel that bond between us." Bri hung her head. "They said my only Fate was the one of my birth—to take the crown."

"That doesn't mean you won't have love, Bri," Carys said softly.

Bri lifted her gaze to meet Carys's blue eyes. "Then it means that for the both of us."

"You'd make a good Queen, Bri." Carys shifted the conversation away from that open wound with a smirk. "But I will make a better one."

"You're by far my biggest competition." Bri flashed a toothy grin. "You didn't grow up in Wynreach, but you come from high-class fae. You have ancestral ties to the Northern and Southern Courts and good relationships with the rulers of every court. You have family ties to the Eastern humans, and you're a warrior—smart, cunning, but kind." Bri shrugged. "I could see them all voting for you."

"They wouldn't pick me over a Golden Eagle," Carys snickered. "Not with that moniker. That name has done half the work for you."

"Then there's Tal, of course." Her gaze darted back down at the name of her twin.

"If charm alone could win the throne, he may be the victor." Carys chuckled, swatting through a cloud of insects hovering in the damp air. "He's healed and in Wynreach now, so you know." Bri nodded stiffly and Carys shook her head. "Gods, you two are so bloody stubborn."

"I didn't do anything wrong," Bri snapped.

"You two fight all the time," Carys said. "Can't you both just move on already? I know you miss him."

"He thinks I'm wrong for coming here, but if we hadn't come Lina would probably be dead by now. I made the right choice in listening to Delta. He should understand that."

"Maybe winning the Eastern crown will be easier than I thought with you two at odds," Carys taunted.

Bri didn't reply, straightening her shoulders as she watched another length of road twist into view. "How many more hours?"

"I'd say another two." Carys looked to the swirling storm clouds on the horizon. She nudged her horse with her calf, urging it to pick up the pace. "I think we'll beat the rains."

"Well, now you've doomed us to the rains," Bri grumbled, touching her fingertips to her forehead in a silent prayer to undo the bad luck Carys just wished upon them.

Carys chuckled as she swapped the reins in her hands. "For someone so determined to prove her destiny wrong, that's an awfully superstitious thing to say."

Bri frowned and Carys's smile broadened. "Maybe it's better we ride in silence."

~

The shoreline glowed molten silver, the afternoon sun making the sand shimmer like a thousand coins. Water softly lapped the shores of the sheltered bay. The storm clouds seemed to pass them by, heading toward the port towns at the bottom of the Western Court.

Bri had never stayed in Silver Sands Harbor before, only passing through the southern border on her way to other places, but it was truly magnificent, unlike anything she'd ever seen. The harbor straddled the border between the Western and Southern Courts, a glittering gem mostly uninhabited apart from the library to the west and the gold mines to the south.

They left the horses and carriage at the base of a thin trail zigzagging up to the white marble balustrade overlooking the ledge. A pack of three scruffy looking dogs greeted them, howling and booming threatening barks, all the while wagging their tails.

"We should have brought a donkey," Carys heaved, pinching her side as they set down Lina's trunk. "This was meant to be a holiday."

"There's nobody around for miles," Lina panted, cresting the top of the path and dropping to sit on the inbuilt bench. "I could have carried my own trunk."

The shaggy brown and black dogs, so enthusiastic only moments ago, collapsed into the shade of the stone patio. Their tongues lolled out of the sides of their mouths as they panted. Where had they come from? Though they were in need of a brush, they looked well-fed.

Carys peered up the hillside to the library. "That place has seen better days."

The copper-domed library sat on the hill high above them, covered in a film of silver dust. An aged, white marble house was built into the hillside below. Originally designated for the librarians who maintained the collections, the dwelling as well as the Silver Sands library both now appeared abandoned. The brown witches who curated the tomes were probably all called away during the many years after the Siege of Yexshire. Once the red witches' numbers dwindled, the witch hunters started looking for any witch that wasn't attached to a rich fae family. They were easily sold to the North for a few coins. No free witch was safe back then and this library would have been the perfect spot for kidnapping witches.

Bri surveyed the stone patio, adjusting her pack on her shoulders. Smooth gray tables and benches seemed hewn from the earth themselves. Wisps of sheer curtains still clung to the columns that led into the house—little more than tattered scraps now.

A perpetual fountain sat to the right, its water browning over the years but still spraying in crisscross patterns. It must have been a remnant of red witch magic. Eventually the fountain would sputter out, though Bri didn't know if that would happen years or decades into the future. The fountain reminded her that there was a time before the Siege of Yexshire, when red witches used their magic to make beautiful things. It seemed so strange to her. Most could barely remember the world before.

"You made it," a voice called from the shadows of the house. The dogs thumped their tails in a chorus at the sound, but they didn't get up.

Out stepped a tall fae whose silver hair belied his young features. A scar snaked from the bottom of his jaw into his tunic. He flashed the travelers a warm, cavalier grin as he strode over to greet them.

"Bern!" Carys wrapped him in a warm hug and he chuckled. "What are you doing here?"

"You can't come to Silver Sands and expect me not to greet you." His warm laugh boomed across the marble. "I heard you were visiting, and I decided to join you."

Lina stood and gave him a swift hug. "I thought you resided in Yexshire now as the head councilor of the Queen."

"I do," he said, looking out to a white and silver manor carved into the far hillside. It peered over the water from beyond the Southern Court border. "But my family's home is still here. Your being here gave me an excuse to visit. Now that the southern road through the High Mountain Court is cleared, it wasn't that long of a journey."

"Neelo wasn't supposed to tell anyone," Bri said, pulling his pale gaze to her.

"They didn't," Bern said with a shrug. "But I happen to know more than a few witches with the gift of Sight and they Saw you here."

"Great," Bri muttered. "That's not what we need right now. We need to keep Cole close; maybe he can make it harder for the witches to See us."

"Speaking of." Carys tipped her head to the mop of blond hair cresting up the trail.

Cole heaved jagged breaths as he climbed the last steps onto the patio. His long legs were nothing compared to the fae's strength.

"Let me help you with that," Bern said, rushing over to him and lifting his pack off his shoulders.

"Thanks," Cole breathed, his eyes snagging on Bern's. He paused before holding out his hand. "I'm Cole Doledir. Head healer to the royal family."

Bern's cheeks dimpled as he shook Cole's hand. "Bern Hemarr, right hand to the Queen and King of the High Mountain Court."

Lina and Bri exchanged secret glances.

"How many rooms does this place have?" Carys asked, pulling their focus back to her.

"Seven," Bern said. "They're modest dwellings, but I managed to spruce them up before you arrived. Come on, I'll show you."

He waved them into the cliffside house. Bri stole one more glance out to the horizon, dread pooling in her gut. She prayed that the wrong blue witches hadn't Seen them here. Coming with a smaller entourage felt like a mistake, but coming with the same Western guards who might be traitors felt like a misstep too. Maybe she could convince Lina to leave the Western Court until they knew who to trust, though she doubted the Princess would accept. She'd see it as abandoning her kingdom. Bri shook her head at the shimmering turquoise sea, unable to think of a single safe path forward.

CHAPTER TWENTY-SIX

Bri took the room next to Lina's on the southern side. It barely had space for the bed that Bern had crammed into it. Had Bern stripped his family home of chattels to furnish the house? She wouldn't put it past him.

After splashing water from the basin on her face, she changed into a lighter tunic that didn't smell like horse's ass. It was crumpled from the ride, but at least they'd avoided the storm and her tunic hadn't been drenched by the rain. Sniffing her armpit, she shrugged. She'd bathe after food and wine.

Bri eyed the thin trail leading up to the library as she ambled across the arched walkway to dinner. The copper-domed edifice sat beyond the eddies of harbor air that could dampen the books. Bri wondered what lay inside, but the library would have to wait until morning. Bern told them no candles were allowed and, given the arid surroundings, Bri didn't blame him. If one twig caught fire, the entirety of the cliffs would alight.

She stepped back out into the balmy air of the patio, pulled by the smell of freshly baked bread. A lone guest sat at the table, a large book in their hands. The Heir of Saxbridge wore a light black jacket and stone-gray trousers, thick smudges of kohl lining their eyes.

"Neelo Emberspear," Bri said with a chuckle, swaggering onto the terrace and dropping into a seat across from them. "Are we all hiding from the mistakes of our mothers, then?"

Neelo's thick lashes lifted as they looked up from their book. They carefully placed a marker between the pages and set the book on the table. "Something like that."

"Well, I'm glad to see you, regardless," Bri added with a sigh.

"The West not all you imagined?" Neelo asked, turning to survey the turquoise waters and across to the teal pennants atop Bern's family home.

Though the territory had never been officially claimed, both the Southern and Western sovereigns mined the region for its precious metals.

Bri's gaze dropped to the table. Chunks of herb bread sat on a platter, surrounding bowls of olive oil, dried spices, and hummus. Grinning, Bri grabbed piece of bread, dipping it in the oil and then the saffron-colored spice mixture. The flavors lit up her tongue, the spices blending perfectly with the airy bread.

"Have I mentioned I'm glad you're here?" Bri asked through a mouthful of food.

Neelo's cheeks dimpled as they grabbed the open bottle of wine at the center of the table and poured Bri a glass. "When I heard you were coming," they said, "I knew I couldn't let you survive on the inevitable hard cheese and jerky you soldiers bring with you everywhere."

A middle-aged woman scurried out onto the terrace, holding a tray with more flatbread and dips. She had brown skin, the same shade of umber as Neelo's own, her straight black hair pulled into a high bun and tied with colorful thread.

"Rish!" Bri beamed at her.

"Oh, you're early," she said, setting the tray down between the two of them. "Here, this will get you started."

Rish was Neelo's personal green witch and had been serving the Heir of Saxbridge for as long as Bri could remember. Just as Lina had Cole and Rua had Aneryn, Neelo had Rish. Bri supposed Remy's head witch was Fenrin now, though it would be expected of her to pick a red witch, and the lanky blond was a Western brown witch like Cole. Remy bucked traditions, anyway; her Court was one of her own making.

Bri winked at the green witch. "Thank you, Rish."

The witch batted away Bri's thanks. "Please," she said, smoothing her hand down her sage green apron. "I delight when the Twin Eagles come to dine. No one appreciates my cooking more fervently than you and your brother."

Bri opened her mouth to speak but Neelo beat her to it. "It's just Bri this time," they said. "And the others, but . . . Talhan isn't here."

"Oh." Rish furrowed her brow but didn't push any further. "Well, I better get back to the kitchens; dinner won't cook itself."

Bri watched the green witch wander back into the white stone building as the setting sun illuminated the tiles in shades of pink and gold. Bri grabbed another piece of bread, dipping it into the sauce. She hummed at the zesty lemon flavor. Rish was truly magical. Neelo stared out at the sunset, swirling their glass of wine.

"Have you heard from him?" Bri asked finally.

"He's recovering," Neelo replied. "He's already in the East."

This is what Bri loved about Neelo Emberspear. Neelo seemed the most quiet of the fae royalty but they also knew the most about the ongoings of Okrith.

"And how is the East?"

"Surprisingly well," they said, taking a slow sip of wine. "Carys did a good job getting them in line."

"Thank you," Carys said, traipsing onto the terrace in a midnight-blue dress that belonged at a royal ball and not a library campsite. "What?"

"Was that in your pack?" Bri's eyes scanned the gown. "Where did you even get that?"

"My morning runs to the markets weren't just for fried bread." She chuckled, sitting on the other side of Neelo and leaning in to give the Heir of Saxbridge a kiss on the cheek. "Hi."

Neelo smirked at the dress. "You can take the girl out of Saxbridge . . ."

Carys and Neelo were lifelong friends. Carys grew up in the province just outside the Southern capital, and her parents had been some of the Queen's favorite courtiers.

"The markets in Swifthill are magnificent, but nothing beats Saxbridge," she said, giving Neelo a grin.

Neelo moved their book from the table into their lap. "That goes without saying."

"Ugh," Bri said with an exasperated sigh. "When you two get together it always turns into a Saxbridge love fest."

"That is something very different where we come from," Carys jeered.

Indeed, the capital was known for its debauchery. You couldn't throw a stone without hitting a celebration. No matter the time of day, somewhere in Saxbridge the parties raged on. Neelo was the antithesis of that loud merriment, and yet, despite not partaking, they seemed to love their court. Bri wondered what it would be like when the heir became the sovereign. Their mother, Queen Emberspear, lived like the Goddess of Wine and Cheer. Neelo's rule would be very different.

Footsteps sounded on the tiles. "What have I missed?" Bern approached the table holding two more bottles of wine. The three dogs followed him out, swarming around his feet.

Snatching a bottle from his grasp, Bri said, "These two chatting about the Southern Court."

"Good thing I'm here, then; otherwise you'd be talking to your glass of wine all night." He chuckled, about to sit when Lina and Cole arrived.

Bri craned her neck past him to see them standing under the archway. The sight of Lina hit her like a crashing wave. She wore a bright red dress patterned with sapphire and burnt-orange thread. It was a simple summer outfit, perfect for traveling as the fabric wasn't easily crumpled, but the way that it fit her . . . The front fabric wove across her ample chest, creating diamond cutouts of dark brown skin that pressed through the holes. It flowed down from her waist, billowing around her large hips and draping to the floor. She was brighter here, as if the colors of her soul were a more vibrant hue. The change in attire had shed a layer off her regal countenance and now she was wholly ethereal.

"Bri?"

"What?" Bri's attention snapped back toward Carys.

"Do you prefer Southern or Eastern?" Carys asked as Neelo smirked into their glass.

"Southern," Bri said, not knowing what they were referring to but assuming between the two of them, the answer would inevitably be Southern.

As Lina stepped from the archway, Cole moved to leave them.

Bern cut him off. "Wait," the silver-haired fae said. "Why don't you join us?"

Cole adjusted his spectacles, looking down at the courtier with a humble smile. He debated the offer for a moment before saying, "Thank you."

As Lina sat beside her, Bri contemplated praising the Princess's dress but then thought better of it. She decided instead to focus her attention on the platter of food in front of her. Twirling the stem of her wine glass, she took a steadying breath. The sumptuous wine and balmy sea air wasn't helping. Her wayward attention superseded all logic, lost to the sensations of the evening. She needed to get a grip, but as the intoxicating scent of jasmine and rose oil wafted toward her, she had to swallow the lump in her throat. She thought of the feel of her lips against Lina's own, her mind drifting to where else she'd like her lips to explore.

Bern and Cole sat at the end of the table, where Bern opened a bottle of wine between them.

"I thought we were bringing our own provisions," Lina said, dipping a piece of flatbread in oil and then the spices in the same combination as Bri had. "But seeing as there's more than wine, I'm guessing Rish is hiding somewhere around here too."

She brought the oil-soaked bread to her mouth, a pleasurable hum coming from her lips. Bri almost bit her wineglass in half, clenching her fist around the linen napkin in her lap. Gods, that sound. Why did Lina have to make that sound? Their enjoyable evening was going to be reduced to utter torture.

"I'm here!" Rish called, hefting a pot in her hands. Bern rushed over to her, but she jutted her chin to his chair in a silent command for him to sit back down. She placed the pot in the center of the table, pulling a ladle and spoons from the front pocket of her apron. Unceremoniously dropping them on the table, she turned to Lina. "My Princess!" she exclaimed, giving Lina a kiss on each cheek. "Your beauty grows with every day. It has been far too long, *mea raga*."

Lina held Rish's hands, beaming up at her. Rish seemed special to them all. How few of them received motherly warmth from anyone else? None of their own parents fussed over them like Rish did.

"Sit this course with us at least," Lina said, gesturing to the last empty chair. Rish looked like she was going to refuse, but Lina gave her a look and the witch laughed.

Cupping Lina's cheek, she said, "Okay, okay, the second course can wait a moment." She took the tea towel from her shoulder and dropped it onto the table, leaning in to Lina. "Now, how are you? Tell me everything."

Lina chuckled, the breathy sound making the hairs on Bri's arms stand on end. At least her attention was fully on Rish now.

The second the food was placed on the table, one of the dogs appeared and rested its head on Bri's lap. He had lighter fur around his nose and eyebrows, giving him a permanently surprised expression.

She chortled at those pleading eyes then picked out a piece of meat from the stew. The moment she did, his ears perked up as his tail thrashed wildly.

"Not too many pieces," Bern said with a laugh. "Or he'll be sick."

"Are the dogs yours?"

"Family dogs," he said. "They've come over with me from the manor. Not much of guard dogs, they'll sooner lick a burglar to death, but they'll warn they're coming at least."

Lina reached down, patting the side of one of the other dogs that lay beside her chair. "Better than nothing," she said, scratching the dog behind the ear in just the right way that made him lean into it and close his eyes. "You can sleep outside my door," Lina added with a whisper, and Bri smiled at the way she spoke to the dog directly.

Bri swigged back her glass of wine, bouncing her leg under the table.

She watched Lina's hand, perfectly endearing, as it scratched under the dog's chin. She didn't realize she was scowling until she glanced at Carys and found her friend biting her lip, trying not to smile. She let out a long sigh through her nose and grabbed another piece of flatbread. Why were the most beautiful and thrilling things also the most torturous?

~

The giant copper doors were already ajar when they arrived at the library of Silver Sands. The dogs had followed them up the rocky trail and were now lying in the shade of the entry overhang.

Bri tried not to look at Lina during breakfast and the walk up the hill, but it was an exercise in futility. Lina had picked a patterned linen dress with a slit that went up to the top of her thigh, and with every step and every flash of her leg, Bri was certain Lina had selected the dress to kill her. Gods, those thighs. She clenched her jaw so tightly the muscles ached.

She shook her head, her expression swinging from smiles to scowls and back again. Everything that was once steady in her felt like a violently swinging pendulum, giddy and aching and everything in between.

They'd fallen asleep on the terrace in the wee hours of the morning, all of them chatting until the sun threatened to rise in the sky. There was too much to catch up on. So many things had happened in the past few months that Bri continued listening even after her eyes grew too heavy to keep open. It was a short-lived but deep and peaceful slumber. When she woke, it was with a soft smile and not a jolt.

The group poured into the library, surveying the dusty stacks that ran in neat lines across the main floor. The air was stale and heavy with the scent of old books. Spiraling staircases framed the side walls, leading to the upper floors. The ceiling vaulted in the center up toward the copper roof that had faded to a shade of sea-foam green from years of exposure to the elements.

"What are we looking for, exactly?" Neelo asked, tracing their finger down the dusty spines of a book. Something ignited in their gaze as they scanned the books. This must have been the most sacred of any temple to Neelo—a library filled with books they hadn't yet read.

"Anything about the violet witches," Cole replied, adjusting his spectacles. "Or anything about poisons."

Bern guffawed. "In a library filled with witches' books . . . I think a great many will mention poisons."

"I'm looking specifically for poisons that can be inhaled or absorbed through the skin," Cole said, eyeing the five of them. "Between all of us we should be able to do it." He turned toward Lina. "You said we had until your coronation. I think we'll need every minute."

She nodded. "I'll start on the third floor of the western wing, work my way down."

"I'll take the east," Neelo said, staring up at the ceiling.

They split apart, Bri taking the floor below Lina. She moved to the end of the hallway, checking the furthest room first, but it was only a storage cupboard filled with buckets, rags, and brooms. The next room along had half shelves containing thick, leather-bound books. She pulled out the first tome, coughing into her elbow as dust filtered into the air. Many years had clearly passed since the last time this room was visited.

She inspected the book in her hands—a collection of nursery rhymes written in the witches' language of Mhenbic. She flipped through pages filled mostly by drawings and a few words. It felt strange to think about witches reading to their witchlings at night, in happy times when they weren't on the run or fearing for their safety.

Bri wondered if the red witches read books to Rua as a child or if Heather read them to Remy. What must it have been like for them? The two High Mountain fae were both raised by witches . . . though in very different ways. Bri knew she was lucky to have both of her parents still alive when so few could say the same. It made her feel guilty that she didn't appreciate them more. She thought to her shared moment with Lina in the atrium of her room. Lina knew what it was to mourn that relationship with her mother long before she passed. If anyone understood what it was like, it was her.

She set the tome back and picked up another storybook—a golden dragon on the cover—that reminded her of one she had as a child. She and Tal had begged their nurse to read *Dragon's Sacrifice* to them over and over. The title in Mhenbic snagged her attention. *Air Ev.* Is that what it meant? "Dragon's sacrifice"? She pressed her lips together. Maybe Lina had grown up loving the story just as much. That she would choose those witch's words as her alias only further endeared her to Bri, and Bri loved thinking that she discovered Lina's secret nod to the childhood story.

Ev. "Dragon." Gods, that's what Lina felt like—a dragon—beautiful and mighty and utterly devastating. She'd trapped Bri in her golden claws the moment she'd pulled back her hood in those markets.

Bri glanced at the titles down the spines. The room seemed filled with children's books. With a sigh, she abandoned the book on the top shelf and exited the room. There'd be no spell books in there. She checked the next room but only found a sitting area full of rickety old desks and chairs.

Lina's footsteps sounded on the creaking floorboards above her and, without thought, she deserted her search of witches' books to go find the Princess.

CHAPTER TWENTY-SEVEN

Bri licked her lips. The thin, dry air seemed to make them constantly chapped. The narrow slats of the window didn't allow for much breeze but the copper-flecked sandstone kept the room cool. She found Lina scouring the rows of towering shelves, seeking out the smaller annexes on the floor above.

"Are you giving up already?" Lina asked, propping her elbow on the low shelf as she flipped the pages of a yellowing tome. The filtered light reflected off the angled ceiling, casting a blissful morning glow around Lina, and Bri was certain the Gods had done it just to torment her.

Bri flipped her dagger mindlessly in her hands. Lounging in a chair beside the shelf, she strung one leg up over the armrest. "I've read every spine on the floor below," she said, yawning. "Mostly children's books. Not a single one sounds like a violet witch book. I thought I'd take a break."

Lina's lips quirked. "We only just arrived."

Bri shrugged. She didn't know why she didn't mention the tale of *Air Ev,* suddenly having the urge to call Lina her dragon. But there was a second definition to the word *Air,* which in Mhenbic meant "sacrifice." That part was what made Bri hold her tongue. Lina had been born with a prophecy that her sacrifices would bring her honor and glory . . . and Bri couldn't bear to give her that moniker. To put the burden of that word on her . . . How much would Lina sacrifice for her kingdom? Bri already knew the answer: everything.

"Reading the spines isn't enough to know what is inside. They might still have something of value," Lina insisted, tracing a finger across the worn page in front of her. "Some of these books are ancient. This one mentions a full moon gathering with all five witch covens. It's probably hundreds of years old."

"And does it say how an arrogant fae princeling can wield the magic of an extinct coven?" Bri mused, resting her head back in the chair. Perhaps she could rest. The dull quiet of the library was pulling her into its heady undertow.

"Ah yes," Lina said, flipping a page and emphatically pointing to the middle. Bri straightened with a jump. "The chapter on how to defeat Augustus Norwood, huzzah!"

Bri shook her head, flashing her foxlike grin. "I think I'm rubbing off on you."

Biting her lip, Lina looked coyly back to Bri. "I hope you continue to do so."

Sleep abandoned, Bri lifted her head, fully aware that her cheeks were burning. She sheathed her dagger and leaned forward in her chair, her eyes heating at Lina's wanton gaze. "What are you thinking about right now?"

"You," Lina said. "That moment in the cellar."

Bri's grin turned predatory. "I think that's the first time I've been in a wine cellar and didn't give a single thought to the wine."

Lina twisted, resting her forearm along the shelf and giving Bri a full look at the front of her dress again. Bri's eyes savored every inch of skin that peeked, from her sandaled feet to the top of her thigh.

"Admiring my dress?" Lina asked breathlessly.

Bri rose from her chair and stalked over to the door. Lina's lips parted as Bri held her stare from across the room and turned the lock.

"I can't stop thinking about it," Lina rasped, watching Bri. "You and me."

Those soft words cut straight to the core of her. Bri had never encountered anyone like Lina—soft and warm, strong and brave. She was the most perfect balance, letting it all shine through her with such intensity that one couldn't help but reflect it all back.

"Neither can I." Bri prowled closer, each step a promise of what she might do when she reached her. "I'm glad you and I chose to be . . ."

"Close?" Lina whispered with a secret lover's smile.

Bri's breath hitched. "I want to be a lot closer." Her words were filled with a thundering need.

Lina's eyes glimmered as she drew near, but Bri paused. Whatever this molten thing was between them was not friendship, but it had no other name. There was no misunderstanding, no assumption between them, that this magnetic pull would last. It would be a quick flame, burning them up and leaving its scars, but they'd move on. They both knew they had to. Bri had a destiny to make in the East, and Lina had a people to unite with her upcoming nuptials, but Bri was sick of pretending she didn't feel completely enraptured by the Princess. In a few weeks they would be parting ways, but Gods could they make their time count.

"I don't want whatever this is between us to end up hurting you," Bri murmured, searching Lina's face.

Lina's hand lifted and swept Bri's hair off her forehead, mirroring her action the day they'd nearly drowned. "It will," she whispered back.

One more step. That's all it would take, and then her lips would be on Lina's, her aching hands would be roving Lina's curves, and the line that was drawn in that cellar would forever be crossed.

Bri's eyes guttered. "I wish I could be everything to you, give you everything you need—"

"What I need," Lina cut her off with her warm, husky voice. "Too many people concern themselves with what I need." She hooked her finger into Bri's belt and pulled her that single step closer, until Bri could feel Lina's breath on her lips, the soft fabric of Lina's dress against her leathers, the quickening thump of her heartbeat in her ears. Lina's pupils widened, dilating until only the barest rim of brown circled her wanton gaze. She licked her parted lips and whispered, "If you don't touch me right now, I'm going to combust."

At her command, Bri's hands darted to either side of Lina, caging her in. Her chest came forward and Bri pinned her supple body to the shelf behind her. Bri gloried in Lina's mischievous smile, letting Bri be the predator even though they both knew Lina was no mouse. Lina's soft curves pressed against Bri's hard muscle, the sensation more glorious than a hot bath or a delicious meal, like the pillowy comfort of slipping into a warm bed. The shape of Lina's body outlined against Bri's own was the greatest sort of bliss. Bumps lifted across her arms, a tingling shooting from the crown of her head straight down to her core.

Their chests rose and fell in unison as Bri stared into Lina's midnight eyes. Even in a library full of tomes, she was certain she'd find no words to describe this feeling. It existed beyond logic, beyond books or poems or songs. It was only ever meant to be felt . . . and all Bri knew was that she wanted more of it.

Lowering her head slowly until she was a whisper away, she waited for Lina to make the final move. The heady smell of jasmine wafted from her perfumed skin as Lina lifted her chin. Her full lips brushed against Bri's own, and that taunting, sweet kiss made a hungry groan rise up Bri's throat.

Lina smiled against Bri's mouth, seemingly aware of the power she held in that moment. With one more agonizingly delicate kiss, their spark ignited into a blaze.

Bri's hand snaked up to cup Lina's neck as she enveloped her in a burning kiss. Lina's giggle of surprise melted into a moan as Bri's tongue swept into her mouth.

No more taunting.

Bri's chest rose and fell faster, stealing the breath from her as their mouths fused together. Golden flashes of delight echoed through her body as Lina's hips twisted, grinding into Bri's muscled thigh. Bri's free hand roamed up Lina's curves, her thumb sweeping up the swell of Lina's breasts and across her hardened nipple that peaked through the fabric of her dress. Slowly, she circled that stiff bud as Lina's breaths shifted into pleasured hums.

Gods, the sounds she made were Bri's undoing. Turning her hips away, Bri broke their kiss, her swollen lips parting as she stared down at Lina's half-hooded eyes. She was so deep in the current of desire now, too strong to swim against it anymore.

"Do you know what has been torturing me all day?" Bri rasped.

"What?"

Bri's fingers traced up Lina's bare knee, roaming higher. "This slit in your skirt." Her fingers circled higher up Lina's soft thigh. "Every time I saw a flash of your skin . . ." Her hand drifted under Lina's dress and reached the soft fabric between her legs, dipping under her belly and into the waistband. "All I could think about was doing this."

Lina gasped as Bri's fingers stroked down through her soft hair. She widened her stance to give Bri access to her hot, wet core. Bri groaned as her fingers slid up and down, dipping into Lina's wetness and spreading it over her. She moved in slow, tantalizing sweeps, circling that sweet button between Lina's legs.

Moaning, Lina pushed herself harder into Bri's hand, making her snarl with pleasure. Each sweep of her fingers toward Lina's entrance made Lina tilt her hips further as if angling them alone would convince Bri to move them inside her. Biting her lip, Bri shuddered at the soft moans escaping Lina's mouth.

Her other hand returned to circling Lina's nipple, wringing out the sounds from Lina's parted lips until she couldn't keep away from them anymore. As her mouth met Lina's, Bri pushed two fingers inside of her, swallowing the moan escaping from Lina's mouth. She let that sound fill every cell of her body as she began working her fingers, massaging Lina's inner folds as her thumb continued circling Lina's bundle of nerves.

"Gods, Bri." Lina mewled into her mouth, the pitch climbing as Bri knew she was climbing higher toward her release. Lina began moving herself along Bri's fingers, demanding more frantic thrusts.

Obliging with a feral growl, Bri moved her hands faster, her own body humming with a building desire as Lina's breathing grew ragged.

The far doorknob clicked, the locked door thudding in its frame but remaining shut. They both froze, Bri's fingers stilling inside Lina.

"You two in there?" Neelo's voiced called through the door.

"Coming," Lina called breathlessly, trying and failing to even her voice. With a grin, Bri began moving her fingers again, making Lina's words come out as a groan. "Give us a minute."

"Oh, fuck no," Neelo cursed, their footsteps sounding down the hallway.

Bri chuckled against Lina's lips.

"So you don't mind people knowing about this?" Lina asked, even as she began rocking her hips again, climbing back up toward that precipice she had been teetering on the edge of.

"Let them think what they want." Bri laughed against her neck, brushing kisses up to her ear. "We know what we are doing."

Lina swallowed, her chest heaving. "And what are we doing?"

"We are enjoying each other while we can," Bri murmured against her lips.

Lina threw her head back, grinding her hips into Bri's hand. "Gods, I enjoy you."

Bri huffed a laugh before dipping her head to trail kisses down Lina's bosom. "I can see that," she said, voice dripping with desire. With one hand, she freed Lina's breast from her dress, licking across her budded nipple. Lina threaded her fingers through Bri's hair, holding Bri's mouth to her chest as Bri's tongue circled her.

"Yes," she panted, the word barely escaping from her throat. "Don't stop."

Bri's heart hammered in her chest at that command, knowing she was bringing Lina higher still. She kept the rhythm, pumping in and out of Lina, working Lina with her fingers and mouth. In two more panting breaths, Lina's fingers tightened in Bri's hair until her legs began trembling. Her high gasps broke into a throaty groan as her body seized, her hot core clamping around Bri's fingers. Bri kept moving, stretching out each little sound until Lina's muscles finally relaxed, her whole body sighing. Pleasure pulsed through Bri, a throbbing ache perfectly tuned to that sound.

Lina pulled Bri's face back to hers, kissing Bri as if she might taste her pleasure. Bri's hands wrapped around Lina, gathering her into her arms, as loud footsteps echoed up the stairs.

Bri knew from the sound it was Carys intentionally stomping up each step to announce her arrival. Neelo had probably told her what they had encountered when they tried to enter before.

A swift bang sounded on the door and Carys said, "Bri, we've found something."

Bri let out a long breath as Lina adjusted her dress. The Princess lifted on her toes and brushed a final kiss to Bri's lips. "I will be exacting my revenge tonight." She gave Bri a wicked grin that had her aching for nightfall and that promise fulfilled.

"Coming, Car," Bri shouted, her shoulders drooping as Lina chuckled at the disappointed look on her face.

"Out of this room or in your pants?" Carys called through the door.

Bri rolled her eyes, storming over to the door and unlocking it. Carys leaned against the frame, her arms folded across her chest as she quirked her brow at Bri.

"I'm not in the mood, Carys," Bri gritted out.

Carys snorted. "Oh, I know exactly what kind of mood you're in." She leaned past Bri and gave Lina a wink. Bri knew Carys would be discreet, Neelo too, but it meant something that they knew. "There's something here that you have to see."

"You found a violet witch book?" Bri asked as Lina left the bookshelf, adjusting her chest one more time before stepping up beside them.

"We found a notebook," Carys replied, shaking her head. "Come look."

Bri hung her head in resignation, trying to ignore the sounds of ecstasy that still sang in her mind. For once, she looked forward to nightfall.

CHAPTER TWENTY-EIGHT

The group gathered around Cole, who stood leaning against a high table. His fingers traced line after line of text, his mouth agape. The midday sun highlighted him against the open doorway, revealing his paling face and widening eyes.

"What's this journal?" Lina asked, reaching the other side of the table.

Bern shot her a look, a mischievous grin pulling up on his lips. So it wasn't a secret at all, then. Everyone knew.

"It's incredible," Cole murmured, flipping to the first page and showing them the name.

"Adisa Monroe," Bri read out. "Who's that?"

"You remember that great-great-grandmother I was telling you about?" Cole's eyebrows shot up to his hairline. "This is her. This is *her* journal!"

"It seems the witches collected all manner of witch relics here," Neelo said, looking down the stacks. "Like a memorial to their old way of life."

"I found a room of children's books in the western wing," Bri whispered. "It was eerie."

"This journal was in an alcove on the main floor, just sitting right there." Cole pointed to the side without looking up from the notebook. "Bern found it. I can't believe it's here."

"You said she was a famous witch," Carys said. "It makes sense that they would keep it."

"She was a violet witch, after all." Cole swallowed, his cheeks staining red as emotion overcame him. "I always thought my mother was joking, bragging about this violet witch ancestor but . . . but it's really true."

"So you're part violet witch?" Bern cocked his head.

"Maybe that's why you have such an interest in concocting new potions," Lina said with a smirk. "It's in your blood."

"Enough to cast violet witch spells?" Carys asked, drawing looks from the group. "What? How far down the bloodline does this violet witch magic go? If he could wield it, maybe there are others out there who could too."

"It's hard to read her handwriting," Cole said. "It's written in very old Mhenbic, but it looks like this is the journal where she kept the notes about her potions. It'll take me some time to decipher it all."

"We should keep looking for more while you read this." Carys nodded. "You're the only one who can fluently read Mhenbic."

"I can read Mhenbic," Neelo said, arching their brow. "You can't?"

"I can understand it . . . mostly," Carys said with a frown. "But reading the words on the page is more difficult."

"Of course you'd be able to read Mhenbic," Lina tutted to Neelo. "Reading is like your first language."

Neelo's gaze dropped to the stack of books in their hands and their cheeks dimpled.

"Are those more books of interest?" Bri asked, nodding to the stack in their hands.

"No," they replied. "Just ones I want to read tonight."

Bri noted the paw print on the cover of the top book. "One about wolves?"

"Lions," Neelo said. "Eastern mountain lions."

Carys chortled, sweeping her braid off her shoulder. "The libraries at Saxbridge getting boring for you?"

"I've read every book in Saxbridge." Neelo gave her a sideways glance. "Most of them twice."

"Of course you have." Carys rolled her eyes. "Right, let's keep looking." She snagged Bri by the elbow before she could turn to follow Lina. "Why don't you help me look over here?"

Bri scowled at her friend.

Bern clapped Cole on the shoulder before heading off in the other direction. "I'm glad you found this part of your family's legacy."

Bri frowned as Carys dragged her into the stacks. "Legacy" was a word she'd heard far too often in her childhood. It seemed to be the only thing that mattered to her parents. She watched as Lina climbed back up the stairs. The Princess didn't turn in her direction, but she did gather the fabric at her hip and tug it up with the next step, flashing a peek of thigh. It was such a subtle movement, but Lina knew exactly what she was doing, judging by the cheeky smirk that played on her lips.

Those lips.

Gods, what Bri would give to freeze this moment in time with Lina, this fleeting togetherness seeming to slip from Bri's fingers like catching raindrops in a tempest. Maybe that's what made it so thrilling—knowing how soon it would end.

～

The shadows deepened until they could no longer read the spines of the books. Relenting for the night, they arrived to a veritable feast upon returning to the house below the library.

Rish had outdone herself again. Relishes, spiced crackers, and vinegar cucumbers sat waiting on the table with more delicious smells wafting from the kitchens. Tapered candles lit the table but the full moon was so bright, it highlighted the entire bay.

They collapsed into their chairs, exhausted from the day of hunting through the stacks. Carys had kept Bri to task for the rest of the day, and when Bri closed her eyes, all she saw were stacks and stacks of books.

"What does it say?" Bern asked, nodding to Cole as he sat.

The brown witch still hunched over his grandmother's journal. He lifted his eyes, a glazed expression on his face from too many hours focused on the words. "She was insane." The group chuckled but he shook his head, his eyes hollow. "She was doing experiments for her High Priestess."

That information tempered the group.

"Experiments?" Lina frowned. "Like the ones they did on the blue witches?"

"No, not exactly. She was trying to push the boundaries of their violet magic, see how far it could take them, dabbling in magic that is banned nowadays or forgotten to time." Cole swallowed, color rising in his cheeks. "I think she's the reason her coven is all gone."

Bri grabbed the open wine bottle in front of her and began pouring everyone drinks. "How is she responsible?"

"She invented so many new spells," Cole said, flipping through the journal and tracing his fingers along the letters and symbols. "Some incredible ones, though some didn't work at all. She wanted to see if she could manifest other witch powers, make monsters, control witches' minds, even become immortal." He opened the book to a page scrawled with drawings of flowers and minuscule scribbling. The scratchings and splotches of ink made the text look frantically written, chaotic and disturbing.

As Cole turned the page, Bri's eyes dropped to the smudged etching in the corner: a lion with tusks and horns. "Gods," she breathed. "Did she create that beast in the woods?"

Neelo's eyes narrowed at the drawing and then back to their own book. "You've encountered a beast like that?"

"After we visited the witch hunters, a horde of golden-masked soldiers appeared, along with this creature." She leaned across the table and tapped the image.

"Shit," Bern muttered. His expression darkened, a far-off look on his face, and Bri wondered where he had gone in his mind. "That is ancient, dark magic. The same sort of power that forged the Immortal Blade and the rest of the witches' talismans. There's a reason the modern witches wanted it left in the past."

"There must be other accounts of her magic back in the Eastern Court," Lina mused. "Maybe she wrote a whole book of spells. If this information is in Augustus Norwood's hands, perhaps he can resurrect her magic without her."

"He'd still need a violet witch, wouldn't he?" Bern rubbed his hand along his stubbled jaw.

Bri folded her arms. "Maybe the Witches' Glass is enough of a magical conduit to use on other types of witches?"

"Was she successful in her other experiments?" Carys asked Cole.

"Mostly no," he said. "There's lots of journal entries about her anger toward the High Priestess for not letting her continue with certain experiments. 'It was only a few girls that died,'" he read, raising his eyebrows at them. "'Think what we could become. We could be the most powerful coven in all of Okrith if Baba wasn't so scared.'"

"That still doesn't explain why you think she's the reason they're all gone," Neelo said, dipping their flatbread into a thick red sauce while keeping their eyes on the book in their hands.

"She created a spell for the witches who wanted daughters," Cole said, and Carys stifled a gasp. "They all wanted daughters, of course, since they often have more powerful magic." He accepted the glass of wine from Bern with a nod. "What they didn't know was those daughters could only produce daughters, and so on. They tried joining with other witches, but it diluted their violet magic . . ." Cole shook his head, swigging back his wine. "It's fascinating magic. I'd never think to combine herbs with our powers this way. It's so similar to brown witch magic, but so strange. It's beautiful spell casting, like I've never seen before." He darted a glance to the fae around him. "But, I mean, of course it's a terrible thing."

Lina chuckled. "We won't begrudge you of all people getting caught up in the alchemy of ancient magic." She leaned back in her chair. "It doesn't surprise me at all that you're related."

"The way my mother spoke of Adisa Monroe was like she was this magical ancestor, a mythical tale that had grown so large I didn't believe it anymore. She'd tell us the story every Harvest Moon when we'd visit the graves of our family." Cole's cheeks dimpled. "My mother's magic seemed brown like mine . . . but I never thought to look too closely. Maybe it had a purple hue that I didn't spot, diluted by the brown witches in her line."

His eyes and hands flared a bronzed shade of brown. The group studied the color, trying to discern if it had a hint of purple but it was impossible to spot. Maybe it was a shade darker than Fenrin's brown witch magic . . . No, Bri was grasping at straws.

"If this Adisa Monroe was the wild spell maker you say she was," Bri said, setting down her glass, "maybe she invented this new poison. It smelled floral." She shrugged. "And the purple smoke, she might have played some part in that too."

"I wouldn't put it past her," Cole said, smirking down at the book. "Her experiments became more and more aggressive over time." He thumbed through the last few pages. "The notebook ends soon, though . . . I wonder if there are more in the library."

"We'll check in the morning." Carys yawned, stretching her arms.

"Oh, here," Neelo said, setting a golden necklace with a giant emerald in front of Lina.

"Oh my . . ." Carys gaped at the huge gem that the heir had placed down with the casualness of someone passing a bread roll. "What's this for?"

"Lina told everyone that she went to Saxbridge to shop for her coronation," Neelo said. "You can say you bought this."

"Gods, you must have a bloody treasure trove under your palace," Bri muttered.

Carys snorted. "You have no idea."

Lina lifted the necklace and put it on. A knot tightened in Bri's throat as her eyes dipped from the emerald down Lina's chest. Her fingers curled, craving to touch Lina again.

"Consider it an early wedding present from my mother," Neelo said with a grin that told everyone their mother had no idea this necklace had gone missing.

Bri choked on her wine, covering it with a cough. Wedding. For a blissful moment, she'd forgotten that Lina was engaged to Tem. It felt so odd, so wrong, that Lina would marry him that Bri must have shoved the thought away entirely.

"Thank you," Lina said, touching the emerald, and Bri's heart sank further. Not the slightest bit of hesitation in Lina's thanks.

A bowl of roasted almonds appeared before her, offered from Carys. She took a handful with a scowl, trying to hide her disappointment. What had she wanted Lina to say? That she'd canceled her engagement? For what? Bri would be leaving as soon as the assassins were under her thumb and a crown was on Lina's head.

She'd make her own way and find her own crown. Still, the thought made her stomach sour. She knew it was unfair that she didn't want anyone else to have Lina, but she couldn't deny the jealousy that roiled in her gut.

With a sigh, she refilled her glass. Lina's hand drifted under the table to her knee, the feeling electrifying every nerve in her body. Her fingers pressed in—a reminder of her plan to exact her revenge—and Bri's heart stuttered.

Gods burn her.

CHAPTER TWENTY-NINE

The door creaked open and Lina peered through the crack. "Guarding my door?"

Bri leaned against the far wall, the drinks still buzzing through her veins. She hadn't been guarding the door, merely pausing, pondering. Her feet had found their way to Lina's room almost instinctively, as if wherever the Princess slept was where Bri should sleep too. She didn't want to admit that it was the growing flame between them that gave her pause, so instead she simply said, "Yes."

"No one knows we're here. Besides, the dogs would alert us to anyone coming up the hill," Lina said, opening the door and revealing her silk nightdress.

Bri's heart leapt into her throat as her eyes dropped to the plunging neckline.

"Do you want to come in?" Lina's lips twisted into a wicked grin.

"More than I want air in my lungs," Bri growled, shoving off from the wall and prowling through the open door.

The moment she breached the threshold, Lina shoved her back against the slamming door, her belly and breasts pressing Bri against the hard wood. Lifting on her tiptoes, Lina brushed a hot kiss to Bri's lips, her tongue licking against the seam of Bri's mouth as her hands skimmed up Bri's sides.

"I think I promised revenge," she murmured against Bri's lips.

The endless hours of lust had nearly burned Bri alive. Still, she pulled her lips from Lina's and whispered, "Gods, this is going to end badly for both of us."

"I don't care anymore," Lina said against Bri's mouth, nipping at her bottom lip. "Take off your clothes."

Bri snarled, yanking her tunic over her head with haste. Lina chuckled at Bri's swift actions, her eyes dropping as Bri shucked her boots and unbuckled her belt. Lina's eyes roved Bri up and down as she stepped out of her trousers, wearing nothing but a fitted undervest and shorts.

"The way I make you feel in my silk nightgown," Lina whispered, tracing her fingers across her lacy neckline, "is how you make me feel wearing that."

Bri's core clenched. Gods, Lina was more intoxicating than any drink or potion in all of Okrith. Everything about her seemed perfectly designed to torment Bri. She rubbed her hand across the back of her neck, letting Lina admire her muscular physique.

"I'm hiking out to the point tomorrow," Lina said, and Bri paused, surprised by the turn in conversation. "I want to watch the sunrise over the Sea of Callipho. It's tradition every time I come here."

"How many times have you been here?"

"A handful," she said. "Whenever we were passing through or staying with Bern's family, we'd hike out there."

"Who's we?"

"My father and I."

"Oh." Bri leaned her head back against the doorframe.

Lina's father, King Thorne, had died many years ago. Bri remembered hearing of his passing, how all of the high-born fae had flocked to the Western Court for his funeral . . . apart from the Catullus family, of course. Her mother had made a show of mourning the King, hanging black flags out the front of their castle, but secretly she knew her mother was delighted. One less Thorne standing in the way of her daughter taking the crown.

"It's not a far walk, if you want to join me?" Lina offered.

"I'm not much of a morning person," Bri snickered. "But for you, I think I'd make an exception."

"Dawn is only in a couple of hours." Lina grinned. "We'll need to leave soon." She pressed in closer, her breath on Bri's lips.

Bri swallowed. "How shall we pass the time until then?"

Lina's chest rose and fell, each breath brushing the fabric of her nightdress against Bri's vest. "I have a few ideas," she whispered.

Bri inched closer, her lips skimming over Lina's, goading her to close the distance. Lina paused, waiting another breath before kissing her. Heat flooded through Bri at the taste of Lina's tongue. Lina pressed Bri into the door again, one hand cupping her neck as the other skimmed down her body.

Lina's husky voice whispered, "Do you want me to touch you?"

"Yes," Bri breathed, her hands falling from Lina's back to her ass and digging in.

Lina's hand drifted from Bri's hip to the waistband of her undershorts, drifting back and forth. Bri groaned at the provoking touches, her own hand dropping to the back of Lina's thigh and tracing up and down in an equally taunting way. Lina's breathing hitched at the sensation and she gave in, dropping her fingers into Bri's undershorts and pressing down on her throbbing bundle of nerves.

Bri jerked at the movement, sucking in a sharp breath. She ground into Lina's hand, moving her hips against Lina's fingers in the rhythm she liked as her eyes rolled back and heat pooled in her core. Lina began to move, matching Bri's tempo, deftly working Bri as her lips fell to Bri's neck. Her teeth tested Bri's flesh, inflicting the slightest pinch of pain as she dragged her teeth over Bri's pulse, and Bri groaned louder, bucking into Lina's fingers.

Lina repeated the action, drawing a rumbling moan from Bri's chest as she panted, "Faster."

Lina obeyed, her fingers moving up and down at double the

pace. Bri's fingers clenched tighter into Lina's ass and Lina let out a deep moan that sent Bri tumbling over the edge of her release. She barked out a cry that Lina caught on her lips, breathing in Bri's orgasm with a wanton kiss. Bri's body twitched, wringing out the last echoes of ecstasy before her eyes flew open and landed on Lina's pleased expression. Lina's fingers stilled at the ferocity in Bri's eyes.

"My turn," she growled.

Pushing from the door, she cupped the back of Lina's neck and they stumbled over toward the bed. Their mouths enveloped each other in scorching kisses as Lina perched herself on the edge of her mattress.

Bri's hands skimmed over the silk of Lina's nightgown. "You knew exactly what you were doing, opening the door in this fucking slip."

"Figured it was worth a try." Lina smiled against her lips.

"It worked," Bri groaned, slipping the straps over Lina's shoulders and yanking the thin fabric up. "Gods, did it work." She dropped the slip to the floor.

Silk pooled around Lina's feet and she kicked it to the side. Bri's heart thundered in her chest as she looked Lina up and down, her shameless gaze lingering on every dip and curve of Lina's gorgeous body. Drifting back up to Lina's dark eyes, she held Lina's lustful stare for a beat, her crooked grin silently promising to make Lina feel just as euphoric as she had been moments before.

Bri pulled her vest over her head and slid down her undershorts, watching as Lina's eyes roved her broad figure. They stood there, bare before each other, and Bri knew this was the edge of something new. She was already free-falling, but now she knew she'd never touch the ground again. Something about being bare, stripped back of every mask, feeling her skin against Lina's own—that felt an awful lot like sealing her fate.

With one final breath, she closed the distance, the feeling of Lina's warm skin against hers igniting a fire in her core. If she could feel only one sensation for the rest of her life, it would be the silken brush of Lina's smooth, warm skin against her own.

Lina's heated softness zinged bolts of desire through Bri as she slowly lowered Lina onto the bed, prowling on top of her. Her lips met Lina's again with a soft kiss, breathing in her night-blooming scent. She skimmed her hand down to Lina's breast, her thumb circling her peaked nipple just as she had done in the library. She was rewarded with the same sweet moan.

She absorbed each breathy sound with her lips, her knee riding up between Lina's ample thighs until her muscled leg pressed against Lina's core. Tilting her hips, Lina ground herself into Bri's leg as her hands roved Bri's muscled back and down to Bri's ass. Lina's fingers pressed in on Bri's muscled backside, rolling Bri's hips along with her own.

Bri's mouth left Lina's, trailing kisses down her neck and over the swell of her breasts. Her tongue circled Lina's nipple, pulling it between her teeth and making Lina gasp from under her. She grinned and did it again, relishing in the sounds she elicited from Lina.

Her hands and mouth roamed lower, over the curve of Lina's belly and down to the inside of her thigh. Lina's chest heaved, knowing exactly where Bri was moving. Bri traced taunting circles with her tongue along Lina's thigh as her hands reached Lina's knees and spread them wider.

Desire coursed through her as she hovered her mouth over Lina, holding her still as Lina tried to close the distance between her wanting core and Bri's lips. She grinned at Lina's shameless writhing, desperate for the promise of her mouth to be fulfilled. Finally, Bri relented, lowering down.

The first slide of her tongue made Lina suck in a sharp breath, a guttural noise catching in her throat. Bri groaned, tasting Lina as her tongue lapped in slow sweeps up and down. Lina's hand reached for Bri, threading her fingers into Bri's hair as Bri found a rhythm with her tongue that made Lina's breath hitch over and over. Lina fisted one hand into the sheets to keep from shattering.

Each sound from Lina's lips rose an octave, lifting Bri higher along with her. Bri's hands strayed from Lina's knees, one sliding down toward Lina's core, the other to her own.

Her finger paused at Lina's entrance, the anticipation alone making Lina buck her hips again.

"Yes," she moaned and Bri slowly dipped her finger inside Lina's wet heat.

Her tongue moved faster as she added a second finger to Lina's molten core. Her fingers stroked Lina's inner walls, slowly in and out at first, steadying the tempo of Lina's own desperate writhing until Bri matched each pump of her fingers to the flicks of her tongue.

Bri's other hand circled between her own legs, another wave of desire cresting within herself at the sound of Lina's pleasure. Each moan made her core throb, music perfectly tuned to her incessantly building desire.

Lina's back arched and Bri knew she was getting closer. She kept her steady rhythm, pulling each ecstatic note from Lina's lungs.

"Gods, yes," Lina mewled, and Bri pumped her fingers quicker as her tongue lashed Lina in fast, sweeping circles.

"Yes, Bri," Lina cried out, and Bri groaned at the sound of her name against Lina's bundle of nerves, the vibrations making Lina scream out Bri's name again. Lina crashed over the edge in a euphoric moan and Bri tumbled over with her.

Bri's fingers and tongue kept moving as Lina's muscles clenched around her, stretching her pleasure out in rolling waves. Lina's moans dropped to panting breaths as her muscles finally released and she collapsed back into her pillow.

Bri kissed her way back up to Lina's belly, collapsing her face against Lina's warm skin, enjoying the way it rose and fell with each of her slowing breaths.

Moments passed with only the sound of their satisfied panting filling the silence. Lina idly traced the line of Bri's pointed ear as Bri's arm hugged around Lina's thigh, leaning her cheek and lips into her skin. The rush of comfort poured through her.

"This might be my favorite place in the whole world," she murmured sleepily into Lina's skin.

"You sound even more tired than me." Lina chuckled lightly.

"For some reason I'm sleepy," Bri murmured into her soft flesh.

"Me too," Lina whispered with a yawn. Her fingers massaged through Bri's hair.

"Hmm," Bri hummed, the pleasant drowsiness pulling her under.

She wasn't sure if Lina whispered something else or she imagined it as dreams of jasmine and midnight eyes pulled her under.

CHAPTER THIRTY

The predawn sky was always a time of relief—a time when Bri finally felt safe to rest—but not this morning, not as she was awoken from her steady slumber by a sweet voice in her ear saying it was time to go. She'd grumbled, and Lina had told her she didn't have to come, but Bri got up anyway and followed her.

As the shadows pulled back and the obsidian sky turned to charcoal gray, the muscles in Bri's core clenched, remembering their passionate night before and how easily she had drifted off to sleep.

Normally, even when exhausted, she'd have to coach herself to sleep, forcing her mind to think of something until stubbornness pulled her under. With Lina, she just closed her eyes and she was gone. They'd both gotten up in the night to relieve themselves, shifting from the position they'd fallen asleep in to lying side by side. She'd curled around Lina's back, burying her face in Lina's neck, her arm gently slung over Lina's side. Tucked against that gorgeous Princess . . . it was the best sleep of her life.

Carys walked out onto the quiet patio, wearing her fitted running garb. She pulled up short as she eyed Bri tying her bootlaces.

Glancing out to the harbor where the sun would soon rise, she asked, "You're not going to sleep?"

"Lina wants to hike out to the point," Bri said as if it were answer enough.

"Bri." Carys's voice was cutting as she said her name.

"What?"

Carys crossed her arms, her large blue eyes piercing into Bri. "What are you doing?"

"Going for a hike," Bri muttered, moving to her other boot's laces. "I'm Lina's guard. I'm not letting her hike through the Western forests alone."

"You could have told her no."

Bri huffed. "She would have just gone without me."

"Listen, this is more than I thought—"

"If you're going to give me another lecture about *good things*, Car, I already know," Bri cut in, looking up at her friend.

"You're normally good at finding people as unattached to you as you are to them," Carys murmured, rubbing her anxious hands down her legs. "But this . . . this isn't casual, Bri."

"It's only for a couple more weeks," Bri replied. "We'll find the Queen's killers and go our separate ways." She searched her friend's face. "We both know it'll hurt but neither of us wants to end it now."

"Ugh," Carys chided. "This is a disaster."

"I know."

"I knew you'd fall for someone like her," she sighed, dropping into the chair across from Bri and resting her head in her hands. Carys seemed more concerned for her than Bri did for herself.

"Like what?"

"You're always fixing people, Bri," Carys murmured. "You care about people so much—too much. But Lina doesn't need you to fix her, and you don't know what to do with that."

"Everyone needs help sometimes," Bri countered.

"Yes, but she doesn't need you, she *wants* you. She chose you because of that, not because of what you could give to her." Carys groaned, fretting for her. "There is no amount of support, or riches, or friendship that she couldn't find somewhere else, but she chose to be with you for however brief a time simply because she wants to. There's nothing there to fix."

Bri's gut clenched. It was true, she always had more to offer a partner than they had in return. She had the upper hand, even with Delta, and it made saying goodbye all the easier. She could brush off those feelings, but there was something raw and real about this that she'd scarcely felt before.

"Ugh, shit," Carys muttered.

"You're more worried about this than me." Bri gave a half-hearted grin.

"Yeah, because you're still all doe-eyed over her. I'm here with two feet in reality, knowing that I'm going to have to pick up the pieces when you two stomp all over each other's hearts!"

"It'll be fine." Bri waved off her friend's stormy temperament.

"No, Bri, it won't." Carys shot up out of the chair, heading to the open archway. Looking over her shoulder, she gestured to the empty spot on Bri's belt where her amber dagger used to be. "How long did it take you to get over the last girl you loved?"

Bri opened her mouth but couldn't summon a witty retort.

Love. Perhaps the feeling wasn't so nameless after all.

"You want to go east and prove you're worthy of a crown," Carys continued, whirling as if she changed her mind and wasn't done lecturing Bri. "She wants a coronation and to establish her reign. How does that end?"

"Car—"

"This is different than the others." Carys cut her off. "I know you know that."

"What am I supposed to do? The second she is crowned, she'll be gone. Then what am I meant to do? Follow her? Pine for her?" Bri rubbed the back of her neck, frustration tensing her muscles. "I can't, Carys. I have my own destiny."

"This is going to hurt, Bri." Carys gave her a warning look.

"It's too late." Bri shrugged with a bitter laugh. "I'm already doomed."

Carys frowned at her, letting out one more frustrated sigh, and then left without another word. Bri wanted to protest that this thing with Lina wasn't the same, wanted to chase her friend down the hillside and explain all the ways that she was wrong . . . but that eagerness to prove herself only incriminated her further.

Shuffling feet sounded down the hall and Lina appeared. "Ready?"

Bri's mouth fell open as she scanned up Lina's body. She'd never get used to the sight of her, equally enrapturing in gowns and battle garb. Lina wore the same clothing she had on the day they trained in Swifthill. A new axe was strapped to her back, the same bronzed cord and vicious teeth lashed below the curving blades. The buckles of her leather harness crossed over her chest, her fitted top smoothing her generous curves. Leather sandals laced up her muscled calves to her knee and she wore a thick skirt of braided leather that revealed her thick thighs.

Rubbing her hand down her face, Bri groaned.

"What?" Lina asked, raising her brow.

"*Why* do you have to look like that?" Bri took a steadying breath. She was ready to rip Lina's clothes off right then and there.

Lina chuckled but didn't answer. Her eyes twinkling, Lina headed toward the stairs as Bri eyed the battle-axe strapped to her back. No wonder she had those legs, carrying such a heavy weapon all the time.

Bri stood. "Are you sure you want to bring your axe?"

Lina's eyes dropped to the knives and daggers strapped to Bri's belt and thighs. "Would you leave your weapons behind?"

Bri grinned wickedly. "Never."

"Nor would I," Lina said in that husky voice of hers that made Bri's toes curl.

She was completely possessed by this Princess. Carys was right; Lina didn't even need Bri to defend her. She didn't need her at all. So why? Bri mindlessly shook her head, drunk on the sight of this goddess before her. She was glad Carys wasn't there to see the foolish look on her face.

～

They trekked the thin trail along the western cliffs of Silver Sands Harbor out toward the point. The thick canopy of lush trees cast cool shadows in the predawn light. The air was more humid there at the southern edge of the Western Court. The earth wasn't as dusty, the plants less jagged and drought-resistant. Here the savanna turned into jungle; another day's trek into the Southern Court and they'd be in the heart of the rainforest.

The soft song of waking birds drifted down from the towering canopy and leaves rustled from the gentle breeze bustling up from the harbor. Every few paces they'd hear another creature scuttling just beyond their sight through the underbrush. Traversing small dips and valleys, the path was never flat. Bri spent much of the hike looking for gnarling roots bisecting the trail. Lina took the lead, moving at a steady, unyielding clip.

The Princess called over her shoulder, "We'll break at the waterfall. We're almost there."

"Thank the Gods." Bri mopped her sweaty brow with her tunic. "If we break, we'll miss the sunrise, though."

"I've seen it before," Lina said. "You sound like you could use the rest."

Bri picked up her pace to catch up, trying to prove Lina wrong. It wasn't the exertion of the trek but the thick air that slowed her down. "How many times have you done this hike?"

"A few. I can't remember," Lina said, her voice dropping an octave. "Darrow and I used to hike this trail together too after my father died."

"Darrow?" Bri asked, hustling forward until she was right behind Lina.

She was surprised at the thought of the silver-haired councilor hiking anywhere. He seemed far more at home hosting stately dinners than trekking through the forest.

Lina chuckled a panting breath. The sounds of rushing water grew as they neared the waterfall. As they turned one last corner, the dense forest parted to reveal a shimmering azure pond. Miniature waterfalls cascaded down the hillside in little steps as colorful birds flitted from tree to tree. The mist cast rainbows of light all around the falling water, creating an otherworldly oasis.

"He was like a father to me after my own died," Lina replied, navigating toward a large, smooth stone and perching herself on it.

Bri sat beside her and fished her waterskin off her belt. "Here."

"I don't think my mother expected Darrow and I to be close." Lina took a swig from Bri's waterskin and returned it. She leaned back on her hands. "He was around in my mother's council by virtue of his family name, but when my father died, they grew closer."

"Were they lovers?"

"I honestly don't know." Lina shrugged. "But he loved her, of that I'm certain."

"A family trait," Bri muttered, thinking of Tem's own confessions of love toward Lina.

"My mother would have never admitted she cared for my father— too headstrong to reveal her grief. But when he died, her leniency to Hennen Vostemur began," Lina whispered as a spray of rolling mist coated her skin. "She pulled our troops from the border, let Valtene fend for themselves as a disputed territory, allowed the witch hunters to roam freely through our lands, capturing the last of the red witches. I don't know if it was heartbreak or she had just given up hope . . . but things changed after he died."

"She never wanted a consort or more children?" Bri mused.

"I don't think she even wanted me; she was just upholding her duty." She laughed lightly but Bri felt the sting in her words.

"How could anyone not want you?"

The words tumbled from her lips before she could think them through. Lina's eyes darted to Bri's, softening as she held them. Bri knew what those words meant to Lina. Bri didn't want her because she was a Princess or a warrior or a Thorne . . . Bri only wanted Lina.

Gods. The words were so clear in her mind, though she feared she'd never speak them: she only wanted Lina.

Bri broke the spell locking their eyes, peering back out to the secret oasis surrounding them. Instead of revealing the thoughts in her head, she said, "I know what it's like to have a mother who sees you as a means to an end."

Lina bobbed her chin. "She left others to raise me. I don't know why she had me at all," Lina said. "She could have just named an heir."

"Is that what you'll do?"

"No." Lina's gaze dropped to her hands. "No, I'm going to have a family one day. You?"

Bri noted the way Lina forced an air of casualness into her voice, careful not to ask too directly. It made Bri smirk.

"One day," she said. "Yes."

She didn't know how she knew the answer, or why. It was in the same way Carys knew for certain she didn't want her own children in her future. Perhaps there was an inner wisdom, some magic that spoke only to their souls. Bri didn't know how she'd accomplish it or when, but she'd envisioned a life with children running around, with laughter filling the halls by day and fantastical stories being whispered around the fires by night.

Bri leaned down to her pack, taking the waxed cloth out from the front pocket. She unwrapped the parcel Rish had made for them the night before. Two perfectly shaped pies filled with chutney and cheese sat inside along with two apples.

Lina grinned as Bri passed her the flaky pastry. "Rish is determined to spoil every last one of us."

Listening to the rush of water and twittering birds, they ate in companionable silence. The sun rose, brightening the sky as the shadows receded.

Rish's food was as decadent and delicious as always; she had even packed little bite-sized sugared rolls as a dessert. The green witch had stayed up into the middle of the night to put together the parcel for them. Bri glanced sideways at Lina. It was something neither of their mothers would ever have done.

"What was she like, Aurella?" Lina asked, leaning back on her elbows. She asked it in such a carefree manner, as if chatting about the weather. She turned her face up toward the morning sunlight, a soft grin pulling on her lips as the rays kissed her skin.

Bri's eyes darted toward her. "Nobody asks me that."

Lina looked at Bri apologetically. "If you don't want to talk—"

"No, no," Bri cut in. "It's weird acting like she never existed. But I think people don't want to ask me because they think it'll hurt . . ."

and it does. It did. I thought my talking about her might upset them too."

"Because you're more comfortable taking care of them than letting them take care of you," Lina said, making Bri frown. "I'm not judging, I'm commiserating."

"I know," she muttered, still grumpy that Lina had so easily cut to the heart of her. They both were uncomfortable receiving the care they so readily gave to others. She leaned back, letting the warming stone below her bake into her shoulder blades. "Aurella was one of those people who always had a story to tell. She could converse with anyone, so easily liked by everyone around her. She was good with a sword, though she was so young. I reckon with a few more years of practice she would have been mighty."

Lina chuckled. "With you as a sparring partner, I'm sure she would have."

"Part of me thinks she was drawn to the Golden Eagle, to the legend that existed somewhere outside of me." Bri ruminated over the thoughts she'd never said aloud. She stared up at the clouds blowing past the swaying canopy of trees. "I knew part of her loved me for my family's name, but part of it was just for me too. . . . She treated me like I painted the sun in the sky, and that adoration was bewitching. I don't know what it was she saw in me—"

"I do," Lina whispered, making Bri turn her face against the warm stone to stare into her endless eyes.

"I loved her," Bri murmured. "If that's the right word. It was its own kind of love—thrilling and sudden—a quick burst of passion. I hadn't thought there was any other kind." She didn't say the words desperate to break free, instead saying, "When I think about her, I brace for that sharp sting of pain, but it's not there anymore. It saddens me that she's gone, but it doesn't hurt the same."

"And you feel guilty for it?"

"It feels like I'm forgetting her somehow, for it not to hurt anymore." Bri brushed her hair off her forehead. "I know that's ridiculous."

"It's not," Lina said with a soft shake of her head. "Nothing that you feel is ridiculous. It's hard knowing how to act once people are gone. We remember them as something other than what they were in this life, as if putting them up on a pedestal will take away that pain. It's okay to let it be. It's okay to keep going."

"Your mother . . ."

"As soon as she died, the praise came flooding in—how she was an amazing ruler, kind and strong." Lina turned her head, their noses nearly touching. "It wasn't true. They would have never said those things about her if she had survived."

"Sometimes I wonder if the person I'm holding on so tightly to never existed," Bri whispered. "If her memory became something other than what she really was to me."

"As if only the good memories are allowed to exist anymore," Lina said with a nod. Searching Bri's eyes, she let out a long sigh. "It feels strange to have someone to talk to like this. I think you may be the only one."

"I can imagine it wouldn't have been a welcome comment in your council if you said that the Queen was sometimes a shit mother." Bri's grin widened as Lina chuckled. "It must have been impossible—the expectations put on the only child and heir."

"When you're a princess, your value is in how you make other people look. How good you can be, how untroubled." Lina's lips twisted to the side. "You aren't viewed as a person in your own right. That's how people see me—only as an extension of someone else's glory."

"I see you," Bri whispered, and Lina's eyes guttered for such a brief moment that Bri wondered if she'd imagined it. In a blink, Lina's face returned to a mischievous smirk.

"I promise if you die first, I'll remember all of you," Lina teased. "Not just the good bits."

Bri's face went solemn at those words, and she swept a hand up to touch Lina's bottom lip. "I pray to all the Gods that I go before you," she whispered. "Because even if I could survive knowing you were no longer part of this world, I never want to."

Lina lifted her hand to Bri's hip. "Then let's pray that the Gods take us at the same time, when we're old Queens and our great-grandchildren are already being born into the world."

Bri's eyes softened as she wondered if Lina meant two Queens— one of the East and one of the West . . . or two Queens together. The thought sparked a flash of light in her so bright she had to clench her teeth. The thought of them having children, of being a family, of filling their lives with the steadiest, deepest kind of love . . . She shoved down that feeling rising within her, too fragile to even think about.

Lina's gaze dropped to her lips, but instead of leaning forward, she sat up and climbed off the rock. "Let me show you the view."

Bri lifted up on one elbow, her eyes drifting from the gilded beads in Lina's hair to her sandaled feet. "I like the view from here fine, thanks."

Lina snickered, hooking her axe back onto her shoulder harness and turning again toward the trail. "Well, if you want to keep gawking, you're going to have to follow me."

"To the edges of the earth, Your Highness," Bri quipped, hastily climbing off the rock. The sound of Lina's laughter made her stomach flip.

Lina rolled the waistband of her skirt over—once, twice—until the strips of leather grazed the very tops of her thighs. A rumbling growl shook through Bri at the sight.

"A little incentive to keep up," Lina called over her shoulder.

Bri bit back a snarl as she stalked after the Princess, knowing for certain she'd follow those swishing hips to the ends of the earth and straight over the edge.

CHAPTER THIRTY-ONE

Storm clouds gathered on the far horizon. Just a little further and Bri and Lina would make it to the lookout and the sweeping vistas of the Sea of Callipho. A small smile tugged on Bri's lips. Her sweaty hair was plastered back on her head, drying quickly in the whipping breeze. With the rushing air, the scent of rain, and the beautiful fae leading the way, she felt deeply grounded, as if her soul had rooted into the soil. She understood now why this place was so special to Lina.

The calm was sharply interrupted by the snick of Lina's axe leaving her harness. Bri's eyes snapped up. She heard the muffled shout before her eyes landed on the three soldiers wearing thin silver chest plates etched in the old Northern Court crest.

Bri's mind flashed back to the same soldiers fighting for Balorn in Valtene. On instinct, she unsheathed two of her daggers and bent her knees, bracing herself.

"How the fuck did you get all the way out here?" she snarled, stepping in closer to Lina.

The soldiers seemed just as surprised to have stumbled upon them. They stared at each other for one heartbeat, then another, before the farthest soldier turned and bolted.

"Stop!" Bri shouted, her legs tensing as she tried to decide if she should go after him or stay and protect Lina.

"Go," Lina hissed. "I'll deal with these two."

Bri barreled into the forest, sprinting after the fleeing soldier. She heard the clang of blades clashing behind her and pushed down on her desire to turn back. Lina was a good fighter, some might even say better than Bri. She'd be able to take two soldiers, but regardless of skill, sometimes victory in battle was a matter of luck, and one misstep would mean death even for the best trained warriors.

Acid burned up Bri's throat as she gained on the soldier. He dashed in the direction of the cliffs, nearing a steep trail cut into the earth that led to the silver beaches far below. Bri finally caught up, grabbing him by the hair and yanking him to the ground.

His heavy armor collided into the stone, and he let out a grunt as the air knocked out of his lungs. Bri dropped her knee onto his chest, cracking it against the steel but pinning him to the ground. She held the tip of her dagger to his throat.

"Start talking," she commanded.

His eyes bugged in his head as he frantically shook it. "I-I can't," he stammered. "Sh-she'll—"

"Who's 'she'?"

"The High Priestess." He sucked in gasping breaths.

Bri's heart pounded in her ears. "Which High Priestess?"

His hand, grasping a knife, flew up toward his neck. Bri grabbed his wrist to stop him from impaling himself with his own blade. The tip of his knife nicked his skin and a thin trail of blood dripped into the leaves below his head.

"She can torture people like no others, get into their minds, turn us into monsters. Please," he pleaded, bucking against Bri.

Bri shoved him back down. "Who is she?"

"The High Priestess of the violet witches," he whispered. "Baba Monroe."

Time seemed to freeze as Bri turned that name over in her mind. "Monroe."

The guard made a choking gasp, pulling her attention back to him.

His eyes rolled back in his head as blood poured from his ears and mouth. The tiny cut on his neck fizzled, rotting a giant black hole into his flesh as his body went limp.

Bri leapt back from his poisoned corpse, her eyes landing on the knife in his hand. The steel was dulled by a thick film covering the metal, the same as the cutlery in the castle. Bri's stomach soured thinking of the blackened leaves in Cole's office. She gagged at the wound that now circled the dead soldier's neck, spiderwebs of inky black climbing up his jawline. Was this what the Queen had looked like when she died?

"Bri?" Lina's voice called through the trees and Bri shot up from her crouch, running back toward the trail.

She pushed through the dense foliage, stumbling out onto the path where Lina stood. Bri's chest heaved as she stared down at two lifeless soldiers, pools of burgundy staining the earth beneath them. Lina harnessed her bloodied axe and looked up at Bri.

Her face was splattered in blood, her dark eyes brimming over with emotion. In two steps Bri was in front of her, grabbing her by the neck and pulling her into a fiery kiss. Bri needed to feel her warmth, breathe in her sweet scent, and know for certain she was okay.

"Are you hurt?" she murmured onto Lina's lips.

"No," Lina whispered, pulling Bri tighter against her. "You?"

"No," Bri panted, resting her forehead against Lina's. "What in the Gods' names just happened?"

The clank of metal sounded far in the distance and their heads turned toward the lookout up ahead.

Lina released Bri and hustled up the little incline toward the parted trees and endless stretch of blue. She gasped and dropped down into a crouch. At the sound, Bri fell onto her belly and crawled up to see what had caused Lina alarm.

Air whooshed from her lungs at the sight: twelve ships, sails lowered, anchored in the choppy waters beyond the bay. She narrowed her eyes at the fleet. Even a single merchant vessel docked there would be peculiar, but twelve?

"Look," Lina whispered, pointing to the launch boat being lowered into the water.

Bri could barely make out the bodies crammed into the boat, swathes of blond and auburn hair and pale faces. An elderly woman sat at the front, her silver hair flowing over her shoulders, and a black spot rested against her chest.

"A totem pouch," Bri murmured. "Do you think she's one of the violet witches?"

Lina ducked behind the tree, peeking out as another ship lowered a boat into the water. "How did they know we were here?"

"A blue witch's vision?" Bri guessed, shaking her head. "Shit. I knew it wasn't safe to come here alone. We need to get out of here. Now."

"Bri." Lina pointed out to the third boat lowering into the water. "Is that?"

She squinted at the slender figure with a mop of blond hair and she froze. "Augustus Norwood." She'd never thought the sight of the little blond brat would instill such fear, but now . . . She yanked on Lina's arm. "We've got to go."

"But . . . what if they sack the library?" Lina whirled and began to run, following Bri back down the trail at double the pace.

"They probably will," Bri barked, adrenaline filling her veins as she ran. "We need to get everyone out of here, especially you."

"Why do they keep coming for me?" Lina snarled, her axe slamming against her back with each leap. "I'm no threat to the East."

Bri glanced over her shoulder to make sure Lina was right behind. She slowed, pacing herself. The boats weren't even launched yet, and it would take hours to row against the turbulent waters and reach the shoreline from that distance.

"He wants your crown," Bri said. "Augustus told Rua he had plans for the West and South. With them and the East, he could easily overtake the last two kingdoms. He wants it all."

"But doesn't the Northern Court Queen possess the Immortal Blade?" Lina sucked in ragged breaths but pushed faster.

They swooped past the waterfall, barely giving it a passing glance. They'd have to remember it fondly later. First, they had to survive.

"Even if Rua has the Immortal Blade, she can't stop attacks on her people coming from all sides," Bri panted. "There are only so many places she can be at once." They crested the undulating trail, careful to avoid roots and rabbit warrens. "Still, Murreneir is probably the safest place in Okrith right now. Rua is holding a ball for the Spring Equinox. Remy and Hale will be in attendance, along with some of the most powerful fae and allies. You'll be safe there."

"I'm not leaving the Western Court," Lina snarled.

"You're attending a royal event that you were invited to," Bri hissed. "Like any good Queen would."

"That was low," Lina muttered.

"Whatever gets you to say yes," Bri huffed.

She knew Lina's desire to be a good ruler would supplant her pride. Lina wanted so badly to be a good Queen; it was evident in all of her choices. She strived to prove her worth, and if Bri could leverage that into protecting her, then so be it.

"Queen Emberspear is going," Bri added, hoping that detail would nudge Lina over the edge into agreement. "Normally she just sends Neelo, but seeing as it is the first royal engagement of the new sovereigns of the North, she's leaving the Southern Court to attend. It would be the perfect time to discuss your joint efforts to keep Augustus's plans from coming to fruition."

"You're sounding a lot like Darrow now. This bloody harness," Lina growled, unhooking her axe from her back and gripping it in her hands. "Better."

"I know you don't want to think about this but"—Bri took in a sharp breath, bracing for the inevitable fight that would come from her words—"can you trust Darrow?"

"Yes," Lina cut in before Bri could even finish speaking.

"Lina—"

"No," she snapped. "He almost died trying to protect my mother.

You should have seen his devastation. I know he seems angry all the time and he is, but you didn't know him before she died. He isn't a good enough actor to be so thoroughly destroyed by her passing."

"He was the one who suggested we come here." Bri's legs burned, forcing her to slow to a jog, but she didn't stop. "Right into a trap."

"You said yourself it could have been blue witches," Lina countered. "Why aren't you accusing Delta? She was there that night too."

"Because I trust her," Bri said.

"Because you still love her," Lina hissed.

Bri halted, whirling around so quick Lina almost smacked into her. "I never loved Delta." Her chest heaved. "I only ever loved one person and she's dead, buried in an unmarked grave, her dagger at the bottom of a river."

Lina's eyes guttered. "I see."

Bri scrubbed her hand down her face, instantly regretting the lie, knowing it was a cruel thing to say. This was the conversation she'd been dreading. Their lust had overridden their senses and now their brains were finally catching up. "I'm not the only one with *entanglements*. What about Tem? Aren't you still engaged?"

"I am."

The hurt in Lina's eyes flooded through Bri, and Bri fought the urge to reach out and grab her.

"We need to keep moving." Bri swallowed. "Warn the others. We can talk later."

"There's nothing more to say," Lina whispered, pushing past Bri and picking up her pace down the trail again.

Bri hadn't felt a single thing when she dropped that amber dagger . . . but watching Lina walk away right then, each step was a stomp to the center of her chest.

She cursed all the Gods. First, to safety. Then she could mourn another thing that never was.

~

The dogs were the first to note something was amiss. Their howling barks echoed from the cliffside and Bri and Lina's friends' heads quickly popped out the windows and over the balustrades. Bri shouted the news up to them, even as she took the cliff steps two at a time. Her pulse hammered through her whole body and she thought she might be sick, but she kept pushing. The rest of the group disappeared into the house before she reached the landing, hastening to depart.

Her argument with Lina echoed below the surface of her mind, even as she rushed to get everyone out. She tried to focus on the task at hand, but that memory stained her every movement, like the ringing of a lone funeral bell that only her ears could hear.

Everyone made quick work of packing their things, the silence brimming with tension as they rushed to saddle the horses and pack Rish's cookery into her open wagon. Bern abandoned his family's furniture, muttering that they could buy more as he carried Cole's pack down the steep path. They spotted the boats rowing into the mouth of the harbor just as they hitched the last horse. Each stroke of those oars was like a beating war drum, counting down the minutes until the impending attack.

"Be safe." Bern gave Bri a tight hug, pulling her hypnotic gaze from the boats. She didn't respond as he mounted his horse and whistled for his dogs.

The road that wrapped around Silver Sands led in two directions and the group split in half again. Bri glanced back at Lina's carriage and her hands clenched as she wondered if Lina was crying inside. The thought shredded her. She shouldn't have said those things; her fear pushed Lina away before Lina could decide to end things herself. Setting her intention to apologize when they were safe, Bri swallowed and gave a final nod to Bern.

Bern's horse trotted off, kicking up dust as the open wagon driven by Neelo and Rish trailed behind. Long days of travel were ahead of them. They'd venture back to the Southern Court to collect the Queen and then journey north for the Spring Equinox celebrations. Bern would stay in Yexshire to brief Remy and Hale and take over for them while they attended the festivities in Murreneir.

"See you in a few days," Neelo farewelled, keeping a wary eye on the boats rowing toward shore.

The choppy waves jostled the boats, those rowing the oars falling out of rhythm as they battled to enter the calmer waters of the harbor.

Bri and Carys turned their horses back toward the western road. The trail hugged the High Mountains, driving straight up toward the Northern Court. It was the fastest way to Murreneir . . . and the fastest way to safety.

Bri glanced at the glittering harbor one last time. The boats drew nearer, close enough to make out the faces of the soldiers on them. She stared at Augustus Norwood's pinched, thin lips, sensing his fury even from the distance. He must have known by the time his boats hit the silver sand, Lina would be long gone, but instead of doubling back, his boats continued toward shore. Bri thought back to the many tantrums she'd witnessed from the young prince. She wouldn't be surprised if he razed the whole library in his anger.

The carriage sprung to life and Carys's and Bri's horses quickly followed. Each clomp of hooves and creak of carriage wheels was weighted by how narrowly they'd avoided an attack. If they hadn't spotted those scouts . . . Bri didn't know if they could have defended against the number of soldiers crammed into those boats. If Augustus had brought more of that noxious purple smoke, their group would have been trapped on the cliff, unable to flee.

Lina's face flashed into Bri's mind. She'd never seen her words hit someone like that—the worst weapon she could wield, the most cruel. It was a skill she'd unwittingly learned from her mother. Helvia Catullus always knew just the right barbs, collecting weaknesses and secrets to employ when she needed them. Bri hated that she'd done the same thing to Lina, that somehow her mother's influence still tainted her existence.

The air thinned as they drove back into the arid landscapes, the greenery yellowing as the sun baked it.

They'd traveled for nearly an hour before Carys spoke. "You okay?" The words barely came out of her mouth.

Bri swallowed, rolling her shoulders. "You were right."

"I wish I weren't," Carys said too gently.

Bri gripped the reins so tightly she was certain they'd leave a permanent outline on her palm. "Gods, me too."

CHAPTER THIRTY-TWO

He tried to stab himself," Bri said, propping her elbows on her knees as she leaned toward the warming fire.

They'd left the horses and carriage closer to the trail and hiked uphill to camp for the night. The forests hugging the High Mountains were damp with springtime rain, the temperature still frigid compared to where they'd just departed. They'd barely found enough dry wood to start a fire.

"Tried?" Carys asked, arching her eyebrow. She held her fingers out toward the flames.

"He cut himself," Bri grumbled. "Just a scratch before I stopped him, but . . ."

"The blade was poisoned?" Cole guessed.

Bri nodded, carefully avoiding Lina's gaze. Each time her shape snagged on Bri's periphery, it felt like a knife stabbing into her side all over again. Just the thought of Lina's pained eyes made breathing hard. They'd just been nearly killed by Augustus Norwood, ancient magic was stirring in the world, and she didn't care one whit.

How could she hide it all when she really wanted to scream to the Gods and punch her knuckles into the nearest tree trunk? Curse the fickle Gods and the wishy-washy prophecies of the blue witches. How much pain could everyone have avoided if they'd never known their true destinies?

"We should fae fire Rua," Carys said. "Tell her we're coming."

"No," Lina cut in.

Bri focused harder on the smoke in front of her, forcing herself not to look. She knew one glance would ruin her, her emotions already seizing control of her muscles. The way she sat, the way she spoke, the way she choked on her own breath . . . it all felt wrong. Willing stillness into her agitated body, she clasped her hands together to keep them from shaking.

"It's too risky," Lina said. "There are too many players in this game now."

"We can trust Rua," Carys insisted.

"But can you trust every guard attending her fae fires not to whisper of this call?" Lina countered. "Knowing that we are alive is already more information than I am willing to give. Bern will inform them in person, but for now I don't want our location known."

Bri was going to open her mouth to correct Lina, that Bern was heading toward Remy, not Rua, but then she thought better of it. She wondered if the mistake was an intentional ploy to get a rise out of her. She wouldn't put it past Lina to try to goad her into speaking.

"Agreed," Cole said, gripping the journal in his hand. "There are location spells in here. Maybe they can track us through our magic too. We need to be careful."

"Monroe," Bri whispered, her eyes widening at the flames.

"What?" Carys shifted from where she was perched on a rotten stump to look at Bri.

"That was your ancestor's name, wasn't it?" Bri narrowed her eyes at Cole over the crackling flames.

"Yes," he replied tentatively, tilting his head.

"And are there any more Monroes alive?"

"Not that I know of." He furrowed his brow, looking up to the sky as if trying to recollect. "My mother was the last Monroe in our family. My siblings and I took my father's surname. Why?"

Bri shrugged. "Just curious."

She felt Carys's eyes assessing her. Her friend would know she had more to say, but she'd tell Carys later. Right now, Cole was the closest person tied to the Queen's murder and she didn't want him knowing of her suspicion. If he was involved, though, it would have been foolish to so openly admit his connection to the name. . . . Perhaps he was inadvertently connected. If Delta and Saika had taught Bri anything, it was that the Western Court was filled with secrets. She'd keep gently prodding Cole and see if anything came of it.

"How long did it take the soldier to die?" Cole asked, pulling their attention back to him.

"A minute or less." Bri rubbed her shoulder. "Why?"

"I wonder if his weapon was tipped with a more powerful poison or"—Cole adjusted his spectacles—"or if entering the bloodstream makes the poison work faster."

"Gods, could you imagine an army with poison-tipped blades?" Carys asked. "It would win any battle."

"What about an antidote?" Lina asked Cole, the sound of her warm, smooth voice making Bri tense.

"I've been experimenting with the residual poisons but have yet to find anything that truly works." He shook his head. "So far I've only found ways to slow the poison's spread . . . but that would only lead to a slower death."

"Shit," Bri growled, kicking at the wet leaves with her boot.

"The ancient covens were ruthless," Cole said. "They made vicious poisons and forged weapons that could fell entire armies. . . . There's a reason modern witches decided to leave that dark, ancient magic in the past. No more amulets. No more rings."

Lina tutted, crossing her arms. "After all that's happened to witches since the Siege of Yexshire, I don't blame them for wanting to revive that ancient power again."

"Most of them can't," Cole said, removing his spectacles to rub his eyes. "Most of that ancient magic died hundreds of years ago. I don't know if any sparks of it live within us anymore. Even if we were able to read the spells, I don't know if there's a witch alive who could cast them."

"Well there's at least one who can," Lina muttered.

Bri glanced at Lina before she could stop herself. A deep-seated ache throbbed through her at the sight of the gorgeous Princess. Still in her fighting leathers, blood still clinging to her skin, Lina stared hypnotically into the flame. Her eyes filled with golden-red firelight. It would take nothing, one raise of Bri's arm, to reach out and rub her thumb across Lina's bottom lip, to feel the steady waves of her breath against Bri's chest.

Lina's eyes flicked to Bri and instantly dropped when she realized Bri was staring back. She swallowed, rubbing her hands down her bare legs. "We should rest. It'll be a long day's travel again tomorrow."

She stood and moved over to where her cloak lay like a blanket next to the fire. Carys grumbled something and moved to do the same. There'd be nothing more than the stale bread and dried meat they'd shared to fill their bellies this evening. Bri missed Rish's cooking already.

Lying on her cloak, Bri folded her arms across her chest and stared up at the starless sky. It would be a long night of nothing but replaying that senseless fight in her head. The horrors of that dying soldier's face would wash over her again and again, but the look in Lina's wounded eyes would gnaw at her forever. Knowing Lina lay just across the fire, also unable to sleep, made it all so much worse. She muttered a curse into the night and closed her eyes, pretending to sleep.

Bri lay awake, staring at the looming mist as the moon strained to peek through the thick blanket of clouds. Carys's and Cole's heavy rhythmic breaths joined the chorus of chirping crickets and hooting owls. The air was thick with the promise of fresh rain and moisture lingered in the dense trees. Bri rolled from side to side, the damp ground seeping into her clothes as she tried to chase down sleep. The harder she fought it, the more it evaded her. It was a night just like this one, in another kingdom, when she and Aurella had been attacked and Aurella was killed. Bri searched a forest just like this one in her dreams, her blackened vision struggling to make out the silhouettes of attackers hiding just beyond the firelight.

Lina rose from her position across the fire and ventured off into the woods toward the stream. Bri's ears strained, listening to the sound of her footsteps until they faded into the distance. Their argument echoed in her mind. They were two unstoppable forces circling in opposite directions, and yet, here they collided. Lina had plans for her court, and Bri only got in the way of them. Bri had a destiny of her own making too, but being pulled into Lina's orbit felt unparalleled, the gravity around her too strong for Bri to resist. There was no one like her. She was fierce but tender, powerful but soft, and so devastatingly magnetizing that being with her would be worth a broken heart, so long as Lina was the one to break it.

Bri let out another frustrated sigh, listening for Lina's footsteps but not hearing her return. Her senses heightened. It shouldn't take that long to relieve herself. Bri sat up, rubbing her hand in her eye socket. She grabbed her boots and shook them in a practiced way from her weeks in Swifthill. When nothing scuttled out, she yanked them back on and headed off in the direction of the stream.

The scent of moss and dewy leaves filled the air but the sound of sniffing made her halt. Lina sat leaning against a tree trunk, her bare feet submerged in the winding stream. She glanced over her shoulder at Bri and the moonlight gleamed off her tear-stained cheeks. Hanging her head, Bri walked over and sat beside Lina. It was the deepest sort of pain, far worse than the sting of a blade—knowing she'd been the one to hurt Lina.

"I'm sorry," Bri whispered, leaning into Lina's side. "I was scared and . . . I didn't mean any of it."

"Me too," Lina echoed, swiping her knuckle under her eye.

Bri pulled off her boots and slid her feet in the cool water beside Lina's. What appeared to be once a small creek was now a rushing stream, eddies of cool spring water rushing down from the High Mountains hovering in the distance.

"We knew it would end," Lina murmured, sniffing again and clenching her jaw as if trying to stop the tears.

That soft pained sound broke Bri. She slowly lifted her hand and wiped away Lina's tears, placing a kiss below each of her eyes. "Maybe in another life, you could have been mine."

Lina pressed her lips together tighter to keep more tears from falling. Okrith was at war and the years had been hard for everyone, but these were the moments that hurt the deepest—not the sweeping battles and daring escapes. This was raw, delicate, precious, the emotions cutting right down to the bone. Whether Lina's tears were from frustration or sorrow, Bri didn't judge Lina for letting them fall, not when she didn't have the courage to let herself break like that again.

"My people love Darrow," Lina whispered. "Their family is woven into the very fabric of the Western Court. The Wystrons have been our closest allies forever. When you suggested it was him, I just snapped. . . . I'm sorry." She dropped her head in her hands. "I want so badly to do what's right for my people. I feel like aligning with a strong family would do the most good for my Court, whether I like it or not."

"*Sacrifice will bring honor and glory,*" Bri whispered, repeating the blue witch prophecy from the day of Lina's birth. "I wish the Fates had never whispered such things. I wish we could have lived without the looming storm clouds of who we were meant to be."

"My mother always said that a Queen should love her people more than anyone else." Lina plucked a weed from the silty stream bed and tossed it into the current. "When what you want and what's right are at odds, people suffer." Her eyes tracked the weed as it floated away. "I think I understand now."

Bri's eyes scanned her face, pain bracketing her expression. "I do too."

Lina turned and held her stare as Bri swallowed, unable to say the words but feeling them dying to be spoken. Her eyes finally dropped to Bri's lips and Bri sprung forward. She grabbed the back of Lina's neck, pulling their mouths together in a burning, desperate kiss. Those warm lips felt so familiar against her own, the taste of Lina's tongue branded into her senses.

"I'm sorry," Lina murmured against Bri's lips.

Bri's kiss cut Lina off, her mouth telling Lina the words she so desperately wanted to say. The proclamations deep in her soul rose to just below the surface—one breath, one slip, and they'd be out, damning her forever.

Nothing mattered in that moment but the taste of Lina's lips, the relief of her forgiveness, and the fear that flowed into frenzied desire.

Lina's arms wrapped around Bri as Lina turned to face her, and Bri's foot glided across the mossy, wet earth as she slid her leg under Lina's. She pulled Lina tighter, needing the press of her body, the comfort of her skin. She dipped her nose to Lina's neck, breathing deeply that jasmine scent as her lips skimmed to Lina's ear.

"You are a goddess," she whispered, her hands roving down Lina's curves.

Lina moaned and Bri's hand dropped to Lina's thigh, squeezing her warm flesh. Lina's hips lifted, her belly meeting Bri's as she shifted closer. Lina's hand eagerly dipped into Bri's trousers and Bri sucked in a sharp breath. Fingers glided over her core, and Bri pressed into Lina's hand, a groan pulling from deep in her chest. Every circle of Lina's fingers set Bri's whole body aflame.

Bri's hand on Lina's thigh rose higher, dipping under her taunting leather skirt and pushing aside her undergarments. Bri's fingers deftly found Lina's wet center, spreading her liquid heat up and down. The backs of their hands pressed against each other and they ground their hips in unison, the breathy moans pushing Bri higher. She dipped her fingers inside Lina, making her gasp. Lina dropped her head forward, biting into Bri's shoulder to stifle her moans as her finger circled Bri faster.

The panic of the day turned into lust-filled heat as Lina hungrily kissed Lina, her hips rocking, writhing, as Bri pumped her fingers into Lina's wet core.

"Lina," Bri panted, and Lina bit down on Bri's shoulder to muffle her high-pitched moan.

The feeling of Lina's teeth marking her skin sent Bri spiraling over the edge. Her bark of pleasure caught in her throat as her climax roared through her. Lina rode Bri's fingers faster, pushing herself over that precipice as she bit down harder. Her core clenched around Bri's fingers and she moaned into Bri's skin, the sound stretching Bri's orgasm out in rolling waves of pleasure.

Bri prayed her fae magic would never heal the bruise on her shoulder. She needed something to remember that this was real.

When the grips of her release finally waned, she dropped her sweaty brow onto Lina's shoulder. She swallowed thickly as her chest heaved.

"Fuck," she groaned. "I don't ever want to let you go."

"Let's survive Murreneir first." Lina's fingers threaded through her hair in slow, massaging strokes, her other still resting in the waistband of Bri's undershorts. "Then we'll worry about what comes next."

Bri nodded into Lina's shoulder, wanting to laugh and cry all at once, but instead, she just held Lina and breathed.

CHAPTER THIRTY-THREE

The rocking carriage jostled Bri awake and she groaned, burying her face further into Lina's belly. Lina stroked her hands through Bri's hair, murmuring something she couldn't hear. Carys had insisted she ride with Lina to "protect" her ... but she knew her friend must have heard their shared moment by the stream the night before.

Bri was so exhausted from the trek, from the fight, from the many years of little sleep, the world had begun to tilt on its axis. Riding a horse probably wasn't a good idea.

"How long have I been asleep?" she asked, rolling from her side to her back until her head rested on Lina's ample thigh.

Lina smiled down at her, serene, more beautiful than any painting. No sculptor or artist would ever be able to capture her perfectly. Perhaps they could capture the gorgeous curve of her lips, the dimples of her rounded cheeks, her long, thick lashes, and the ring of deep bronze in her eyes when the sun caught them in just the right light. But this spark in Bri's chest, this tiny flash of hope, this desperate yearning that flamed every time Lina whispered her name, that would never be replicated.

How could Lina be so fierce one moment and so calm the next? Her capacity to balance all of the things—the ones Bri floundered to contain—was more impressive than any fighting skill or royal prowess. Bri had always felt like one singular note, and Lina was a whole chorus.

"Not long," Lina whispered. "A few hours. We're probably nearing the border soon."

Bri lifted her arm and stroked the tasseled edges of Lina's coat sleeve, rubbing the delicate fabric between her thumb and forefinger. "The first time you've been in the Northern Court in how many years?"

"Gods, over a decade," she murmured. "It wasn't long after the Siege of Yexshire that my mother demanded I stay in Swifthill."

"Swifthill seems like a good place to grow up, though," Bri said. "Children playing in the fountains, eating sweets from the markets."

"It was," Lina said. "Until I grew up enough to want more than what lay within the sandstone walls. When I have children, they'll see every corner of Okrith. They'll never have to wonder what lies beyond the horizon." Her voice grew softer as her fingers slowed in Bri's hair. "They'll never have to wonder if they're loved because I'll tell them every day."

Those words tugged at Bri's aching heart. "My mother wasn't one for words of love either," she murmured, rubbing her hand up Lina's forearm.

"I forget sometimes that our mothers were once friends." Lina's braids swayed, the light clink of the gilded coils punctuating each rock of the carriage. "Do you think you'll ever visit her again?"

"I don't know." Bri sighed. "Are you going to tell me I should be the bigger person? That I should set aside our differences in case I never have another chance?"

"No." Lina's lips curved down, and her stroking fingers paused. "Close your eyes."

Bri furrowed her brow. "What?"

Lina's laugh made Bri's head wobble. "Just do it."

Bri peeked one eye at her and then begrudgingly closed them.

"Imagine ten years from now, to a moment in time. You're happy, the happiest you could possibly imagine," Lina whispered. "You're surrounded by friends and loved ones. A party. Focus on this celebration. Can you picture it?"

"Yes," Bri murmured.

"Is your mother there?"

Bri's eyes opened at Lina and she frowned. "No."

Lina's face turned wistful. "Then maybe the fear of not having more time with her isn't a good enough reason to bring her back into your life."

Bri's eyes flickered. "But Tal's there."

Lina stroked the hair off Bri's forehead one strand at a time, absently playing with it. "I think you have that answer then too." Bri frowned and Lina traced the lines with a grin. "You hate that I'm right, don't you?"

Bri reached up, snaking her hand around Lina's neck and lifting up as she pulled Lina down in a brief, soft kiss.

Lina chuckled against Bri's lips. "I think this is the only acceptable way to be silenced."

Bri pushed up higher on her elbow and kissed Lina deeper before pulling away. "I wish we had more time to be Lina and Bri before our Fates and meddling destinies tore us apart."

"We always knew we had only a heartbeat," Lina whispered, tracing Bri's lips with her fingers as she searched her eyes. "From before even that moment in the cellar, we knew it, didn't we? One blink and it would all be gone."

"I don't think I'll ever be ready to say goodbye to you." Bri's eyelids grew heavy as she tucked her cheek against Lina's soft, warm flesh.

"First Murreneir," Lina whispered back, though they both knew they were only delaying the inevitable. "Then the rest."

It was another day of slow travel through the Northern Court before they arrived in Murreneir. The region was still gripped by winter's chill, and small patches of snow and ice clung to the shadows, but the terrain had shifted from a blanket of white to rolling hills of green. Spring flowers bloomed in yellows and creams along the hillsides. The shaggy cattle had been sent out to pasture, where they grazed the new shoots.

A hawk screeched high above them, and Bri pulled up the velvet sash. Peering out the window, she searched for the bird circling the carriage. She knew at once it was Ehiris—Thador's hawk. The beautiful bird belonged to Aneryn now that Thador had passed.

She craned her neck to the far hillside, spotting a midnight-blue cloak standing before a giant castle. Her mouth dropped open as she stared at the stunning palace. Rambling roses covered the exterior stone, probably coaxed to life by the green witches tending the vibrant gardens. The sharp gray towers and pointed archways sat in stark juxtaposition to the soft foliage. How fitting for the King and Queen of the Northern Court. Renwick and Rua were a strange juxtaposition of hard and soft too—cutting and delicate all at once.

Ehiris circled back, landing on the outstretched arm of the blue witch on the hill. Bri wondered how Aneryn fared in her new position as head blue witch to the King and Queen. Aneryn had served Renwick her entire life and she and Rua had quickly become best friends. Bri hoped the strain of life had eased for them. She'd left Rua at the precipice of something, the broken, budding Princess just beginning to bloom into a Queen.

Every arched window glowed with candlelight, welcoming them like a beacon on the flattened summit. By the time the carriage reached the brand-new stables, the sun was beginning to set. Bri barely had a moment to step out of the carriage before she was bombarded by her friends.

"You made it!" Remy said, bowling into her with a giant hug.

Bri squeezed her friend tightly and then turned to Hale, giving him an equally tight hug. "You look well! How is the High Mountain Court?"

"Wonderful," he said with a charming, wolflike grin. "Though it would be far better if you and Carys were still there."

Bri smiled, clapping him on the shoulder one more time before releasing him and turning to Rua. "Your Majesty," Bri said with a mocking bow before pulling her friend into a hug.

"Don't start with that," Rua snapped though her face split into a wide smile. "I knew you wouldn't let me live it down."

"Aren't you meant to be receiving me in your grand hall?" Bri arched her brow, looking between Rua and Remy. "I don't think Queens are meant to greet visitors in their stables."

"When you win the Eastern crown," Rua taunted, "then you can tell us what a Queen does and doesn't do."

The group moved on to hug Carys and greet Lina as she followed Bri out of the carriage. Spring rains pelted the sides of the stables, and Carys was soaked from head to toe, but their friends hugged her anyway. As the group shuffled past her to greet the others, Bri spotted another figure leaning against a splintering beam.

Seeing him was like a punch to the chest. The same golden-amber eyes and auburn hair as her own—Talhan—her twin.

He looked straight down to his boots as she approached, kicking up straw as she shuffled over. Each step felt like an eternity. When she'd left, Talhan had been so terribly injured, she thought he might not survive. Fenrin had saved his life with his brown witch magic while Renwick had whispered something in his ear, something, she knew, that had kept him holding on. She suspected what it was but never had a chance to confirm it before their falling out. Their argument flashed through her, making her shoulders droop.

"Hi," he said, barely getting the word out.

"Hi," Bri replied, jutting her jaw to the side. "I—"

Talhan grabbed her and pulled her into a hug before she could finish her thought, crushing her with his muscled arms as she laughed. He buried his head in her shoulder and squeezed her so tightly she thought he might crack her ribs, but she didn't care, hugging him back with equal force.

"I missed you," he muttered.

"Same."

Carys came over, slinging an arm over each of their shoulders. "Save it until we have a bottle of wine in our hands," she said. "I'm starving."

Bri turned back to find Lina chatting with Remy, the High Mountain Queen making Lina laugh as she murmured something to her. Clasping his hands behind his back, Cole stood anxiously beside them. Remy smiled at the brown witch, a curious look on her face as she sized him up. Lina's eyes lifted and she smirked as she spotted Bri and Talhan. Bri's expression softened, knowing Lina could feel every ounce of her relief. The world didn't feel right with the Twin Eagles at odds. A million more words flew between Bri and Talhan than those they uttered out loud. They both knew that hug was an apology, and it was why Bri was forever grateful to have a sibling—a person who could say the harshest truths and still be easily forgiven.

"Your home is beautiful," Lina said, turning to Rua and Renwick.

The Vostemur King stood behind Rua, his arms wrapped around her shoulders and his expression warmer than Bri had ever seen. He still had those sharp edges, fine tailored clothing, and not a hair astray from the smoothed back knot gathered at the nape of his neck, but he seemed more at ease than the Prince she once knew.

"Thank you." Rua leaned her head back into Renwick. "I'm glad you were able to come for our first celebration."

"It's been a long time since I've celebrated the Spring Equinox," Lina said, stepping to the side as servants came to unhitch the horses. "Thank you for inviting me. I hope that my reign will mean closer ties to the other courts of Okrith." Lina grinned down at the sapphire ring on Rua's finger. "And congratulations on your wedding."

Rua cringed, looking around the group as Renwick huffed a laugh and kissed her temple. "I'm sorry we didn't invite anyone."

"No one comes for the prayers," Talhan said, pushing to the front of the group. "They come for the food. Speaking of, let's go before I eat one of your horses."

The smell of freshly baked bread and spiced meats beckoned them into the warm interior as they laughed. Bri dropped back to Lina's side and brushed her fingers against the back of Lina's hand. When Lina echoed the action, a secret smile tugged on her lips.

CHAPTER THIRTY-FOUR

Rua took her hosting duties far more seriously than Bri had expected. Bri knew Rua would hate to have anyone note her eagerness to fill her new role, though, so she kept her mouth shut. The whole wing of guest rooms was beautifully appointed in traditional Northern Court decor with hints of Rua's upbringing displayed in the mountain frescoes and crimson details. The castle seemed to pay homage to the town of Murreneir too. An eye-catching mixture of redwood and gray stone, the castle should have appeared an odd clash, but instead it was harmonious and beautiful.

Gratefully, Bri and Carys were given rooms on either side of Lina, with Cole across the hall. It was a move noted by all their crew: putting a brown witch in the guest wing with the fae. Just like the High Mountain royals, Renwick and Rua seemed determined to carve out a new path for their court. The rigid hierarchies that Hennen Vostemur had toiled endlessly to define were starting to fade away.

They changed clothes quickly before dinner. Carys's hair was still wet but freshly braided. Bri swapped her tunic and trousers for a fresh pair, but not bothering more than that. This dinner was amongst friends. Their group had arrived a day early for the festivities. The rest of the guests would come the following day, and Bri was grateful they had this time together before the palace was overrun. How many more times in her life would all of her favorite people be under one roof? She prayed to the Gods it was many.

Renwick and Rua sat at the head of the table in the formal dining room, and, while they both looked immaculate, Bri noted Renwick's loosened collar and how Rua favored a detailed tunic and trousers over a gown. The two of them stole glances at each other throughout the meal, and Bri plied herself with wine, trying not to steal just as many glances at the gorgeous Western Princess sitting across from her. Lina had worn her blue and gold dress, the one that dipped down in a salacious V and hung from the very edge of her broad shoulders. Bri bet she could slip her pinky finger under one shoulder and the whole garment would fall off.

Lina's eyes flicked up, and Bri realized she was gawking at her. Her cheeks burning, Bri darted her gaze away, toward the head of the table. The Northern Queen cocked an eyebrow at her, not missing a thing, and Bri rolled her eyes at the smug look on Rua's face.

"I've heard from Bern this morning," Remy said, pulling the many little conversations into one. "He should be arriving tomorrow, along with the Heir of Saxbridge and Queen Emberspear."

A flash of lightning strobed through the shut curtains and thunder rumbled through the room a moment later. The wild spring weather lashed at the shuttered windows.

"Queen Emberspear?" Lina said with a chuckle, ignoring the storm. "Have you locked up the armory and the wine cellar? Perhaps the apothecary too?"

The group laughed, giving knowing nods. Wherever the Southern Court Queen went, a trail of depravity would inevitably follow.

"I should probably warn our brown witch healer," Renwick muttered, the muscle on his cheek popping out.

"Evie can handle it," Rua said with a wave of her hand.

"Bern told us that the library was sacked." Remy's tone grew apologetic as she looked at Cole and then Aneryn, noting the two witches at the table. "Most of the books survived, but it seems like they were looking for something."

"They were looking for Lina," Bri growled.

"Then why bother with the library?" Rua asked.

"Frustration?" Carys offered. "Who knows. They were so close to hitting the shore before we got out of there. I'm just glad they were spotted before it was too late."

Remy shuddered, shaking her head. "Augustus Norwood always seems one step ahead."

"You give him too much credit," Hale snarled. "This plot is not his doing. He's just the puppet of someone else."

Bri nodded in agreement. She'd known the spoiled princeling his entire life, just as Hale had. She understood Hale's relief at learning he wasn't in fact related to the fallen Eastern King. His mother was having an affair—with her Fated of all people—and Gedwin Norwood had conspired to keep them apart. When the King's blue witch oracle prophesied that Hale would be Fated to a High Mountain Princess, Gedwin had claimed Hale as his son in order to profit off the union. Gedwin had allowed the Catullus family into his court for the same reason: he was betting on all the future rulers of Okrith before they were even crowned. Of Gedwin's two legitimate heirs, Bellenus and Augustus, only Augustus remained. The pompous Prince was the perfect figurehead for someone else to use to attain power—it was easy to inflate his ego and steer him in their own devious directions.

"Augustus surrounds himself with powerful magic," Aneryn said, her eyes flickering a shade of sapphire. "Whoever is wielding it is probably the one pulling his strings. Whenever I try to See him, all I see is purple smoke."

"He did seem fond of the stuff," Rua growled. "If it canceled out the power of the Immortal Blade, it might cancel out all of our powers."

Lina patted the corner of her mouth with her napkin, the cream fabric staining burgundy from her painted lips, and Bri had to remind herself again not to stare.

She cleared her throat, unbuttoning the collar of her tunic. "We were chased by a poison smoke that looked much the same."

"But that one didn't nullify magic," Carys said. "It killed people. The poison created caustic burns."

Cole shook his head as he pushed the fish around his plate with his fork. "It's possible there are different varieties. Maybe the smoke is the conduit for the violet witches' spells?" He looked down the row of waiting faces. "So far most of the ingredients appear to be the same. It's why finding an antidote to the powder itself has proved useless. It's only one piece of the puzzle. Maybe the spell that enchants it determines how it is used?"

"Violet witches," Lina murmured. "After all this time."

"If my ancestor's journal is to be believed," Cole said. "There was a time when they wanted to rule over all other witch covens. Adisa Monroe thought the violet witches had enough power to do it. Her notes are filled with her anger about being discouraged from conducting her experiments. . . . She died hundreds of years ago, but perhaps that's still the belief held by violet witches today."

"And finally they have a young, desperate Prince to help them," Hale said with a curl of his lip. "Augustus would promise them anything to regain his armies and his throne. He'll let them cast all kinds of dark magic in order to get what he wants."

"He doesn't realize what beast he is unleashing," Aneryn spat, looking at the amulet of Aelusien hanging around Remy's neck and to the *Shil-de* ring on Hale's finger. "There's a reason those talismans were left in the past. Think what would happen to this realm if there were hundreds of them."

"You said there were no more Monroes?" Bri asked Cole again.

"Yes?" Cole furrowed his brow. "That I know of, at least."

"Monroe?" Hale leaned down the table, looking at Bri. "That's my mother's middle name."

Her lips pinched to the side as she considered his words. Hale's mother, Kira, was a fae, not a witch. Bri glanced at Renwick—though being able to tell who was part witch was harder than she'd realized. Maybe Kira knew something about Baba Monroe, the High Priestess.

Bri took a long swig of wine, letting it burn the back of her throat. There's no way Kira would have conspired with a Norwood. It couldn't be her. Something wasn't adding up.

"Are you going to tell us what's going on, Bri?" Hale asked, his gray eyes piercing into her.

Bri looked up and down the table, her eyes landing on Lina again. These were her friends—her family. She should tell them what that dying soldier said about Baba Monroe . . . and yet, the words caught in her throat for a moment. Too many threads were being knotted together and she couldn't untangle them all. She took a steadying breath.

"One of the scouts who attacked us," she said before taking another long sip of wine. "He told me that the High Priestess was named Baba Monroe."

Gasps rang out, sharp whispered conversations springing up around them. Silverware clanked onto porcelain plates as everyone stopped eating to listen. They all turned toward Hale, but it was Remy who spoke.

"Your mother's fae, not a violet witch," Remy said, voicing Bri's own doubts. "She'd never help Gedwin Norwood's child after the way he treated Hale and her."

"How is your mum?" Bri asked, thinking of the gorgeous, green-eyed fae.

Kira was like a sea goddess living in the far reaches of Haastmouth Beach, banished there by the Eastern King. Bri had accompanied Hale to visit his mother a few times when they were children, spending the summers swimming in the rolling ocean waves and running across the rocky stone beaches. That all ended when Hale was appointed a commander of his father's armies, but Bri still thought of Kira and those summers fondly.

Remy leaned down the table with a smirk. "She has a boyfriend."

"Rem." Hale rolled his eyes at the gasps of delight from Carys and Talhan.

"Really?" Carys leaned in further, intrigued. "One of those fishermen in Haastmouth?"

Remy nodded. "Timmy."

"No way." Carys grinned.

"I'm happy for her," Bri said, chuckling at Hale's reddening cheeks. "It takes a special kind of strength . . ."

Her words faded off and the group instantly sobered. Hale reached for Remy's hand, Renwick doing the same with Rua, as if her words threatened the magic that tied them together. To ever move on after losing her Fated, even if it had been three decades . . . She was proud of Kira for permitting an ember of happiness in her life after all she'd been through.

"Could it be an alias?" Talhan asked, pulling the group away from their somber thoughts. He tipped his head toward Cole. "Paying homage to this ancestor of yours?"

His face paling, Cole leaned down the table, looking at Hale. "What was your mother's name?"

"Kira," Hale said tightly.

Cole's eyebrows lifted. "I don't recognize that name but . . . There was a family tree in the journal." Cole pushed back from his chair. "I'll go get it."

Renwick pinched the bridge of his nose as the servants came to collect the dinner plates. "I thought after my father's and uncle's deaths, there would be peace."

Rua placed her hand on his forearm. "There will be." She gave him a confident nod, not a single shred of doubt in her visage.

"I thought I was impressive, building the palace of Yexshire in a handful of weeks," Remy said to Renwick. "But this place is even furnished."

Renwick huffed a laugh. "I called in some favors."

"How goes the East?" Bri asked Talhan.

He gave an exaggerated eye roll. "Exceedingly dull."

Carys propped her elbow on the table with a smirk. "Which is why you should leave the dull business of ruling a kingdom to someone like me."

Talhan winked at her. "Not a chance."

"It's not fair that both of you have had a chance to go east and make yourselves known to the new council," Bri groused. "You already have a head start in the autumn elections."

"Please." Talhan snorted, dropping his napkin on the table. "You have a prophecy on your side. The people will flock to you."

"See?" Carys gave Bri a pointed look as she sipped from her goblet.

"What do the other rulers of Okrith think?" Aneryn asked, eyeing between the crowns of the Northern, Western, and High Mountain Courts. "Who would you most like to see on the throne?" Her flashing blue eyes landed on Remy.

"You can't make me pick!" Remy laughed, holding up her hands in defense. "Let the people of Wynreach decide. I'd be happy with any of these three."

"Any other contenders?" Aneryn cocked her head.

Carys shrugged. "No real competition so far. A few courtiers from around the realm, but they're low-level players, with not much fighting skill or connections." She watched as the servants carried in plates of dark chocolate cake and placed one in front of her. "I think they're mostly entering because they figured they might as well. It might secure them better standing with whoever ends up being elected."

Bri ate a forkful of cake, the table humming collectively at the delicious chocolate dessert, layered with caramel buttercream.

She grinned as Lina savored the decadent, rich cake. The way Lina slowly pulled the fork from her lips made Bri's hand clench tighter around her own cutlery. A tiny bit of frosting clung to the corner of Lina's mouth, and Bri had the overwhelming urge to lean across the table and wipe it off. She bet Lina's tongue would taste of sugar and caramel.

The desserts vanished far faster than the dinner, until the room was filled with the sound of cutlery scraping across porcelain. The cake was so delicious, Bri had half a mind to lick the plate clean. She looked at Talhan's pinched brows and knew he was debating doing the same thing.

"If Cole doesn't hurry up, I'm going to eat his slice too," Carys said, tipping her chin to Cole's untouched plate.

The room froze as if everyone was doing the calculations. How long had the brown witch been gone? The bedrooms were only a short walk from the dining room. . . .

Bri dropped her fork and pushed up from her chair a split second before the rest. They all bolted down the hall, Talhan falling into stride beside her.

"Maybe he's just having a shit," he grumbled.

Bri ignored her twin, the hairs on her arm standing on end. Something didn't feel right. She was the first to reach the cracked door. She barreled into Cole's room, the rest of the group stumbling in after her.

The room was empty.

"Curse the Gods," Talhan snarled.

Cole's clothes and books were gone, along with his pack. A freshly snuffed-out candle trailed smoke into the air and two silver *druni* sat on the bedside table. Bri's stomach plummeted as she stared at the witch coins stamped with the phases of the moon. Leaving them behind was called a witch's goodbye.

Renwick barked orders down the hall to his guards as the room filled with muttered curses. Bri clenched her fists and kicked over the table. The sound of the silver coins scattering across the floor mocked her with every spinning clink. Those two *druni* meant Cole was gone.

CHAPTER THIRTY-FIVE

Bri raced down the halls, the sight of Lina's carefully tidied room roaring through her mind. The second she spotted the made bed and the missing cloak, she knew what had happened. Bri barreled into the stables, and her eyes quickly landed on Lina saddling one of Renwick's giant horses.

"Airev strikes again?" she asked, trying to not sound winded. Lina frantically readied the horse. Her cloak hood was pulled to the tip of her nose and her hand axe was strapped to her belt. Gone was the tempered Princess, and in her place once more was the headstrong nighttime thief.

Rain bucketed down, pouring like waterfalls from the windowsills. Bri had to shout above the roar of water to be heard.

"You can't go charging out into this storm by yourself," Bri implored. "This isn't Swifthill."

"No, so I'll probably be safer," Lina gritted out bitterly.

"Lina." Bri stepped in front of her. Lina moved to duck past her but Bri sidestepped again. "They'll find him."

"I want to find him myself and chop his fucking head off," Lina growled. "I trusted him."

"In Swifthill, Airev might be able to blend in," Bri said. "But even glamoured and cloaked, you're dressed like a Westerner in the North-ern Court. You can't track him down on your own. People will know who you are." She pulled back Lina's hood to look into her wrathful eyes. "For all we know, he could be leading you straight into a trap. Please."

Lina glowered at the word. "Why'd you have to go and say that."

"Because I knew it would work." Bri's lips twisted up. "Because the only person I'll ever beg is you."

Lina's eyes flared for a split second before the anger bled back into her expression. Bri could read every inch of Cole's betrayal on Lina's face. Had they really been bringing a traitor with them this whole time? Was everything Cole had done to help them a lie?

"Something about this doesn't make sense, Lina." Bri shook her head, placing a steadying hand on Lina's forearm. "Why would he tell us so much? Why wouldn't he have broken off from us sooner? He had so many opportunities. Why would he try so hard to save Delta when getting her out of the way would have been the smarter choice?"

"I don't know," Lina hissed, clenching and unclenching her fists. "Which is why I need to find him."

"I think the talk of Baba Monroe spooked him," Bri confessed. "I think he might know something, something worth fleeing over." She took a step closer, backing Lina up against the stable wall. "Let Ren-wick's guards find him, the ones that know this countryside. They will return with answers. Come back inside." Lina clenched her jaw, staring hard at Bri, but Bri continued. "It's safer to stay here in a fortress than scouring the hillsides at night in the pouring rain."

Bri slid her arm up Lina's side, delighting in the way Lina's eyelids drooped as she pressed into Lina's soft curves. Her lips found Lina's neck and Lina arched into the sensation. Her tongue slid over Lina's collarbone and her teeth tested the soft flesh on Lina's shoulder in mir-ror to the bruise that now proudly bloomed below Bri's tunic.

"Come inside," she whispered against Lina's skin, trailing kisses up Lina's neck.

"You are very persuasive," Lina moaned, her hands lifting of their own accord and snaking around Bri's back.

Bri grinned, nipping at the lobe of Lina's ear. "I know."

"I wish this never had to end," Lina murmured, raking her fingers down Bri's back.

Bri pulled away and met Lina's gaze, afraid to say the words that had been on the tip of her tongue since their fight in Silver Sands. She took a breath, terrified that Lina would laugh at her for even saying it, but she summoned every ounce of courage and said, "If I gave you a reason to call off your engagement, would you?"

Lina blinked at her, that split second feeling like hours as Bri tried to read her expression. She steeled herself for Lina's rebuff.

"Yes," Lina said, eyes falling back to Bri's lips.

Yes.

Her head swam. Her heart burst. *Yes.*

Bri crashed her lips back into Lina's, desperate to feel every ounce of that *yes* echoing through her body. Maybe she was being careless. Maybe she was spitting in the face of the Fates themselves . . . but in that moment, she didn't care. She'd damn herself for one more heartbeat with Lina—just to feel the rush of being a single sound in Lina's symphony.

"Yes," Lina moaned again.

Bri swept her tongue into Lina's mouth and she groaned, dipping her hands under Lina's tunic and sliding up to the swell of her breasts. Her core clenched at Lina's soft breath, that slight hitch electrifying her as her thumb grazed Lina's chest. Her cloak parting, Lina tilted her hips as Bri pressed in closer, pinning Lina to the stable wall with her knee between Lina's legs.

A sweet moan sang against Bri's tongue as Lina rolled her hips against Bri's thigh. That sound made her lose all control, dropping her hands to Lina's belt and deftly unbuckling it. In one swift movement, she yanked Lina's trousers and undergarments down to the knee. There was no taunting, no waiting, as she dropped to her knees, desperate to taste Lina's arousal on her tongue. Her fingers slid down Lina's core, parting Lina as her tongue followed.

Lina threw her head back, biting into her fist to stifle a throaty gasp. Bri worked her into a frenzy, the panic of thinking Lina had run off morphing into sharp, unleashed desire. Her fingers found Lina's warm, wet entrance and Bri dipped them inside her. The action made Lina lift onto her tiptoes, practically climbing the wall at the sensation. Bri knew from Lina's ratcheting breaths she wouldn't hold on long, already making the sounds that pulled from her lungs when she was so close to shattering.

Bri's tongue circled, alternating between broad sweeping strokes and short teasing flicks that made Lina pant. Lina's free hand found Bri's neck, fisting in her short hair. Bri's fingers pumped faster as Lina rode her mouth, chasing ecstasy with increasing desperation. Bri hooked her fingers, hitting a spot that made Lina's hips jerk, and then she was breaking, her flooded core clenching over and over around Bri's fingers. Lina's muffled screams were barely audible over the storming rain as her hips stuttered around Bri's wet mouth.

Lina dropped her fist, covered in teeth marks, and Bri released her, kissing across her thigh. Lina's head fell forward as she dropped back onto flat feet and pulled in long, heavy breaths of air.

"That was . . ."

The stable door opened, and the muttering of two voices sounded to the side. Bri and Lina froze, Lina's eyes filling with a sudden embarrassment that made Bri press her lips together to keep from laughing.

"Well, tell them to turn back," Rua hissed from beyond the stable wall.

Bri lifted her fingers to her lips, slowly sliding Lina's trousers back up. Lina shook her head, a silent laugh making her shoulders shake as Bri slowly returned Lina's clothes and buckled her belt. Bri dropped her forehead into Lina's hip, giving the fabric one last kiss before standing. Bri lifted onto her toes and peeked through the gap in the boards above her head.

"Really? That's how you're going to handle this?" Aneryn snapped at Rua, the hawk on her shoulder bristling. The witch's eyes and hands flickered a sapphire blue as her vision waned.

"Handle what?" Bri asked by way of greeting. The two jerked toward Bri and Lina as they turned the corner.

Aneryn's eyes darted between them and Rua's nostrils flared, but they didn't say anything, too lost in their squabble. Bri bit the inside of her lip as she glanced at Lina's flushed face.

"I'm sending them away, Bri. I'll handle it," Rua said.

"Who?" Bri asked. She and Lina moved back toward the stable door; Airev had abandoned her plot entirely for the euphoria of Bri's mischievous mouth.

Rua looked down at her hands and clenched her jaw. "Your parents are coming to the ball tomorrow night."

Bri's eyes widened. "Excuse me?"

"We didn't invite them directly," Aneryn said. "But we did send out invitations to the heads of each court and . . . somehow they took that to mean they were invited."

Bri rolled her eyes. "Of course they did."

"They're in Brufdoran now; Aneryn just Saw them," Rua said. "I'll have one of the messengers fae fire them and tell them to turn back."

Aneryn leaned into her friend. "Ru—"

"You'd rather they come?" Rua raised her brows.

Aneryn shrugged. "You invited Hale's mother. And Neelo's."

"Yeah, but everyone likes Hale's mother." Rua gestured wildly. "And Neelo's mother is a Queen, and none of the rest of us have parents around to decide whether or not they should garner an invite." Rua's mouth dropped open, realizing her slip of the tongue a moment too late. She gave Lina an apologetic glance. "Sorry."

Lina chuckled, shaking her head. "Gods help anyone who is your enemy, Rua. You're fiercely loyal to your friends." Her gaze dropped to the Immortal Blade on Rua's hip and back up to her eyes. "I respect that."

Aneryn folded her arms and looked at Bri. "What would you have us do?"

Bri scratched the side of her head, frowning at the floor. "You're making me decide?"

"I think we should send them away," Rua said, folding her arms in the exact same way as Aneryn's, the two of them looking like twins.

"And I think we should suck it up and let them attend the new King and Queen's ball." Aneryn gave Rua a pointed glance as if reminding her that she was a Queen now. "It is the gracious and diplomatic thing to do."

"You'd make a better Queen than me, Aneryn," Rua muttered, and the blue witch gave a cheeky grin.

Bri let out a long sigh and looked pleadingly at Lina. "What would you do?"

"It's not my decision to make." Lina grinned at Bri's scowl. "But"—Bri's shoulders sagged in relief that the Princess had more to say—"if it were me, I'd let them come, only so that I wouldn't have to hear them whine about it for the rest of my life or use it against me later. Gracious, yes, but selfish too. Let the suffering only last for three days instead of an eternity."

Bri knew before Lina even spoke that she'd have considered every outcome and chosen the best one.

"They can come . . ." Bri gave a definitive nod of her head. "And I'll try to avoid them as much as possible." She rubbed the back of her neck, her muscles already bunching at the thought of having to speak to her mother. "Someone should warn Tal too."

"Not me," Rua said at the same time Aneryn said, "Nope."

Bri pinched the bridge of her nose. "You two are insufferable."

"Talhan is in Renwick's study." Rua grinned. "They're bleeding the High Mountain King of his coins."

Lina guffawed. "Who let Hale near a card table?"

"They're waiting to hear back from Renwick's scouts," Aneryn said with a shrug.

Lina perked up at that, taking a step closer. "Have they heard anything yet?"

"Just one message. They found Renwick's stolen horse abandoned halfway to Vurstyn." Aneryn's eyes flashed blue as if she were Seeing Renwick's guards in real time. "Looks like he swapped the horse for another, but they're still following his trail southward."

"He better not make it across the border," Bri snarled. "That traitorous piece of shit." She looked at Aneryn. "Can you See anything else?"

"He has some sort of protection magic." Aneryn shook her head and her eyes faded back to dark brown. "It's similar to the violet witches' purple smoke—"

"Of course it is," Bri growled. "He's part violet witch. Gods, why hadn't we considered that?"

"Why would he tell you that, then?" Rua cocked her head, voicing Bri's own concern. "He may be a spy or a traitor, but I don't understand why he'd share that with you."

"Maybe he got off on it." Exasperated, Bri brushed her hair off her forehead. "Maybe he liked toying with us and twisting the truth, or maybe he was forced by Baba Monroe to stay with us, spying and relaying information back."

"It must be how they knew to find you in Silver Sands," Rua said, speaking to Lina. "As your personal healer, he's probably closer to you than anyone."

Lina's eyes searched Rua's and she nodded, her voice filling with menace. "Just let me know when they find him."

"Come play a hand," Rua offered, glancing at Bri. "We can break the news to Talhan together."

Bri snickered. "How gracious, Your Majesty."

"I'll unsaddle the horse." Aneryn held up a hand as Bri moved to step over the threshold. "Maybe you two should go freshen up first."

Lina grimaced and Bri winked at Lina as she tried to contain her laugh. "Point taken."

CHAPTER THIRTY-SIX

Renwick's study was as refined and well-appointed as Bri had expected...apart from the mob of drunken fae gathered around the large card table.

Renwick shuffled the cards in his hands. "Shall I deal you in?" he asked, nodding to the empty chairs between Talhan and Hale.

"Gods, it's just like Saxbridge," Lina said with a mocking grin, eyeing Remy sitting on Hale's lap. "I should have known you two were Fated right then."

Remy's hand brushed across Hale's neck as she shrugged. "I'm keeping him from losing all of the High Mountain Court's gold."

Rua sat beside her Fated, sweeping her wavy brown hair over her shoulder and placing her elbows on the table. "I'd make him give it back."

Chuckling, Aneryn lifted Ehiris off her shoulder and placed the hawk on a perch nailed between two shelves.

"Have your guards found Cole yet?" Lina asked, pulling all eyes to her.

Renwick's emerald gaze dropped from her to the cards in his hand. "Not yet."

"They'll find him," Talhan reassured. "How far can a witch get in a storm?" He glanced at Aneryn. "No offense."

She tsked. "I'm not the only one with witch blood in this room."

"Ugh." Talhan chortled, his deep laugh shaking through him. "Half of you have witch magic in some way or another. At this point, I can't keep up."

A knock sounded on the door, and they all turned to it, hoping for some news about Cole.

"Enter," Renwick called, and a soldier clad in the new Northern Court uniform opened the door.

"There was a message from the fae fire, Your Majesty," the guard said with a bow.

Everyone paused, leaning in.

"Word on Cole?" Bri asked.

"It was from the Western Court council checking on the Princess." The guard glanced at Lina. "They asked Her Highness to call back at her nearest convenience."

Bri bit the inside of her lip. When had Lina told her council that she had come to Murreneir? Did they know about what happened in Silver Sands? Had someone else in the palace notified the Western council?

"You can do it here," Renwick said, tipping his head to the fire behind him. "They probably want to make sure you survived the storms."

Before Lina could agree, the fae guard nodded and stepped up to the roaring fire at Renwick's back. He whispered the magical conjuring words and the flames turned a bright green. Lina frowned but stood, ambling over to the fireplace to speak with her councilors.

"Word has come from the South," Remy said. "Fenrin contacted me earlier."

Bri noted the way Aneryn perked up at the brown witch's name. She leaned over the table to look at Remy.

"The southern storms have wrecked Augustus's fleet," Hale said. "He was foolish to try to take the southern route this time of year. It looks like the weather has been our champion."

"Why don't I feel comforted?" Bri asked, her eyes darting between the cards in her hands and Lina crouched beside the fire.

A voice flickered out from the flames. Tem's voice.

"Are you all right? Are you hurt?" Concern coated his warm tone. "Have they found him yet?"

The conversation around Bri dimmed as she honed her fae hearing, hooking into the conversation Lina whispered into the flames.

"I'm all right, Tem," she said softly, knowing the rest of them could hear but still keeping her voice low. "We're safe."

"That lying bastard," Tem growled. "It was Cole this whole time?"

"I don't know," Lina said. "There's still a lot of unanswered questions."

"I'll alert Delta and Yaest now." His voice hardened with resolve. "He won't step foot in Swifthill without your guards knowing, Lina, I promise you that."

"You did good work," Darrow's voice sounded from the hearth. "Whether intentional or not, you stomped out the rat, and now it's time to come claim your victory."

"Give her time," Tem said. "Let her celebrate with the Northern royals. We'll prepare for your coronation and our wedding for when you return."

All eyes in the room darted toward Bri and she snickered, knowing that they had all been eavesdropping too. It wouldn't matter how much she scrubbed with soap, they probably could all smell Lina's jasmine and rose oil clinging to her clothes and hair. Judging by their surprised expressions, it seemed none of them knew Lina was engaged.

Bri held her breath, waiting for Lina to give some sign of refusal, that *yes* still ringing like a honeyed song in her mind.

But Lina only said, "I'll be home soon. Stay well."

Remy nibbled at her lip. Rua scowled at her cards. Talhan's eyebrows lifted expectantly. Bri knew all of their tells—how to read each of their expressions—and right then, she wished she could vanish from the card table instead of bearing the weight of their pity.

There were a million good reasons why Lina wouldn't have ended her engagement right then and there—these eavesdropping cads being one of them—but still, it stung.

Lina returned, sitting beside Bri and picking up her cards. Her knee pressed into Bri's from under the table, and the tightness in Bri's muscles eased as she pressed hers back. It was all Lina needed to do to let Bri know she understood what Bri must be feeling.

"Swifthill has eyes out for Cole," Lina announced to the table as if they didn't already know.

"The guards last spotted Cole racing southeast," Rua said. "I don't think he's returning to Swifthill. It looked like he was cutting inland toward the High Mountains."

Remy snorted. "A terrible idea."

Hale idly rubbed his thumb up and down the outside of her arm. "He clearly has no plan if he's headed that way. There's nothing but unforgiving forests and icy peaks. He'll sooner freeze to death than get up and over one of those summits."

"I don't understand what made him bolt like that." Lina considered her cards and then Hale. "What truth had we been circling that made him abandon his ploy?"

"Something about his ancestor," Rua said, shaking her head. "But he'd been so forthcoming. . . . It's bizarre."

Bri's hand dropped under the table and she squeezed Lina's knee. Lina pulled her bottom lip between her teeth at the action before Bri released Lina's knee and returned her hand to her cards.

Talhan sneezed—a fake sneeze. It was convincing enough that no one else noticed it, but Bri knew. It was something they'd made up as children to mean "I see you." He'd spotted her hand drifting below the table and was calling her out on it in a way only he could.

She gave him a sideways glance and he smirked. When was the last time they'd used that little code? Probably when she was pickpocketing from their father's coin purse or swiping her finger through the frosting of an uncut birthday cake. They'd created so many little shorthands between them over the years that sometimes they had people convinced they could truly read each other's minds.

Relief cracked through her again that they were no longer fighting. Talhan knew her like nobody else. He'd seen the way Bri was treated as a child. He knew how hard-won becoming the person she wanted to be was.

Looking at her now, no one could probably imagine that for many years she was forced to wear dresses and ribbons in her long hair. Bri was paraded around like a doll and punished when she didn't play the part. She wasn't always brash and defiant; those traits slowly rose to the surface out of survival and necessity. Bri had loved daggers over dresses and would rather learn to fight than how to wave a fan. Talhan was the one who'd saved her. He'd shared his weapons and recounted his fight training to her and spar with her; he'd sneak her his clothes to wear and she'd take his place in the training rings when they were too little for people to tell them apart. Even then, their tutors feared them—the eagle children.

Talhan coughed pointedly, bringing Bri's mind back to the present, and she tossed two of her cards in to Renwick. She shot her brother a grateful glance and he nodded, seemingly knowing exactly what she was thinking about. Lina threw in one card to Renwick, her other hand dropping under the table to squeeze Bri's knee in return.

When Bri met Lina's gaze, she knew the Princess saw it all too. Lina saw those swirling thoughts in Bri's mind even if she didn't know what memories they were. Knowing that Talhan wasn't the only one who could see beneath her gruff exterior made Bri soften. She didn't like admitting she was ever anything other than the cavalier soldier she was lauded for being, but for some reason, she felt like she could tell Lina anything and not be judged. The embarrassment she expected to flare within her at the thought didn't. Something about Lina made it easy—easy to be together, easy to be herself, easy to bare her truths. She'd never felt that before, not even with Aurella. All those things she guarded so tightly seemed to feel lighter, to float off her as if Lina pulled the weight from the room.

"Thank the Gods," Talhan said as the door opened and two servants walked in carrying trays of goblets and pitchers of wine.

"This is nice," Carys said, draping her arm over the back of her chair. "All of us together again. Certainly nicer than a root cellar."

The group snickered and Renwick arched his brow in confusion, meeting Lina's gaze. "I don't know what they're talking about either," he muttered.

"It happened in Yexshire," Aneryn said.

Renwick blinked at the blue witch. "You were there too?"

Rua chuckled, sweeping Renwick's ash-blond hair behind his pointed ear. "I promise we'll include you next time we're drinking in a root cellar."

He narrowed his eyes at her sarcastic comment, which only made her widen her grin.

"When Neelo arrives," Carys said, looking around the table, "we'll have the five crowns of Okrith under one roof."

"And who is the fifth?" Aneryn asked.

"It's me, isn't it, blue?" Talhan said, leaning back in his chair and swigging from his goblet.

"Perhaps," Aneryn demurred.

Carys leaned her elbows on the table. "Do you know who will win the crown?"

Aneryn tipped her head to the side. "Perhaps," she said again.

Talhan snickered. "That's a no, then."

"Maybe," Aneryn said, peeking over her cards at them. "Or maybe I just don't want to disappoint all of you."

Renwick's cheeks dimpled as the Eagles and Carys frowned. "This is the problem with the Fates," he said. "She could tell you all of your futures and you'd either argue with her as if she weaves the threads herself, or you'd get mad at her if that future doesn't come to pass."

"The better question would be: What future do you want her to whisper?" Rua's eyes lifted to Bri. "I think the answer to that would be far more telling."

Bri grabbed for her goblet, letting the maroon liquid burn down her throat. She tossed in her losing cards and dropped her hand under the table again, uncaring if everyone noticed as she threaded her fingers through Lina's, holding Lina's hand in her lap. She already knew what future she wanted the Fates to whisper.

CHAPTER THIRTY-SEVEN

The floral scent of the Spring Equinox ball welcomed the guests before they even stepped through the wide archway. Above, night-blooming flowers twined through open windows and climbed along the vaulted ceilings. A riot of brilliant spring colors adorned the hall—garlands of pink and yellow, brilliant bouquets of red and blue, and a rainbow of petals cascading down the aisle to the dance floor.

The heady scent was intoxicating—mixed with the smell of honeyed wine and fresh fruit pastries. Light music danced along the stone, mingling with the banter of party guests. A long wooden table stretched across the dais where half of Bri's friends already sat, peering over the crowd. Bri spotted Aneryn dancing with the green witch Laris, the two of them laughing as they missed the steps to the dance. It warmed her to see an easy smile on Aneryn's face. The witches had once shunned her, but the green witch holding her hands didn't seem to care.

Rua stepped down from the dais to greet Bri. She wore a beautiful red and gold tunic with long belled sleeves and her dark hair was twisted half back and held in place with shimmering sapphire clips.

Instead of her usual crown, gilded flowers perched atop her head. Bri smirked, thinking of Remy's wedding and how much Rua had hated her outfit. Now, she looked in complete control—equally fierce and beautiful.

Rua and Bri bowed to each other before Rua said, "Apologies, I would have made space for your parents at the head table . . ." She flashed a playful grin. "But that many place settings would have ruined the ornamentation."

Bri held in her snicker as she scanned the room. She spotted her parents mingling in a corner and her stomach sank. Her mother looked like she hadn't aged a day—the same dark brown hair, amber eyes, and thin lips. The numerous jewels upon her fingers glinted in the light as she regaled a story upon an unsuspecting gaggle of old ladies. Bri's father stood behind her mother, a vacant glaze in his eyes. The Twin Eagles had their father's tall stature and aquiline nose, a hint of his red hair in their own auburn locks. Two heads taller than the rest of the crowd, her father was as silent and brooding as ever, letting her mother take control of every conversation.

"That is quite all right, Your Majesty." Bri chuckled as Rua gave her a conspiratorial glance. "I'm sure they'll enjoy mingling more, anyway."

"Excellent." Rua gestured to the head table, following Bri back up onto the dais.

Bri walked to the seat between Talhan and Carys, her eyes searching for Lina in the crowd but not spotting her. Talhan wore a full crown of budding white flowers, his hooded eyes painted with gold and his limbs swaying. She wondered if he'd already drank the Northern castle dry.

"Having fun without me?" Bri asked as she dropped into the chair beside him.

"I had to greet our parents upon their arrival," Talhan slurred with a smile. "I have been drinking ever since."

"One of the few ways to survive them," Bri jeered, eyeing their parents again. Their father's eyes remained downcast while their mother did all the talking. He liked it that way—seemingly holding himself above their mother's meddlesome ways. Bri had long wondered how different their lives could have been if her father had enough backbone to hamper her mother's efforts.

She leaned forward and looked down the table, noticing Neelo had arrived. The Heir of Saxbridge had their eyes firmly glued to a large tome in their hands while their mother talked loudly to Hale. Queen Emberspear was as stunning as ever, with umber brown skin and long, flowing black hair. Her thick lashes were painted with kohl and her lips were a crimson red. She wore a gown with a plunging neckline, its forest-green hue an homage to the patron color of her Court as well as the green witch coven. She was vibrant and vulgar in equal measure as she unashamedly adjusted her chest in her revealing dress.

Neelo seemed stiffer than usual, their shoulders bunched up around their ears as they shrunk in their seat and focused on their book. No wonder Neelo had seized the opportunity to travel to Silver Sands. Being around Queen Emberspear and her excesses—parties, orgies, dangerous stunts—was fun and thrilling in small doses, but to live around her must be terrible, especially for someone who enjoyed quiet pastimes like Neelo.

Carys nudged Bri with her elbow and Bri looked up to the arched doorway. Her heart stopped when she saw who stood there, silhouetted against the torchlight.

Lina Thorne: Warrior. Queen. Goddess.

She wore a shimmering bronze gown that hugged her plentiful bust and flowed out in draped waves to her sandaled feet. A matching bronze circlet wrapped around her forehead, a spherical diamond hanging from the center. Her face was painted in matching metallic highlights that made her dark eyes sparkle, but one other tiny detail took Bri's breath away: the slit in Lina's dress that rose all the way up to her hip, revealing the amethyst dagger strapped to her thigh.

Bri's eyes drifted up Lina's body as heat pooled in her core. The way that cold dagger pressed into Lina's soft thigh . . . She looked up into Lina's eyes, finding the goddess staring back at her.

Talhan slid his goblet in front of Bri. "Here. You're looking parched."

"Shut up," Bri snapped, the spell broken.

"Do you remember—"

"Yes," Bri said, not needing him to finish his thought. She remembered the agreement they'd made as children, what they would do for each other when it was time, the things they held for each other in safekeeping.

Lina sauntered up to the dais, each step offering a peek at the dagger and making Bri's heart stutter. The Princess could stab Bri straight through with that dagger and Bri would only thank her for it. Lina bowed to the other sovereigns seated at the table and took her place between Carys and Renwick. Bri leaned so far over the table that Carys had to pull her back to keep Bri from lighting her hair on the flickering tapers. She gave Lina a look and Lina smirked back coyly, knowing exactly what she was doing by wearing *that* dress with *that* dagger.

"I see the West has been a fun adventure for you," Talhan taunted.

Bri scowled at her twin. "Something like that."

With a huff, Carys tossed back her wine. Queen Emberspear stood, her eyes hooded and her movements flowing. She tapped her knife against her glass, making the musicians pause and the dancers halt.

"Oh Gods," Carys muttered, watching the Queen. "What havoc is she about to wreak?"

Bri shook her head, bracing herself.

"A toast to Murreneir and the King and Queen of the Northern Court." She lifted her goblet, her voice easily carrying over the cheers. Despite her drunken movements, she spoke with the clear, lyrical tone of the royalty.

Bri cocked her head at the Queen as she lifted her cigarette to her lips and puffed on it. Sickly white smoke rose into the air all around her and her eyelids drooped further. Bri's stomach turned, thinking of the many nights in Saxbridge with Hale smoking the mind-altering herb that was so common in the South.

"A new age is dawning in Okrith." Queen Emberspear braced her hand on the table to keep from tipping over and Neelo shrunk an inch further in their chair, not looking up from their book. "I knew all of your parents." She glanced down the table, eyeing Remy, Hale, Rua, Renwick, and Lina in turn. Her gaze lingered on Lina, a flash of sorrow on her face. "And one by one, I've watched them fall."

The crowd murmured, whispers skittering through the vast hall. As the voices trailed off, the Queen spoke again.

"I have decided it is time to step down and let my child take their rightful throne," she said, her voice rising to a shout to be heard over the frantic murmurs and whispered gossip. "But my last act as Queen will be to see that the Heir of Saxbridge doesn't have to rule alone."

Neelo's shoulders tensed. Their eyes stopped scanning the letters on the page. It was the only indication of surprise that they gave.

"This room is filled with the best stock in all of Okrith," Queen Emberspear called out to the jeering crowd as if she were selecting a new horse. Remy and Hale exchanged worried glances, Rua and Renwick doing the same. "A duel! Any contender who wishes to compete for my child's hand, step forward now."

Casting wide-eyed looks down the table, the friends all stared at each other with worried, bemused expressions, even as the crowd laughed and applauded at the Queen's antics. What was she doing?

Carys leaned into Neelo, muttering, "Should we stop her?"

"That'll only make it worse," Neelo whispered back, their lips barely moving. "This isn't the first time she's done this. Just let her play her game, and I'll shoot down whoever she picks later."

Carys blinked at Neelo for a moment before bobbing her head. How many times had the Queen tried to sell off their hand in marriage? How many drunken bets or misguided games had almost cost Neelo their future?

A few cheers rang out as one by one people began stepping out onto the open dance floor and bowing to the Queen. Bri glanced to Talhan on her right, his face an unseemly shade of scarlet as he clenched his napkin in his hand.

Queen Emberspear grinned, gleefully delighted, and Bri wondered if this was a premeditated plan or if she had just come up with it on the spot. Only the Queen of the Southern Court could bring her wild games with her wherever she went with no repercussions.

The Queen raised her napkin in the air, holding it by the corner. "To the victor belong the spoils."

Bri cringed at the word "spoils," clenching her knife as Talhan kicked her under the table. No, she wasn't allowed to stab the Queen.

The moment the napkin left Queen Emberspear's hand, the room erupted into a giant brawl. None of the courtiers wore their armor or weapons. The sound of fists striking meaty flesh accompanied the barks of pain and growls of aggression. A few immediately stepped back off the dance floor, the first strike to the face or gut enough to dissuade them from this foolish pursuit. Several carried on, a few dropping to the ground, knocked out by a wayward blow. The fight stumbled up the steps toward the raised table and Bri kicked out, knocking the fighters to the side.

One struggled backward to where Talhan sat at the edge of the table, and Bri's twin shoved away the courtier about to crash into him. The red-haired fae whipped around, landing a blow to Talhan's jaw in a brutal sucker punch. Talhan kicked back from his chair, fuming, and socked the redhead square in the nose. He crumpled as Talhan ducked under another swinging fist.

Three half-drunk courtiers converged on Talhan at once and he spun, booting the knee of one while grabbing another in the crook of his arm. One clawed at him, foolish enough to try to attack the Eagle. In one swift move, Talhan seized him by the throat and squeezed, choking the fae until his eyes rolled back. Talhan dropped him, focusing his attention on the last attacker. The fae dropped into a low stance as if making to tackle Talhan and Talhan guffawed, grabbing the fae by the hair and slamming his head down into his knee. The crowd groaned at the wet smack of the blow.

He spun, checking for any other harebrained courtiers, but the floor was bare, having cleared out at the sight of his fighting skill.

"Talhan Catullus," Queen Emberspear boomed. Everyone paused as her face split into a catlike grin. "Congratulations."

Talhan's eyes bugged at her as he looked around the circling crowd, where there surely should have been other brawlers. He'd been forced into the fray and now here he was—the unwitting victor.

Gaping, Bri shook her head at her twin. "It's not real," she mouthed. "Just play along."

Talhan narrowed his eyes at her and then looked back to the Queen. "My honor, Your Majesty," he said with faux valor, placing his fist over his heart and bowing deeply.

With an unceremonious thwack, Neelo shut their book and stood, hastening out the side door. The crowd's eyes tracked them as they moved, whispered chatter rising again. No one moved except Talhan, who raced after Neelo into the hall.

"We'll let them celebrate in private," Queen Emberspear tittered, and the throng erupted into brash laughter.

The rest of the table scowled at the unruly Queen. She sat and puffed on her cigarette, a crooked grin twisting her lips. The only one whose sharp features didn't shift was Renwick, his stoic expression more practiced, but the rest of them glowered at her.

Queen Emberspear raised her eyebrows at Carys and shrugged. "What?"

Carys frowned but didn't reply, grabbing her goblet and taking a deep swig. She was smart enough to know that displeasing the Southern Court Queen was a bad idea. She leaned in toward Bri and whispered, "Did Talhan just accidentally get engaged?"

Bri snorted. "I don't know who I feel more sorry for, him or Neelo."

"Neelo, definitely." Carys chuckled. "Don't worry. They'll set him straight. Queen Emberspear will probably forget this whole thing happened by tomorrow morning anyway."

Bri grinned, her eyes lingering on the doorway that Neelo had disappeared through. "We shall see."

CHAPTER THIRTY-EIGHT

They dined on the finest of Northern Court fare—a sumptuous meal of fresh fish, quail eggs, and roasted vegetables. The wine kept flowing until the plates were carted away and desserts were passed around through the dancing crowds by servers.

Talhan and Neelo never returned.

Queen Emberspear didn't seem to notice, going through an entire pouch of rolled cigarettes and a whole pitcher of wine by herself. Bri noted how Hale's chair continued to inch away from the Queen's over the course of the evening, until Remy granted him a reprieve by inviting him to dance.

Bri caught Lina watching her from down the table and smirked. "Dance?" she mouthed, tipping her head to the crowd.

With a nearly imperceptible shake of her head, Lina patted her lips with her napkin and rose, sauntering out the side doorway. Bri's eyebrows lifted, watching that metallic fabric sway as Lina strolled away.

Following Bri's line of sight, Carys groused, "Well, I guess I'm going to go dance."

Bri gave her friend a wink and they both stood, Carys moving toward the dance floor and Bri heading toward the hallway.

The room beyond the great hall was silent, though Bri's ears rang from the absence of the clamorous party. She spotted Lina half-way down the hall, leaning out the open window to smell the night-blooming roses.

"You look . . ." She smiled as the Princess turned, and she scanned Lina from her crisscrossing sandals to the bronze circlet on her head. Bri's heart raced as she took in every inch of Lina. "The Moon herself would be jealous."

Lina looked Bri up and down. "You're not so bad yourself."

The air between them thickened, charged with this brand-new hope that fluttered in Bri's chest and filled her veins. Like teetering on a high rope, she felt desperate to have her feet on solid ground again. Bri took another step toward Lina, their chests brushing together as their wine-laden breaths intertwined. She peered down into those dark, endless eyes, an eternity seeming to stretch out within them as her fingers found Lina's exposed thigh. Her fingertips grazed Lina's flesh, slowly lifting toward the dagger as Lina's lips parted.

"You did this just for me, didn't you?" Bri whispered, her fingers tracing the outline of the scabbard.

"Yes," Lina panted, her eyelids growing heavy as Bri's fingers drifted higher.

Bri lowered her head, her mouth meeting Lina's as the soft kiss sent tingles straight down her spine. She let out a low groan as that sweet jasmine filled her, those full lips enveloping her own.

"Ha!" A shrill laugh echoed through the quiet, and Bri snarled before even turning to see who it was.

Helvia Catullus, her mother, stood a few paces away, grinning at them as if she'd just won a bet.

"Maybe it was the heart of the sovereign the oracles saw you stealing, my dear," she said in that grating nasal tone that was still familiar even after so many years. "Though I don't think even the Fates could have predicted this."

If ever there was a voice that could douse ice on Bri's flames, it would be the voice of Helvia Catullus.

Bri's lip curled. "Go away, Mother."

"I was just merely—"

Lina took three menacing steps toward Helvia, her mother's amber eyes widening as Lina growled, "She said *go away.*"

Bri's heart flared at the fire in Lina's eyes. No one had ever stood up to Helvia on Bri's behalf, not even Talhan. Her twin had found ways of helping her over the years but he knew he'd be punished just as badly, perhaps even worse, if he ever raised his voice to their mother. But here was Lina, snarling in the face of the parent who'd tortured Bri instead of loved her. Despite being inches shorter than her mother, Lina stared her down with every ounce of the Princess's royal ferocity.

Bri's mother sneered at Lina. "I can't say this was the way I had hoped Bri would take the throne, but if we must."

"There is no *we,*" Bri snarled and stalked toward Helvia, who retreated a step. Bri's words were a lethal promise as she muttered, "If I find out you had anything to do with the Queen's murder, I'll cut your throat myself."

Her mother's mouth dropped open. "You think *I* did this?"

"You hated my mother," Lina hissed.

"She banished me from my homeland!" Helvia whirled on Lina, those amber eyes storming a shade darker than Bri's own. "She sent me away with day-old babes in my arms. Tell me, Abalina, would you have done the same if you were Queen?"

Lina paused before saying, "No." But that hesitation cracked through Bri. She'd considered it for a moment.

"Your mother and I were friends," Helvia said, lifting her chin. "I trusted her and she sent me away. So yes, I spat upon her name and rallied people to support my children over hers. I used King Norwood's interest in Bri's prophecy to gain us favor and standing in the East, and I worked to make my family what it is. *Her Majesty* needed to know that she'd made a mistake, see that we were thriving." She shook her head and swallowed. "I wanted her to *apologize* to me, not to die."

"You waged a campaign against Queen Thorne," Bri said. "What she did was wrong, but you were no better."

Her mother scoffed. "I did what needed to be done to protect my family."

Bri rolled her eyes, having heard that excuse so many times over the years, especially after her mother had lambasted her with barbed words and putdowns. Never in her life had she been good enough for Helvia Catullus, and it had taken Bri far too long to realize she could wear all the gowns and baubles, paint her eyes and demure behind a fan, and still, it would never be good enough.

"You were only protecting yourself," Bri gritted out.

"I was protecting our legacy," Helvia hissed, her tone and posture so similar to Bri's that it made Bri's anger flare even brighter. "And you and your brother went and undid all of my hard work by pledging your swords to that bastard, Hale Norwood."

Bri released a growl that made her mother retreat another step. Good. Let her fear her daughter. Let that question of what Bri could do if pushed too far keep her from one more stinging comment. Bri could handle the jabs at her expense, but if Helvia spoke ill of Hale one more time . . . Let her wonder if Bri's dagger would end up in her side. Hale was Bri's true family, not this selfish scandalmonger standing before her now.

Memories of her childhood flooded back to her at the sound of her mother's scratching voice: the years of harsh words and disappointment, the expectations of greatness that she could never quite live up to. Bri remembered the days when Helvia wouldn't let her eat until she perfected the steps of the Western dances. She still felt the switch being lashed across the back of her hands when she didn't write letters to the high-born fae families, thanking them for their continued fealty to the Catullus name. She'd never told anyone how bad her *training* became. Only Talhan knew. It was why he never stopped her from pledging her sword to Hale. Her mother's actions loomed over her worse than any prophecy and, now that Bri was free of her, she'd be damned if she gave Helvia what she wanted after all these years: her daughter on the Western throne.

"I never had a desire to take a throne that wasn't mine," Bri snarled. "But now that Hale is the King of another kingdom, and the Eastern crown is unclaimed, it's clear *that* is what the Fates whispered on the day of my birth."

"So you have no plans to stay with the Western Princess then?" Helvia's face twisted into a wicked smirk, and suddenly Bri realized she'd walked right into her mother's trap.

Lina froze beside Bri and her heart plummeted. They'd been speaking of a future, together, and Bri's words had just undone all of it. She couldn't claim the Eastern crown and stay by Lina's side. She couldn't do both. At some point she'd have to choose, and every moment, every breath, she teetered between the opposing desires. But right then, with the person who'd tortured her for this goal standing in front of her, she couldn't give Helvia what she wanted, not after she'd spent her whole life fighting to free herself from her mother's oppressive grip.

Bri paused, a damning pause that she knew Lina felt in every cell of her body.

"Excuse me," Lina said, turning and leaving.

"Lina," Bri called after her.

"Whatever it takes, Briata." Her mother's chilling voice echoed down the hallway and she halted. "That girl is weak. It is you who will seize the Western crown."

Bri whirled at her mother, unsheathing her dagger in one quick move and pointing it straight at Helvia's chest.

"Go on. One more word," she growled, pressing the tip into Helvia's sternum until her mother silently shook her head. An infuriating smirk flashed across Helvia's face. "There is not one sliver of good in you, is there? Not a single scrap."

Bri was so close to pressing the blade a little further, just so her mother would know she could do it. She could prove she wasn't a helpless child anymore, but at the sound of Lina's thundering footsteps, Bri paused. Her mother might be the sort of person who deserved a dagger to the heart, but Bri wasn't the sort of person who killed for spite. She wouldn't do it—not for her mother, but for herself.

She dropped the dagger, giving her mother one last hateful look as she said, "All the good that I possess, I made for myself."

～

Bri threw open Lina's bedroom door, finding the Princess directing two servants to take her things as she grabbed armfuls of her garments.

"Get out," Bri commanded, not taking her eyes from Lina. The servants stopped what they were doing and immediately left, a flicker of relief on their faces. Bri's heavy breaths sounded too quiet in the frozen silence stretching out between them. "This is it?"

"Cole isn't in Swifthill. The city is safe." Lina tossed her clothing into her open trunk. "My people need a Queen, and I've been wasting time attending parties. I should be in my kingdom right now."

Bri's heart thundered in her chest. Her mouth was so dry she could hardly speak. "Am I coming with you?"

Her cheeks burned. It didn't feel right to let Lina go. Nothing about it felt right. Cole wasn't acting alone, the ride back to Swifthill might still be dangerous, and she'd promised Delta she'd protect Lina . . . but most of all, Bri wasn't ready to say goodbye. For one damning moment she thought it might be okay, that they might find a way to be together.

Lina whipped her head toward Bri, her eyes piercing straight into Bri's soul. "I don't know, Bri, are you? Because one second you're asking me to end my engagement, and the next, you're telling your mother that you believe you're destined to rule another kingdom."

"I'm trying—" Bri scowled, covering her face with her hands and taking a breath. "It's complicated between us for so many reasons. I can't give you children, for one."

"Absolutely anyone I want could give me a child." Lina rolled her eyes. "I could pick any one of my citizens and they would do it gladly—to boast that they sired a future sovereign. That doesn't mean they need to be my consort. . . . You said that yourself."

"You've thought about this," Bri whispered.

Lina took a shallow breath. "I have."

"Lina . . ." Bri took a step toward her.

Lina put up her hand, halting Bri. "I just need to know. Do you want all of me or not? Because this"—she waved to the circlet around her

302

head and down her flowing gown—"all of this is part of who I am. And I'm willing to share it with you ... but I won't give up my crown, Bri. I can't. I was meant to rule the West."

Bri stiffened. "And what if I was meant to rule the East?"

"Were you? Do you really believe that?" Lina's eyes brimmed with damning tears. "Or are you just too afraid to love me?"

Lina's words cracked Bri open.

"You're not like me, Lina. You are made of all the things that are good in this world. You have such a good heart and you so badly want what's best for your people that you're willing to sacrifice everything for them." Bri shook her head and Lina's shoulders deflated, the words seeming to crash into her. "I understand now why you picked the name Airev." She looked down at her clenched fists, her voice dropping an octave. "You deserve someone that will give you everything, someone who will sacrifice just as much for you as you do for them, someone like Tem."

"You think Tem will be better for me than you?" Lina let out a bitter laugh. "How chivalrous. One day you'll know that chivalry is nothing more than thinly veiled cruelty."

"He loves you and—"

"And you don't?" Her voice cracked and the sound was like a knife between Bri's ribs.

"I didn't say that. I just—"

The broken, hopeless look in Lina's eyes destroyed Bri. It ached deeper than anything Bri had ever felt before—knowing she was the reason for Lina's pain.

"My court is falling apart. I need someone now," Lina shouted, tears welling in her eyes. "I was foolish to rush you into that spot."

Bri's eyes flared. "So you just needed me to fill that role then?"

"I'm not talking about you being my mistress. I'm talking about you being my wife!" Lina screamed, storming past Bri to the door. "I wanted to share everything with you. Gods, if you think you're just filling a role, you're even more of a fool than I am."

She threw open the door, revealing the two wide-eyed servants waiting in the hallway. "Take my trunk to the carriage," Lina said, pointing back into the room and wiping her eyes. "I'm leaving. Now."

Bri followed Lina into the hall, signaling the guard posted at the stairwell. "Get three of your best," Bri ordered. "They'll accompany the Princess back to Swifthill." Lina opened her mouth to protest but Bri said, "Cole is still out there. Rua would happily send you with this protection, considering you're leaving me behind."

"Don't you dare," Lina seethed. "This is *your* choice, not mine." She stormed down the hall, throwing over her shoulder, "I hope you're very happy in the East, where you belong, Briata Catullus."

Bri's heart sank with each step until the last wisp of bronze fabric disappeared around the bend. She bit her lip until she tasted blood, trying to force down the rising tide that roiled within her, but she couldn't. She blustered to the door of her room, needing to get inside before her heart exploded.

CHAPTER THIRTY-NINE

She slammed the door behind her, storming to the far wall and punching her fist straight into the stone. Her knuckles screamed in pain but she didn't care, slamming them into the wall again and again.

A burning wave radiated from her chest, searing her from the inside. Bri ground her teeth together so hard she thought one might crack as she wailed her other fist against the wall. She painted the stone red. How had she fucked this up so badly? How had she gotten so lost in someone else?

Her skin shredded away, and blood slickened the stone wall as she shattered the delicate bones in her hand. She didn't care if she could never use it again. Nothing mattered. Talhan was right. She should have never gone to the West.

Bri faintly heard the door open but she didn't stop until Carys grabbed her. The second her friend's arms were around her, she crumbled, tears streaming down her cheeks as a shuddering sob escaped her lips. She buried her head in Carys's shoulder, clenching the back of her friend's dress in her bloodied fists.

Her knees buckled and Carys guided her down to the floor, holding Bri's head against her. Carys murmured words into her tunic that she couldn't hear over the roaring waves of pain, as if her very soul were screaming.

Carys held her so tightly, the heavy pressure of her muscled arms the only thing keeping Bri from falling into the gaping pit within herself. Her friend seemed to know, pulling her tighter still, letting her know she wouldn't let go. Her tunic was wet—tears, saliva, snot— there was nothing glamorous or poetic about the violent storm raging within her, purging her soul of the rancorous sorrow.

Lina was gone.

And it was her fault.

Those two torturous thoughts rolled over and over through her mind. She deserved every ounce of the pain that crushed her now.

The door opened again—the sounds distant, the voices underwater. Bri only vaguely noted that Rua and Remy had walked in. They didn't say anything as they stalked over and sat on the other side of Bri. Rua pulled her knees to her chest, hugging her legs and staring out over the room. It was the same position she'd sat in on the floor of her tent on the ice lake encampment, except Rua had been the one crying then and Bri was the stalwart light in her tempest.

The room filled with the sound of her wet, sniffing breaths. A weighted silence. And they'd never know truly what it meant to her, to have them sit there and listen to her cry. Sitting there in that stillness spoke straight into the deepest parts of her soul: We're here. We see you. We won't let you fall.

Bri released Carys and dropped her head into her hands. She spat onto the floor, the metallic tang of blood in her mouth as she wrung out the poisonous pain that coursed through her body.

It was something far more primal than logic or words—so overwhelming, so all-consuming—this feeling that seemed to split her soul in two. She'd never felt anything like it. Not with Aurella. Not ever. It was as if someone had carved a hole in the center of her chest, an aching, gaping wound so sharp she could scarcely breathe. She panted more gasps of air, trying to regain control. Her knuckles dripped blood onto her trouser leg, but her friends didn't move, only sat silently beside her, permitting that moment to wash herself of the agony.

The minutes rolled on, each tormenting wave cresting and then ebbing until finally she lifted her head with a sniff. At that subtle movement, Carys rose, disappearing into the bathing chamber and returning with a wet cloth. She took Bri's hand and held the cold compress to her swollen knuckles. Despite the stinging, Bri didn't so much as flinch.

"You must think I'm an idiot," Bri muttered, looking at Rua through wet lashes.

Rua raised her eyebrows. "Wasn't it me saying the same thing to you not so many weeks ago?"

"We can take turns." Remy huffed, slinging her arm around her sister. "Just so long as we don't all fall apart at once, I think we'll be okay."

"Agreed." Tears sprung to Bri's eyes again. She rubbed the heel of her palm against her chest. "Gods, it hurts."

They all knew she didn't mean her hand.

"I understand," Carys said, her voice wobbling.

Bri glanced at her, knowing she was speaking of Ersan—a wound within her that even after several years had never truly healed. Bri wondered if thinking of this moment would make her own voice crack and bring tears to her eyes forever.

Leaning her arm into her friend, Bri said, "I know you do." She wiped her sleeve under her eyes, glancing at each of them with a nod of silent thanks.

Rua pulled a deck of cards out of her pocket. "Two kings?"

Snickering, Remy watched as her sister shuffled the deck. "Renwick is rubbing off on you."

"Ha. You should have seen her on the ice lakes." Bri chuckled, the sound feeling suddenly foreign to her ears. "She bested him in every single hand. No wonder they were Fated."

"You think the Gods gifted us both with a love of cards?" Rua jeered, dealing out the cards as Remy shifted across from her to make a circle.

Bri released a slow breath, looking at the pile of cards Rua dealt and back to her bloodied knuckles that trailed rivulets of crimson down to her fingertips. "I think I might ruin this deck."

"Please." Rua waved her hand. "I have a dozen more."

"Something of a collector now?" Remy teased.

"Well, now I know what to get you for a wedding present." Carys grinned. "I know this painter back east who does royal portraits. . . . He'd be perfect."

"Oh Gods, you're going to put my face on a deck of cards, aren't you?" Rua shot her a look.

Carys's smile turned devious. "You, and Remy, and Neelo, and . . ." She covered her trailing thoughts with a cough.

"And Lina," Bri whispered, the Princess's name burning up her throat.

"Shit, sorry," Carys muttered.

Bri shook her head, focusing on the cards in her hand. Her trembling fingers struggled to hold them. Pain flared up within her in unexpected waves. One moment she thought she'd regained composure, and the next her eyes were welling again.

She struggled through the first round, letting the others' banter carry on without her glum input. Bri knew they were doing it for her, making idle conversation to pull her from the depths of her despair, but she was grateful for it. She'd probably have ruined her hand beyond repair if they weren't there, bearing witness to her pain. The blood had stopped flowing, her fae healing already working its magic to scab over her wounds.

She knew her friends understood. Even in her suffering, she wasn't alone, and a festering question nagged at the back of her mind: Who was there to comfort Lina right now?

CHAPTER FORTY

Everything had turned gray inside Bri. Every time she jolted awake, tears would spring to her eyes, that burning physical reaction beyond her control. Never had her body acted of its own accord like that, each new bout of loss pulling at her strings.

Remy's arm wrapped around her as she tucked in tighter, Carys and Rua on her other side. The three of them had slept the night in Bri's bed, gowns and all, as if keeping guard from the inevitable nightmares.

"It's a bit too soon to be hitting on her, Rem, don't you think?" Carys taunted.

Remy snorted, tucking her chin over Bri's shoulder. "In another life, I'd be like a moth to the flame."

Bri's lips begrudgingly twisted up.

"Ah, is that a smile?" Carys asked ruefully.

"No." Bri's smirk faded and she shut her eyes, burying her face back into the pillow.

The day passed in a sorrowful blur, time warping until the sun began setting again. Bri felt as if she were in the deepest ocean, as if she couldn't come up for air. The lines between reality and dreams smudged until she didn't know where she was anymore. Everything smelled of jasmine. Every sound was Lina's voice. Wave after crashing wave smashed into her, breaking her down until she ceased to exist.

"Everybody out," Talhan growled. The door unceremoniously slammed shut behind him. "You've got kingdoms to rule and guests to entertain. Let me talk to my sister."

Bri scowled, scrubbing a hand down her face and blinking away her bleary vision. Her head rang with the sound of her twin's booming voice. Her three friends begrudgingly got up. Rua looked back at Bri, raising her eyebrows in question, and Bri gave her a nod. *Yes, it's okay to go,* she silently told her.

Talhan stood with his arms crossed at the foot of her bed. His normally charming, cheeky grin was absent, a hard look in its place. He'd turned into the intimidating fae warrior she fought beside on many a battlefield.

"What?" Bri snapped.

Talhan's eyes sharpened, an eagle ready to strike. "What are you doing?"

"I was sleeping."

"You know that's not what I mean," his deep voice rumbled. "What are you doing with Lina?"

"Nothing." Bri gritted her teeth to keep her voice from shaking. Just hearing Lina's name made her body rebel. "If that wasn't already obvious from her leaving here without me."

"I knew you'd get your head stuck this far up your own ass without me," he snarled, making Bri sit up and toss him a lewd gesture. He flashed a menacing grin, seemingly happy to see that spark of life within her.

"She wants to get married, and she's willing to marry Tem to do it," Bri hissed. "She wants to cement her legacy. She wants a crown and a consort."

"But she would have married you if you hadn't been such a dick," Talhan guessed. "Why wouldn't you want that, Bri? To have someone love you, to love them back?"

"I will make my own destiny."

"Fuck destiny," Talhan spat, taking another step. "What do you want, Bri? A crown? You could have one."

"Not one that I've earned," she snarled.

"You had already earned it until you stomped all over Lina's heart because of your own foolish pride." Talhan shifted on his feet like he was a pacing wildcat.

Her voice broke and she clenched her fists in frustration. "I let her go."

"So go apologize and win her back, you bloody idiot," Talhan snarled. Bri chucked her pillow at him and he easily dodged it. "What do you want more, Bri, a throne or her?"

The muscles in her jaw ached from grinding her teeth so hard as tears slid down her cheeks. What would she want if she hadn't been told? If the currents of Fate and her mother's meddling hadn't tossed her to and fro . . . She closed her eyes and imagined the future, the same future she'd envisioned while resting her head in Lina's lap.

Finally, she spoke the words that had been echoing in the back of her mind the past day. "A throne means nothing without her beside me."

Talhan let his hulking arms drop to his side, his face softening. "Then why are you still here?"

Aneryn burst into the room. The two of them twisted toward her, staring at the witch's flickering blue eyes and the sapphire flames licking up from her hands. Behind her, the rest of their friends hung in the doorframe, having not gotten far before the blue witch came running.

"What is it?" Rua asked from the hallway. "What do you See?"

"The Western Princess is in danger," Aneryn panted, locking her flickering eyes with Bri.

Blood drained from Bri's face, her limbs numbing as she leapt out of bed. "Cole?"

"I don't know," Aneryn breathed, her brow furrowing in frustration. "I don't See anyone, just this thick purple smoke." She grimaced as if even the thought of it stung her throat. Her eyes cleared of the flickering blue and she narrowed them at Bri. "But I hear things . . ." Her voice dropped to barely a whisper. "I hear her screaming."

The cold, sharp sting of those words slapped Bri in the face. She darted to the wardrobe as the rest of the group stumbled in.

"We'll go ready the horses," Remy said.

"I'll go get my blade," Rua echoed.

Bri turned to them with panicked eyes. "But your party?"

"Fuck the party," Rua said. "We're coming." She darted a look at Aneryn. "Aneryn can host."

The blue witch gave her a tight nod. The others bolted to their rooms, and Bri was dressed and ready to depart in the blink of an eye. Each movement was haunted by the imagined screams in her head. They had to get to Swifthill before Aneryn's vision came to pass.

~

They raced through the damp Northern Court on horseback. Renwick's giant black steeds ate up the distance at twice the pace of the smaller Western horses Bri and the others had ridden northward. What a sight they must have been—seven of the most renowned fae in all of Okrith barreling through the little country towns. Bri didn't care about the gaping stares and the waving scarves as they roared into villages and back out again. All she could think about were those midnight eyes wide with fear, that husky warm voice morphing into screams of pain. Her visions darkened her every breath.

They'd pushed their horses to the brink of collapse before finally relenting and stopping in Valtene to swap them out. It would be slower going on the Western horses, but at least they were bred to handle the arid terrain.

Bri's clothes were sodden, her skin damp and her soul chilled to the bone. They planned to grab fresh clothes and quick provisions that they could eat on horseback while the stable hands readied their new mounts. An hour break—no more—Remy had promised her, but she didn't have an hour. She didn't have a single heartbeat to spare. She needed to know Lina was safe again before she could exist at all.

Bri was tightening the saddlebag on her horse's flank when she heard the crunching of straw and scuff of boots behind her. The others had rushed to the tavern to relieve themselves after their long ride through the night. Another full day's ride lay ahead of them. She smoothed a hand down her horse's neck as Talhan's telltale footsteps approached.

"No amount of prayers will get that horse to make it all the way to Swifthill in one go," he said. Bri turned just in time to catch the bread roll he chucked to her. "Nor you if you don't eat something."

"I can't stop," Bri said, tucking the roll in her pocket.

Talhan watched her frantic movements and frowned. "Bri."

She knew what her twin was going to say. He'd push her even when others were afraid to, and he'd tell her when she was being a fool.

Guilt swarmed her every sense as she checked the buckles over again.

"We'll get to her in time," Talhan promised.

"You don't know that," Bri snapped. "They could have killed her on the road, dumped her body before they even reached Swifthill. . . . What if Cole ambushed her? Gods, how had I not seen it?"

"They were all suspicious," Talhan said, taking another step and rubbing his hand down her horse's muzzle. She noted the move—how he put himself between her horse and the stable door. He could grab the reins and stop her from leaving. "How could you have known it was Cole? From the brief moments I spoke with him, he seemed like a nice person."

"When Mother showed up, I . . ." Bri balled her fists, thinking of that cocky grin on her mother's face—how she knew she was backing Bri into a corner with her every word. Helvia knew Bri would destroy herself, her happiness, rather than let her mother be right. "I pushed away every instinct I had. I pushed *her* away. Lina wanted a life together and I said no."

"Mother has that effect on people," Talhan gritted out. "You swore to yourself you'd never give her the Western crown, and now you're in love with the person who wears it."

"She seemed so delighted that Lina and I were getting closer." Bri huffed, the scabs on her knuckles cracking as she clenched her fists. "And equally delighted to drive a wedge between us. It's like she could see the crown in her reach and I didn't want to give it to her."

"Of all people, she knows the right wounds to press on." Talhan frowned, giving her a nudge. "I'm sure you'll find another way of disappointing our parents."

"But I was the one who succumbed." Bri rubbed the back of her neck as she scowled. "I should have been stronger, should have told Mother no, that I loved Lina and we'd figure it out. Gods."

She looked to the wall as if she might punch it, but her knuckles barked at her just from balling her injured hand into a fist. If she were human or witch, she probably would have irreparably injured herself. That she was healing at all was a miracle she didn't deserve. If Lina died because of her, because she'd broken her vow to protect Lina, nothing else would matter. It wasn't the same as before, not at all; this was wholly different, far deeper than anything she'd ever known.

"I loved Aurella, I did, but this . . ." She placed her palm to the center of her chest, pushing down hard on her sternum. "It feels like my soul has been ripped in two."

"I know that feeling," Talhan whispered, his gaze dropping to his boots. "It was just outside here in Valtene." He placed his hand to his gut. "I thought I was dying, but I couldn't let go. Our souls are tied to this world by the people we love, Fated or not." His face darkened, his expression strained. "Why are the best things the ones we're too afraid to get right?"

Bri's eyes guttered. "I sent her to her death because I was too scared to love her." She swallowed, forcing back the tears that threatened to well. Panic rose above her grief. She turned and mounted her horse. "It's why I can't stop now."

"Okay." Her twin blinked at her and nodded, turning to the horse beside hers. "Let's go."

CHAPTER FORTY-ONE

The spring storms torrented down upon Bri and Talhan. They rode like the Goddess of Death was chasing them, racing through the walls of rain. Bri prayed to all the Gods that the muddied earth didn't slide out from under her horse's hooves as she spurred her onward. The rest of her comrades were right on her tail, having slogged the ride into two unending days. Glimpses of the crew following Bri and Talhan appeared at spots along the trail, slowly gaining on them as the Twin Eagles struggled to navigate the foreign terrain. Every hill she crested, Bri would spot her comrades in the valley behind, spurning on their stubborn horses to catch up. She had hoped around every bend that they would overtake Lina on her journey home, but, as the days stretched on, they found no royal caravan and Bri began to fear for the worst.

Blinking against the downpour, she mopped her wet hair from her face. Only the bright streaks of lightning illuminated the city before them. Another flash and then the rolling boom of thunder. Swifthill sat in heavy darkness up ahead, the domed roofs morphed into cascading waterfalls as the gutters filled with rain. No lights flickered; the windows were closed and curtains were drawn against the storm.

The others behind her struggled to control their horses, but Bri's

315

horse kept going. Patting the mare's neck in exhausted gratitude, she decided then and there that she would buy this horse from its owner if they survived.

The gate to the city was closed, the giant iron grate blocking the path. Slowing her horse to a halt, Bri peered through the rain.

"Hello?" she shouted, trying to find a guard manning their post but seeing none. Dread turned her stomach to acid. Where were the guards? Sheltering from the storm? "HELLO?"

The onslaught of rain lessened to a drizzle and then fell harder again as the storm clouds blustered over them.

"We hear you, Catullus," a muffled voice called as a masked figure stepped out from behind the wall.

Terror seized her as she stared at the masked lion's face. "Let us in."

The rain eased so that she could hear him chuckle. "No."

"Where are the guards?"

"You think we killed them?" He laughed again, his shoulders shaking. "We didn't kill the guards, Catullus; we *are* the guards. It's not only the palace that keeps personal soldiers."

Her mind racing, she prayed that Lina was still alive as she heard the rest of the horses clomping toward her. The whizz of rushing air sounded beside her right ear and the masked soldier went down. The crimson fletching of an arrow protruded from his throat, the arrow having shot almost straight through him.

"Gods," Bri cursed, glancing over at Remy. "How did you make that shot through the grate in the rain?"

Remy shrugged as Hale smirked at her. "Practice."

"Now how are we going to get in?" Talhan called from behind them.

Rua led her horse to the sandstone wall. She lifted her feet out of the stirrups and crouched atop the saddle.

"Rua!" Renwick warned her, but it was too late.

She leapt, clinging to the craggy sandstone. Her boot slipped and they all flinched, but her fingers clung to the rocky outcropping. She scuttled like a spider up to the parapets, unsheathing the Immortal

Blade as her boots landed on the solid stone. There was not a single cry, only the muted thump of bodies hitting the ground.

Renwick dismounted his horse, hustling to the gate and waiting there with his hand on the hilt of his sword. He blinked back the rain, his eyes scanning wildly for Rua. With a creaking groan, the iron gate lifted, higher and higher. It halted halfway to the towering arch above, and Rua stepped out from behind the wall, wiping strands of wet hair off her face. When she rounded the corner, her smile faltered as she met Renwick's furious gaze. Bri braced for the lecture Rua was about to receive, but instead Renwick grabbed her and pulled her into a fierce kiss.

Talhan snorted, looking at Hale. "I don't know which of the two of you is worse."

Breaking their kiss, Renwick held Rua against him, his voice a low rumble of relief as he said, "Stop. Doing. That."

Remy shook her head, and, reaching out with her red witch magic, she lifted the gate the rest of the way. Her eyes flickered a brilliant red as her flaming hand lifted into the air.

Rua grinned wickedly at her sister, the look telling them all she knew she could have used her red witch magic too, but instead chose to scale the wall. Hale had a witty retort ready but it died on the wind. Bri was already moving, navigating her horse under the gap. They could laugh about their victory once they'd claimed it.

Bri raced her tired horse forward, and the rest followed, skirting the outer edges of the city and onto the narrow road to the castle.

As the group neared the stables, Bri's gasp caught in her throat. Dozens of saddled horses sheltered under the awnings as masked soldiers guarded the stable door.

Shit. They were already here.

"We will battle our way in through the front," Carys called to Bri. "You and Tal go around and find Lina."

Bri could barely hear her over the roaring of blood in her ears. She turned to her twin, tipping her head. "This way."

She dropped from her horse, letting it bolt off into the gardens. She landed in a crouch and stood, her brother repeating the action a moment after her.

A shout rang out up ahead as the rest of their group barreled into the stables, distracting the guards. Rua and Renwick raced up behind the others, the Immortal Blade still in Rua's grip. They would be okay, Bri told herself, even as she pushed her legs to the point of burning. She and Talhan ran around the outer walls, winding through the shadowed gardens, concealed by the heavy mist left in the storm's wake. Panting, they reached the furthest tower, the top branches of a tree bursting from the dome.

"Here," she breathed as shouts rang out from the stables. The battle was beginning and she had to get to Lina quickly.

The high arched windows of the Queen's chamber flickered with soft firelight. There. Bri knew Lina would have pushed to be crowned immediately upon her return. She'd be in that room . . . if she was still alive.

Craning his neck up to the towering window, Talhan cursed. "We really have to climb that?" He whined as if he were being asked to finish his greens. "We could go up through the interior."

"It will be barricaded with guards at every corner," Bri said, already climbing over the bottom balcony. "This is faster." She looked up again, sizing up the climb. "It's balcony, window, balcony, ledge, window, and then that nick in the stone to climb into the archway."

"A nick in the fucking stone," Talhan grumbled, even as he climbed. "I wish you and I were still fighting."

"No you don't." Bri grunted as she hoisted herself up to the second-story window ledge.

"No I don't," Talhan echoed, moving with a litheness that belied his lumbering frame.

Bri gripped the rain-slicked stone so tightly her fingertips bled. As one boot slipped out from under her, she placed the toe of her other foot into the nick in the stone and leapt. Her thighs burned as she sprung from the stone and her fingers gripped the highest window ledge. She got one hand over, using that purchase to lock her elbow over the sill. Rolling, she swung her leg over and tumbled unceremoniously through the window, crashing into the frame.

Glass shattered around her as she tumbled forward. Grabbing her dagger, she bolted to her feet. Five wide-eyed faces gaped at her.

"Bri?" Lina gasped.

Relief flooded through Bri at the sound of Lina's voice, so potent she thought her stomach might rebel. Lina sat on her bronze throne, her battle-axe resting against the arm and the hollow eyes of the ram skull staring out over the room.

Her braids were gone, her hair now a billowy halo of tight black curls. She wore a flowing golden gown and beaded ceremonial chest plate. Beside her, on a pedestal, sat a gold and bronze crown. Its needle-like spikes glinted in the dimmed light.

"Thank the Gods you're here," Delta growled. "Though you should have been here *with* Lina, not after her."

She stood in front of Saika, her thin sword gripped tightly in her hand. Across the room, Darrow and Tem had their weapons drawn too, guarding the locked door. They all jolted as something collided with the doorframe. Fists pounded and the wood groaned.

"They attacked hours ago," Delta continued, briefing Bri as if she were a soldier under her command. "At least fifty of them. We fell back to the royal chambers, but it won't be long until they breach this door."

"Do they have witch magic with them?" Bri asked, scanning Delta up and down. She stood rod straight, a soldier ready for battle, but Bri didn't know how well she'd hold herself in this fight, having only recently recovered from her surgery.

Delta shook her head. "Not that we've seen."

Even without magic to contend with, fifty fae soldiers were too many to handle on their own. Where were the castle guards? Why hadn't they been prepared for this ambush? Had they known their attackers? They needed to buy time until Bri's other friends reached the door.

"Shit," Talhan muttered as he fell across the broken glass. In her panic, Bri had forgotten he was behind her. "Thanks for the help."

Waving him off, Bri held her gaze on Lina's. "Rua's here. We've got the Immortal Blade now."

Lina's eyes stormed in a swirl of emotions that made the rest of the room pause. Bri didn't know if Lina heard a word she'd said. She opened her mouth, eager to say the words rolling through her mind, but Delta spoke.

"They attacked the guards from all sides. So many masks . . ." Delta glanced sideways at Bri, guilt on her face. "We left them out there to fight off the attackers."

"We were preparing to die." Darrow's throat bobbed, his voice quavering. "I don't understand it."

"But now we are saved." Tem's voice was barely a whisper as he peered across the room to Lina. "We should crown you at once, Your Highness. Let this be your first victory as Queen."

Something in the way he said it made Bri look at him twice, and her heart plummeted to her feet. Bile rose in her throat as she eyed the purple flower in Tem's breast pocket.

Blooming amethyst.

"You," she breathed, her limbs filling with fire as the shock blanketed her skin.

"What?" Tem's brow furrowed.

"It was you," Bri whispered, taking a shaking step forward as he retreated toward the door. Her mind raced. "I should have known it was you."

"What was me? I don't know what you're talking about." Tem sheathed his blade and lifted his hands out to her as if trying to hush a skittish horse.

"Why is that flower in your pocket?" Possessed, she stepped forward again as her mind whirred. "It's the same flower that you gifted Delta when she was recovering. . . ."

"Bri, what are you doing?" Lina rose from her throne, her brows knitting together.

"And what of it?" Tem asked, looking to the others like Bri had lost her mind.

"The flower is called blooming amethyst and is used in violet witch magic. It only grows on the banks of the Crushwold River . . . or at least it used to." Her voice dropped an octave as she prowled forward. "The soldier we caught had a packet of its seeds on his person." *To sow the seeds of rebellion.*

"I don't know what any of that has to do with me liking a flower," Tem scoffed.

"Where did you get the flowers?" Bri cocked her head. "I didn't see them growing in the gardens." Her eyes dipped down to his neck. "And what about your necklace?"

He narrowed his eyes. "My necklace?"

"Lina thought that soldier had stolen it from you, but it was his own necklace, wasn't it? Do you all have one? Just in case you need to take your own life?" Bri felt Talhan shift closer to her side. Lina gaped between her and Tem as Bri spoke. "His necklace was so scuffed, I couldn't make out the symbols as clearly as yours. It's not a wolf paw at all, is it? It's a lion paw." She cocked her head. "The guards at the gate said the royals aren't the only ones to keep guards. . . . Delta, do any other families in Swifthill have their own guards?"

"Only the Wystrons," Delta hissed.

Bri kept her eyes glued to Tem's horrified face. "Why do you have a lion paw necklace, the same as the assassins wear, and bouquets of the same rare flower that was used to murder your Queen?"

Tem held his hands up higher as Bri took another step. "I-I—" He paused, blinking at her as the room hung in frozen silence.

Then he smiled.

Slowly clapping his hands together in mock applause, he said, "Well done, you." His chuckle was low and sinister, his innocent mask contorting into a crooked grin. "I honestly didn't think you would figure it out. Too love drunk to see what was right in front of you."

Darrow stepped toward his son. "Tem, what—"

"Silence," Tem snapped at his father as his eyes filled with wrath. "You were too weak to do what was necessary, Father. *I* will usher in a new dawn for this kingdom." Lina's eyes widened in horror as he took another step backward, reaching for the door handle. "As the Queen's consort, I will rule the Western Court . . . once you all are dead."

"No!" Delta shouted, but it was too late.

The lock flipped and a swarm of soldiers erupted into the room.

CHAPTER FORTY-TWO

With a curse, Bri darted forward, slicing and hacking her way toward Lina as the masked soldiers crowded the room. In a heartbeat, Lina grabbed her axe, her arms bulging as she choked up on the grip.

"The others will be here any minute; we just have to stay alive until they reach us." Bri shouted to be heard over the clang of swords. Widening her stance, the wall of soldiers collided into them. "No heroics."

Lina was as fast as an asp, lifting her axe and dropping it at an angle as though chopping wood. Blood sprayed as she whirled, the other side of her double axe colliding with an attacker's knee. His leg cracked, the knee bending at a horrific angle, but she didn't stop. One after another, she hacked away at them like they were wheat to a scythe. Bri wanted to stop and watch her glorious tirade, but too many more were pouring in through the door.

Talhan navigated toward the wall, guarding his back as he took on five soldiers at once. Dozens swept into the room and Bri lost sight of him.

She ducked under a wide punch, her dagger coming up between her attacker's ribs. Bri took a half step back, kicking him into the next attacker behind him. A rogue sword swung at her, knocking her dagger out of her hands, but she swiftly grabbed another from her belt. She cursed herself, realizing she hadn't put her knife in her boot in her haste to depart. This dagger was her last weapon; the drying blood made her hand stick to the hilt.

The floor was slick with gore, the stench of blood and bile filling the hot room as the crush of bodies made the fighting more frantic. She could just make out Delta's head beside Talhan. Saika cowered behind them weaponless, her whole body trembling from head to toe. Bri glanced sideways at Lina, dancing around her attackers and pushing some out as she pulled others in. Complete control and power. Never would Lina cower behind her, and never would she ask Lina to. They could ride off into any battle side by side. Watching the Princess swing her axe, Bri knew here was exactly where she was meant to be—not in the East, but fighting by Lina's side.

With the barricades of the dead and wounded, it was easier to control the number of assailants attacking at once. The room thinned as more and more bodies went down. Clusters of fighting broke out, fractioning off from the giant melee.

"Look out!" Lina shouted, and Bri whirled just in time to block Tem's blade.

The courtier's face was scrunched into a look of rage. He stabbed at her again. "You," he seethed. "You Eagles ruin everything."

"You planned to play the mourning widower, didn't you?" Bri blocked his next blow, surprised by his strength. "Too bad your ruse was discovered."

"Not yet," he said, slashing at her side but only nicking the fabric.

He laughed as Bri stumbled backward, feigning a misstep that made him lower his guard. She lunged forward, and he narrowly missed her strike.

"If I'm the lone survivor when your friends arrive, they'll never know." He ducked under her swing. "They'll find me crying and heartbroken and give me my crown. The West will still be mine."

He was reckless but skilled, attacking with the desperation of someone knowing that they had to win. He faked a kick and Bri bent to drop out of striking distance, just as his fist collided with her jaw.

Spots flashed in her vision as blood filled her mouth. Instinctively ducking, she narrowly avoided the killing blow, feeling the blade sweep across her hair.

"Bri!" Lina screamed, hacking her way toward Bri, but another two soldiers got in between them, redirecting her attention.

Slashing blindly, Bri landed her dagger down on Tem's forearm. He yelped out a pained cry as his leg smashed into her calf. Bri fell onto one knee as his shin collided with her ear. Her dagger dropped from her grip, scattering across the floor, and she lifted her arms, bracing for the strike.

Grinning, Tem lifted his sword. A blade slashed across his bicep and he turned to find Darrow holding up the sanguine sword. He lifted the tip and pointed it at Tem.

Tem gave Bri a kick in the guts, knocking the air out of her before turning to his father. "You would kill your own son?"

Bri dragged herself across the floor toward her dagger as Darrow replied, "If I must."

"I knew I couldn't bring you into these plans." Tem scowled. "You were always too soft-hearted when it came to the Queen. I knew you would never come to the winning side."

Bri's fingers reached for the hilt, moving slowly so as to not draw Tem's attention, but the dagger was still too far from her grasp.

"You have lost, Tem," Darrow hissed. "How many fools from our household did you needlessly bring into this battle? The powers of the Northern and High Mountain Court are at our doorstep now."

"As our enemy, not as our ally." Tem tapped his blade in a taunting gesture along Darrow's sword. "Augustus Norwood is the future of Okrith. All will bow to him."

"How many long nights did you fret to me that the West was alone in this world?" Darrow's brows dropped heavy over his eyes as he lowered his sword. "Did you really think Norwood would let you rule this Court? You swore your sword to Queen Thorne. The Gods will remember that. Put your blade down, Tem. You don't need to die."

"Don't speak to me as if I'm a child," he spat.

"You're not a child." Darrow shook his head. "You're a coward and a fool. Now, put your sword down."

Screams echoed from down the hallway; the others were nearly there. Darrow turned toward the sound, a fatal decision as Tem took one swift step and impaled his father through the chest. Darrow's eyes bugged, betrayal filling his wide gaze as he stared at his son. Rivulets of crimson blood dripped from his gaping lips, and he coughed a spluttering, wet breath.

"The Gods will remember this too," Darrow whispered, dropping to his knees.

Twisting onto all fours, Bri clambered forward, grabbing the dagger. The whoosh of a sword sounded beside her and she rolled, narrowly avoiding the strike as Tem's steel clanged against stone. Pivoting in toward his body, she sliced out, stabbing into his thigh. He gasped and stumbled backward. Blood spurted from the wound, pouring down his leg faster than she'd ever seen a body bleed out, and she knew it was a fatal blow. The copper mist rained down from his thigh as he retreated, pressing a trembling hand to his leg to stanch the bleeding.

Bri scrambled back to her feet with a groan, watching Tem's bloodless face as he tripped back against the wall and slid to a seat on the wet stone. He collapsed beside his father's lifeless body. Bri knew that vacant look all too well. He was already one foot into the afterlife.

She turned just in time to see Lina delivering a killing blow to one soldier as another slammed the hilt of his sword into her wrist. Lina growled, her axe clattering to the floor as she clutched her arm. Retreating a step, she scanned for a weapon she could wield with one hand. Her eyes landed on the amethyst dagger set on the arm of her throne but it was too far away.

Taking another step back from the advancing soldier, Lina bumped into the pedestal where her crown sat. In desperation, she whirled, grabbing the bronze crown and swinging it. Its deadly spikes stabbed into her attacker's arm. Bri gaped at the viciousness of the clawed weapon as Lina pulled back and swung the crown again, piercing it into the soldier's neck. Blood bubbled as he clutched the weeping wound and he fell to his knees.

"My duty is done," a shaking voice sounded from behind Bri.

She spun, finding Tem's pallid face. He held the purple flower from his jacket pocket, twirling the bruised stem in his bloodied hands.

Bri's brow furrowed. "What?"

He lifted the flower and sniffed it, his eyes rolling back for a moment before he blinked and then stared at her again. A soft grin covered his face, one so familiar. The kindest fae, that's what she had thought he was, a lovesick puppy, harmless. He rested his head back against the stone wall. As he breathed in the sweet-scented flower once more, his eyes flitted past Bri and he said, "I won."

Bri followed the direction of his gaze to where Lina stood, holding the crown in her good hand, waiting for the last attacker to approach.

When Bri spotted it, her heart stopped—the soapy film along the inner rim of the crown, easily misinterpreted as being dulled from wear. The same sheen as on the cutlery in Cole's office and the blade of the scout in Silver Sands. Her heart leapt into her throat as she screamed, darting forward.

Lina's pupils dilated until the dark brown of her irises disappeared. Her face was vacant, utterly hollow apart from her pinched brows. Bri vaulted over the piles of dead bodies, dashing to Lina and seizing the crown from her grasp. The crown clattered across the floor, the sound too loud in the now quiet room.

Lina's legs crumpled under her as Bri darted out, grabbing her just before she fell. The tiles were too slick and Bri's boots slipped so she landed with her legs stretched out and Lina's head cushioned against her thigh.

She held her trembling, bloody hands to Lina's cheeks. "Lina." Her voice cracked, watching those dark pupils scanning the ceiling as if the Gods were beckoning her skyward.

Lina's eyes flitted to Bri's face. "You came after me," she whispered, the pained sound shredding Bri in two.

"I never should have let you go." Bri's eyes welled as she nodded. "I'm sorry. I'm so sorry, Lina. I should have fought for us. I was too much of a coward to tell you." Her bloodied thumbs swept crimson streaks across Lina's cheeks. "I love you."

"But the East?" A trickle of black blood trailed from Lina's ear and her lips parted on a gasp.

Scrunching her face, Bri swallowed, trying to stop the tears as she gritted out, "Forget the East."

"I thought you wanted to be the master of your own Fate," Lina murmured.

"I am." Her hands bracketed Lina's face as she bent and kissed her. A soft, slow kiss—the one she'd been too afraid to do the first time Lina fell asleep in Bri's lap. When she pulled back, Lina's eyes were glimmering too, the clash of joy and sorrow so potent Bri could feel it hanging in the air between them.

Bri spoke the truth that flowed through her: "I don't care what the Fates whisper; all I hear is your name."

A tear slid down the side of Lina's face as her lips pulled up. Her voice trembled as she whispered, "Hold my hand."

The pleading fear in her voice stabbed through Bri as she grabbed Lina's hand and squeezed it. Lina blinked and another tear fell, this one a shocking crimson red.

"Hang on, Lina," Bri's voice broke, tears spilling down her cheeks. "You are fierce, my dragon. Fight it."

Lina's eyes fluttered shut and Bri squeezed her hand tighter.

"We will find a way to fix you, Lina, just, please, hang on." Bri wept, uncaring if they all witnessed her tears. No one mattered in that moment except the Princess whose hand she held.

Lina's breathing slowed. "I don't know if I can."

"You can. You must," Bri sobbed, shaking Lina to try to rouse her. She bent and brushed another salty kiss to her lips, tasting the metallic tang of blood. "I'm going to hold you every night until you drift off to sleep in my arms." Another tear slid down her cheek as she promised the future she saw every time she closed her eyes. "You're going to marry me. We'll plant the seeds of our children in this castle and watch them grow until they crack through the roof. We'll be a family, Lina, just please, Gods, hang on."

Lina took a shuddering breath. Her eyes strained open as she wiped away Bri's tear. "I would deny the Goddess of Death herself, Bri, if it would ease your pain."

The tears slipped heavier from Bri's eyes as she watched Lina battle to stay awake, hanging on for Bri and not for herself. The sound of rushing footsteps pounded into the room.

"We found someone." It was the biting voice of Renwick.

Craning her neck, Bri saw that he held an elderly woman by the neckline of her dress. He shoved her into the room, the totem bag around her neck bouncing against her chest.

Remy, Hale, and Carys marched through the doorway, Rua taking up the rear and holding the Immortal Blade tight in her grip. Her eyes were clear and she held her chin high. In only a matter of minutes, the rest of the group had made it to the room, but still it was too late.

"Who are you?" Talhan asked the woman, stepping over a body to reach her.

The witch's gray hair hung over her eyes as she peered up at him with a leering, crazed smile. Puffing up her chest, she lifted her hands skyward. "You know who I am," she snarled as deep violet flames circled her fingertips. Her glowing eyes turned an eerie shade of purple. "You've been reading my journal."

CHAPTER FORTY-THREE

"Baba Monroe," Talhan whispered.

The High Priestess of the violet witches lifted her chin at the name. The whole room remained frozen, the echoes of battle still strumming through the charged air.

"The journal of Adisa Monroe was from hundreds of years ago," Carys said, stepping further into the circle.

"Yes," the witch said, her sharp eyes looking sideways at Carys. She had a nasally, age-addled voice, wrinkles around her pinched mouth, and wiry, unkempt gray hair, but her expression was formidable, even in a room of highly trained fae.

"You really did it, then?" Carys asked. "You found a way to live forever?"

"Not forever," she muttered bitterly, glancing at the *Shil-de* ring on Hale's finger. "Witch magic has always blurred the lines of life and death. The High Priestesses who came before me were too afraid to push our magic like our ancestors had. They were simpering, weak things who would rather make pretty smelling candles and braid flowers into their hair than conjure curses and grow their powers." Her lip curled as she leered around the room. "Look what that cowardice did to my coven."

Talhan took a step forward. The witch didn't cower or even blink at the move. "If you have lived for centuries, why return now?"

"Magic is not an endless well. I took my time." The way she said it made it clear she was leaving something out. There were reasons beyond biding her time that prevented her from resurrecting her coven. Her eyes scanned the space, searching for something. "I regained my power over the centuries and planted the seeds of a violet witch rebellion."

" 'To sow the seeds of rebellion,' " Carys muttered the words written on the seed packet found in the traitor's bag. "All of this is your doing? You and Norwood."

The witch's face split into a wicked grin. "The young Prince Norwood's ambitions will reestablish our home court as the power it should have always been. He was wise to accept my aid." She glanced at Rua and then Remy. "Wiser than your brother."

They all rocked backward, as if that revelation had caused a wave of magic to push them over.

"You knew Raffiel?" Remy asked, her chest rising and falling sharply.

"No," Baba Monroe said with a sneer. "But I received his message loud and clear."

"What message?" Rua's hand drifted to the Immortal Blade. "What does that mean?"

Lina's shuddering breath interrupted the witch's diatribe. There was no time to hear her deranged stories, not when Lina was barely breathing.

"Did you create this poison?" Bri growled, pulling everyone's attention to her.

The witch turned her violet glare toward Bri, a smile twisting her pale lips. "I did." She spoke with such unnerving pride. "A terrible way to go. What my soldiers get is far more concentrated, only seconds to end them." Her eyes dropped to Lina. "They don't spend their last hours in agony, frantically screaming for a way to reverse it, unlike my enemies."

Bri's throat constricted. "And can you reverse it?"

The witch flashed a feral smile. "I can."

Bri's eyes guttered, a painful flicker of hope sparking within her.

"Do it, then," Bri commanded, absently stroking her thumb down Lina's cheek as the Princess stared vacantly toward the sky again. The blood on her thumbs mixed with the metallic paint on Lina's cheekbones, making a swirl of sparkling constellations down her face.

"I will need my dagger." The witch scanned the room again, her eyes landing on the amethyst blade resting on Lina's throne. "And a blood promise that you will let me leave unharmed and unfollowed if I save her."

Rua stepped forward before the witch's words even finished, gripping the Immortal Blade in her hand and tugging. She sliced across her palm, blood welling as Renwick gritted his teeth. She held out her bleeding hand to the witch.

Baba Monroe shook Rua's hand with a mirthless smile. She turned to Bri, expectantly lifting her eyebrows. "My dagger?"

Lina's eyes rolled back, her breathing jagged, as she let out a heartbreaking cry. Bri's hands gripped her tighter, the sounds of Lina's agony making more hot tears stream down her cheeks. Hale rushed to the throne and pulled the dagger from its sheath.

Holding out her palm coated in Rua's blood, the witch took the amethyst blade from him. As her hand touched the purple stones, her magic flared and her eyes glowed an unsettling shade of mauve. She sighed as if the magic stones soothed something within her. Steadying her breath, she looked down at Lina.

Baba Monroe loosened the purse strings of her totem bag and reached inside, retrieving a dried flower petal. Looming over Bri and Lina, she screwed her eyes shut, muttering the Mhenbic words of a spell long forgotten to all but her. She held out her fist, crushing the petal in her hand as she continued her muttering, and with a final word, she released it. Fragments of shredded flower danced down like falling autumnal leaves, and tiny skitters of violet lighting strobed across the particles.

As the powder brushed across Lina's face, she gasped and snapped upright.

The dam broke in Bri once more and she sobbed, watching the life return to Lina's face. She yanked Lina into a tight embrace as she buried her head into Lina's shoulder.

She watched from their fierce hold as the witch turned and made her way past the cautious crew.

Talhan stepped to block her exit and Rua doubled over, clenching her stomach. The witch grinned as Remy hastily jerked Talhan out of the way.

"Let her go," she hissed. "We can kill her another day when Rua won't pay the price."

"Wise, Your Majesty," the witch sang, ambling forward with a casual grace as if she knew she would go unharmed. She glanced over her shoulder, her eyes looking to each of them before landing back on Bri. "Think to your choices, rulers of Okrith," she said with a predatory slowness. "Yield to the East or we shall see you on the battlefield."

She spoke the words as if casting a spell, a promise that she was certain would be fulfilled. Looking around the room, her eyes shifted from Bri to Remy and then settled on Hale. The violet magic flared in her eyes as she stared at him. "Tell the rest of my grandchildren it's time to come home."

Hale's brows pinched in confusion as she grinned at them one last time and left, sauntering down the hall with the easy air of victory.

CHAPTER FORTY-FOUR

The friends sat on the western steps of the palace, watching the sunrise together as they ate and drank. It didn't feel right to sit at a grand table. They needed the feeling of the solid ground below them and the steady reverence of the wilderness waking for the day. Birds twittered and rustled from the trees, singing their morning songs.

Talhan split open a steamy cinnamon loaf and passed out the pieces. The kitchen staff had spoiled them with food, showering their gratitude upon the group with their decadent breakfast. By hiding in cabinets and barring themselves in rooms, fewer of the palace staff had lost their lives than Bri had expected, but the carnage was still horrific.

Most of the guards were dead or gravely wounded. Baba Omly had rushed over in the night, along with a host of brown witches. Renwick had called upon his own brown witch healer and Remy to Fenrin to come to the Western Court and aid the recovery efforts. The brown witches continued to tend the wounded even as the others sat and ate.

Bri reached down and threaded her fingers through Lina's as she laid her head on Lina's shoulder. It felt wrong to rest after such a night. Baba Omly had gently but firmly shooed them away. Bodies were being wrapped and shrouds hung across the windows again; there'd been only the barest reprieve before the castle was plunged back into mourning.

They sat in silence, not a single word passing between them, until the stench of the drying blood on their clothes made them rise and go bathe. Bri wished the feeling wasn't so familiar to her—the boneless shock of near death. They all drifted like ghosts through the palace, their minds still reliving the horrors of what had just happened as they bathed and changed their clothes. It felt like too common an action to Bri—washing, dressing, brushing her hair—after she'd just taken so many lives.

She was still washing blood from her skin when Talhan arrived at Lina's chambers to bid them farewell.

"I wish you could stay for the funerals," Bri said into her twin's shoulder. "But I know you need to head south."

Talhan looked at her, his cheeks dimpling as he nodded. They hadn't spoken about what had transpired between him and Neelo when he chased after the Heir of Saxbridge the night of the ball . . . but Bri had her suspicions and she wasn't going to push him.

"Who'd have thought." He grinned, shaking his head. "If Mother had known, I think you'd have received a lot less of her energy."

"We could have split her meddling between the two of us." Bri chuckled, the smile dying on her face as she looked to the window covered in a black shroud.

"I'll keep an eye out for Norwood," Talhan said. "I'll let you know if we catch sight of his fleet."

"And Cole." Bri frowned. "Even if he's not directly serving Baba Monroe, he knows more than he's telling us. Keep an eye out for him as well. His trail went into the foothills of the High Mountains, but who knows where he went from there."

"Probably East to reunite with his grandmother."

"Maybe." Bri shifted, staring at the ceiling. "Maybe we should move the competition for the Eastern crown sooner."

"Carys's odds have just vastly improved with you in the West and me in the South," Talhan said, adjusting the shoulder straps of his pack.

Bri narrowed her eyes at him. "Do you think you'll do it? Marry Neelo?"

Talhan shrugged as if it weren't a life-changing question. "Depends on them."

"Just don't pull a Rua and get married without me," Bri said with a smirk.

Talhan shook his head, giving her one last hug, and she felt the small tug on her jacket pocket. "Never. You have to be there standing beside me." He pulled back and looked her in the eyes, giving her a knowing nod as she felt the outline of the object in her pocket. "Bring me mine when it's time."

Before Bri could reply, the door to the atrium opened and Lina strode in, her eyes softening at the two of them.

"I will," Bri whispered, looking Lina up and down. Her eyes were still puffy with tears.

Lina walked right up to Talhan and hugged him. "I'm sorry we couldn't get to know each other under better circumstances," she said. "But I look forward to making up for lost time in the future, Talhan Catullus."

"As do I," he said with a cheeky smile. Releasing her, he stepped back and looked between the two of them. "Take care of my sister."

Lina bowed her head. "I will."

He gave Bri a wink and left. It was bittersweet watching him walk away. She was excited for him, for the future he was heading toward, but was also sad they'd be apart again.

Lina's arm slipped around Bri's waist. "When the realm is at peace, we'll see each other often—Solstices and Equinoxes, weddings and birthdays . . ." She pulled Bri's hip into her side, molding into her curves like the piece of a puzzle. "We'll visit so often, we'll all be sick of each other."

Bri's lips tugged at the sides, her arm wrapping around Lina's shoulders as she guided her to the bench seat and they looked up at Lina's tree. They sat in the same spot as they had many nights ago, when Lina poured her heart out and grieved her mother, after which they had slept side by side for the first time. This space would forever be sacred to Bri, as would the Queen beside her—a place where they could be real and raw and vulnerable, where they could be brave enough to whisper their truths and shed their tears.

"When I was dying," Lina whispered, and Bri's fingers constricted on her arm. The words were like a punch to the gut. "Everything felt muted, the sounds around me jumbled . . . I don't know if the things you said to me were real or imagined."

Bri reached into her pocket, the small object burning a hole in her side since Talhan's hug, and she knew exactly what it would be.

"It was real," Bri said as she produced a gold ring, a halo of diamonds circling the band. Lina gasped, looking down at it and then back up to Bri.

"Sometimes I imagined it—being loved," Bri said, fiddling with the ring in her hand. "So vividly in my head, that feeling of being held, being home in someone's arms. Someone I loved unconditionally, who I'd do the hardest things for, harder than waging battles or fighting off beasts. Real things. Like owning up to my mistakes and admitting I was wrong." She looked into Lina's welling eyes and the sight made hers pinprick with tears. "Saying how deeply sorry I am for causing you pain."

Lina placed her hand on Bri's cheek.

"I meant everything I said last night," she whispered, choking back the tears as the memory of Lina's vacant eyes flashed in her mind. "I only want you. I want you to know the same peace I feel every time you lie down beside me. I want you to feel as loved as you make me feel. I don't know what spells the Fates weave, but sometimes our choices are stronger than any magic, and I choose you, Lina. Always."

"Always," Lina whispered as a tear slid down her cheek. Bri got down on one knee, holding the ring aloft. "I don't know if I'm allowed to propose to a Queen," she said with a smirk, "but I'm going to risk it." Lina chuckled, beaming down at her from where she knelt. "Will you marry me?" Bri bit the corner of her lip, nervous after all that had happened that maybe Lina would still say no.

Lina waited a beat, her smile as radiant as the rising sun. "Yes."

Bri leapt up, her hands cupping Lina's face as she pulled Lina's lips to hers. "I love you," she whispered, tears of joy and relief streaking down her cheeks.

"I love you too," Lina said, her lips meeting Bri's again.

Emotions brimmed over, filling her until she was bursting as she slid the ring onto Lina's finger. She wiggled it over Lina's knuckle, relieved when it was the perfect fit.

"Thank the Gods." She chuckled.

"*When* did you have time to buy a ring?" Lina asked, beaming down at her hand as she twisted the band from side to side.

"I bought this ring when I was twelve years old," Bri murmured. "Talhan's been hanging on to it for me. We agreed if we were to ever get married, we wouldn't use any of our family's heirlooms, that we'd make our own legacies."

A smile twisted on Lina's lips. "It's beautiful."

"You should see the one he picked."

"I can already imagine." Lina smiled, wiping the tears from Bri's cheeks, the tenderness of the action immediately making more fall.

"I don't think I've ever cried this much in my life," Bri said with a sheepish chuckle. "With your every word and action, you hold the strings to my heart."

Lina kissed Bri's cheek and then the shell of her ear, whispering, "As do you, my Queen."

CHAPTER FORTY-FIVE

Lina's sob cut through the silence as the pyres burned all along
the cliffside. Bri held onto her tighter at the sound of her cries,
circling a hand slowly around Lina's back as she purged the
pain from her soul. It was what Bri wished she could have done the day
of the Queen's funeral.

Dozens of pyres lit the evening sky and the clouds turned burnt
orange as smoke filled the air. The people of the city had all come. Hundreds gathered in the clearing, thousands more along the land bridge
leading toward the palace. Black pennants bobbed through the crowds
like a sea of onyx waves. Burial songs erupted unprompted and prayers
were shouted to the sky. Keening wails echoed from the far-off parapets of the city walls.

"How did we get to this place?" Lina whispered as she stared at Darrow's funeral pyre. "How long will it take for the West to feel like one
kingdom united again?"

"As long as it takes," Bri murmured back, squeezing Lina's shoulder.
"Bit by bit until one day, you realize you're no longer asking yourself
that question."

Lina hung her head.

All—ally and enemy—were burned then laid to rest. Delta had

wanted to hang Tem from the castle walls, to let the vultures have him, but Lina refused. Delta and her loyal guards had stamped out the threat in Swifthill, scourging the last of Tem's comrades from the city in a matter of hours. As soon as his companions had heard Tem was gone, they knew the jig was up. Some surrendered, some fled, others used their poison necklaces rather than face the shame of what they'd done. Lina was wise, knowing that the residents of Swifthill grieved for what had happened. How many of them had lost a loved one? Whether the dead had been protecting Lina or trying to destroy her didn't matter to the families who mourned. Bringing the city back from this trauma was an impossible task, but if anyone could do it, Lina Thorne could.

A tear slid down Bri's cheek as she stroked Lina's back. Bri would hold Lina up when she was breaking, and she knew Lina would do the same for her. That is who they were to each other. Together they would always be beautifully vulnerable and equally strong, carrying the other when one was hurting. They were shining souls already, but together they chose to be incandescent, that choice more powerful than any the Fates could conjure.

Bri caught sight of someone in the crowd and whispered, "Look."

Lina lifted her head, following Bri's line of sight and landing on a woman rocking side to side rhythmically, a baby wrapped to her chest. Lina sniffed as she spotted Nelle standing amongst a band of brown witches, all dressed in their ceremonial brown robes, their totem pouches hanging from their necks. Nelle noted their eyes on her and bowed, giving a soft, warm smile. She seemed confident, at ease, not as tightly coiled as when they had last seen her. With a mob of witches at her back, she looked like she could take on the world.

Lina adjusted the crown on her head—a new crown made for her of dented bronze and gold.

"I like this one better," Bri softly teased. "I'd always be worried that you'd impale me with the other."

Lina huffed, giving Bri a begrudging smirk. "I'm sure I could do it with this one too if I tried hard enough."

Bri pressed her lips together to keep from smiling. It felt like laughter should be the opposite of tears, but the rawness of both bubbled to the surface in times like these. It was unexpected and absurd to smile, but they'd survived. Gods, they'd survived.

"So the eagle seized the crown from its sovereign," Lina said from the corner of her mouth. "Would have been nice if the oracles had told us it was a poisoned crown."

"Bloody blue witches," Bri whispered.

They'd never found Cole, and Augustus Norwood's fleet still lingering near the coast of Silver Sands. At some point, he'd be forced to come to shore to restock his supplies, but who knew how many months he could survive circling Okrith before then. The games for the Eastern crown would draw him out. Soon all eyes would be turning to the East.

Bri's hand dropped from Lina's shoulder and she threaded her fingers through Lina's. "I wish I could curse the Fates, but since this twisting road led me here, I cannot hate them." She kissed the back of Lina's hand, her lips brushing against her soft skin. "The way I love you is a magic all its own, Fated or not, and its more than I dared to dream of."

"I love you too," Lina whispered. "More than I knew I ever could. You see me beyond my crown or name, beyond my wealth or power, just as I see you." She squeezed Bri's hand. "My mother was wrong about loving a person above her people. Everyone needs someone who loves them above all, who treats them like they painted the moon in the sky. That kind of love amplifies all others. If anything, I love my people more for it."

"Everything feels bigger now." Bri rubbed her thumb over the back of Lina's hand, playing with the gold band around her finger. "You and me."

"That sounds an awful lot like a vow," Lina said.

"It is." Bri's face softened as the crowds began to dwindle and the smoke thinned. "And you know how seriously I take my vows."

Pressing her own lips together Lina let her eyes drift down Bri's face to her lips. Bri knew Lina was fighting the urge to kiss her. Their eyes met again.

"You and me," Lina vowed.

Lina's eyes landed on one of her guards and she nodded to him, beckoning him over. As he approached, he took something off his belt and handed it to Lina.

"What's this?" Bri asked as Lina passed her the weapon. She turned over the hand axe, beautifully tied in bronze string, sharp jagged hooks at each of its curved edges. The handle was tipped in gold and the grip fit perfectly in her hand. Carved into the neck was the word *Airev*, metallic bronze filling the grooves of the letters.

"A gift," Lina said, smiling at Bri's astonished expression. "You have enough daggers. If you're going to be sticking around in the West, you need a proper Western axe."

Bri shook her head in disbelief at the beautiful weapon, already eager to practice with it in the training rings.

"It's perfect, thank you." Emotion filled her words as she looked into Lina's eyes. She slid the handle through her belt, enjoying the tugging weight that settled on her right hip.

"After the ceremony, we should go test it out," Lina murmured, her dimples belying her regal expression.

"Gods, I love you," Bri said, trying and failing to keep a broad smile from splitting her face.

She couldn't stop saying it—the words setting her free a little more each time. She loved Lina. She loved her endlessly and irrevocably. In this land of scorching sunlight, red earth, and orange sunsets, she'd finally found home.

ACKNOWLEDGMENTS

Thank you to all of my family for your love and support. To my husband, Glen, thank you for encouraging me and helping puzzle our days together to make this dream work for our family. Who knew we'd be here all those many years ago in Guatemala? To my amazing children—I hope you are always beautifully vulnerable and equally strong!

To my rock-star Mountaineers, thank you for being my biggest cheerleaders, celebrating my books, and encouraging so many people around the world to read them! You are the most incredible group of readers and I wish I could gift each and every one of you a battle-axe! ;)

To my amazing agent, Jessica Watterson, thank you for encouraging me and championing my stories! I am so grateful for you and all of your support. (Here's to many more excited 4 am messages in the future! Thank you for understanding me pre-coffee.)

Thank you to David Pomerico and the incredible team at Harper Voyager for taking on this series and believing in my stories. I'm honored to be among the amazing group of Voyager authors and I'm very excited for our future together!

Thank you to all of my amazing patrons! I love taking you on new adventures every month! A very special thank you to Krista M,

ACKNOWLEDGMENTS

Virginia P, Drea D, Tanja Æ, and Jordyn D! Your support means the world to me, and I greatly appreciate you!

Thank you to Salt & Sage, Aria J, Norma, Cat and my podcast wife, Kate, for helping make this book the best it could be!

To my Welly author friends, Anne, Moira, and Rachael, I am so grateful to have met you and share this journey with you! I cherish our friendship and every time after we get together I always feel on top of the world! Thank you for always being there for me on this wild ride!

And thank you to everyone who has gotten this far into the acknowledgements and hasn't judged me for my over-excessive use of exclamation points!!!

Thank you for reading Bri's story! The journey continues in *The Evergreen Heir,* The Five Crowns of Okrith Book Four. Turn the page for a sneak peek!

Don't miss any of the adventure—Read all of the Okrith Novellas for FREE by signing up to A.K. Mulford's newsletter!

www.akmulford.com

THE EVERGREEN HEIR

Neelo's fingers trembled as they traced down the spines of the old tomes. They took a steadying breath, and then another, letting the old book smell steady them.

They couldn't marry him.

It had happened so fast: their mother inciting another brawl to win the title of Neelo's betrothed, the instant, blundering chaos, and somehow Talhan Catullus getting pulled into the fray. The look on Talhan's face flashed through Neelo's mind again. When it was over, he'd just stared at them. Shocked, the cavalier smirk normally on his face wiped clean and something deeper, something that burned into Neelo, had filled Talhan's gaze instead.

Why did it have to be him? Of all the people Neelo could have easily dismissed . . . why did it have to be the Golden Eagle himself? He was one of the few people in Neelo's life who didn't make them feel like a weed amongst roses, and now their mother had ruined that for them.

Queen Emberspear's increasingly desperate bids to play matchmaker were growing weary already, but this time, she'd really messed up. Their mother had started pushing for Neelo's coronation the moment they came of age, and it had been a constant battle to convince the Queen to remain on her throne. They refused to allow her to give up so easily. It wasn't her time to go.

Neelo paused, fingers lingering on a title they'd never read before: *The Witch of Haastmouth*. A tingle shot through them as they selected the midnight blue book from the tall shelf, and flicked through the pages.

The momentary reprieve disappeared at the sound of the door opening.

They rushed down the stacks, hoping to disappear amongst the rows, but as they turned the corner, swift footsteps followed. They managed to climb up four steps of a rolling ladder before Talhan Catullus turned the corner and they froze.

"I knew I'd find you here." He smirked as his honeyed eyes landed upon them. Crossing his arms and leaning into the shelf, he asked, "Were you about to hide from me on top of that bookshelf?"

Neelo's voice dripped with sarcasm as they gave him a scornful look. "I was dusting."

Talhan's smile disappeared into something more contemplative, and Neelo's pulse began to race.

"Neelo," Talhan whispered, making their stomach clench at the sound of their name on his lips. "I—"

"She'll forget in the morning," Neelo cut him off. Bristling, they took a further step down the ladder and met Talhan's eyes. Those eyes . . . like pools of amber—the sun just after dawn.

Neelo hated that look in his eyes as his lips parted and he said, "Oh?"

"Don't worry. I'm not going to let her tie you to me like that," Neelo reassured him, gripping the rail of the ladder tighter. "I won't let her do that to you."

Talhan took another step closer, his hand perching on the shelf beside Neelo's waist. "And what if I want to be tied to you?"

Heart stuttering, they shook their head. "What you'd be getting yourself into . . . you don't understand what that means."

"Then show me what it means." His low gravelly voice made their toes curl in their boots. "What if I come visit Saxbridge? I could stay for the summer and—"

"In the heat?" Neelo scoffed. "You Easterners melt into a puddle in the Southern summer. It's the worst time to—"

"Neelo," Talhan said their name again, like a chant, like a prayer.

"Okay, yes." They sighed, folding their arms tightly across their chest. "Come visit. In the summer." They rolled their eyes. "Then you'll understand why this is a bad idea."

Talhan smirked, shuffling closer still. He lifted his hand and for a moment, Neelo thought he might touch their black velvet jacket, but his hand dropped lower and he plucked the book from their hands.

"Have you managed to find one you haven't yet read?" he asked, smoothing his large calloused hand over the linen-bound tome. Gods, the way he touched that cover, as if that little witch story was worthy of such reverence. It made Neelo's own palms buzz as if they could still feel the texture of the fabric beneath their own fingertips.

"We shall see." Neelo let out a soft chuckle. "Sometimes it's a translated title from Mhenbic or Yexshiri and I've actually read the story before in another language."

Talhan's eyebrows shot up. "You can read in Yexshiri?"

"Of course." Neelo's lip curved to one side, the closest to a grin they seemed to be able to muster. "Can't you?"

"I can barely read Ific," Talhan said ruefully.

He passed the book back to Neelo. As they took it, Talhan's pointer finger grazed the back of their hand, trailing slowly away. Neelo's breath hitched at the small, intimate gesture. Their eyes dropped back to the book and Talhan reached out again, his finger gently touching their chin and lifting their gaze.

"I—"

The door burst open followed by the sound of heeled boots clicking across the polished wood floor. Talhan retreated a step as Rish turned the corner. Neelo's personal attendant looked harried. Sweeping her black locks off her face, the green witch adjusted her gossamer emerald shawl around her shoulders like a green songbird ruffling her feathers.

Neelo's face morphed back to its normal sharp countenance. "What's she done this time?"

"Forgive me," Rish panted, a sheen of sweat covering her flushed cheeks. "Do you remember that time in Westdale?"

"Gods," Neelo cursed, giving Talhan a quick apologetic look. "I need to go."

Talhan took a step toward Rish. "Where's Rua? Why can't she handle this?"

"She's with Bri," Rish said, already turning toward the door.

He quirked his brow. "And where's Bri?"

Neelo stepped off the ladder and pushed passed Talhan. "I'm coming. Don't worry."

"Wait," Talhan said, taking Neelo by the hand, his brows pinching together in concern.

Neelo looked down to where their hands touched and swallowed as the sensation made their whole body buzz. "I'll see you in Saxbridge," they whispered, yanking their hand away and thundering off after their green witch.

ABOUT THE AUTHOR

A.K. Mulford is a bestselling fantasy author and former wildlife biologist who swapped rehabilitating monkeys for writing novels. She/ They are inspired to create diverse stories that transport readers to new realms, making them fall in love with fantasy for the first time or all over again. She now lives in New Zealand with her husband and two young human primates, creating lovable fantasy characters and making ridiculous TikToks (@akmulfordauthor).